Once Upon A Dream

Prince Ewezie Odira
+2348068141254

Once Upon A Dream

Dream-Dream

PHANDIRA

authorHOUSE®

AuthorHouse™ UK
1663 Liberty Drive
Bloomington, IN 47403 USA
www.authorhouse.co.uk
Phone: 0800.197.4150

Published by AuthorHouse 11/24/2014

ISBN: 978-1-4969-8870-6 (sc)
ISBN: 978-1-4969-8871-3 (e)

1

THERE was once a dream, though it wasn't mine but I had it all the same, and I still have it. It is neither a religious vision of doom or blessings, nor a political speech on promises or propaganda; for it is only a dream.

You and I are here, and hereafter in this dream, you and I shall be called 'we', as it would be on planet earth, and yes, we are in a dream, a dream-dream, for that is all it is.

We or our dreams? At times one cannot tell which is vaguer. The picture of things is not yet clear but we have been made to understand that today is the first of January, in the year F.G. 300. As we must have guessed, the B.C. came and went, so too did the Anno Domini and the new calendar system is already three hundred years old. Yes, we are that far off our present consciousness.

The F.G. is an abbreviation for *Finem Gratiæ,* a lost language's way of saying 'the end of grace'. We feel this language isn't lost because we are still here, dreaming a dream.

The sky is almost green and the atmosphere is not exactly clear, though we don't see anything painting it up but it is not quite the same as the lost earth. Ah, the lost earth. It has been precisely one thousand six hundred and twenty years since earth was lost and almost totally forgotten. The planet Moffat where mankind inhabited after earth is quite a folktale by young storytellers without adult supervision. So yes, the past existence of earth is always a fascinating topic of argument among scholars.

There is always no concrete evidence to prove that life began on earth and anyone who succeeds in finding any new detail at all may be *godded* – an award given in one's honour after death to dub one a god; one of whom is *god Aleone Axebury,* a *webarcheologist* who scientifically proved beyond eight hundred and seventy-nine unreasonable doubts, save one, that there was once a company called '*Yahoo*'.

There are many other gods here and there for one reason or two others, and some great achievers are already in line to be godded once they die. We must have heard of knights, yes, the real knights when they were in shining armours, and the next knights – the wealthy ones with shining wallets. Then came the *archknights,* the *archlords,* and there are a few *angels,* like *Angel Anita McZean* of *Temporia, Moffat,* who, in A.D. 3973, saved the entire citizens of a country in Moffat from burning alive during the *Belgorian War of Fire.* No, don't faint in awe; a country in Moffat was just a few houses and a shopping mall.

Though there are yet to be living archangels among men, we do have saints – an honour which was for the holy dead until the living believers became so self-righteous, so highly placed above pastors, deacons, reverends, bishops and popes that they were canonized and made saints once they had their own congregation to lead. We are indeed awaiting the first sets of archsaints and Emmanuels – gods living among men.

The most renowned saint is *Saint Mary-Jane III,* the head of the Universal Church. Along with her, in the *Western King's Council of Saints,* are a hundred and seventy other living saints who are heads of various Christian denominations.

Mary-Jane III has already been tipped to become the first archsaint of mankind for her immense contributions in maintaining peace among the nations of the *Eastern World,* the *Mid-Moral World* and the *Western Free World.*

One would have thought that the horrible effects of the wars on the lost earth should have taught mankind to live in peace. The last blast destroyed a lot of things, including all the lessons to be learnt. The lost earth saw terrorism and war, crime, envy and hatred so severe and frequent that there was no single day left to commit a new atrocity, for every single date on earth has been set aside as a sad memorial for two disasters or more.

But mankind picked up quickly again in Moffat – a shrinking planet named after its discoverer, *god Daniel Moffat.* There were a lot of technological and medical breakthroughs because four out of every four-and-half persons were geniuses. It rather became a lawful act for many centuries to gun down a fool until the late *Saint Francsec* stopped the killing of fools in A.D 3680 and the beautiful Peace Ambassador *Saint K.K Jamima,* in A.D 3850, put a final end to the use of guns and weapons in any form of war or hate. In one of her popular messages, Saint Jamima said, "love itself is complicated; let's try practising that rather than dying for complicated wars." She was shot that same year, and that was the last complicated bullet to be shot in Moffat. Her message of peace came a little too late as a radical prophet, *Saint Alloy Chlnnu,* claimed that Moffat will be destroyed in less than 200 years, unless mankind can live in peace. Mankind did live in peace but it wasn't enough to keep Moffat from shrinking. Scientists estimated that by A.D 4004, the last of Moffat must have vanished into the thin air.

Everyone went about their businesses in Moffat, which was just around the corner, thru a few doors and houses, all destinations were close by. There was no need for streets because there was no space for it and with no space, no cars. Manual scooters and skates were the best means of transportation and that alone shot up the level of domestic accidents by eight hundred percent. People had no need to leave their homes all the time, thanks to computer gadgets and social networks, unless one had a date at the *Central Restaurant* – the only site in Moffat visited by relationship pilgrims. The round building wasn't made round with blocks; save for the frames, it was all doors numbering in hundreds for all men from all over the planet coming in and going out. It belonged to *Lord Alpha Rho,* an ancestor of *Lord Omicron Rho,* one of the wealthiest men alive.

Now, this cramped, compact Moffat should encourage togetherness, yes? No! Not when your neighbour refuses to open his door, forcing you to take a longer route to wherever it is you suddenly wish to visit.

Once upon a time, in A.D 3972, or shall it be said twice upon two times, considering he and his father before him had once been forgiven for the same hideous act, *Sir Iliya Arth-Belgore,* the president of one certain nation – a group of neighbouring houses of course, set off again thru many miles and millions of houses just to punch the face of the president of the free world for inflating the price of cow milk, the only source of protein on Moffat. A fierce war broke out a few months later, and like humans do, even without the use of guns, many people were killed and the emotional Moffat was completely devastated. A couple of decades later, mankind was on the move again to another planet.

In A.D 4000, an astronaut, *god Rory Onward,* convinced the survivors on Moffat that he was instructed by a voice in space to build spaceships that will convey everyone out of the shrinking Moffat. All aboard, numbering a few millions, the ships stumbled into another planet. Rory Onward was totally convinced in his mind that God had brought them to heaven. With a Bible in one hand, eager to explain the absence of the angels and Saint Peter in particular, god Onward suddenly heard a voice say him, "Genesis 1:28." He opened the passage quickly, hoping to get some words that could turn out to mean 'welcome to Heaven', 'the key is under the flower pot' or 'chill, Peter is on the way'. He couldn't believe his eyes when they snapped upon 'be fruitful, increase, fill the planet, and rule'. He dimmed his eyes in disappointment and let out the word, "Oh". The large expectant crowd cheered in a fanatic frenzy and till this day, this new habitat is called the planet Oh.

Well, that is the story the comedians usually put up. The more serious minded historians claim the name Oh was coined from god Rory Onward's signature which was a beautifully scripted letter 'O'. There was no need arguing why his first name Rory wasn't used, considering that around the time mankind was only out of the lost earth, just over one percent of the population could still pronounce the letter 'R'.

It all started as joke by over-pampered kids and pretty skinny lousy girls way back in the nineteenth/twentieth century of the lost earth. The kids call the hopping carrot-loving mammal a *'wabbit'* and those ladies will prefer to be called *'vewy pwetty pwincesses'*. The worst is not that 'R' is no longer pronounced, a good number of people on the planet Oh sometimes don't type the letter R. School teachers often ask kids about the two alphabets that have the same pronunciation. Smart kids, like the little *Miss Sextine Rho,* will quickly respond, "The letter *aaw* and the letter *debeau.*" Her father, Lord Omicron Rho, takes a few extra seconds to ensure his name is always spelt correctly at the receptionist's desk.

"I am Lord *Omicwon Woe,*" he'll say and then add, "the cwon is with an aaw and Woe is aaw, aych, oh."

We, however, cannot totally blame pampered kids and skinny girls for the loss of the letter R's dignity because over the years, English itself stopped being popular. It went from one language to another and to another and then back to English again. Unfortunately for R, Russian didn't take centre stage; we would have been left with more Rs than *necessarrry.*

The inability to pronounce a certain letter isn't the only atrocity committed against the language structure. For one, the word 'are' is quietly vanishing from all the right places while 'my' is being taken over by 'me', and 'me' also replaces 'I' occasionally. Constant chatting among young people since the lost earth age has created entirely new words, words that were usually acronyms or just abbreviations.

People on the planet Oh actually do verbally say the word 'LOL' when they wish to inform someone that something quite funny has just been said or done. Just like saying 'fall', *lol* does sound like *'lall'*. Like the receptionist who will smile back at Lord Omicron Rho and say, "Lol sir, I can spell Omicwon."

We don't get surprised when we hear people say *'Ohemgee', 'Aideekay', and 'Seemesh'* and when something is really amusing they scream, *'Lahmao!'* We understand they're simply saying, 'Oh My God', 'I Don't Know', 'Shaking My Head' and 'Laugh My Arse Off'.

One would expect this language from kids and teenagers alone but it becomes necessary to recall that the adults of today were the youths of yesterday, and there is no time to get rid of any youthful language. The people on the planet

Oh have a lot on their mind. With the maximum lifespan of man dropping to seventy years, maturity happens at a very young age. Primary and secondary education last for just a year and the next three years is used to attain degrees in at least two professional courses. At the age of seven, if your kid is not a health care provider or an architect or an engineer or an entertainer or all of them at once, you might just be seen as a bad parent.

Advancing from these professional courses lands one in an *exceptional* course – crazy job titles like *Explanationist, Questionnaire, Inspirationist,* and the peak of one's career is a *Jack of all Trades* status, a status Lord Omicron Rho and a few other gentlemen possess.

Lord Omicron Rho is a mechanical engineer, a gadget engineer, an architect, an astronaut, a botanist and ten other professions written in his extended curriculum vitae. His pregnant wife, *Dame Nissi Rho,* is simply a historian, a lawyer, an accountant, an aesthete, a quintessentialist, a master chef and very nearly a *sahmxist* – a sit-at-home mother.

Their eight year old son, *Lexis Rho,* is already an architect and a *gadget imagineer.* He's almost done becoming an astronaut and a mechanical engineer, walking in his beloved father's footprints. Sextine, his three year old sister, just got enrolled to study Medicine and Automobile Imagineering, and in the future she will wish to be a fictionist; a profession her mother believes is a mockery of history.

We are not totally astonished by the brilliance and intelligence of this generation; even Lord Omicron Rho isn't flattered by the receptionist's name on her digital nametag: *Dr. Fran Evensong.* Their knowledge acquisition has been made easier by the invention of the BEM nearly fifteen centuries ago. The *Brain's External Memory* is responsible for the slightly visible exoskeleton lining the back of the heads of the few hairless people around. People with hair do have the BEM hidden properly.

The BEM stores ten times the information that can be stored in the normal brain and this information is easily accessible by the users. Very strict school teachers often encourage their students to turn off their BEMs during examinations. There are about four BEM companies; we can bet their headquarters are in every hospital, hunting newborn babies who are yet to own a BEM.

When Dame Nissi gives birth to her baby girl *Leontine,* Lord Omicron will opt to hire the less popular BEM company, *Vexim,* to equip the little Miss Leontine Rho with her first external brain memory device.

These brain boosters are not the only companies stalking newborns. The *Digit Keepers* are often mistaken for journalists chasing after some famous celebrity. Way back on earth, digit keepers would have been called bankers. Change is constant. We've gone from cowries to coins to paper money, and from one cashless policy to another, paper money ceased to exist. All a man slaves for is to eat good food and have high figures in his digits account, not forgetting to love and be loved of course.

The economy on Oh is generally okay. If a nation were to be running the digit keeping system on the lost earth, one digit would have worth three dollars. The prices of many commodities are high; everything ever sold was made by one professional or more.

A maximum lifespan of seventy years usually doesn't bother anyone, there's a huge amount of time to get there. A seventy year old man on the planet Oh will mathematically be just above ninety-five years old on the lost earth. On Oh, it takes four hundred days to make a year, and thirty hours to make each of those days. There are eight days in a week and thirteen months in a year.

This additional day and month was born out of man's lazy desire to rest. Just between Friday and Saturday comes a lazy day called *Trägeday*. Hardworking teachers claim the day was named after how tragic the development was. Historians believe it is from the old German way of saying 'sleep', sort of. But scientists simply say an extra day was needed to balance the maths in the time it takes the miraculous planet Oh to go round the sun. The extra lazy month, *Hipnoary*, falls between January and February. It has just sixteen days unlike every other month that has thirty-two days. Like we rightly guessed, Hipnoary was named after Hypnos, the Greek god of sleep; nobody disputes this.

Lord Omicron looks down from Dr. Fran Evensong's nametag to his sophisticated wristwatch. We hate to imagine that it is neither *Rolex* nor *Longines*, but we get the idea they've tried to last the test of time, beyond the lost earth and Moffat. The timepiece looks rather unusual to us. The clock hanging on the wall appears the same and it's about 15 minutes past 10 a.m. and that is fifteen minutes into the New Year. Lord Omicron has just missed all the fireworks and his family who had been waiting in the resort park.

His wristwatch and the clock on the wall both keep a decimal time. They have the numbers 1 to 10, with 10 and 5 dividing the area from north to south into two equal halves filled by 6, 7, 8 and 9 on the left and 1, 2, 3, and 4 on the right. It is easy to guess that the planet Oh has just ten hours of morning and ten hours of night, and the other ten hours? That's purely afternoon – when it appears to be that the sun stands still for ten hours especially over the nations of the Western Free World. The Eastern World experiences the slow ten hours in the morning while the Mid-Moral World experiences this at night – that's why they are nicknamed the dark nations; a rather racist tag, considering that every nation indeed has ten hours of the night every day.

The time system still maintains the ante meridiem (before noon) and post meridiem (after noon) to disambiguate hours of the day in the ten hour clock. *Tempore meridiem* (during noon) classifies the middle ten hours of bright afternoon. This three-stage time format was reintroduced in F.G. 2 by *god Aleqi Quinton* as the smart Miss Sextine Rho will always confirm to her teacher during the frequent brief Q&A sessions.

2 "I'M sowie I'm taking your time... I just want to be sure where your family is at the moment."

"You know me family?" Lord Omicron asks the receptionist.

"Sure sir, you vewy popular here, and the whole planet has been waiting for you."

Lord Omicron puffs and looks around. "I doubt anyone was waiting."

"Lol sir... company policy. We don't allow journalists in."

"Seemesh," Lord Omicron shakes his head calmly.

"Ok sir, Suite seventy-five. Welcome back to Oh and welcome to Phantom Wesort." She offers to shake Lord Omicron's hand, "I'm Doctor Fwan Evensong, Fwan with an aaw."

Lord Omicron giggles as he shakes her hand briefly.

He sets off like a mean gentleman and once he takes the turn into a lonely hallway, his pace and joy increase geometrically. This sums up Lord Omicron Rho's behaviour. Once in public, he's seen as a serious minded fellow but when alone or with his kids, he's no better than a playful cartoon character suffering from excess energy and *sugar explosion*.

The thirty year old lord is one of the wealthiest jacks of all trades alive. He is often criticized by the media on how he uses his excess digits. To this he once wrote, "Accusations of the rich! When you spend, you be called proud; when you keep your digits to yourself, you be called stingy. These two are better than being accused of poverty by the devil... you will pay with your life." Well, that didn't go down too nicely with a lot of people. Lord Omicron Rho was later crowned 'The Arrogant Man of the Year, F.G. 296'.

In Suite 75, Dame Nissi Rho stands in front of the window, caressing her heavy stomach as she looks to the near-green sky, just above the huge *Saint Adaora's Hospital* across the street. She sees the bright golden rectangular light that is visible once in a while in the months of January and Hipnoary. Explanationists, due to their acquired education and skill in explaining the unexplainable, have over the years argued louder than everyone else and hence have proven beyond every audible and reasonable doubt that the bright golden rectangular light is, in their own fact, the precious golden gates of Heaven. We are yet to touch it.

Lexis Rho is sitting on a fine desk trying to teach the little Sextine how to play the game of *Quess* – a four player chess game. Yes, chess-chess. It survived all the wars because it mentored all the wars.

Sextine is staring speechlessly at the quess board – the normal chess chequerboard of sixty-four squares, in an eight by eight arrangement, with extensions of thirty-two chequered squares in a four by eight grid on the four sides (this is called the base).

We understand this mini quess lecture is meant to be a natural learning process. Sextine's BEM is essentially deactivated and placed on the desk. At her age, let alone the age she's living in, Sextine can only think of sleeping, screaming, and sleeping. Almost everything she has known is stored in the BEM.

Sextine reaches out for her BEM but Lexis stops her.

"Leave the BEM alone, they won't let you compete with it."

Whatever that means, Sextine is disappointed.

"Let's go over this again," Lexis says as he points at the crowded quess board. "This is the king, the queen, the pwince, the pwincess – she's the only piece that can checkmate the king without help; the two castles, the two bishops, the two knights, the archbishop, the lord, the lady-in-waiting, the dame, the sweeper or assassin, the saint, the spy or saboteur – you will have to be wise to spot it; and of course fifteen silly pawns scattered all of over the war zone."

Sextine's eyes are on her mother.

"Sugar, you listening?" Lexis taps Sextine.

Dame Nissi looks back into the room, a mission aimed at rescuing Sextine from her brain draining brother. She rather becomes startled when she sees her husband standing inside the room. Dame Nissi is speechlessly happy and her kids are yet to know why.

Lexis and Sextine look towards the door. Lexis' mood brightens up almost immediately as he screams, "popmy!" Sextine is not even wondering why she doesn't understand any of these.

'Popmy!" Lexis screams out again as he stands up quickly and runs joyously towards Lord Omicron.

Dame Nissi's pregnancy won't let her move any faster than she is moving at the moment. We understand that not only does Dame Nissi have a massive baby coming soon, it will be out of fashion for the child to call her 'mom.'

Gone are the millennia when the male parent was called poppa, papa, father, daddy or dad. An African slang 'popsi' has been in vogue on the lost earth and more recently it has metamorphosed to 'popmy.' No, it wasn't inspired by a man's responsibility of popping champagne during family dinners because that will mean 'momxy' was inspired by a woman's auto-ability to be Momus – the Greek god of fault-finding, unfair criticism and mockery.

Lord Omicron's long hug with Lexis allows Dame Nissi more time to come closer.

"I can't move any faster," She mutters in an attempt to let him know how much she missed him.

"No," Lord Omicron breaks the hug with Lexis. "I was coming to get you. I've missed you so much."

Dame Nissi's wry smile doesn't believe him that much.

"The baby, she'll be here next Twägeday."

"Wow!"

"You wow like you don't know."

"Nissi? Of course I know," Lord Omicron says quickly.

Dame Nissi is a great conversation pilot. She's only interested in letting Lord Omicron know how much he doesn't know about certain things, things she is actually meant to let him know. She gives him a yeah-right-I-don't-believe-you one-cheek smile. Lord Omicron is forced to elaborate on that.

"Sugar, not that I know the exact expected date of birth but I'm aware you this heavy."

"I am this heavy? That language is archaic and impolite on babies."

"Sewiously?"

"Yes! What planet have you been on? Saying I'm heavy looks as if I'm with an unwanted load. I am not heavy Omicwon, I am simply pwegnant."

Lord Omicron's face is lightened up with a smile to which Dame Nissi tries not to smile back. Lord Omicron takes her hand and helps her sit on the bed as he takes a long look at the motionless Sextine.

"Is Sextine sick? he asks, sitting beside the emotionless Dame Nissi.

"Why?"

"She saw me, didn't she?" Lord Omicron asks.

Lexis is suddenly now aware why Sextine did not understand his quess lecture without her BEM. Her entire language knowledge is saved on her BEM, and from the way she's looking at them, we too understand her entire day to day behaviour is saved on the BEM. Lord Omicron is about to learn the worse as Lexis and Dame Nissi respond to his question simultaneously.

"Her BEM is deactivated," says Lexis.

"She doesn't know you," Dame Nissi says unapologetically.

"She doesn't know me?" Lord Omicron is almost furious. "Nissi, I don't understand what you mean by that."

"Anyone who doesn't understand what I just said doesn't understand basic English."

"You being sarcastic, you know that?"

"Look who's talking... the arwogant man of the year FG 296."

"Nissi, that was four years ago!"

"You were here when Sextine was born, wight? Don't blame me for that. I'm weally stwessed up... this pwegnancy..."

"... Don't use the baby as an excuse," Lord Omicron interrupts her.

"Oh that is not an excuse! Can't you see I am indeed pwegnant? You don't know what it feels like!"

"I know exactly what it feels like, me've been in the simulator five times! So please, take it like man!"

"I AM NOT A MAN!" Dame Nissi screams at the top of her voice.

"I meant man, as in mankind... humanity."

"Sewiously Omicwon, what planet have you been on? You dwiving me cwazy."

Tired of talking, Dame Nissi is just about to lean on Lord Omicron before he drops a huge surprise.

"I've been on the lost earth, Nissi. We found earth."

Dame Nissi is stunned; her eyes piercing thru her husband's lips, rereading the words he just spoke.

"You found... you found... you found the lost earth?" Dame Nissi stutters.

The entire Space Agencies on Oh have been waiting for the arrival of Lord Omicron's crew. The crew had sent a message that they found something interesting – a class eight information which on a normal day will attract various presidents to the meeting. Due to huge disappointments over the years, only a handful of government officials and a whole lot of questionnaires and evidence-seeking scientists are waiting on the crew.

The crew's arrival was delayed after crew members opted to go home to freshen up first; there was no rush to announce something no one would believe. Dame Nissi's baby is just about to delay proceedings even further.

"Ah!" Dame Nissi groans with her hand on her stomach.

"What's the matter?" Lord Omicron asks.

"The baby... Leontine."

"Leontine," Lord Omicron repeats the baby's name as if he's just hearing it for the first time.

"Yes, the baby, Leontine. She kicked."

"Maybe she's happy to hear we found the lost earth."

Dame Nissi isn't only disappointed to know that her husband doesn't understand that the baby is coming, and it is indeed time to panic, she's also sad that he doesn't understand the baby that is coming.

"Omicwon, the baby can't hear anything."

"No of course, that was... yes, she can hear us." Lord Omicron is confused the more and ignorantly tries to defend himself.

"Omicwon, Leontine will be deaf, wemember? That's what the doctors said, they can't fix it either."

Lord Omicron is dumbfounded. "I don't understand," he mutters.

Dame Nissi is frustrated and in pains. "You don't even understand anything any longer, do you?"

"Chillax Leontine," Lord Omicron says as he reaches out to pamper the restless Nissi.

"My name is not Leontine!"

"Me is not talking to you," Lord Omicron argues. "I'm talking to the baby..."

"She can't hear you!" Dame Nissi is almost in tears before she recollects herself; not totally sure she's getting enough oxygen. "God damn you Omicwon."

"You don't mean that. Sugar, I'm sowie, just twy and calm down."

Dame Nissi flares up again. "Quit telling me to calm down, you can't tell the baby to calm down. The baby is coming!"

"She's coming?" Lord Omicron is now officially panicking. "You should have told me many sentences ago!"

Dame Nissi sighs at Lord Omicron's confused state.

"Where is the teleport station awound here?" Lord Omicron asks yet another dumb question.

"Oh dear dear dear!" Dame Nissi speaks desperately, "you don't teleport pwegnant women. Get me to a hospital!"

"Yes," Lord Omicron hits his head with his hand. "Um, I'll get a doctor, it will be easier. Yes, the weceptionist is a doctor. I will find her."

Lord Omicron takes a couple of steps away from his complaining wife as Lexis tries to comfort her. He ignores her request for a nurse, a *babypetter*, a nutritionist and a baptizer too.

Lord Omicron taps his wrist watch and an array of small translucent rectangular screens pop up orderly, floating just above the wrist watch. Lord Omicron has never been more confused than this. It has been months since he used this gadget and he's getting the easiest protocol all wrong. Waiting for answers from his BEM, he catches a glimpse of Sextine again and she's just staring back at him.

"Lexis, go and activate your sister's BEM. I don't like the way she's looking at me."

That's not what Dame Nissi is expecting to hear and she reminds her husband accordingly as Lexis walks over to Sextine.

"The doctor dear... and the hospital staff..."

"Ah yes," Lord Omicron has just remembered how to operate this gadget he is wearing.

We understand that this is just a phone, or so we apparently understand – the *Sapien*.

"Sapien," Lord Omicron calls out to it.

"Yes, boss," it replies in a baritone voice.

"Search for contact, Doctor Fwan Evensong."

"Boss, spell Fwan."

"Ef, aaw, ei, en."

"Found Doctor Fwan Evensong, Phantom Wesort, the *State of Genia, Sexat*," the sapien responds immediately.

"Yes, call her," Lord Omicron instructs the sapien.

"Not understood boss, no her found. Say that again."

"Call Doctor Fwan Evensong," Lord Omicron requests again with his eyes now on his restless wife.

Lexis has just practically resurrected Sextine after reactivating her BEM. She screams out in joy for her father.

"Popmy!" Sextine yells, running towards Lord Omicron.

Lord Omicron turns to her; he's happy all the same.

"My sweetheart," he says as Sextine gives him a hug. "Momxy is going to have a baby."

The sapien records that last speech as an explanation to Lord Omicron's last command and Lord Omicron has never seen his sapien this helpless.

"Boss, speak some more. I have found Doctor Fwan Evensong."

"Yes!" Lord Omicron breaks the hug with Sextine. "Call her, sapien, call Doctor Fwan Evensong."

"Boss, speak some more."

Dame Nissi realises why the sapien is confused and she attempts to fix it.

"Sapien," she calls out softly.

Lord Omicron's sapien takes an extra second to process the unknown voice while Dame Nissi's sapien responds immediately.

"Sapien activated," Dame Nissi's sapien responds in an electronic female voice.

"You not me boss," Lord Omicron's sapien objects to Dame Nissi's call.

"Omicwon," Dame Nissi chooses to speak to a human being. "Save the contact first before you call her."

"Oh," Lord Omicron realises his mistake.

"Not understood boss," Dame Nissi's sapien responds to her statement.

"Sapien," Lord Omicron calls out again and before he could say another word, both sapiens respond instantly.

"Yes, boss," his sapien replies.

'You not me boss," Dame Nissi's sapien objects.

The official noisemakers on this planet are these sapiens. They respond to anyone who says the word 'sapien', making it almost impossible to place a sapien-command in public without alerting every other sapien nearby. A new generation of sapiens are on the way though, and this time you can baptize your own gadget.

Lord Omicron ignores Dame Nissi's sapien. We are quite glad Lexis' sapien is still deactivated from the New Year's event they attended earlier.

"Save contact, Doctor Fwan Evensong," Lord Omicron instructs his sapien.

"Contact saved, boss."

"Call Doctor Fwan Evensong," Lord Omicron instructs it immediately.

"Doctor Fwan will speak if she can," the sapien responds.

Lord Omicron walks impatiently towards Dame Nissi and holds unto her hand.

"Lord Woe?" Dr. Fran Evensong speaks up, rather sounding very surprised. "Is evewything alwight?"

Lord Omicron speaks nervously into the air, "yes yes, no no, my wife is having a baby... you a doctor, we need help."

"And other important staff too," Dame Nissi adds.

"Oh dear," Dr. Fran quickly offers a surprising solution. "Saint Adaowa's Hospital is just acwoss the stweet, quite visible from Suite seventy-five"

Lord Omicron dashes towards the window to confirm.

"Ha! And I've been looking at it all night," Dame Nissi says, feeling disappointed.

"I'll get a twolley fwom them and I'll meet you halfway," Dr. Fran suggests.

"That will be fantastic," Lord Omicron agrees. "We on our way."

3 LORD Omicron helps his wife up while Lexis and Sextine only succeed in blocking their path.

"Both of you should just sit over there, thanks for the help."

"No no," Dame Nissi objects, "they are coming with us."

"I'll come and get them later, they are slowing us down."

"No no, Omicwon," Dame Nissi strongly objects. "It's vewy wisky, this place is a wesort."

"Okay okay," agrees Lord Omicron. "Both of you just tag along nicely."

Lexis and Sextine walk quietly beside their parents as they make their way towards the elevator as fast as they can.

"What if halfway is midair on our way down in the elevator?" Dame Nissi asks worriedly.

"Don't be widiculous," Lord Omicron giggles. "Doctor Fwan is not an engineer."

"Who can tell these days?" says Dame Nissi. "She might have made her calculations and she could be determined to actually meet us halfway."

"That will be a thweat to my pwincess if it happens. I will hunt and kill her with my saint."

Dame Nissi and Lexis giggle. Lord Omicron has just said something impossible in the game of quess. It is pretty very difficult to really threaten the highly dynamic princess, whereas the saint cannot kill or be killed.

The elevator arrives at the reception and the doors open. Dr. Fran is already waiting with the trolley.

"Halfway is still up there," Dr. Fran jokes as they quickly help Dame Nissi sit on the trolley, "I had to wait here."

"I told you she calculated it," says Dame Nissi.

"Lol Dame Woe, I am not mad."

"Ha! But you a doctor; put one and two together, baby."

"I believe that is what you and your hubby have done, baby," Dr. Fran points at Dame Nissi's stomach.

Dame Nissi tries, and she still can't help but laugh really hard. Lord Omicron is only happy to see her ignoring the pain at last, but not for long. Dame Nissi doesn't believe they are going as fast as they can to the hospital.

"Can't we go any faster?" she yells.

"Nissi, we alweady there," Lord Omicron reveals.

"If it's there it means it's not here!"

"We are here... at the hospital," Lord Omicron assures her.

Dame Nissi takes a breath of hope but she's soon yelling again when an automated trolley robot takes over the duties of pushing the trolley. Dame Nissi ignores the fact that robot is moving thru the hallway a lot faster than her human helpers.

"No no!" Dame Nissi screams, "I don't want that thing near me. You know how they malfunction."

Lord Omicron and Dr. Fran are still trying to catch up with the trolley. This gives them a little time to cook up reassuring words for the sceptical Dame Nissi. Lord Omicron carries Sextine in his arms while Lexis mans up and keeps up with the speed.

The doctor-on-call suddenly joins them from nowhere – a tall lady in her early 30s.

"This beauty has never malfunctioned," she says, sending mild shivers on the Rhos. "She is perfectly fine."

"It doesn't matter," Dame Nissi objects immediately. "I don't like these things. Is there no nurse or somebody? I am going to have a baby!"

"It's New Year's Day my dear, look awound. Nobody works on New Year's Day... I'm the only one here."

"No no," Dame Nissi says to her husband as she takes quick breaths, "are you sure she's even human? The nurses at least, they've been useful when I had our kids."

"I can assure you," the doctor says, "I am a nurse too."

"What if I need an anaesthesiologist?"

"I am an anaesthesiologist too."

"Oh that's fabulous," Dame Nissi mocks the doctor. "What of a baptizer?"

The doctor smiles and says, "I was formerly an archdeacon, so I am still licensed to baptize."

"Impwessive," Lord Omicron chips in.

"Yea... and a lot more. I am just two pwofessions away fwom officially becoming a jack of all twades. So chillax, you are in safe hands. I am *Pwofessor Knight Nightingale.*"

They could all afford to smile mildly as the robot makes the last turn towards one of the delivery rooms. Lord Omicron sees two young men and a lady sitting opposite the door with three huge metal cases beside them.

"I thought you said you are the only one here?"

"Of course," Professor Knight responds quickly. "Those awen't hospital personnel... the young lady is an agent of the digit keeping company, *Vault*... glad her other competitors are out having a nice time. Those gentlemen with her are agents of *Fahwenheit* and Vexim, both BEM companies. They will be stalking your baby *tomorning.*"

The robot stops the trolley right in front of the door and Professor Knight goes ahead of them.

"Doctor Evensong, help it open the door," Professor Knight requests.

Dr. Fran follows her quickly and the Rhos are just about to wonder why Professor Knight won't open the door herself when they see her pass thru the closed door. Dame Nissi almost lets out her heart thru her agape mouth.

"It's a hologwam," Lord Omicron quickly explains the situation as Dame Nissi calms herself.

Dr. Fran opens the door and the robot brings in the trolley. Dame Nissi takes a good look at Professor Knight standing in the middle of the room.

"Are you actually here or you are not actually here?"

"I am actually not here," Professor Knight replies with a raised shoulder.

"You are almost a jack of all twades and you are nowhere close to the twade. Where are you?" Dame Nissi asks the perfect hologram of Professor Knight.

"There are nine other patients who need attention... as a matter of fact I'm in my office. I am simply telling their families what to do. They all do have a doctor within the family, so it's easy."

"Saint Adaowa, pway for us," Dame Nissi whispers.

"Saint Adaowa is still alive," Professor Knight educates Dame Nissi.

"Well, that makes it better," says Dame Nissi. "I don't twust dead people who are alweady walking in Heaven. They may not care more than a doctor will."

"Saint Adaowa is not a member of the universal church anyway, so even if she's dead... Saint Maywy-Jane the third says only saints who were once Universalites are given the unction to intercede for mortal men. Perhaps dear, Doctor Evensong is physically here. She works here as a part-time physician and this is certainly one of those times."

"I am not a Universalite," Dame Nissi says in pains, "I am simply going to have a baby..."

"Yes my dear," Professor Knight agrees, "we are all set whenever you are set too."

"Me Gee!" Dame Nissi yells, "I've been set! I've been waiting to get here!"

"But we've all been here too."

"You are a hologwam, pwofessor, you be just here to talk."

Professor Knight signals Dr. Fran to get on with the job as she moves over to the side of the room.

"All the boys can leave now," the professor says.

Lord Omicron's facial expression is trying to ask why but there are no matching words to challenge that final decision. He takes Lexis and leaves the delivery room. They are immediately approached by the BEM company agents.

"Sir," both of them are about to begin their memorized pick-up lines.

"It's lord," Lord Omicron interrupts them swiftly.

"Lord," they switch at once, not minding how inappropriate that sounds.

"I have alweady made up my mind," Lord Omicron says again.

The two young men are quiet, already tired from the day's work. The Fahrenheit agent is smiling; since his company is the most subscribed BEM provider on the planet. It takes a pretty awkward situation to accept Vexim.

The Vexim agent is just about to walk away.

"Haven't you sold any BEM today?" Lord Omicron asks the dejected Vexim agent.

"I have," he responds sluggishly.

"Quite a few I guess."

"Eleven."

"Not bad," Lord Omicron suggests.

The Fahrenheit agent tries not to laugh.

"Not when Fahwenheit sells eighty-two."

Lord Omicron smiles. "But Vexim is doing well in the middle nations... doesn't that make up for this?"

The Vexim agent is only wishing to take his seat now.

"You should know that's insignificant. Fahwenheit sells more in the east and west."

"But then I'm not happy with Fahwenheit," Lord Omicron drops a bomb.

"Excuse me?" the Fahrenheit agent speaks up.

"No, me annoyance can't possibly be your business, you just a salesman. You don't make Fahwenheit, be sure I would have kicked you a long time ago."

"May I ask why?"

"You may ask," says Lord Omicron.

"Why?"

"Did you see my little girl? Lord Omicron asks. "Without the BEM, she doesn't know who I am."

"You definitely misusing the BEM," the Fahrenheit agent says with the smile of a genius.

"So, your best thought is that I, as old as I am, cannot use the BEM pwoperly on my kids?"

"Yes, why not sir? With all due wespect..."

"You've alweady diswespected me more than twice," Lord Omicron interrupts the Fahrenheit agent. "How come my son can play quess without the BEM?"

"And your son's BEM is not Fahwenheit?"

"It is."

"I don't get the point any longer."

"You just as dumb as you look, with all due wespect," Lord Omicron says bullishly. "The BEM works fine on my son, but not on my daughter while you claim I don't know how to use the BEM, as useless as your point is and still you don't get the point any longer. You did get it for a little 'long', didn't you?"

"The BEM is just helping your daughter," argues the Fahrenheit agent. "At her age she can't know a lot. The BEM collects all the information and as the years go by it will slowly synchwonise with her bwain and educate her. It is a slow pwocess."

Lord Omicron nods. "A slow pwocess... collects all the information, seemesh."

"Let me just explain how it works," offers the Fahrenheit agent and this enrages Lord Omicron the more.

"I KNOW EXACTLY HOW THE BEM WORKS! I know exactly how evewy BEM works... I am only wondewing how your company makes its own policies and if the people are aware of the new behaviour of these things stealing information with a pwomise to educate the owner later... sewiously?"

"Your daughter must have seen you before you bought her the BEM. It is nobody's fault your image didn't stick to her head."

Lord Omicron is not going to respond to that. It is just one of those monopolists reading him his limited rights with utter arrogance to the best of his arrogant knowledge.

Lord Omicron is not meeting such people for the first time. One of his crew members, *Sir Nnia Den,* owns *HoloCorp* – the biggest and virtually the only hologram company in existence.

Sir Nnia Den is jokingly called an evil genius sometimes; the fact is that he is seriously an evil genius all the time. His first version of the hologram was used to steal the ideas of other competing hologram makers. His father, *Lord Remy L. Den,* left him a lot of digits as inheritance, making life easier for him to scoop up ideas and develop them immediately while the real owners are still begging for sponsorship. His best invention so far is the Holo-X which allows users to control a maximum of ten identical holograms simultaneously. Holo-X is only allowed for use in hospitals and security agencies. It is his best invention because he's still hiding the Holo-X^3 – a more dangerous gadget that grants the user's hologram the ability to touch and grab things. His company, on paper, employs 8,800 people. In reality, that's roughly 800 people and 8,000 Holo-X/Holo-X^3 generated holograms.

Sir Nnia Den is a member of the crew that just found the lost earth. Unlike the rest of the crew members, only Sir Nnia returned with any form of evidence that they were truly on the lost earth – a dusty classy twelve inch tablet probably named after a thirtieth century vegetable.

Just as Lord Omicron is about ignoring one arrogant monopolist, Sir Nnia calls him on his sapien.

"Sir Nnia Den wishes to speak with you," the sapien alerts Lord Omicron with a quiet vibration accompanying its baritone voice.

"Accept," Lord Omicron says reluctantly.

The video call sets up immediately and Lord Omicron is unconcerned about anyone listening to the conversation. If you need to talk privately on Oh, best you teleport or send in your hologram.

"Where on Oh are you?" Sir Nnia asks quickly as he walks towards the reception of Phantom Resort.

"Sir Nnia, my wife is having a baby."

"She had to do that tonight?"

"Don't be silly..."

"Lol, pay me no mind. I'm aware they feel the urge more than poo. So, will you answer the question now?"

"What question?" asks Lord Omicron.

"Where on Oh are you?" Sir Nnia says slowly.

"Saint Adaowa's Hospital..."

Dr. Fran emerges from the delivery room; she's not particularly happy. This worries Lord Omicron and he puts Sir Nnia off.

"We'll bubble later, have to go."

"I am coming over in ten seconds... found a teleport system here..."

The call terminates and Lord Omicron stares at Dr. Fran, hoping to read her mind.

"Where is Nissi?" he mutters in confusion.

"Inside, she's fine... just a little issue with the baby."

"She's alive too, wight?" Lord Omicron finds his voice.

"The baby? Yes she is."

"Didn't they teach you to smile when you've got good news?"

"Lord Woe, there's a little issue..."

Lord Omicron ignores her and signals the agents of Vault and Vexim to come with him. The sales agents pick up their respective metal cases and follow Lord Omicron, Lexis, and Dr. Fran into the delivery room.

Dame Nissi is looking pale and visibly worried about the baby who is strapped to the sophisticated translucent *Yonder Baby Surveyor* machine. The most glaring data on this machine is the Life Expectancy of the baby written in red – '24 years and 36 days.' This is three times lower than the maximum life expectancy of this generation.

Lord Omicron is more concerned about his wife. He overlooks the baby, the machine, and the alarming date. Straight to Dame Nissi's bed, he gives her a warm hug. This doesn't brighten up Dame Nissi's countenance.

"The baby..." Dame Nissi mutters.

"Ah yes, the baby," Lord Omicron says with a fading smile, realising Dame Nissi doesn't look happy. He looks at Professor Knight, "still here?"

"Not litewally," she tells him.

Lord Omicron summons courage to find out why Dame Nissi and other ladies in the room are cold and quiet, including the little Miss Sextine Rho whose BEM is apparently still activated at this point. Lord Omicron looks at the machine; the life expectancy figures cannot be hidden.

"Twenty-four years and thirty-six days until what happens?" he asks aimlessly.

No one responds and Lord Omicron walks towards the machine.

"Why is she tied to the Baby Surveyor, won't that influence the data?" Lord Omicron asks, hoping to gain a year or two from the machine.

The question does need an answer and Professor Knight is not reluctant to speak.

"She has *Floating Syndwome,* but that's not an issue."

Lord Omicron nods, neither happy nor sad.

The Floating Syndrome hasn't really been a problem anymore to mankind. Due to man's need to increase their centre of gravity since leaving the lost earth, the bones have become more of iron than calcium phosphate, though the bone iron is completely coated by bone calcium. The human skull doesn't evolve into this Iron-Calcium Complex. The lack of the heavier iron-calcium bones causes a newborn to float at birth, hence the tag, 'Floating Syndrome' – a syndrome that also affects nonliving things. Every other thing made by man is electronic and computerized, making it digitally possible to set a standard value of gravity that will prevent products from floating in the air.

"I am coming over with the ICC vaccine to solve the situation," adds Professor Knight.

Professor Knight walks in thru the door holding a syringe for the baby and her hologram vanishes into her sapien.

Sir Nnia Den also walks in thru the door and everyone looks at him.

"Sir Nnia," Lord Omicron acknowledges his presence.

"Did anyone pwomise to steal your baby?" Sir Nnia reacts to the way they looked at him, and the baby strapped on the machine.

"This is no time for sarcasm, Sir Nnia."

"Who is this man?" Dame Nissi asks about Sir Nnia.

Professor Knight proceeds to inject the baby. She's very aware of whom Sir Nnia Den is; the lecture isn't for her. She has supported a lot of his methods in the past and also represented him in the court of law on many occasions.

Lord Omicron responds to his wife immediately, with Sir Nnia spreading out his hands beside his laps, hoping Lord Omicron will dish out enough praises for him to lap up.

"Sugar, you should know Sir Nnia Den... a member of my team.... he..."

"I shouldn't know him," Dame Nissi interrupts him.

"Of course, not necessary..."

Sir Nnia stands arms akimbo.

"I've given the baby the vaccine," Professor Knight tries to regain their attention.

"Please untie her too," Lord Omicron requests, "it could be affecting that life expectancy *ish*."

"I asked her not to get that data at all," Dame Nissi says *sadly-coldly*. "I did ask her not to."

"Wait babe, you did ask who?" Lord Omicron points at Professor Knight and Dr. Fran. "Which of you did she tell not to use that damn thing?"

"Unfortunately, she asked me," confesses Professor Knight with a bold smile.

Sir Nnia giggles, upsetting Dame Nissi the more.

"Leave this moment, Sir Nnia."

"Lord Omicwon?"

"Yes, just give us some time. This is family matter."

Sir Nnia bows out towards the door and he looks disgustingly at the Vault and Vexim agents. "What about these two, outcast Woes?"

Lord Omicron's stern look could kill the extinct lions over and over again. Sir Nnia raises his hands in a rare apology and exits the room.

"You will do well to wipe that smile off your face," Lord Omicron verbally attacks Professor Knight. "How dare you dis my wife this way?"

"There's no way I would have known the baby's life expectancy will be low," Professor Knight defends her actions.

"You didn't know? Didn't you study the baby's pwofile before embarking on this?"

"I did all that; I know she'll be deaf, that's all her pwofile documented."

"And at birth she floated... can't you add that too to your bwain?"

"Lord Omicwon, if your wife knows as much as I do about the baby, which I'm sure she does, why is she being expectant? Why didn't she add that too to her own bwain?!"

"Oh you bloody loop head!!!" Lord Omicron screams and just about to take a step towards Professor Knight.

"We all full of blood," Professor Knight wonders quietly.

"Omicwon!" Dame Nissi calls out to him. "Omicwon" she adds with a more subtle voice, "let the obvious dog keep sleeping, let it go."

"Hmm," Professor Knight is unrepentantly speechless as she walks out of the room, "I'll be in my office."

"I'm sowie Lord and Dame Woe," Dr. Fran apologises.

"Boss," Lord Omicron's sapien brings in news, "you on the news, ninety-eight percent match."

Lord Omicron knows he has to ignore the mood in the room for a while. He raises his sapien and accepts to see the news. "Show me," he commands.

The sapien pops up a video feed. Lord Omicron sees a picture of himself at the top corner of the screen. We also see Sir Nnia Den, Professor Knight Nightingale and many other people gathered behind the reporter in a conference hall.

The headline reads, 'BREAKING: CREW EPSILON RETURNS TO OH WITH ASTONISHING NEWS'.

"We are waiting for this event to finally commence," the reporter says. "Some of the cwew members are yet to be here. Lord Omicwon Woe, the man on your scween, is the captain of *Epsilon*; we just learnt his wife had a baby moments ago in this hospital, that pwompted the sudden venue change fwom Phantom Wesort. Sir Nnia Den is alweady here. Other members of the six-man team are *Lady Ose Neo, Archpwofessor Lux Eden, Sir Luminescence Wellington,* and of course our darling heir to the thwone of the Western Nations, the King's daughter, *Pwincess Lotem-Zeta II.* We'll take a break while we wait for the event to begin."

Lord Omicron clicks off the news and turns to his attentive wife.

"How do you get them to alert you when you are on the news?" Dame Nissi asks him.

"I think that's done automatically."

"No no... yes, mine does that for me since I'm the owner. How do I make her tell me when you are on the news?"

Lord Omicron is a bit confused but the Vexim agent saves the moment.

"You tell the gadget to give you news alerts on Lord Omicwon."

"You just tell her?" Dame Nissi asks.

"We tell them evewything," says Lord Omicron.

"What is the exact command?"

"Set up news alert," the Vexim agent explains. "Then it will ask you to choose the contact, and then you say his name. She'll use his pictures on the eagle to cwoss match faces that pop up in the news thirty/eight."

Dame Nissi smiles, a smile that calms everyone in the room who may have even been breathing carefully just to please the heartbroken Dame. Lord Omicron is infected with the smile immediately and he joins her on the bed, gently caressing their son, Lexis.

Lord Omicron signals Dr. Fran to bring the baby. She moves quickly.

"There are not many gadgets to choose fwom," Lord Omicron tells Dame Nissi, "just a digit keeper, Vault, and a BEM company, Vexim."

"Vexim?" Dame Nissi tries to recollect the name. "That's not the common one, wight?"

"Fahwenheit is... they are getting a few things bad and I won't like the whole family to be on Fahwenheit."

"Getting suspicious again?" asks Dame Nissi, "Anyway, I get the point. You have to go to the confewence hall now... the entire world is waiting for you."

"No, I want us to finish with Leontine first..."

Dame Nissi insists, "I am here... forget what that baby survey said. We have so many years to spend with her..." "And you found the lost earth!" adds Dame Nissi with a smile.

"You've still not told me why you love the idea of the lost earth this much."

"The pictures, Omicwon," Dame Nissi whispers to his hearing alone, "it means my ancestors were not mad handing them down fwom genewations to genewations. It means I can have the gallewy I dweam of; people will surely want to see those pictures over and over again."

Lord Omicron smiles. "And I am glad this will make you happy." He stands and adds, "I'll be going over there, and I'll make sure it is quick."

"Please do," Dame Nissi responds.

"And hey," Lord Omicron says to the Vexim agent, "make sure that BEM doesn't overwide my daughter's natuwal learning ability." "And," he turns to Dame Nissi, "let him check Sextine's BEM please. Whatever that gadget is doing seems to be illegal to me."

"I'll let him do that. Good luck."

Lord Omicron nods and exits the room.

4 LORD Omicron runs into the entourage of the Crown Princess, Lotem-Zeta II. We altogether almost believe this is a serious official procession until Lord Omicron begins snooping amongst the numerous guards, trying to find the hidden princess.

The 28 year old almost dark skinned heir to the throne is not exactly petite; it simply takes taller guards to keep her away from searching eyes. The guards are aware of Lord Omicron's friendship with the princess so they practically pretend nobody is breaking their orderly procession.

"Your highness?" Lord Omicron whispers before he finally spots her. He stands tall beside her, both looking very mean but simply gossiping.

"Lord Omicwon, have you heard?" the princess asks with an embedded mischievous excitement.

"Heard what?"

"Lady Ose Neo has been sainted."

"What? How? Who appointed her a saint? Your popmy?"

"Lol, my popmy ain't cwazy. The sugar appointed herself."

"Ha! Yet another self-pwoclaimed saint in the universe. She does have followers? What was her claim?"

"That she met an angel on the lost earth," Princess Lotem-Zeta at this point is trying not to laugh, "and the angel gave her messages for the people of Oh."

"We only just came in a few hours ago and Lady Ose Neo is alweady a saint? I bet I'll be godded after this event."

"If they believe you, if you sound like one, then I myself will declare you be an archgod."

"A god of gods perhaps," Lord Omicron jokes.

"Lol, Saint Ose Neo... hmm, I wonder what Sir Nnia will make of this."

"That evil genius will enjoy this. It sounds like one of his inventions."

They giggle on as they reach the crowded conference hall.

The principle officials, about thirty men and women, are seated on the high table. One of the officials is unashamedly in her pyjamas, clearly protesting the timing of this event.

Princess Lotem-Zeta and Lord Omicron breakaway from the guards to join the rest of the crew just beside the desk reserved for them. Sir Nnia and Archprofessor Lux Eden are all smiles; they all give a slight bow to the princess.

"I hope this will be fast," the princess complains immediately, "my daughter is waiting for me."

"Shouldn't that girl be eight years old now?" Sir Nnia asks in his usual rude fashion.

"That girl?" Sir Luminescence speaks up for the crown princess. He is one of the few who got knighted for defending the throne of the Western Nations, not just for a couple of outstanding achievements. "Her name is Pwincess Zeta Alma-Beauty Maywy Sigma, gwanddaughter of King Sigma the sixth. You should addwess her pwoperly, mm?"

Princess Lotem-Zeta could afford a very wide happy grin, bending over to Lady Ose Neo and acknowledging her silent greetings by rubbing the new saint's back.

Professor Knight Nightingale is one of the officials on the high table. She announces the presence of the minister of space – *Archlord John-Johnson J.J Johnson,* a tall john to behold.

The hall is silent and everyone could hear Lord Omicron complain about Professor Knight.

"What is that lady doing here?" he asks, trying so hard to keep his voice and anger down.

"She's part of the space ministwy, she has always been there. That's Pwofessor Knight Nightingale."

Archlord Johnson gives up on his short patience for Lord Omicron to finish nagging. "When you are done, let the team captain speak up please."

"I am the team captain!" Lord Omicron's voice is quite loud in rage.

Princess Lotem-Zeta pinches him on the leg. "You be calm now sugar, speak lordly."

"I am Lord Omicwon Woe," he says in a respectful voice. "I am the captain of Epsilon."

"Yes then," Archlord Johnson says after clearing his throat, "I am Archlord John-Johnson J.J Johnson, the minister of space. With me here are cabinet members, wepwesentatives fwom space agencies, concerned scientists, concerned explanationists, and concerned questionnaires."

Each group obliges to the minister's informal roll call by raising their hands when their group is mentioned. The scientists are all suited up, most without seats standing around the seated few.

"We are here to welcome Epsilon," the minister continues, "to hear what they discovered, and if possible, see what they discovered."

Lord Omicron takes over the people's attention. "Epsilon took off fwom Oh on the thirty-first of September, two-nine-nine."

"What is your name, sir?" One of the questionnaires interrupts Lord Omicron.

"Um... Lord Omicwon Woe. Woe is aaw, aych, oh."

"How old are you, Lord Woe?" the questionnaire asks again.

"Thirty years old," Lord Omicron replies quickly.

"You marwied, Lord Woe?" asks a female questionnaire in a more polite manner.

"Yes, I am," he replies, adding, "with thwee kids," in anticipation of the next question. We notice another questionnaire visibly reserves his question.

"You are the captain of the team?" asks yet another questionnaire.

"Yes! I said..."

"How many journeys have you embarked on with the team?" another questionnaire cuts him short.

"Fifty-two space journeys," he responds.

"Is this your first mission as team captain?"

"No, it is..."

"How many out of the fifty-two were you team captain?"

"All of them," Lord Omicron responds.

Princess Lotem-Zeta is visibly fed up with the questions. She stands beside Lord Omicron in a silent protest. A number of questionnaires become less enthusiastic to ask another question, yet a few press on.

"How long have you been team captain?" asks a female questionnaire.

"Fifteen years..."

"Same team members since then?"

"Can we pwoceed?" Princess Lotem-Zeta asks.

"This is my pwoceeding," the minister says, "with all due wespect. You two can sit now."

Princess Lotem-Zeta reluctantly joins Lord Omicron in sitting.

"You know," she whispers to him, "those double Js in his name are just to hide the stupidity of having more Johns in one name."

Lord Omicron laughs quietly. This clearly prevents the minister from speaking; he's not ready to ignore them.

"When you two are done basking in your egos, we may move on."

"Excuse me!" Princess Lotem-Zeta is strongly offended and she stands to her feet. Her guards take a couple of steps towards her. "Mr Minister, I believe I must have heard you poorly."

"Don't you think you should be wealthy enough not to have a poor state of hearwing?" Archlord Johnson mocks the princess.

"This is insane, have you got no knowledge of who you are?"

"You should have simply asked pwoperly about me, your highness."

"I know damn too well about your stupid being!" the princess announces.

"Then you should know you are expected to sit here and follow due pwocess."

Lord Omicron pulls gently on the princess' cloths and she bends over to him.

"Let it be, pwincess," he whispers.

"I can have this man cwucified for insulting me," the princess whispers strongly.

"No, you won't, that will be murder."

"You can call it whatever you wish, as long as it has him dead forwever." She takes her seat. "I wonder why Saint Fwancsec stopped the killing of fools."

"My Pwincess, a lord is hardly a fool let alone an archlord."

"Now I could have you killed too, Lord Omicwon."

"Now that's betwayal," Lord Omicron says immediately.

"You betwaying me alweady! Archlord Johnson is a fool, agwee?"

"Agweed," Lord Omicron accepts to please the princess.

"Lord Omicwon Woe," Professor Knight calls out. "Can you now give us little details of your last journey?"

Lord Omicron takes a few seconds staring at Professor Knight, wondering why he should respond to her question.

"A pwofessor of what exactly are you?" Lord Omicron asks.

Professor Knight smiles. "I am a pwofessor of all the pwofessions I've embarked on, including space science and astwonomy. Unlike your team member Archpwofessor Lux Eden, I declined the title of Archpwofessor."

"Pwofessor Nightingale!" Archprofessor Lux Eden speaks up immediately. "Please don't say that again. You not an Archpwofessor because you never had the balls and you still don't have the balls."

"Without those balls I'm still twice your worth, Archpwofessor Lux Eden."

"This is gwadually turning into multiple duels," an explanationist speaks up "and it stems fwom the lack of belief that the lost earth may have been found."

There's a brief silence in the hall. The minister signals Lord Omicron to carry on.

Lord Omicron clears his throat and speaks calmly. "The team of six on Epsilon left Oh on Fwiday, the thirty-first of September, two-nine-nine. We, however, did encounter minor navigation issues."

"What was the issue?" asks a questionnaire.

"Shut up!" The entire Epsilon team, apart from Lady Ose Neo, respond to the questionnaire in one loud voice.

"Though we are still sure of the course," Lord Omicron continues, "it is important we say that we indeed stumbled upon it accidently. That particular course led us to the lost earth."

There is a sudden unrest in the hall, everyone questioning every other person, and the questionnaires are of course answering questions with questions. The minister tries to no avail to call everyone to order; surely nobody's name happens to be 'ladies and gentlemen', not even at the fifth time of asking.

"Is there any evidence to support your claim?" a scientist shouts.

All eyes are on Lord Omicron, all mouths just in that thin line between open and close, no, not ajar, and with all ears waiting to hear a big yes.

"Um, Sir Nnia Den was placed in charge of collecting evidence," Lord Omicron reveals.

"So, you placed Sir Nnia in charge... why not you?" asks another questionnaire.

"I was going to study our course," Lord Omicron responds, "just to be sure I understood how we stumbled upon the lost earth."

"To study the course?" asks yet another questionnaire. "You were so not awed by this lost earth, you actually ignored it to study a wecorded course?"

"Yes, of course, I wasn't pwepared to be lost there."

"Have you seen the lost earth before you stumbled upon it?"

"No."

"How is it that something you've never seen before couldn't get hold of your attention?" asks another questionnaire.

"Because I've lived my whole life without paying any attention to it, since I've never seen it before. Maybe next time I'd be fascinated by it."

"The team captain," explains an explanationist, "Lord Omicwon owes Epsilon a safe weturn to Oh and to the State of Genia, the capital of Sexat, hence Lord Omicwon had to be sure of the course."

"I believe Sir Nnia Den is capable enough to shoulder the wesponsibility of collecting evidence. Sir Nnia?" the minister calls on the evil genius.

Sir Nnia stands slowly as other crew members look around him, hoping to see any sign of any evidence collected from the lost earth. Undoubtedly there is no evidence, for Sir Nnia Den stands empty handed and empty spaced, but full of an arrogant courage to say what he has to say.

"Yes, I somewhat have bad news," Sir Nnia begins. "I did not collect any evidence."

There is serious murmuring in the room. Many of the scientists standing around the high table vacate the room in disappointment. Lord Omicron's mouth is left wide open in surprise, leaving the rest of the crew staring curiously at him, rather more surprised at the wideness of his mouth.

"BECAUSE!" Sir Nnia adds in a loud voice.

Lord Omicron eases his joints and mutters to the princess. "There is a because..."

"Seemesh, this is unbelievable," the princess tells him. "The evil genius stwikes again."

The room is now almost quiet and with all eyes on Sir Nnia's lips, he continues gracefully.

"Because, I was not sure if the things I saw were safe to be bwought home. I thought if Lord Omicwon Woe can assure us that we can find our way home, then the most important thing is to tell our people what we saw out there."

"This is totally stupid!' a scientist protests. "He came to 'tell' us what he saw!"

"They were not sure of the hazards the lost earth could be containing," explains an explanationist, "so, instead of dying in an attempt to collect evidence, they decided it was best to tell us what they found, with hope that we will get to see it in the future."

"Were they not with gadgets to check if the lost earth is hazardous or not?" asks a questionnaire.

"You should know," Sir Nnia responds, "the lost earth could have a more advanced technology than ours. It was not worth the wisk, considerwing we can get to it more pwepared to collect evidence."

"Sir Nnia Den," the minister calls him, "this ministwy is not financed with stones. We need evidence that will justify us financing the next twip to the lost earth to collect evidence."

"This is simple, Archlord Johnson," argues Sir Nnia. "The ministwy will basically finance our normal twip as usual and we'll simply choose to stumble upon the lost earth again by mistake..."

Princess Lotem-Zeta cannot believe she finds Sir Nnia funny. She blows up her cheeks, sucking up the laughter. The real citizens of the 'free' world could afford to giggle quietly. Archlord Johnson stares angrily at the entire crew.

"You think this is a joke?" the minister asks sternly.

The room is quiet; it is clearly no longer a joke.

"Basking in your foolishness," the minister continues, "you expect us to finance you for another fictitious journey. And as dumb as you all are, none of you came back with anything. Did you even twy bweathing the air on the lost earth without your masks? Did you? Sir Luminescence?"

"Yes, Archlord Johnson, it was oxygen." Sir Luminescence responds.

"I suppose you don't have any evidence too."

"I'm afwaid I don't, Archlord Johnson."

"Archpwofessor Lux Eden, any evidence?"

Lux Eden shakes his head, "no."

The minister looks at the princess. "Any evidence, Pwincess Lotem-Zeta?"

"None, Archlord Johnson," she responds.

The minister turns to Lady Ose Neo. "Lady Ose Neo?"

"Saint Ose Neo," the new saint corrects the old archlord.

"Pardon?" the minister almost voicelessly demands.

"My name is Saint Ose Neo. God bless you."

"Can you explain why we still have your name here as Lady Ose Neo?"

"Lady Ose Neo was sainted just a few moments ago after her team got back to Oh." An explanationist is quick to answer.

We are yet to understand that this is exactly why they get paid. If the explanations they render best convey the message or reasoning of the *explainee,* the tabs are kept by the sapien after which it makes a request to transfer digits to the explanationist.

"Why were you sainted?" a questionnaire asks. That's one bill for the minister and the scientists to pay.

"I believe an angel with the word of the Lord came to me on the lost earth," says Lady Ose Neo. "Soon I'll give you all the messages he gave me."

"But there's no pwoof of the lost earth," argues the minister. "How then can we accept you as a saint?"

"Archlord John-Johnson J.J Johnson," Lady Ose Neo speaks his name in her accustomed troublemaking voice.

The princess is quite elated.

"You want evidence," Lady Ose Neo continues. "It is said that old things have passed away and behold I am a new cweature. Hmm, not that I'm boasting in the sins of my past life but you know damn too well the normal Ose Neo won't sit hushed and watch you insult me team and evewything that is important to us." She then speaks softly, the voice of the new creature she has become, one that still makes the princess smile broadly. "That is all I have to say, and please, change your data. I am now to be addwessed as *Saint Ose Neo* of Genia, Sexat in the western fwee world. God bless you."

Lady Ose Neo from now, the 1st of January, 300, is unarguably to be known as Saint Ose Neo – the one who met an angel on the lost earth, a planet that still remains lost.

"I'll take that to be you have no evidence of the lost earth too," concludes the minster, "and with no evidence, I am afwaid we wasted our time coming here."

We seem to have forgotten the protesting lady in her pyjamas. Her loud "HA!" attracts all the attention again and the minister closes the event by apologising to her.

"*Archduchess Penelope Lontor*, sowie for wasting your time. Goodbye evewyone."

And just as though the grand wizard has announced the adjournment of a witches and wizards' gathering, nearly half of those in attendance, including the pyjamas-protesting Archduchess Penelope Lontor, literally disappear into thin air. Their holograms have been terminated. The remaining 'real people' in the room, including all the scientists, make their way to the door. The princess' guards shield her and the rest of the crew away from news reporters. A couple of zealous believers still found their way to Saint Ose Neo just to kiss her hand.

The closest rendezvous for Team Epsilon to regroup is in Dame Nissi's delivery room, and without discussing or agreeing, they all make their way to the room. Lord Omicron opens the door.

Dame Nissi is watching the event on the screen over her sapien with Dr. Fran. Lexis and Sextine are fast asleep.

Dame Nissi smiles at her husband as the crew enter the room and we could hear the news reporter thru Dame Nissi's sapien announcing the sack of Archlord Johnson as the minister of space. Everyone ignores the news.

"Pwesident Leonard Eddy-Tome has announced the immediate dismissal of Archlord Johnson as the minister of space," the reporter announces. "This might be the aftermath of the archlord's spat with Cwown Pwincess Lotem-Zeta a few moments ago. Pwofessor Knight Nightingale has been placed as the supervising minister of space until daybweak at least. Let's hear what she has to say..."

Lord Omicron gives his wife a hug and the sapien screen turns off in the process.

"How is the baby?" he asks.

"She's doing fine. We haven't seen anyone to baptize her yet."

"I can do that," Saint Ose Neo offers.

Everyone waits on Lord Omicron to make a quick decision; one that should be influenced by Princess Lotem-Zeta's vibrating eyeballs.

"Yes, why not," Lord Omicron quickly accepts and Princess Lotem-Zeta claps mischievously.

"Please do make it quick," Sir Nnia snaps in.

"You weally should save your voice Sir Nnia!" Lord Omicron barks. "You'll need it after this."

"No, I won't because I'm going home now. I will see you all later and I will tell you then why I bwought back no evidence."

"You actually didn't bwing back any evidence?" asks Sir Luminescence.

"No," Sir Nnia mocks him, "any evidence didn't actually bwing me back. Goodbye."

In as much as they all want to hold back Sir Nnia for more questioning, they are happier he's leaving already. Sir Nnia exits the delivery room and Saint Ose Neo proceeds to take the baby from her bed. Dr. Fran brings her a small bowl of water.

"What will he be called?" Saint Ose Neo asks.

"She... Leontine Bella," Dame Nissi responds.

Saint Ose Neo sprinkles water on the forehead of the baby. "Leontine Bella Woe, I baptize you in the name of the Father, and the Son, and the Holy Spiwit, amen."

It's all smiles in the room, but Archprofessor Lux Eden is being distracted by his sapien. He complains loudly about it.

"This is unbelievable," he says. "These explanationists are charging a hundwed and thirty digits per explanation!"

"What?" Sir Luminescence lifts up his hand to conjure his sapien. "Sapien!" he calls out.

While his sapien gives him the "yes boss" response, other sapiens in the room echo, "you not me boss."

"Ah please don't do that here," the princess complains.

"Get my bills," Sir Luminescence instructs his sapien before turning to the concerned Lux Eden. "How many explanations were you offered?"

"Just one," he says, disappointing everyone around. "Point now is I can't wemember needing an explanation."

"Just one explanation and you distwacted all of us," says Lord Omicron as he collects Leontine from Saint Ose Neo.

"I didn't complain about the number of explanations, I complained about the charge, a hundwed and thirty digits! That's almost the pwice of a new sapien."

"Yes boss," his sapien responds immediately and, inevitably after a second, other sapiens echo, "you not me boss."

"It is a hundwed and sixty digits for these noisemakers," Saint Ose Neo corrects the archprofessor.

Archprofessor Lux Eden looks at the new saint with intent to further buttress his point.

"Let's not argue now," Lord Omicron pleads.

"Of course," agrees Saint Ose Neo with a contractive smile, "old things have passed away."

"The new me murders saints you know," Archprofessor Lux Eden informs the smiling saint.

Saint Ose Neo raises her eyebrows and Princess Lotem-Zeta bursts into laughter.

"Me Gee! Lux Eden, that was... lol!"

"Alwight alwight," Lord Omicron calls for their attention, "I need to take my wife home. I need to see my home too. Today is Saturday; we'll meet at the office on Monday afternoon... by 1 t.m. if that is ok by you all."

"1 t.m. is fine," agrees the princess. "Just that we may not have enough time to bubble then. I have a function in the palace by 5 t.m."

"Lol," Saint Ose Neo giggles, "I thought you'll say 2 t.m. I'm sure we'll be done way before 5 t.m., wight, Lord Omicwon?"

"Absolutely, we don't have much to discuss. I'll inform Sir Nnia about the meeting. Shall we?" Lord Omicron ushers them towards the door.

5 DR. Fran Evensong supports Dame Nissi as they move to the teleport system near the hospital reception. There are five teleporting machines in this system and five of Princess Lotem-Zeta's guards are the first to advance into the machines. Each of them selects the same destination and vanishes.

"Lord Woe?"

"Yes, Doctor Fwan?"

"It won't be safe using the teleport because of Leontine."

"Why is that?" Dame Nissi asks.

"Teleports are dangewous for deaf people, you know, the ears not being functional and all that, they may lose the essential balance."

The Rhos nod in a confusing agreement.

"I'll get one of the wesort's conveyors for hire," Dr. Fran continues. "You can float your family back home. The hire services usually cost thwee hundwed and twenty-five digits. The cars are just close by, come on."

The Rhos pretend not be surprised about the price of hiring a car; the secret agony of being one of the richest families around. They follow Dr. Fran back to Phantom Resort. They watch her speak to the man in charge of the cars and he gives her a remote, pointing to the floating car up ahead.

Dr. Fran hands the remote over to Lord Omicron and bids them farewell. Dame Nissi collects the sleeping Leontine from Lord Omicron as they walk to the conveyor.

The base of the car is just about twenty centimetres above the ground. This allows it to float as fast as 400km/

hr. which is the speed limit here in the State of Genia. Once in a while, people still get arrested for over speeding. There is usually one or no accident every ten years, thanks to the strict measures these conveyors impose on its drivers. One of the greatest safety features is the mind reading ability – one that overrides the driver's decision that could lead to a one percent chance of a driving error. These restrictions include not moving the car at all.

Lexis and Sextine sit at the back while Dame Nissi sits in front, carrying Leontine. Lord Omicron shuts the door for his wife and hops to the driver's seat. He turns on the ignition and the car speaks in a female voice. This excites Dame Nissi; she has never been in a female conveyor. Not to worry, we will never see any difference in a male conveyor.

"Welcome, I am Viva," the car says.

"Wow, a female!" Dame Nissi smiles.

Lexis and Sextine look too tired to talk.

"Yeah, female cars," says Lord Omicron, "I heard they whine a lot."

"Yeah wight. I've never been in one anyway."

The car has been carrying out a lot of activities since the ignition was turned on. The seatbelt, with its lights on, has been strapped across Lord Omicron's chest. It is clearly screening thru the driver's body systems. It shows his alcohol level (1%), Tendency to sleep within the next hour (5%), BEM driving experience (Top class).

"Please turn on safety measures," the car reminds Lord Omicron.

He obliges and clicks on the button.

"Safety measures activated," the car confirms, "float safely."

Lord Omicron taps the 'start engine' button. Viva's engine declines to come on. He clicks it repeatedly and vigorously. Dame Nissi keeps staring at the monitors.

"Wait Omicwon," she says after realising the problem, "the safety measures won't let you start the car."

"Why?"

"Because it's safer if the car doesn't move at all. They must have attuned it to a safety percentage of hundwed percent."

"Widiculous, I'm calling Doctor Evensong."

"No no, you don't need to call her... just turn off the ignition and start again. This time, turn on the engine before accepting the safety measures."

"Female cars," Lord Omicron nags as he turns off the ignition.

"All cars behave like that. When last did you float one of these?"

"God knows it's been many years."

Lord Omicron turns on the ignition. The car welcomes him again and repeats the whole process. It gets to the point of activating the safety measures and Dame Nissi holds back his hand.

"I want to click 'no'," Lord Omicron explains.

"If you click no, it will shut down. Just start the engine and move the car before activating it."

Lord Omicron does exactly what his wife says but Viva has other ideas. The engine indeed comes on but the car refuses to move.

"What is all this?" Lord Omicron is visibly irritated.

"Maybe just accept the safety measures, since the engine is alweady on... and clear your mind too, you might be thinking of something she deems not fit to let you into the stweet."

"Is she cwazy? I am only thinking of Leontine."

"That's it! You cannot think of her, she's deaf you know..."

"What has that got to do with me?" Lord Omicron asks.

"If you have her on your mind, the car might just as well assume you are deaf too."

"Jeez, she's deaf not blind, are you nuts?"

"OMICWON, I'M NOT NUTS!"

Lord Omicron bursts into laughter at the sound his wife's last comment. Dame Nissi is surprisingly laughing quietly.

"Nice whymes, 'I am not nuts'," Lord Omicron mocks Dame Nissi, still trying to control his laughter.

Dame Nissi laughs a little more and then complains immediately. "I think I was at peace when you went away, like damn, you back to make me go cwazy again."

"Don't mind me," Lord Omicron apologises, "I'm sowie." He quickly accepts Viva's safety measures and moves the car. "So much for a female car; how did you guys get here in the first place?"

"My cousin, Sir Louis, he bwought us in his car."

"Hmm, Sir Louis," Lord Omicron responds with a fading smile.

We are yet to understand why he doesn't really like Sir Louis who is Dame Nissi's distant cousin and more importantly, their next door neighbour.

"Yes, he's still vewy much alive, with his lovely wife Lady Louis."

Lord Omicron sighs, "please don't start."

"Lol, you know they adopted a baby," Dame Nissi continues happily.

"How will I know that?"

"Well... you know now. The baby is so cute, they named her Valentine."

"Valentine, a human?" Lord Omicron asks.

"No, not human, just something Lady Louis can bweastfeed."

"They should have named her a Bow, Wow, Woo, Whoa, Hoe, Ha or something."

"That something is Valentine." Dame Nissi concludes.

"Warning," Viva speaks up, "this conversation is getting boring, you may fall asleep."

"Unbelievable!" Dame Nissi exclaims. "And that's the absolute twuth about you."

"What do you mean Nissi? You'll pay attention to this car?"

"Each time I bwing up my family, you just fall asleep."

"Nissi, you are an only child... you don't have a family outside us."

"I have cousins Omicwon, I have uncles and aunts!"

"And I should be bothered about them?"

"There we have it!"

"Warning," Viva speaks up again.

"Oh shut up you car!" Lord Omicron screams back at Viva but she continues nonetheless.

"This conversation is heated up," Viva informs them, "you are getting distwacted."

"Warning," Viva has more notifications, "your mind is clouded. Warning, I am under attack."

"You damn sure are under attack," says the angry Lord Omicron. "Sapien," he calls out for his wrist companion.

The sapien responds at once with the traditional 'yes boss' while Dame Nissi's rejects the call.

"Shut this car up," Lord Omicron commands.

"Identify car model and codes," the sapien requests.

"I don't know, see for yourself," says Lord Omicron as he takes his hands off the wheel to help pair his sapien to Viva.

"Warning," Viva is at it again, "your hands are off the wheel."

Lord Omicron isn't bothered by whatever warning she has, it will take two seconds to introduce her to his weapons grade sapien – a version of the gadget given only to uniform men, astronauts inclusive. He taps the sapien and it pops up the usual array of multiple translucent screens containing information we can't really see or understand. He dips his finger into one of the screens and lifts a small red circle into the car's monitor. Viva responds immediately in a louder voice.

"Warning! A viwus has been detected... warning..." Viva's voice fades away.

"Completed, boss," announces Lord Omicron's sapien and it goes back to sleep.

Lord Omicron keeps his eyes on the road while Dame Nissi keeps her eyes on the increasing speedometer data.

"That's four hundwed and two, Omicwon," Dame Nissi alerts him quietly.

"Ah women, you might have as well started with 'warning'!"

"Well... we are clearly committing a cwime now."

"Warning, boss," Lord Omicron's sapien warns, "you over speeding."

Dame Nissi shakes her head in disappointment. Lord Omicron looks sorry as he drops his speed to 200km/hr, partly because they've entered the residential areas normally characterised by the presence of occasionally choral humming birds called the lilies.

It is still a mystery where the lilies go during the day. Explanationists and saints simply agree the lilies go to eat from God, citing "He provides for the birds of the air." Some scientists and explorers, however, claim the birds fly across the constantly turbulent *Youlv Ocean* – an ocean famed for being so carnivorous that no creature lives in it. Whatever that is said about the lilies, one thing is for sure. Each morning, they fly way out of the range of human eyes and way beyond reach of any tracking device; that's one for gadget innovationists to work on.

The birds are called lilies because they actually look like the extinct lily flowers. It is always a delightful sight to see them return to the ground at night, beautifying the environment with their usual white, pink, orange, and golden colours. You'll be lucky if one lives next to you, and like the Rhos, you'd be glad to have an entire garden of lilies settling down around your home every night.

Lord Omicron drops his speed to 40km/hr as he takes the final turn towards the family house. They are used to seeing a bunch of fascinating lilies but never a bunch of fascinated people staring into the night sky. Something certainly must have gone wrong.

"They are all looking into the sky," Dame Nissi mutters.

"Yes," Lord Omicron responds as he stops the car, "please don't come down yet, let me check it out."

Dame Nissi nods; there's certainly no way she would have agreed to come out with her kids as everyone stares at the sky. Anything coming from the sky will definitely love to snatch one or all of her little children.

She looks on as her husband questions the first man he meets. The man gives Lord Omicron a hug, certainly happy to see him again. If the man's senses can still exchange pleasantries, Dame Nissi begins to believe that nothing dangerous is out there. That will be hard to believe as Lord Omicron just raised his eyebrows and turned sharply towards her cousin's house. She looks towards Sir Louis' house, the few people who are not making random checks on the sky are emotionally busy trying to console the upset Sir Louis whose wife is surprisingly not sitting beside him. Lord Omicron returns to the car not looking worried, he basically doesn't care about Sir Louis.

"What's going on?" Dame Nissi asks.

"A false pwophet came awound," Lord Omicron reveals.

"A FOLF?"

Lord Omicron nods and Dame Nissi could only imagine how terrifying the situation was.

The *folf* is a magnificent creature. It is famed for being the only creature that can swim across the Youlv Ocean. It has a bulky body like a horse and a mean head of a wolf. Its wings are usually twice the body size. With golden eyes and a form of latex skin overlaid with massive amount of wool, it earned the domestic name 'false prophet'. Simply put, it is a flying wolf in sheep clothing.

Lord Omicron is not overly concerned about the folf anymore. He's aware it never strikes twice in the same place during its lifetime.

"Who did it take?" Dame Nissi asks.

"Your little cousin, Valentine Louis..."

"Oh no! I haven't seen Lady Louis, have you seen her awound?"

"Please Nissi, don't ask me about them. We need to go to bed."

"But what was Valentine doing outside by this time? It's just past 3 a.m."

"Now you've asked a vewy important question," Lord Omicron responds excitedly. "Sir Louis has accused Lady Louis of cheating, because poor Valentine was out with her to visit her boyfwend, Master Havvy the dog, when the false pwophet came and snatched her away."

"Lady Louis was cheating? That's terwible."

"What do you expect fwom dogs? Tell your cousin to step up."

"Certainly the topic doesn't bore you any longer."

"Lol... It will get more intewesting because I'm sure Sir Louis will want you to stand for him in court. He has alweady filed for divorce."

"Seemesh," Dame Nissi shakes her head, "I think I'm sleepy now."

Lord Omicron opens the door for his wife while Lexis leads Sextine out of the car. The Rhos are clearly tired as they walk slowly towards their house. Dame Nissi is first to spot a beautiful white dog sitting near the front door of the house.

"Lady Louis?" she calls out to the dog.

"Where?" Lord Omicron raises his head at once and sees the dog. "What's she doing there?"

"Give her a bweak, she just lost her child"

"Nissi, Valentine wasn't basically her child."

"Stop that, you discwiminating against her. My gweat-gwandmomxy was adopted," Dame Nissi argues.

"Lady Louis, go home please," Lord Omicron instructs the dog.

The dog gets up and walks away.

Lord Omicron places his left palm on the door's security scan. The door runs a quick identity check while Dame Nissi keeps her eyes on the departing Lady Louis.

Oh, before it is forgotten, we had just realised that indeed Sir Louis' wife is a dog, yes, a dog-dog. We can all remember how this crazy sequence began if we think hard enough. It is still difficult to see a female human legally married to a male animal. Trust their egos, ladies will want to be asked first. Poor animals, they are yet to learn how to propose.

"Please, state your purpose of visit," the front door throws a surprising request to Lord Omicron.

Lord Omicron is feeling embarrassed; he turns to Dame Nissi.

"Don't mind that thing, it's been faulty many times," Dame Nissi explains.

"Sowie, the Woes are not home," the door says again.

"You see," Dame Nissi points out, "if you had stated your purpose of coming and the lie detector finds you twustworthy, it would have opened the door still knowing we are not home."

"Nissi, how do I get into the house if I'm not home?"

"Don't bother, let me twy. Here... hold Leontine" Dame Nissi hands Leontine over to him. She places her left hand on the door scan and the door opens almost immediately.

"Seemesh," Lord Omicron shakes his head and walks into the house nevertheless.

No doubt the door needs to be fixed. The biggest doubt is if Lord Omicron or any member of his family can stand for another second pondering on the faulty door.

We don't actually get to see the inside of this fine mansion. We simply get our eyes shut out by the door slammed obviously by Lord Omicron, and he snaps his fingers and the lights still obey him by turning on. They actually do obey everybody.

6 MOMENTS later, in a thick forest, we hear a very sorrowful cry. We surely can see Lady Louis sitting in the grass, but the way she's crying is certainly not natural for a dog. Finally, someone confirms our confusion, and it is Dame Nissi. Dressed up in a folf's latex, which is one reason the folves are getting extinct, Dame Nissi looks on Lady Louis with pity. The dog's voice intensifies, her sorrow

deepens, and for a second she's beginning to clearly sound like the baby, Leontine Rho.

"Don't feel sad Lady Louis," Dame Nissi says to the dog as she walks slowly towards her, "listen to you cwy. I told my husband to stop discwiminating against you."

Lady Louis can see Dame Nissi approaching, she can hear the words of consolation, but her sorrowful voice is most definitely not paying attention, she wails even the more.

Dame Nissi stretches out her hand to reach for the dog, a hand which she instantly and fearfully withdraws with a scream at the sight of Lady Louis' dangerously grinning canines.

This dawns on us, for we are just having another dream, a dream in a dream and Dame Nissi is our host. The dog's grin doesn't affect the cry, but it does affect the dream.

Dame Nissi's scream forces her out of the dream and she sits up at once. The sight of a grinning Sextine doesn't help her course. Sextine is sitting on the bed, sitting on both legs, holding the wailing Leontine in her arms. Dame Nissi's vision is still blurry as she stares at Sextine.

"What is wong with you?" she asks Sextine.

Sextine is still grinning, staring back at her mother. Dame Nissi rubs her eyes and gets a clearer picture of Sextine holding Leontine, and her canines are a lot safer.

"What is wong with you?" Dame Nissi asks again.

Sextine doesn't move a muscle and Leontine's cry finally gets Dame Nissi's attention.

"Me Gee Sextine, I can swear by all the gods your BEM is completely out of order. Give me me baby..." Dame Nissi collects Leontine from Sextine. She cradles the baby for a couple of seconds and proceeds to breastfeed her.

The baby is finally quiet and Sextine stops smiling and speaks cheerfully.

"Momxy, you were whimperwing in your sleep."

"I was what? Was that why you were gwinning?" Dame Nissi asks Sextine.

"No I wasn't."

"Heh," Dame Nissi now whimpers, "that was just a teeth show? Impwessive. Where is your popmy young lady?"

"In the lab..."

"Have you had bweakfast?"

"Yes, we've all eaten."

"Can you make me something, I'm hungwy."

"No momxy," Sextine objects, "you put Lexis in charge of emergency bwunch."

"Yes I know that, but I'm asking for emergency bweakfast."

"It is past 2 t.m. momxy, it is bwunch time, and I'm hungwy too."

Dame Nissi looks at the time, it is indeed past 2 t.m. Official brunch time is between 2-3 t.m. in the afternoon. Printing brunch meals needs steadier hands than that of a 3 year old.

"Call Lexis for me," Dame Nissi tells Sextine.

"I'm wight here momxy," Lexis reveals, staggering up from the floor and slowly diving into Dame Nissi on the bed.

"Careful, you'll disturb Leontine," Dame Nissi warns, rubbing Lexis' hair as vigorously as possible; one will feel is it abnormal to have neatly arranged hair.

Lexis rolls down the bed and sets off to get food for everybody, which is not necessarily a difficult task.

Lord Omicron is in his personal gadget laboratory as Sextine pointed out. It will be easy to guess what he's up to considering he has both a high level of skill and a little daughter he'll love to communicate with someday.

We understand Lord Omicron has a brilliant idea, one that doesn't really concern Lexis who is simply in the business of feeding the hungry. *'A glass of milk will certainly be welcomed'* he thinks to himself as he walks quietly towards Lord Omicron. He taps him on the shoulder; though startled, Lord Omicron is very much glad to see the glass of cold milk, and his son of course.

"Lexis!" Lord Omicron grabs the glass of milk from his son's outstretched hand and gently puts his Nissi-redesigned hair in order. "Is momxy up?"

"Yes, Leontine woke her up..."

"Lol, she has started her alarm duty alweady."

Lord Omicron downs the glass of milk and he's full of praise for Lexis. "You are one bwight adowable boy. People will find you so easy to love no matter what you do. Has anyone ever told you that before?"

"Yes, my BEM tells me that always."

"Your BEM?" Lord Omicron conceals his worry that Lexis' BEM could be misbehaving too. "What else has that BEM been saying?"

"She says I can sleep all day and still achieve my dweams."

"Ha!" Lord Omicron raises he eyebrows. "Of course you can sleep all day but what you'll achieve is a lot of dweaming. You see," he speaks more gently, "as men, we must begin early; we must think early, we must plan early to achieve gweat things. We must work day in and day out and of course, finally, we get to end up marwied."

Lexis giggles, "I want to marwy Pwincess Maywy-Zeta."

"Lol dude, you are fwee to tell the pwincess yourself. I am vewy certain her momxy will love you to be her son-in-law."

"Because you her fwend, yeah?"

"Not just that Lexis, I wasn't joking when I said you w'an adowable boy. Pwincess Lotem-Zeta will surely be cool to have you as her son-in-law."

Dame Nissi clears her throat and interrupts the father-son marriage plot as they both turn sharply to her, quick enough to watch her unleash Sextine into the lab. Sextine sets off slowly like an accreditation inspector carefully analysing the smell of the fresh air in the room.

Lord Omicron's eyes stick to Sextine immediately. If all his scientific projects were successfully, it would have been possible to cage Sextine with a blink of his left eye.

Dame Nissi is obviously about to say something, she doesn't clear her throat as a form of exercise. Lord Omicron subconsciously gives his attention to his wife, with both ears and an eye but his finger rises quickly, pointing at the straying Sextine – 'somebody get hold of that virus', if only fingers could speak in F.G. 300.

"What are you doing?" Dame Nissi asks.

"Chatting with Lexis..." Lord Omicron finds a simple answer to match the simple question, and more importantly make his complex wife to simply understand him.

Well, It's not that simple. Of course Dame Nissi wants to know what he's doing in his lab this time, not what he's doing with Lexis.

"Is he some kind of gadget now?" she asks again, painting a clearer picture of the answers she's demanding for.

Dame Nissi is quite determined to free Sextine from her husband's pointed finger. She snaps her fingers at Sextine and signals Lexis to keep her under a little control.

Lexis skips towards the fleeing Sextine and Lord Omicron is relieved the family Is still working as a unit to keep things out of Sextine's reach.

Lord Omicron puts his finger down and smiles. "The heart whispewer," he explains to Dame Nissi, "I'm just noticing a few things I got wong, so I think I can achieve that now."

Dame Nissi is no stranger to that word, 'heart whisperer'. She's only estranged by why her husband will choose to revisit a project that nearly earned him a 'Joseph-the-dreamer' title at the expense of his gadget engineering licence.

"Hmm," Dame Nissi sighs as she puts her arms around Lord Omicron's neck from behind, "fwom what I wemember, you got a few things wight and got many things wong."

"No doubt... I am now saying I can fix a few of those many wongs." Lord Omicron pecks her elbow.

"Why would you want to fix them? I hope you are not being worwied about Leontine?"

"No... I mean yes... no, maybe. If it works, it will help us to communicate with her too, don't you think?"

"I don't think there are many ways people communicate with the deaf, Leontine is not the first. With her BEM, with ours too, it will be vewy easy to learn how to sign"

"Nissi, signing is borwing."

Dame Nissi sighs and taps Lord Omicron's shoulders as she stands erect. "You cannot be so sure, and stop being negative, it's too early."

Lord Omicron nods.

"Lexis has pwinted bwunch... coming to eat?"

Lord Omicron shakes his head, "no, I'll just finish up here first. I'll join you guys later."

"Okay. Sextine, Lexis!" Dame Nissi calls for her invisible children.

They run out from the corner, glowing green. Lexis is still holding the *lumipen* responsible for lighting them up.

Dame Nissi snatches the pen from Lexis. "I've told you to stop playing with this thing, you know how long it will take before it switches off."

Lord Omicron is not bothered by the cheapest and safest thing in his house. The lumipen is an age long beautiful gadget that helps one draw an emergency bulb on any spot being overtaken by darkness. His attention is back to his little project as Dame Nissi leads the kids out.

7 IT is clear a couple of days have gone by. Lord Omicron is dressed differently, with a full glass of milk beside him, still sitting in the same spot, giving attention to the same little project. Dame Nissi steps in carrying Leontine, she bids him goodbye. She's off to the court hearing for the divorce between Sir Louis and Lady Louis the dog where she'll be representing her cousin, Sir Louis.

Dame Nissi steps into her office thru the pretty door just opposite her husband's gadget lab at home. She keeps the quiet Leontine in a cradle before she raises her forearm horizontally and calls up her sapien.

"Yes boss," the sapien responds immediately.

"Initiate hologwam," she instructs the sapien.

"Holo debeau two initiated, state your destination boss."

Dame Nissi has no intentions of being at the court in person; nobody really comes there in person.

"Mawital Court Seven, Dechamp stweet, the state of Genia."

"Destination found, but boss be warned, you asked to avoid Barwister Axel Allen. He is in Mawital Court Seven."

"Yes, he's up against me today."

"Taking your hologwam to Mawital Court Seven."

The Holo W-2 is the best civilian hologram around. Unlike other previous versions by Sir Nnia, Dame Nissi will be able to nurse her child or communicate with someone else without disrupting the behaviour and comportment of the hologram she sent out.

In as much as one is indeed not coming in person, it is quite unprofessional and embarrassing to appear out of the hologram portal on the judge's desk. Sir Louis doesn't mind, he walks out of it and the judge, Theoadam Lifeson, gives him a long stern look. Dame Nissi walks in thru the door and the quick court hearing begins at once. She is hoping she won't have to say anything in the court, the picture of things is always clear these days.

Lady Louis' lawyer, Axel Allen, introduces himself and calls Sir Louis to the podium.

"Why did you marwy Lady Louis the dog?" he asks Sir Louis.

"Because I was in love with her," Sir Louis replies.

"And why are we here today?"

"Because I am no longer in love with her," Sir Louis replies, and Lady Louis whimpers from her seat.

"No moaning..." Judge Theoadam announces.

"So," Barrister Axel Allen continues, "are you in love with someone else?"

"No."

"You can't be saying you fell out of love with your wife without falling in love with someone else."

"Ask it!" Sir Louis flares up in anger. "Ask it how it fell out of love so quickly and publicly had sex with Mr Havvy the dog."

"Your honour, please inform Sir Louis that my client should not be degwaded to the pwonoun of 'it'."

"Sir Louis, be warned," the judge agrees with Axel Allen. "Where you can't say Lady Louis the dog, you use she or her."

"And how are we sure of what she calls me?" Sir Louis asks sarcastically.

"Is that why you want a divorce? Axel Allen asks.

"Isn't it obvious she made me lose faith in her? She had sex publicly with Mr Havvy! Havvy, a stweet dog!"

"Lady Louis said you failed to keep her and her daughter Valentine Louis safe fwom the attack of a false pwophet."

"Lady Louis was out committing adultewy when Valentine was killed. The folf didn't attack them in my house."

"Your honour, no further questions for Sir Louis," the barrister announces. "I'd like to call Lady Louis to the podium."

"Dame Nissi Woe, any questions for Sir Louis?" the judge asks.

Dame Nissi shakes her head, 'no.'

Lady Louis walks majestically to the podium while Sir Louis takes a seat beside Dame Nissi.

"Lady Louis, I'm sowie about the loss of Valentine," Axel begins.

Lady Louis acknowledges with a bark.

"Do you still love your husband?"

Lady Louis whimpers, putting her head down. Murmurings break out in the court.

"Were you in love with Mr Havvy the dog?" Axel asks, pulling up a photo of the dog from his sapien.

Lady Louis barks in affirmative and everybody expresses their shock. Axel Allen wasn't expecting that too.

"Order!" the judge screams. "There is no need beating awound the lilies. Matwimonial love isn't the same as normal love, if not, a man would have a billion wives or a lady a billion husbands. So Sir Louis, as a matter of fact, Mr Havvy the dog is allowed to love your wife, but not allowed to marwy her or have sex with her. So I find your wife, Lady

Louis the dog, guilty of infidelity and I appwove a divorce between you two. You owe her nothing and she owes you nothing. What the court has sepawated, let no one join together. Court dismissed."

Sir Louis speaks quickly to Dame Nissi. "I'm coming over to your place"

Dame Nissi nods, and in a twinkle of an eye, the hologram-filled courtroom is completely empty.

Back in Lord Omicron's lab, Lord Omicron is sweating on stabilizing a small chip inside a completely dissected gadget.

"Boss," his sapien alerts him, "Sir Louis is at the door."

Lord Omicron frowns at the mention of Sir Louis' name.

"His purpose of visit has been declared safe," the sapien continues. "He has come to thank Dame Nissi Woe."

"Ok, let him in. Call Nissi."

"Boss, elabowate on Nissi," the sapien requests, instantly displaying pictures of eight beautiful women, including Dame Nissi Rho.

The sapien is mainly responsible for people's desire to have unique names. You can't afford the confusion that surrounds having a namesake as your friend, a friend's friend or even a family friend of a friend of a friend's family, at least to avoid too many questions from the sapien.

Lord Omicron takes a frustrating glance at all the Nissis and instinctively picks out his beautiful wife's face; "That Nissi, sapien."

"Yes, boss," the sapien responds.

"Call Dame Nissi," he instructs it again.

"Dame Nissi will speak if she can."

"Yes dear?" Dame Nissi's voice resounds thru Lord Omicron's sapien.

"Sir Louis is here to see you."

"He's with me in my office." Dame Nissi informs her husband.

"Hello Lord Woe," Sir Louis greets the animated Lord Omicron who certainly doesn't want to talk to him.

"I am coming over," Lord Omicron says reluctantly.

Lord Omicron terminates the call and drags himself to Dame Nissi's office. Sir Louis is carrying Leontine while Dame Nissi stands beside him. Both of them give Lord Omicron a hopeful look as he steps in. Dame Nissi is not getting the smile she hoped for and she's not reserved to speak her mind.

"Omicwon, please smile, it won't hurt anybody."

Lord Omicron is quick to defend himself. He speaks up, still without a smile. "Can you tell who is jealous of you or mad at you when evewyone is always smiling at you? A smile is always seen a smile, don't smile if you don't mean to."

"So what now, you jealous of me?" Sir Louis asks.

"Jealous of what, Lady Louis the dog?"

"Stop that Omicwon, my cousin has just gone thwu divorce, it hurts."

"Please Nissi, the weason behind the divorce is vewy simple, and it makes it easy for Sir Louis to endure."

"Easy?" Sir Louis wonders. "I have seen couples sepawate for easier weasons."

"Tell me about them," Lord Omicron requests.

"Um," Sir Louis thinks, "Doctor Dechires and his husband Engineer Logan."

"Exactly," Dame Nissi confirms the duo.

"Please," Lord Omicron plays down the hype, "Dechires left Logan because Logan owed someone and didn't tell him, and they ended up having an argument."

"Just one argument!" Dame Nissi stresses, "Just one!"

'Of course!" Lord Omicron insists it's enough for a divorce.

"Haven't you done worse things?" Dame Nissi asks again.

"Haven't 'we', Nissi," Lord Omicron corrects his wife. "I am not marwied to myself."

"Yes, haven't we done worse things? And yet I put up with you. We've had more than ten arguments since we got marwied. Fwom what you saying, I could have walked away in any of those but I chose to stick with you."

"That's why I love you," Lord Omicron professes.

"No no, that's why you are maltweating me."

Lord Omicron tries to speak again but it is almost impossible to interrupt a lady who is trying to make a point.

"What about Avwam and Habiba?" Dame Nissi continues. "Habiba opted out of the marwiage because Avwam didn't eat the dinner she made him."

"Yes, why shouldn't he eat at home?" argues Lord Omicron. "Then what of Sir Moore and Lady Lanx? The man punched his wife! Now that's more like it."

"Oh don't go there! Lady Lanx had a plastic surgewy and Sir Moore couldn't wecognise her. He was simply twying to stay faithful when he pushed her away. The weason for the divorce was because she changed her face to something Sir Moore didn't like, and he won't even wait for a couple of hours for her to undo the changes. The divorce wasn't because Sir Moore punched her. No man even dares touch his wife, it is totally unacceptable."

"Ha! Be dweaming," Lord Omicron responds. "That a man shouldn't touch his wife doesn't mean he should be impwisoned in his own house. If the man wants to step out and the woman is blocking the door, for Sigma's sake she'll get pushed. If she waises her hand to thweaten the man, she sure will get waised fwom the gwound and gwavity will be allowed to finish the job. If she's the first to slap the man then I can bet in the name of all the living saints there's no denying she will get spanked."

"Then that man must be marwied to a man," Dame Nissi suggests. "If you can look at this pwetty body and your hands can land in a blow, you need a total bwain twansplant."

Lord Omicron is wondering where all the 'you's are coming from. He sure can't remember ever thinking of hitting a lady.

"Lol sugar, calm down," Lord Omicron can now afford to smile. "I admit Sir Louis is going thwu a hard time."

Dame Nissi realises how quiet and emotional Sir Louis has been. She rubs his back, a show of compassion. Lord Omicron finally feels sorry for Sir Louis as he pats him on the shoulder and luckily realises that Leontine is staring back at him. He runs his finger down to the baby's right cheek. Dame Nissi could see the desire written all over Lord Omicron's face; a desire to believe that Leontine will certainly hear them someday. She nods at him, a good reason for Lord Omicron to get back to the lab.

"I'll be in my lab," Lord Omicron announces. He walks back to his lab and gets back to work immediately.

The entire day goes by, and the next day; the entire week, and the next week; the entire month and the next month; the entire year and the next year, until we come to understand that ten years has gone by. Ten years of Leontine growing up into a beautiful girl, ten years of Lord Omicron improving on the heart whisperer, ten years of Professor Knight Nightingale ignoring Crew Epsilon, ten years of Sir Nnia Den harnessing the information on the secret tablet, ten years of Dame Nissi Rho running the new Nissi's Gallery, ten years of Sir Louis feeling sorry for himself, ten years of

Saint Ose Neo preaching the Word, and ten years of us, dreaming a dream.

8 WE aren't sure who is recalling the events of last night, but we get the feeling Dame Nissi could be dreaming again. The Rhos just returned from Nissi's Gallery. The nicely arranged living room is a bit darker than usual. Lord Omicron confirms it's been a very cloudy day, less sun to generate enough energy for all the power sapping gadgets around.

"The lights are set on low importance," he explains, "needs more time to power up. Sextine can you paint up a sixty watts light over there?"

Dame Nissi is holding unto Lexis as they move slowly out of the living room, a certain mother-son bond has grown over the years. Sextine grabs a white lumipen and goes over the space Lord Omicron pointed at. Leontine understands what her sister is up, one of her own favourite chores – creating lights. She walks over to Sextine quickly and collects the lumipen before Sextine could draw an additional uncoordinated luminescent line.

"How many?" Leontine signs to her.

"Sixty," Sextine signs back.

Sextine is just about to walk away but Lord Omicron keeps her put with a hug. They watch Leontine paint a beautiful eye-shaped light, correcting the lines Sextine had started. Each shade added about half a watt on the lumipen meter.

"The more things are touched, the more beautiful or ugly they become. What mark do you make on things?" Lord Omicron asks Sextine.

"This is not my thing," Sextine defends herself. "I'm going to bed popmy." She kisses her father goodnight.

Dame Nissi holds Sextine's hand briefly when she crosses the sleepy girl's path on her way back to the living room. She stands beside her husband, watching Leontine put the finishing touches on the light.

The drawing lights up the living room, adorned with flowers and gadgets and a few photographs hanging on the wall, *phovies* actually, because they display a right pointing isosceles triangle signifying they are basically videos waiting to be played; that's before they turn on automatically every morning at 5 a.m. or whatever time the family prefers. One's eyes cannot elude Dame Nissi's baby bump pictures, three in all, arranged according to their ages. Lord Omicron is only seen in the first baby bump phovie, a pointer to how much time he usually spends away from Oh.

To the almost present, the dream-present, Lord Omicron stands up enthusiastically from his seat in the lab. He grabs the heart whisperer – a fragile looking gadget having a heart plug and earplugs.

"Leontine, Nissi," he calls out, unaware of the time.

His family is still asleep, or so does Dame Nissi think. She's certainly not feeling sleepy because she's in a distressing situation, being chased down by the eye Leontine had drawn earlier.

The eye has grown very large, large enough to block the routes of every floating car in town. A large crowd is kept at the edge of what seems to be the Youlv Ocean which surely shouldn't be in town in the first place. Dame Nissi is standing between the eye-evil and the deep turbulent green Youlv Sea.

"What do you want?" she screams at the eye.

"Eye doesn't listen to food," the eye responds. "In fact eye cannot even speak to food! So eye cannot negotiate with food. Eye can only see food; eye wants food in the sea for eye only does seafood."

The eye makes a wobbling move towards Dame Nissi and she screams up from her sleep. She sees Lord Omicron and Leontine staring back at her. A small dim eye-shaped light is on the wall and Dame Nissi realises she's in Leontine's room. Still confused, she squints at Lord Omicron.

"What do you want?" she asks Lord Omicron.

Lord Omicron shows her the heart whisperer.

"In the middle of the night?" Dame Nissi signs as she speaks.

"Don't sign all that," Lord Omicron suggests, "leave Leontine alone."

"No no, you leave Leontine alone," Dame Nissi yet signs as she speaks. "How long will you keep torturwing her with this failed gadget of yours?"

"Nissi, you are overweacting, and it's not even the middle of the night, it's almost 5 a.m."

"And I keep warning you people to stop doing cweepy things awound me when me's asleep. You make me dweam horwible dweams! What is wong with you people?"

"Sowie about that sugar," Lord Omicron apologises.

"Is it working now?" Dame Nissi asks about the heart whisperer.

Lord Omicron shakes his head, "no."

"Then sewiously, stop disturbing my daughter. She cannot hear you with the earplugs in her ears even if the heart magically says something."

This gives Lord Omicron a new clue, perhaps Dame Nissi is right. Even if the heart speaks, the ears won't hear it. Surely the heart speaks and the heart listens. The former isn't the issue, Lord Omicron has successfully listened to his heart speak a language he couldn't decipher. He's only hoping Leontine might be luckier than he is.

"You even listening at all?" Dame Nissi asks in a louder voice.

"Yes, sure." Lord Omicron takes the heart whisperer and kisses the quiet Leontine on her forehead. "I'll be in my lab," he says as he proceeds to dab Dame Nissi's forehead with his. He walks out of the room hurriedly.

"I'm sorry," Dame Nissi signs to Leontine.

"That's alright," Leontine signs back.

The day begins like every other normal day; Yes, Dame Nissi's dream isn't abnormal at all. The Rhos quietly get dressed to go about their businesses. Dame Nissi is worried about Sextine's academic program. The young lady has refused to select a second course of study alongside the modern architecture program she's currently running in *The University in the State of Genia*. Dame Nissi believes this has also influenced Leontine's refusal to add to her Botany and Veterinary Medicine degrees. Leontine is now always stuck in Nissi's Gallery admiring the pictures of things famed to have existed in the lost earth.

Thru a couple of open doors, Dame Nissi sees Sextine about to use their teleport system; she's still bidding Leontine farewell. The quiet ta-ta is almost getting emotional, that's how much their BEMs are telling them they love each other. Dame Nissi is not moved by the show of love, she's more interested in having two career ladies as daughters.

"Sextine!" Dame Nissi calls out. "Don't go anywhere, we need to talk..."

"NO!" Sextine screams back leaving Leontine wondering why she's getting worked up. She signs, "Momxy," and points at Dame Nissi.

Leontine smiles at her mother, she could barely read Dame Nissi's lips from there.

"What do you mean 'no'?" Dame Nissi asks and smiles back at Leontine. "You'll float with me and Leontine; we'll dwop you off in school."

"Just hurwy, I'm late."

Lexis bumps into Dame Nissi and kisses her goodbye. Dame Nissi returns to her room to get dressed.

Going into the teleport system, Lexis has a long animated handshake with Leontine before he pats the disappointed Sextine on her back.

"State your destination," the machine tells Lexis.

"Vexim Headquarters, Unmi, Genia," Lexis responds.

"Destination found. Goodbye."

Lexis is teleported off to his current job as a gadget imagineer at Vexim. He has increased his job time at the company after Lord Omicron bought seventy percent ownership of the BEM company. Lexis is also trying to develop an upgraded BEM that can help him communicate effectively with Leontine. It is always a surprise how this has eluded mankind. You never know what you didn't have until you need it.

In no time, Dame Nissi is ready to leave for her gallery. Sextine sits in front, expecting a long talk from her mother, to whom she's ever ready to respond. Leontine sits at the back and quickly goes about her little hobby of looking out thru the window of a floating car. She hits the glass repeatedly to alert Dame Nissi and Sextine to the nice car that is floating to the opposite direction.

Dame Nissi and Sextine turn immediately, only in time to see the back of the conveyor crested with 'By Sextine Rho'. Sextine sighs, that's one car she wants to forget about.

"Oh your pwoject car!" Dame Nissi exclaims. "Still in circulation."

Dame Nissi realises Sextine isn't particularly happy to see the car she made as a project for her first degree in Automobile Imagineering.

"Me Gee Sextine, smile please. That car was perfect."

"Don't identify with failure momxy, even if you the one that failed, don't identify with yourself."

"Sextine, I don't know where you get your own ideas. You sound like you love to work hard but you don't ever wake up early fwom bed in the first place."

"Ha! *O-Chi-m-o* momxy," Sextine sighs, "you must bwing up my sleeping habit. I've told you my alarm doesn't work, and that bed has its own way of slowing down pwogwess."

"The ticking of the clock is loud enough for the stwong. Only lazy people need an alarm in the morning."

"Yeah I'm lazy, I'm twying to tweat that disorder, don't blame me..."

"Sextine, don't lionize laziness. I'm not blaming you, but you know Leontine looks up to you more."

"And what else am I not doing well?" Sextine asks. "I didn't ask Leo not to get into school for another degwee."

"Oh you know that too. First, you made a late decision to go back to school, and even now, you doing just one course. Your mates are allowed to offer thwee!"

"I'm not me mates, la duh? Education is a waste of talent; all I do there is get set for endless exams."

"That is a lie, they not endless..."

"It is not a lie! I've barely worked as a doctor and an auto imagineer and yet I'm asked to add more qualifications. The earlier I get a fulltime job, the better for us. A stitch in time saves nine, you know."

"Sugar, weak thweads don't make any stitch in time," Dame Nissi points out. "You have to get equipped first, and getting equipped is not a waste of time."

"Getting equipped to earn digits, wight? So what better way than to start now to earn it? How sure are you I'll be stwong enough when I'm finally equipped? I need to make hay while the sun shines, I can study later with the light at night."

"O dear, Sextine... If day and night won't cease, why then should you make all your hay in a day's sunshine?"

Sextine feels helpless trying to argue with her mother. She joins Leontine in looking out thru the window, but that's not her thing. She throws in another question to Dame Nissi, trying to broker a deal.

"If I pick an additional pwofession, can I then study over the eagle?" Sextine asks.

"Online?!" Dame Nissi exclaims. "No no Sextine, we can't pay that high just to kick your education away. You need to have a close intewaction and bubbling with what you studying. You have to touch and feel it."

"Then momxy, get me the Holo-X-cube, it has gwabbing ability."

"I can't expose you to a new madness," Dame Nissi explains. "Take popmy for example, he can't just make discovewies on the eagle because he inputs into the eagle for people to soar and find what he had found thwu intewacting and bubbling with the places he visits. I am a quintessentialist, which is many miles ahead of a consultant *motivationist*, emulate me at least. I cannot be an exemplar without intewacting and bubbling with my clients."

"So then I should become a lawyer?" Sextine asks.

"Law? No, where now is that coming fwom?"

"Momxy, you said I should emulate you and law is an important pwofession."

"No no Sextine," Dame Nissi objects, "lawyers are jobless. If the pwofession is that important, let another man's daughter be that important."

"But you are a lawyer..."

"Yes Sextine, exactly why I'm sure of what I'm telling you. Evewyone is living orderly, evewybody knows who owns what, the government knows the limit of their powers, and the evidence about evewything is always stored somewhere, it has become gweatly unimportant for anyone to come and do a battle of words to pwoof or dispwoof anything."

"I'll be a fictionist then."

"Jeez, this girl. O well, even though you'll wake up someday and fathom you've been a liar all your life, blatantly mocking histowy, being a fictionist still means you need to intewact with people."

"No momxy, I only need to bubble with my wight bwain, I needn't meet anyone before I cook up a tale."

"Sextine, when you meet people, they could inspire you, so yes, fictionists need inspiwation."

"I can simply go for a session with an inspiwationist... he'll unlock my wight bwain perfectly."

"That's more family digits being wasted!" Dame Nissi is clearly frustrated with the argument. "This matter, you see her? She's closed."

Dame Nissi and Sextine manage to steal a couple of glances at each other as they remain quiet for the rest of the float.

Back at the Rhos' mansion, Lord Omicron rushes into the teleport system. He has just been informed by *Archprofessor Knight Nightingale* that Crew Epsilon is back in business and the ministry is willing to allow them return to the lost earth to fetch the evidence they failed to retrieve ten years ago.

Lord Omicron arrives thru the teleport system in the highly industrialised zone of the state, right in front of his own headquarters in Unmi – RHODICULOUS... jacks of all trades, and with the popular slogan, 'we can do anything for you'.

From the big black steps to the entrance of the company, his numerous employees and clients are surprised to see him; this is certainly that once in a green moon. He is quickly joined by his ridiculously animated personal assistant, *Archprofessor Elise Leo Elise.* Some critics claim that one of her many professorship awards is in scientific madness. No, this is not a joke, it is actually the only reason Lord Omicron can stay home all year if he chooses; there's someone who is mad enough to run his company singlehandedly.

"*Hullo* me Lord!" Archprofessor Elise chants at Lord Omicron. "Why have you come to us?"

"Elise! Where are you?" Lord Omicron asks, significantly ignoring his PA, apparently believing it's just a hologram.

"Me's here," Archprofessor Elise tells him.

"Here," Lord Omicron gently grips her shoulders. She's indeed here. "I am surpwised... first time in many years, what bwought you out here?"

"I was just seeing off Sir Nnia Den."

"Sir Nnia?" Lord Omicron looks back at once. "He's one of the people I need to call now. I need to assemble my Epsilon team."

"Can I now tell you why he was here?"

"Of course Elise, after which you call the entire Epsilonians."

"Sir Nnia Den came to buy your seventy percent ownership of Vexim."

"What? And you followed him out here before you tossed him away?"

"Lol boss," Archprofessor Elise giggles, "you don't toss away two-hundwed percent of the value of the entire Vexim."

"I don't care how much he is willing to pay. Just wonder for a minute why on Oh he wants to buy Vexim now."

"Well me lord, that's why I followed him out; I was asking him why. I didn't want to wonder much."

"Seemesh..."

Lord Omicron suddenly catches a glimpse of Archprofessor Elise talking with two men.

"I told you I don't like you meeting clients as a hologwam," Lord Omicron complains.

"Yes boss, they wouldn't know."

"What if they offer you a handshake?'

"I'd shake them... I'll shake them all. It's an x-cube, boss."

"Oh... I see."

"I'm getting one for Lexis too."

"No! Don't ever say that again, my wife might just see it in my mind. She's still sceptical about such things."

Lord Omicron finally gets into his personal office after a hurdle of greetings along the way. The office theme colour of white cannot be hidden, a glowing appearance intensified by the bright daylight piercing thru the windows. Archprofessor Elise is not a fan of bright lights. She skips towards the windows and pulls the red curtains across them. She whispers a quiet call to her sapien and the upgraded sapien version responds immediately, not whispering back however.

"Call Pwincess Lotem-Zeta," she instructs the sapien.

"Pwincess Lotem-Zeta will speak if she can," the sapien announces.

"Yes," Princess Lotem-Zeta speaks up thru the sapien.

"This is Archpwofessor Elise Leo Elise..."

"I know who you are. Tell Omicwon I'm alweady on me way. Is there anything else?"

"Bah me choc'late, your highness," Archprofessor Elise flutters her eyelashes and grins.

The princess suddenly pops out thru the hologram portal Lord Omicron has been setting up. Her emergence startles Archprofessor Elise.

"Too bad I wasn't coming in person," the princess reveals.

Archprofessor Elise pouts in disappointment.

We are now at Nissi's Gallery. Thru the beautiful NG-crested gate opens up a huge busy compound. Magnificent structures arranged strategically and filled with different groups of people being taken around by tour guides. The tallest building is the palm tree-shaped shopping mall, even the nuts are dangling. The restaurant in the middle of the park is a round building shape like a tripod African pot sitting on a metal tripod stand with steps of fire rising thru the firewood decoration under the pot. The biggest dome-shaped building is the main gallery which receives most of the visitors, though the attractiveness and necessity of the African pot cannot be overemphasized. The only difficulty Dame Nissi is having with her gallery is that she can't prove to poke-nosing scientists beyond any doubt that the things within the frames were once in existence on the lost earth. People, however, do enjoy the fiction and fantasy of having a lost earth out there.

In the photo section of the gallery, Dame Nissi is holding unto Leontine as she walks a group of adults thru the gallery. Each article is depicted in an enlarged high resolution photograph and a 3D reconstruction suspended in a glass in front of the photograph. Leontine soon breaks away from Dame Nissi and stops at the 'Oh Section' where she admires the pictures of the false prophet and the very popular *Water Steps*. The Water Steps are naturally occurring pyramidal stairs preceding the Youlv Ocean. This is the only part of the ocean that is normally calm, save for the side of the pyramid facing the ocean itself. The steps enclose a huge cave normally used as a hiding place by folf hunters, or that's what the stories say. Some versions hold that the folf itself lives inside the Water Steps.

Dame Nissi isn't too worried about letting Leontine out of her sight; she's certain she'll be safe enjoying herself with her favourite things in life – nature.

Dame Nissi explains the picture in front of the group she's taking care of. First up is the *Arc de Triomphe*.

"This is the Arc de Twiomphe," she begins, "it was believed that the building was completed awound July of A.D 1836. It was a famous monument in a city called Pawis in the Fwance of the lost earth."

Next up is the *Parc de la Villette,* and we begin to get the feeling that Dame Nissi's ancestors are of French origin. A majority of the photographs she inherited were taken in France of the lost earth.

"This is the Parc de la Villette. It was designed and likely built by one Bernard Tschumi between A.D 1984 to 1987, in the Fwance of the lost earth." "This," Dame Nissi points at the picture of a resplendent football stadium sitting on a river, "is called the Water Table, or the em-aaw-es (MRS) – Messi-Wonaldo Stadium. It was built sometime in A.D 2090 in honour of two famed gods of football, Lionel Messi and Cwistiano Wonaldo, who bwoke so many wecords in the game of football. The stadium is not owned by any particular nation, whereas a form of football is mainly played in some parts of the Mid-Mowal World of Oh, the game we all know as 'kickers'.

Next up is the *Archangel Doves,* a huge statue of an angel wearing a crown of doves and standing on a heap of guns.

"They called this the Archangel Doves; the name didn't go down too well. A group of sculptors fwom the China of the lost earth made this in A.D 2016. It was made in Somalia, a nation in the Afwica of the lost earth, to mark the beginning of peace in Afwica." She sees Leontine spinning around the Oh section of the gallery and she's caught in between a smile and a worrisome look. She ignores the next picture – a huge golden gate; certainly her guests can see it is tagged 'The Gates of Wuzybury, A.D 2035'.

Back in Lord Omicron's office, Archprofessor Elise has succeeded in bringing together the holograms of the crew members of Epsilon. However, she has a bad news. Saint Ose Neo is off for a ten day crusade in Pena, a nation in the Mid Moral World. This leaves Lord Omicron with two problems. He informs the crew that the minister has requested the team be increased to seven members, hoping 'it will add more sanity to the team and help the team remember to collect evidence from the lost earth'. With Saint Ose Neo's absence, there are now two vacancies in the team.

Everyone is thinking of possible replacements while Sir Nnia is suggesting they disobey the minister of space, a suggestion aimed at making Lord Omicron lose his place as crew captain – a plan Archprofessor Knight is well aware of. One may be wealthy enough to own a spaceship but certainly not powerful enough to authorize any space travel.

Archprofessor Elise suddenly realises that Lord Omicron and Princess Lotem-Zeta are both looking at her with an intention to add her to the crew. Archprofessor Elise wouldn't have nominated herself but someone else is clearly thinking what she's thinking and that motion is being seconded by the crown princess.

"No!" Archprofessor Elise exclaims with her eyes wide open.

The rest of the crew are wondering what question she's answering.

"Yes!" Archprofessor Elise screams again. "Yes? Yes? What are you saying?"

"I will like to swap Saint Ose Neo for Archpwofessor Elise Leo Elise," Lord Omicron announces.

Before he finishes that statement, Archprofessor Elise has already ran round the room once, and she keeps running, screaming joyfully. Sir Nnia is unhappy with that decision; he really doesn't need another smarty in the crew.

"No!" Sir Nnia objects at once. "This is madness! She is a mad woman." He turns to Lord Omicron, "You are cwazy... can't you see she's a mad woman?"

"Well," Princess Lotem-Zeta defends the call, "he's cwazy, she's mad, and that makes the team perfect. Normal people like Sir Nnia and I can balance the equation."

Sir Nnia breaths heavily in anger as he listens to the princess.

"What now, are you about to declare me mad?" the princess asks him.

Sir Nnia hisses and goes back to his standing position.

"So, who will be the seventh member?" asks Sir Luminescence after Archprofessor Lux Eden has managed to keep Elise quiet.

Lord Omicron won't think long about this. He has always wanted to bring Lexis along with him.

"Imagineer Lexis Woe," Lord Omicron announces to the crew.

"Your son?!" Sir Nnia flares up again.

"Pull your act together Sir Nnia, you behave like a divorced dog!"

"Sir Luminescence, you dare not insult me!"

"Please gentlemen," Lord Omicron tries to proceed, "if you believe in the significance of Epsilon and our ages, then you should be aware we are not getting any younger. We need to start bwinging in people we twust, people we believe can one day take over the pwestigious affairs of this team."

A nodding competition is certainly going on now and Sir Nnia is simply the referee monitoring the number of times the rest of the crew nod in agreement to Lord Omicron's ideology.

"So what happens to we who have no sons?" Sir Nnia asks.

"I said people you can twust," Lord Omicron tells him, "not sons you gave birth to"

"Perhaps," the princess adds, "I intend bwinging in my little daughter *Kamsi-Elle* someday. She's eight years old, and she's a certified pilot and space specialist."

"Your highness," Sir Nnia is not easily impressed by that feat, "the entire planet is aware of those things. What we don't know now is why exactly we just went fwom being six sewious minded people to seven scallywags destined to fail."

"For once he counts himself in on both ends," says Sir Luminescence."

"Don't bother yourself Sir Nnia, nothing has changed yet. Now, Archpwofessor Knight Nightingale has said we can leave anytime we want. Today is Fwiday."

"Archpwofessor?" mouths Archprofessor Elise who seems to be the only one unaware of Nightingale's new title.

"How long are we going to spend?" asks Archprofessor Lux Eden.

"The speed of the machine has gone up over the years, and we have the exact location. I'm looking at four days tops, unless we choose to get missing again."

"That's a possibility," says Sir Luminescence, "it is not as if we choose it on purpose..."

"You've chosen two mad people on purpose, why not?" Sir Nnia asks.

"Sir Nnia, Elise and Lexis will only observe what we are doing. They won't pilot the spaceship," Lord Omicron explains.

"Yes, today is Fwiday," Princess Lotem-Zeta returns them to the initial topic. "It can't be over the weekend, my family needs me at home."

"Yes," Lord Omicron agrees, "certainly not over the weekend. Monday?"

"The Pwesident of Acanthia is paying us a visit, it falls under my portfolio, and I have to sit in for the king too."

"What's he coming for now again?" Archprofessor Lux Eden asks.

"Pwesident Aminu?" the princess confirms. "Same bugging issue. He wants licence to weaponize digitizers."

"I thought they are alweady allowed thwee seconds of weapons gwade digitizers," Lord Omicron wonders aloud.

"Thwee seconds is hardly enough according to Aminu. He wants it topped."

"Lol, is he planning to invade Sexat?" Sir Luminescence asks.

"Maybe Sexat should stop influencing international laws," Sir Nnia chips in.

"Influencing?" the princess resounds. "That 'influence' is what is keeping evewybody away fwom a weaponized digitizers arms hurdle. God knows if Acanthia upgwades fwom thwee seconds, Jermain will fly up to ten seconds."

"With a king in common, is Jermain not an ally of Sexat anymore?" Sir Nnia asks.

"An ally against whom? Oh is in peace, we all live as equals. There's no point forming cliques." The princess replies.

"Five seconds and one second is weally unequal your highness."

"How does this help us choose a damn date for our journey?" Archprofessor Lux Eden asks.

"Ha," Lord Omicron gives a thankful sigh, "Lux Eden, you should be godded a deity of wemembwance. Monday is out of it, Tuesday then?"

"My wife will be taking her baby bump phovies on Tuesday," Sir Luminescence informs the group.

"Sir Luminescence Wellington is not marwied," claims Sir Nnia.

"It was a pwivate wedding, I was there," Archprofessor Lux Eden tells Sir Nnia.

"She can make the phovies in the morning, you'll catch up with us," Princess Lotem-Zeta suggests to Sir Luminescence.

Sir Luminescence nods in agreement.

"Why don't we then leave it until Wednesday, Ose Neo will be back by then," says Sir Nnia.

"It is a ten days cwusade," Lord Omicron responds.

"Which began on Monday," Sir Nnia continues, "today is day five."

"Saint Ose Neo said she won't be available for any future expeditions," Archprofessor Elise gives a rare insight.

"That's a fine way to cement your place here, hey?" Sir Nnia eyeballs Archprofessor Elise. "You sure you even called Ose in the first place?"

"We will depart on Tuesday, what time?" Archprofessor Lux Eden asks.

Lord Omicron smiles at the number of times they always get carried away. He thinks for a while and suggests, "1 t.m. in the noon."

Everyone waits for Sir Luminescence to nod first before they nod along.

Dame Nissi is getting exhausted back in her gallery and it is not even brunch time yet. She's in the antique section of the gallery, surrounded by digital pictures and 3D reconstructions of earthly things, ranging from a laptop to a car, a 12 hour clock, a bulletproof vest, a sleek mobile phone, a TV wire, and the one she's talking about – a book and a pen.

"These were wyting matewials for a long time. It started fading away gwadually in the twenty-first centuwy of the lost earth. It was weplaced by gadgets and other electwonic stuffs. The knowledge of the book and pen is the inspiwation behind the wyting competition overseen evewy four years by King Sigma the third of the Western Nations."

Dame Nissi's face suddenly brightens up. She has just seen Sextine hug Leontine from behind. Her smile only lasts long enough for her to realise that Sextine is actually back from school too early.

"Excuse me for a moment," Dame Nissi withdraws from the group of tourists, walking towards her daughters.

Sextine breaks the hug with Leontine and spins her around and signs, "How do you not get bored alone?"

"This place is beautiful," Leontine signs back with a broad smile after managing to see Sextine's question thru her spinning vision. She sees Dame Nissi coming and alerts Sextine with a nod towards their mother.

"You back?" Dame Nissi asks.

"We done." Sextine replies.

"So you are back then..."

'Yes," Sextine agrees. "Just got off the teleport, no one is home though."

"It is barely 10:47 t.m." Dame Nissi notifies Sextine. "You'll join us for the tour?"

"Momxy, it will be the millionth time," Sextine complains.

"Say umpteenth, you've not even been here a hundwed times. I wonder why you came here."

"To see Leontine," Sextine signs.

This makes Leontine smile sheepishly again. Dame Nissi shakes her head and leaves the two sisters.

"I paid for a movie, you'll love it," Sextine signs as she speaks.

"Which one?" Leontine signs back.

"Earth Age!"

"Superb!" signs Leontine. "I would have paid for it this weekend. I cannot wait to go home."

"Me too," Sextine signs in agreement.

The long afternoon is quite boring for Sextine while Leontine suddenly becomes a tour guide for a group of adults who can understand the sign language, thanks to their all-knowing BEM devices.

It is not soon night but night comes anyway. At 4:30 p.m., daylight has completely disappeared and the Rhos are already long in the comfort of their home. Not so comfortable for Lord Omicron though, he's desperately trying to understand his heart with the heart whisperer. The rest of the family are sitting round a suspended All-Dimension television monitor (*Intellivision*), watching the movie 'Earth Age', which was basically inspired by a certain movie 'Ice Age 10'.

No one has seen Ice Age 10 but Earth Age is quite entertaining, an easy conclusion to make from Leontine's infectious smile. She's reading the texts on the screen while her brother Lexis would rather enjoy viewing from behind the scenes.

At least we can see a monkey, an elephant and a tiger because we are sure we know these animated animals from somewhere. The monkey, *Ben*, is swinging around the elephant, *Biggy*, who is complaining to the tiger, *Morpheus*, about a certain ruthless lion, *Leo*.

"Your heart is sure swinging in your chest now, eh Ben? Be calm and let me talk," Biggy tries to control the monkey. "Morpheus, Leo said we must move the logs back into the caves."

"No," Morpheus objects, "Leo said you should move the logs."

"Define a team for me," Biggy requests.

"Listen Biggy, no tiger works for a lion."

"Teegah, Morpheus," Ben corrects the tiger. "It is teegah, not tiger."

"I am a tiger... get that into your head once and for all, tiger! You can't teach me what I've been called all my life."

"But your life has only just begun, you are four months old," says Ben.

"Whatever," Morpheus replies. "I'm off to find the zoo, follow me if you care about your family."

Dame Nissi leaves the living room and the voices of the arguing animals fade away. She walks to Lord Omicron's lab and looks thru the open door for some seconds before speaking up.

"You know, the amount of time you spend on this thing, one would think something is so wong with Leontine."

"Nissi, please don't start," Lord Omicron responds tiredly.

"No no, I'm not starting anything. I'm off to bed. Just that I'm sure you understand the picture you are painting to Leontine. She's there with the whole family seeing a movie and she's vewy happy, but soon you'll come along with this thing and when it doesn't work again, you two will feel sowie for each other. Now tell me, do you share her happy moments with her or do you always give her a weason to be sad?"

Lord Omicron nods quietly. If there's something he's afraid of now, it's the fact that he has only one chance to get the heart whisperer right. One more failed attempt and Dame Nissi is sure printing him out as protein supplement for other normal humans.

The night is fast spent and the daylight ushers in a beautiful Trägeday – the only day that is legal for workers to ignore their duty posts in favour of a very long sleep. Little wonder why a lot of things could malfunction today. The Rhos have a family tradition of eating together every Trägeday morning; the major problem is the impossibility of waking up at the same time.

9 LEONTINE is up and hungry, or in the reverse order, it is clear she forgot to eat last night after the Earth Age movie pampered her to bed. She plans on completing the movie today.

Dame Nissi is up next, not exactly happy that Lord Omicron slept in his lab again. She walks into the dining room, surprised to see Leontine munching something we are not very sure of. The kitchen-dining complex looks more like a food manufacturing factory, with numerous synthetic food printers and real food teleports of different shapes and sizes standing against every inch of the wall.

"Me baby," Dame Nissi signs to Leontine, bringing forth the expected smile. She gives Leontine a long kiss on her forehead, most of which is to buy her brain some time to figure out what she'll like for breakfast. She ends the kiss and she's glad to see Sextine stagger into the dining room. "Ah," she sighs, "dear Sextine, you will live long..."

Sextine grins lazily. "What do you want?"

"Anything sugar, just get me anything."

Dame Nissi sits next to Leontine while Sextine goes about getting the food. There is only one soup plate in the tray; this gets Sextine confused.

"Momxy, what happened to the bowl plates?"

Dame Nissi ignores her with a shake of the head. She'll certainly soon find out. It is basically Sextine's fault that the plates always vanish into the air... literally.

We realise Sextine opted for *Luelxy Cereals* over a long list of other cereal companies. The cereals are still pouring into the plate when Lexis is heard coming along, humming an unusual tune.

Dame Nissi is subconsciously shielding her eyes from one of Leontine's custom eye-shaped lumipen lights. Lexis is just about passing the light and Dame Nissi requests he cleans it off.

"Ah! Past it alweady," Lexis replies as he drags himself towards a seat.

Dame Nissi is disappointed and she turns away from him just in time to witness another Sextine Bowl Plate Destructive Disorder. Sextine is now over the *Que Milk Vendor* – a milk printer, and she selects the *Mayor Milk* option. Dame Nissi's eyes are naturally the first to express shock before her lips can join in the act. The often repercussion of Sextine's usual action manifests at once and Dame Nissi can only sigh in disappointment.

The milk burns up the cereal, and everything, including the plate, lights up like a burning phoenix. In three seconds, neither cereals nor milk, nor plate nor fire nor ashes remain.

"I have lost count Sextine, I have just lost count," laments Dame Nissi. "If you're taking Luelxy ceweal, take Luelxy milk or another sister milk. Don't bwing those companies' war into this house."

"Sowie momxy," Sextine begins with an unnecessary apology, "maybe we shouldn't subscwibe to both eastern and western milk companies."

Nobody really knows the true story of the milk beef but it is certainly one of those frozen wars that originated from Moffat after the Belgorian War. The world can share many things freely but their DNA seems to never forget how milk helped destroy planet Moffat.

Sextine stumps swiftly to the *Ramics Dishmaker* and selects for print, five wonderful soup plate designs.

Lord Omicron arrives just in time to snatch Sextine's breakfast; she happily goes to print another. Lord Omicron spends time focusing on Lexis, not quite sure why he's not eating, and why his seat is so close to the table. Dame Nissi didn't see Lexis sit down; she was watching Sextine's milk drama.

"Can you pass me the salt?" Lord Omicron asks Lexis.

"It's closer to you... but what do you need it for?" the surprised Dame Nissi asks. "This is perfectly not in need of salt."

"I know," Lord Omicron acknowledges, "I just want Lexis to pass me the salt."

Everybody understands this; it is the basic hologram test. Dame Nissi had suspected earlier that her real son is still in bed, so she watches with keen interest.

Lord Omicron concludes Lexis isn't here in person and rightly so. "Get your bum-bum down here," he orders.

Lexis sinks thru the seat and crawls the hologram out of the dining room.

Sextine switches back her attention to the breakfast she's making and she turns around to Dame Nissi to announce yet another milk problem. "Momxy! The milk is floating again," she squirms.

Dame Nissi scratches her head vigorously in disappointment. Milk with floating syndrome is actually not an uncommon situation and that is basically the problem; it is almost always happening every Trägeday.

"Call that Luelxy Company," says Dame Nissi. She happens to be the only one with a sapien at the moment.

Leontine is giggling at Sextine as the milk rises slowly from the plate independent of the cereal.

"I think the pwinter has an issue," Lord Omicron suggests.

"Then all other stuff it pwints should float too, don't you think?" Dame Nissi asks. "Sapien!"

"Yes boss," her sapien responds.

"Call Luelxy Milk Company."

"Luelxy will speak if they can."

Leontine is making gestures at her father, asking why she doesn't own a sapien yet to which Lord Omicron apologises at once.

Sextine notices the *Gravitizer* indicator on the machine is blinking, 'it's certainly not the fault of the milk company,' she thinks to herself. It's a little too late to notify Dame Nissi who is already scolding the Luelxy representative for sending in floating milk.

Lexis walks into the dining room laughing hysterically, confirming all the reasons why he had opted to send a hologram to the family breakfast. He is on a video call with his beloved girlfriend, Princess Zeta, the eldest daughter of the Crown Princess Lotem-Zeta III. We can see the pretty Princess Zeta on the screen laughing too. The translucent screen is definitely a piece chipped out of Lexis' sapien, dangling slightly to the left of his head and moving ahead as Lexis moves.

Dame Nissi can barely hear herself. "Lexis, will you be quiet please!" she yells.

That doesn't really help, especially when lovebirds are involved. Lexis and Princess Zeta interpret that as 'hello sweethearts!'

"Is that your momxy?" Princess Zeta asks rhetorically. "Hello Dame Nissi Woe."

"Hello your highness," Dame Nissi probably won't ignore the innocent girl; her family are not even fans of Luelxy milk!

"I'll see you in the afternoon. Love you!" Lexis terminates the call right on time for Dame Nissi to concentrate on the solution for the floating milk.

"I can solve this in two seconds. Just send me the exact coordinates of the milk," the Luelxy milk rep tells Dame Nissi.

"You shouldn't have cweated the pwoblem in the first place," Dame Nissi nags.

As smart as the sapien is, it quickly enlarges the digitizer icon and places it at the middle of the screen.

"I'm swiping out a digitizer now, better sync to the location," says Dame Nissi as she slides her finger across the icon. A three centimetres glossy DNA-lookalike digitizer follows her finger out of the screen. She walks quickly to Sextine's position and throws the digitizer into the milk which is now well above Sextine's head and still rising gradually.

"Got it," reveals the Luelxy rep.

The milk company thru the digitizer is given the right again to adjust the milk; correcting its gravitational value is of paramount importance. Soon the floating milk will falls back into the plate positioned by Sextine. This is one of the few functions of the domestic digitizers, asides aiding in the sharing of files between sapiens and other gadgets. The weapons grade digitizers can be a lot more dangerous. When placed on anything, humans inclusive, these weapons allow the activator to manipulate their 'client' any way they want thru a weapons grade sapien for the amount of time allowed according to the strength of the digitizer.

Sexat is the only nation that owns five-second weapons grade digitizers (WGDs). Acanthia and Jermain are allowed three-second WGDs while other nations who care and those who can afford this feat are allowed one-second WGDs. We can only imagine how much time is needed by an aggressive man to fling his adversary into a lake of fire. Just before we are done twigging all these, Sextine is already sitting with the rest of the family, munching her digitally salvaged breakfast.

"How is you and Zeta doing?" Lord Omicron asks Lexis.

"Fine... bubbling ok. I'll be at their place today."

"Nice. And how is work going?" Lord Omicron asks again.

"Hectic, since you basically became the owner of that company, it became difficult for me to come home early."

"Lol..." Lord Omicron giggles. "When you go to work in the morning, the first thing you do is to make plans on how you will come home otherwise you won't come home."

Lexis giggles along...

"That's why I'm always home whenever I like," Lord Omicron adds.

"You work mainly at home, all day and night," Dame Nissi chips in her major complaint.

"It is certainly better than spending the whole time at Unmi," Lord Omicron defends himself, but Dame Nissi isn't strong yet for any argument this morning so he turns back to Lexis. "We'll be going to the lost earth again on Tuesday. I added you as the seventh member of Epsilon... the minister has appwoved it."

We are not sure if this is good news or bad news or both. Sextine and Dame Nissi hang their milk dripping spoons halfway to their mouths, both staring at Lexis. Sextine is simply amazed while Dame Nissi is more jealous than surprised, Lord Omicron can't tell the difference. All he sees are two angry ladies trying to discourage Lexis. Leontine is unpretentiously following the conversation the best she can.

"YES!" Lexis can no longer hold back his excitement.

"NO!" Dame Nissi counters and Lord Omicron drops his spoon in disappointment.

"YES!" Sextine airs her opinion.

"NO!" Dame Nissi gives Sextine a stern look. "No no no no no no," she ensures the no's go round twice to her opponents.

Lord Omicron is now getting a different feeling about the objection when he notices a hidden smile on Dame Nissi's face.

"Momxy, I'll love to go to the lost earth please," Lexis pleads.

"Of course! Who wouldn't love to? How did you get that chance before me? This is so sad," Dame Nissi covers her eyes.

Lord Omicron sighs and joins Lexis and Sextine to burst into laughter.

"You evil people!" Dame Nissi can't hold back her smile now. "Make sure you take pictures for my gallewy."

"Where is he going to?" Leontine signs to Dame Nissi.

"He is going to the lost earth with popmy," Dame Nissi signs back babyishly.

Leontine flaps her hands in excitement and signs to her father, "Can I come too?"

Dame Nissi raises her eyebrows in surprise and looks expectantly at her husband.

"I'll sort that out... I will see what I can do," Lord Omicron signs. Fair enough, Leontine keeps smiling. "We'll get you your sapien today," he adds.

This makes Leontine even happier and she gives him a big thumbs up.

Lord Omicron drinks up a glass of water and hustles Lexis up to join him as he stands to leave for the gadget stores. "Come on Lexis, you coming with me." He walks over to the ladies and gives each of them a kiss on the head. Lexis utilizes this time to eat what's left in the plate before him.

Thru the living room and out to the family's private teleport system, Lord Omicron and Lexis are good go.

"I hope you switched off the holo portal you used this morning, before your sisters will get surpwising visitors." Lord Omicron says to Lexis.

"Nah, I'll have to be alerted first, it's always on the safety mode."

Lord Omicron steps into the teleport system and clicks the button.

"Please state your destination," the machine requests.

"Unmi gadget market, Unmi, Genia," Lord Omicron states.

"Destination found, goodbye."

Lord Omicron is taken away by the system and Lexis repeats the same procedure and joins him in the empty Unmi gadget market. The locked stores have just reminded Lord Omicron that it's a Trägeday, business will be very slow. He looks ahead and sees the ever reliable *Liebman Gadget,* normally stylized 'Liebman Gaɠet'.

Ɗ (ɠ) is actually gradually being accepted as a new English alphabet, simply because it makes it easier to spell out 'dg' in unimportant words like briɠe, friɠe, weɠe, and doɠe, and for sheer *efizzy* from pompous people, like the former minister of space when he says, "I'm Archlord Johnson with a ɠ." And that's the difference between the rest of the Johns in his Johnny name.

Lord Omicron and Lexis walk into the gadget store. For a man of Lord Omicron's financial status, he's not afraid of being tempted by Liebman's one-in-town wicked gadgets and Lexis is surely playing the devil pointing at anything and everything, even things they already own; one of which prompts a response from Lord Omicron who was only nodding his head previously.

"Look!" Lexis points at a sky-green sexy latex suit attached with similar boots, gloves and facial gear.

"We have more than ten *Performance Enhancing Suits* at home," Lord Omicron reminds Lexis as he advances towards the sapien section.

"Yeah but not the Latex PES V4. Those are super cool."

"Those are super feminine. Your momxy has one alweady. Sextine and Leontine don't need it yet, and you and I will never need it."

They slowly pick between two fancy sapiens, one with extra armbands of different colours. They walk to the receptionist's desk, beholding another huge section of more advanced gadgets. The *Ambrosia Food Printer* catches Lord

Omicron's eye. The floating milk syndrome back at home is something he needs to fix once and for all. Just about to inquire about the printer, he doesn't really understand why a sapien is hanging amongst other gadgets in this section.

"That will be a hundwed and ninety digits," the receptionist informs them about the price of the sapien they are holding.

"Why is that one over there?" Lord Omicron points at the sapien he has been looking at.

"It's weaponized, sir," the receptionist reveals.

"Weaponized? You authowized to sell weaponized gadgets?"

"Yes, only to authowized personnel."

"How much?"

"One thousand, seven hundwed and fifty digits."

Lexis tucks in his lips and nods.

"We'll take it," Lord Omicron announces.

The receptionist marches at once to get the weaponized sapien.

"Should that still be for Leontine?" asks the confused Lexis.

"Sure. Dunno, just feel she needs some more pwotection."

"But nothing has gone wong in decades, the sapien could attwact twouble."

"Nah, nobody will know it's weaponized, chillax."

"Hmm," Lexis chillaxes.

The receptionist returns with the weaponized sapien.

"You didn't ask me to identify myself," Lord Omicron says.

The receptionist smiles, "I know you Lord Woe."

"Oh..."

"Yes, but I'll still need your ID to appwove the sale."

"Sure. Sapien," Lord Omicron calls on his sapien.

"Sapien activated," his sapien responds immediately and of course, Lord Omicron is interrupted by other sapiens that disclaim his authority to command them, more remarkably is the receptionist's name-calling sapien.

"But you not Malcolm Neo," insists the receptionist's sapien.

"Genewate ID," Lord Omicron instructs his sapien, still keen on the receptionist's sapien.

"ID now available," Lord Omicron's sapien announces as it pops up a screen housing a small cube.

Lord Omicron picks out the cube and hands it over to the receptionist. The receptionist places the new sapien on his desk screen and it requests for 'purchase authorization'. He expands the cube to the size of the space provided for the purchase authorization. We can see Lord Omicron's name, image, address and job description.

"Your gadget calls you by name?" Lord Omicron asks the receptionist.

"Yeah, not fun. 'Yes boss' is quite cool."

"How come you didn't give him his own name?"

"Yeah, not exactly a fweak for change. Nobody likes them to be called something else."

While they talk, the receptionist drops Lord Omicron's ID cube on the desk screen and it approves the sale of the sapien. Next up on the screen is the 'ownership registration'.

"You and Saint Ose, family?" Lord Omicron asks the receptionist whose name is obviously Malcolm Neo.

"We are cousins."

Lord Omicron nods.

"The owner's identification?"

"Doctor Leontine Bella Woe," Lord Omicron responds.

Malcolm keys in the name and bills Lord Omicron.

"You've got bills," Lord Omicron's sapien announces.

The screen pops up again showing '1750 digits to Liebman Gaǵet for Sapien WG-298'. Lord Omicron approves the bill for payment and he sees yet another wonder – A BEM device hanging in that same section. Lexis too is now amazed.

"Don't tell me that BEM is weaponized too," Lord Omicron tells Malcolm.

Malcolm giggles, "You should know that alweady sir."

"Unbelievable... what exactly does it do?"

"I think it enhances what the users believe they can do."

"You haven't sold any?"

"No?" Malcolm replies, now wondering if Lord Omicron has lost his own memory.

"Don't mind me asking too much questions," Lord Omicron assures him the questions aren't unnecessary, "who made this?"

"Woediculous, sir," replies Malcolm, now looking more confused than Lord Omicron and Lexis.

"My own Woediculous?" Lord Omicron wonders aloud.

"Yes," Malcolm confirms, "It was made under your company's licence to say the least."

Lord Omicron and Lexis laugh out loud at the apparent joke. Their laughter soon fades away when they realize Malcolm Neo is dead serious.

"Sewiously?" Lord Omicron's wide open eyes are fixed on Malcolm's steady eyes. *"Adonbelivit!"*

"I'm not joking sir," Malcolm reassures him.

"Who exactly in my company invented this? Please don't say it's me."

"Hold on," Malcolm goes thru the shop's inventory on the desk screen and arrives at 'OmniBEM E5.' "According to this," he tells the all-listening father and son, "it was developed, designed, cweated and marketed by Archpwofessor Elise Leo Elise."

"Elise?!" Lord Omicron is completely bemused and we are puzzled too. *Oh that skinny Elise, her ancestors are among those wesponsible for how me's talking wight now... lol. #BlameElise.*

"That epitome of mischief! How much is that? How many do you have here?" Lord Omicron asks quickly.

"This is the only one we've got. It's twenty-two thousand digits."

"Twenty-two... does it elevate man's lifespan or what? I don't know about this development... I have to pull it out of the market."

"Sure," Malcolm moves quickly to get the BEM, "it will make here a lot safer. Evewyone who has ever asked about it ended up buying an extwa PES... you'd feel they plan to invade our store at night."

"OmniBEM E-five," Lord Omicron says to himself. "Seen E one to four?" he asks Lexis.

"Nope," Lexis shakes his head.

"Elise is something else. And I'm sure this thing works perfectly, I don't understand why she didn't show me first, and it goes for a whopping twenty-two thousand digits."

"Actually we didn't pay for this... it's only here for marketing and stuff. Since you are the owner, you don't have to pay us to take it back."

"Have you sold any before?"

"No, we got just one and this is it," Malcolm hands Lord Omicron the OmniBEM E5 package.

Lord Omicron's attention is back to the Ambrosia Food Printer. "How much for that Ambwosia?" he asks Malcolm.

"That will be four thousand four hundwed digits."

Lord Omicron doesn't blink. With no extra word, he takes the new weaponized sapien and BEM, turns around and starts walking away. Lexis raises his shoulders at Malcolm and goes after his father.

"Popmy, you don't like the Ambwosia?"

"The pwice is too high. Food pwinters have never gone above nine hundwed digits no matter who the maker is."

"You can still bargain with the guy, it's not as if he said it's a fixed pwice."

"Hmm, Lexis... if the pwice of a commodity is on the high side to you, please walk away... because announcing to the seller how low you think the pwice should be will only make both of you feel worthless."

Lexis giggles. "But we can afford this... that pwinter is worth it."

"Just because we have all the digits to spend doesn't mean we should spend all the digits we have. What exactly does it do diffewently?" asks Lord Omicron.

"You can make meals fwom scwatch."

"Other pwinters do that."

"No, other pwinters simply give weadymade food. Ambwosia gives you access to uncooked foodstuffs so you can pwepare to taste by just clicking the wight buttons."

"You basically saying it will take more time then..."

"Yes, if you don't like the menu option anymore, that does happen once in a while but it still allows subscwiption to seven independent meal vendors."

"Seven? Impwessive. We'll give them a call when we get home... have them deliver it afterwards."

"Cool!" Lexis is elated.

Lord Omicron looks at the OmniBEM E5 in his hand and realises he hasn't gotten all the answers yet as they walk towards the teleport system.

"Sapien," he calls up his gadget and invariably bothers Lexis'.

"Yes boss," responds Lord Omicron's sapien.

"Video call, Elise Leo Elise."

"Elise Leo Elise will speak if she can."

Lord Omicron's sapien has barely finished speaking when the ever vibrant Archprofessor Elise pops up with her trademark greeting.

"Hullo me lord! And me lord's son..."

The boys are not smiling, with Lexis basically rendering emotional support. Lord Omicron lifts up the weaponized BEM towards his face, high enough to be seen by Archprofessor Elise.

"What's this?" Lord Omicron asks.

Archprofessor Elise looks closely at the pack. "I can't see anything, me lord," she says quite frankly.

"You blind?" Lord Omicron shakes the pack vigorously and asks again, "What is this?"

Archprofessor Elise looks again at the package, we will never see her looking this serious and confused in her lifetime. "Me lord, what is what? You asking me of the whole pack, if me can see her?"

"*Geheh*?" Lord Omicron contracts the *confusionist* virus. He's still trying naturally and BEM-artificially to comprehend what Elise means. He looks at the pack too to be sure he sees what he expects Elise to see. "You damn wight, what do you think I'm saying?"

"Me thought you saw a mistake in the name or something." Archprofessor Elise says happily.

"I will not ask you again. I want to see you in my house in ten seconds!" Lord Omicron terminates the call and enters the teleport system.

"Welcome, state your destination."

"Pwivate station," Lord Omicron tells the machine.

"Enter your password," the machine requests.

Lord Omicron punches in an eight digit password while his sapien alerts him on Archprofessor Elise's request to arrive thru the family teleport system. He approves it before confirming his password to the machine.

"Destination found," the machine announces, "goodbye."

Lord Omicron arrives back home and he sees Archprofessor Elise speaking to the front door, apparently having an argument with the lie detector. Lexis arrives almost immediately and collects Leontine's sapien from Lord Omicron. He skips into the house after having a successful palm print test at the door, leaving Lord Omicron wondering why Archprofessor Elise is still trying to deceive the door. The malfunctioning door has failed to agree with her that Lord Omicron asked her to come over, or perhaps her previous plan to visit must be clouding out the real truth. Lord Omicron can hear her arguing with the door.

"That is a lie, please say again. State your purpose of visit."

"I told you, Lord Omicwon Woe asked me to come."

Lord Omicron grabs Archprofessor Elise's arm and drags her thru the door Lexis had left open. Certainly even the door had no idea it was open but Archprofessor Elise's self-satisfying smirk tells a different story of two malfunctioning creatures happily going about their malfunctioning businesses.

Lord Omicron shuts the door and raises the BEM package to Archprofessor Elise's face. He could hear Sextine in the dining room feeling excited about Leontine's weaponized sapien. Dame Nissi, however, is not comfortable with it.

"A weaponized es!" Dame Nissi murmurs strongly, still comported enough to avoid the word 'sapien'. "If for nothing I'm sure it costs ten times more than the normal ones."

"Why you yelling at me? Popmy bought it, not me," Lexis protests his innocence.

"I'm not yelling Lexis, and you were there when he paid for it, I'm sure you winked at him at least."

Lord Omicron does his best to ignore the complaint as he tries to figure out what has been happening in his own Rhodiculous since he became obsessed with the heart whisperer.

"The pack Elise, start talking."

"But you can see she's the OmniBEM E5, she's weaponized."

"And you did this without letting me know?"

"Me did? No! Me told you evewy step we took. Me sent you a daily video log of the pwogwess. You must wemember the day she was completed, me sent you a video of her... the one me was dancing in her."

"You sent me a video of you dancing Elise, there was no message in it!"

"Me lord, perhaps you were not patient. There was a message after the short dance."

"Short dance? It was a thirty minutes concert! Which marwied man will wisk his marwiage watching a dancing lady?"

"Me was more like celebwating, certainly not doing anything *sweeticing*."

"But you do wealise this is a violation of the Saint Jamima Act? This weapon is highly dangewous."

"A weapon is a weapon me lord. Perhaps the PES is more advanced than she is, that's why me thought you were not intewested in seeing her."

"How are the Performance Enhancing Suits more advanced?" Lord Omicron asks.

"The BEM is just a make-believe. It makes you think you can do a lot of superhuman things. But if your body is not used to those things, there is no way you can pull it off, no matter how convincing the BEM ideas are."

"I don't understand you, Elise."

"An example... if we had a fat lady..."

"Be wealistic here; there be no medically fat ladies in existence."

"Just listen first, me lord. If the lady be fat, and she has a weaponized OmniBEM E5, no matter how stwongly the BEM is convincing her to make a dash and jump a long distance, her fat body won't let her do it. But the PES makes you do anything and evewything."

"Elise, there is always a small start before a quantum leap. If digitizers never got weaponized in the first place, we won't need a fund-wasting body that keeps wegulating the maximum abilities of those weapons."

"Yes of course, but me lord..."

"No buts Elise. This thing doesn't exist, okay?"

"Yes me lord, but..."

"Ah, no buts! This matter, you see her? She's closed."

"Yes me lord," agrees Archprofessor Elise as she staggers and Lord Omicron holds her.

"You good?"

"Yes me lord, was diagnosed of stomach cancer... took the last medicine few minutes ago."

"Sowie. It's gone now, sure?"

"Yeah, took an extwa dose just to avoid a welapse. I need a glass of water that's all."

"Sure, come this way..."

Lord Omicron leads Archprofessor Elise to the dining room where Leontine is first to see him and she gives him a big hug. Archprofessor Elise takes a seat and the sensitive

Doctor Sextine offers the less animated Elise a glass of water and glucose.

"Thanks for the sapien," Leontine signs.

"You welcome," Lord Omicron signs back.

"But I still cannot use it," Leontine signs.

"Why?" Lord Omicron is visibly worried as he looks at Dame Nissi.

"These things work better with voice commands," Dame Nissi reminds Lord Omicron.

"Ah, that's a fact," Lord Omicron recalls. "That is true," he signs to Leontine. "But don't feel bad, the School of Sapien Acupuncture has good data on how to use these things. We will simply buy it and update your BEM and you'll know exactly how to use it."

"No no Omicwon," Dame Nissi objects. "I'm not an advocate of people uploading knowledge they can't defend into their BEMs. It is dangewous to health too. The school teaches how to manually contwol these things in just one day, evewy Saturdays. Tomorwow is Saturday... I'll take her there first; we can then weinforce whatever she learns by updating her BEM with the school's data."

"That's perfect," Lord Omicron signs to Leontine. "You will go to the School of Sapien Acupuncture tomorrow."

Leontine nods happily.

"I'm going to see Pwincess Zeta," Lexis announces immediately with his eyes on the time – 2:25 t.m.

"Can I come?" Sextine screams, abandoning the off-colour Archprofessor Elise.

"No Sextine!" her parents respond together.

"But why?"

"Because Leontine will be lonely here," Dame Nissi explains.

"But you will be here, popmy will be here too."

"No Sextine, I'm sure Lexis is going on a date."

"Not exactly a date momxy," Lexis reveals. "My fwends, *Hanson, Easy,* and *Jax Lilyscent* will be there too."

Lord Omicron remembers the Lilyscent surname. "Jax Lilyscent... the Lilyscent I know?"

"Yes popmy, you've seen us together before."

"They allow a Lilyscent into the palace? I thought they are enemies with the Zeta-Sigmas."

"Oh please Omicwon," Dame Nissi doesn't agree with his thinking. "The boy's popmy wasn't even born when the Lilyscents and Sigmas had their mini pillow fight."

"He's still a Lilyscent, and be careful with him," Lord Omicron warns, "they may also have something against the Woes."

"Haha!" Dame Nissi laughs it off. "We are all the Woes in the world and they haven't done anything against us."

Lord Omicron has just been reminded of his small family. His father was an only child, and his father before him, and his father's father, and to the twentieth generation as far as he could count. He's the first Rho to have more than one child.

10 LEXIS arrives at the King's palace, with Sextine of course. It would take a miracle to force her to stay home just to babysit Leontine – a veterinary doctor and botanist who doesn't really find much fun in human company.

With Lord Omicron back into his lab and accompanied by Archprofessor Elise to help out with some crazy suggestions, Dame Nissi decides to join Leontine in completing the Earth Age movie. This time we see Biggy tutoring Morpheus on how to fight, leaving the frustrated Morpheus insisting he's being trained to be an elephant instead of a tiger... "Teegah!" Ben surely corrects him again.

Lexis meets up with his friends just outside the monumental palace and a guard leads them straight to the princesses' exquisite private living room; they've been expecting them.

The intellivision is on and the room is quite *spoisy* – that trademark noisy atmosphere created by a sporting event. The aggressive kickers commentators won't even pause to breathe, that's how intense the *Oh-Nations Cup* final is. The host nation, Jermain, is up against the world number one, Meotonia.

Sextine and the boys get a warm welcome from Princess Mary-Zeta. It is a simple, "Hi!" from afar, "I'll be with you shortly." As shortly as whenever the ninetieth minute is up. Even the little Princess Kamsi-Elle has been waiting with her new pack of sapien, standing beside her kickers-engrossed mother with her cheeks air-filled in frustration.

Lexis and his friends don't mind, Princess Zeta had already kept a digital quess board suspended in the middle of four seats, the same seats she points at during her electrified welcome note. They pretend not to be in hurry to get to the quess board.

Almost seated, Jax Lilyscent whispers strongly to Lexis. "Lexis, doesn't she know you her boyfwend?"

"I heard that Lilyscent!" Princess Zeta screams from her seat.

Princess Lotem-Zeta wouldn't ignore that name easily. She looks over her shoulder and it's quite easy for her to identify the almost dark-skinned Jax, a descendent of the Lilyscents who were banished from the royal family many years ago. The crown princess doesn't blink and she turns back to the kickers match.

One would wonder how these noble ladies are huge fans of kickers. The game itself is quite violent, a sad tale of the little the people of Oh can remember about football. The sound of the ball when kicked clearly tells it is still made of leather. The players of both teams are padded up and crowned with a safety helmet. Only one player from the yellow kitted Meotonians is running around the enclosed pitch just as the rule states. Seven of the blue/black kitted Jermainis are chasing their lone opponent round the small pitch containing a few number of poles. The Jermainis aim at kicking the ball at the Meotonian player who is adequately skilled at swerving away from the ball. The ball at some point eventually hits the Meotonian player after a perfectly timed looping shot is taken by the captain of Jermain. The game structure is reversed immediately. The Meotonian quickly retrieves the ball and tries to shoot at the fleeing Jermainis. Six of the Jermaini players successfully leave the pitch and the remaining player (the runner) is now being chased with the ball by the Meotonian who is quickly joined by six other Meotonians, seven of whom become the chasers. For a team to win, the time spent running from the ball (runtime) must be higher than the time spent chasing the runner (chasetime).

"Have you ever been in love?" Lexis asks Jax Lilyscent who sits adjacent and gets the quess game started. Lexis is trying to justify why the princess should ignore them for the game.

"Of course," Jax responds. "The longest list one can ever make is the names of ladies I said to me that we love."

"Lol, you certainly don't feel the same way about them all, do you?"

"Yeah, why not? Same feeling that lasts just for a week or so."

"That, my fwend, is lust, not love." Lexis concludes.

"What is the diffewence?" Jax wonders.

"You see," Easy explains, "lust is many years older than love but love happens to be more mature when born."

"EASY!" his friends whisper his name. Easy winks at them. It is fascinating how he's always so sure of himself – an explanationist in the making anyway.

"You can't possibly pwove that lust must pwecede love," Hanson says. "What happens to love at first sight?"

"That is absolutely lust at first sight," Easy responds. "You love people for who they are... you don't know the stwanger, what's there to love? And that line 'I love you' is simply a pwoverb only the old can interpwet it."

"Ha!" Jax sighs. "Lexis you started this, why did you ask me about love?"

"To let you know it is normal we wait for Pwincess Zeta."

"Intewesting. If this was mutual, I believe that kickers match can wait."

"Two mad people can't fall in love with each other," says Lexis, and his friends too laugh quietly at him.

"Lexis the mad," Hanson echoes.

Easy looks around the room again. Sextine is sitting alone with her sapien, swiping thru pictures of Leontine taken in Nissi's Gallery. Princess Kamsi-Elle is still standing beside the crown princess who is more excited about the game than the calmly seated Princess Zeta.

"But you notice she never gets angwy or overexcited. Is that what music does to the soul and body?" Easy asks about Princess Zeta who is a renowned lover of music.

"The whole of Oh knows she loves music, maybe... or just her efizzy is too much." Jax says.

"It is not," Lexis defends the princess' alleged excessive elegance.

"Too much efizzy is never bad anyway... don't know why people keep denying it."

The eight year old Princess Kamsi-Elle is maximally tired of waiting and things are about to get naughty. "Momxy," she tries to get Princess Lotem-Zeta's attention.

Princess Zeta looks worryingly at her little sister; she has been expecting a drama.

"Hold on sugar, the game is ending soon," Princess Lotem-Zeta pleads with Kamsi-Elle.

Kamsi-Elle looks at the game time, 84:40. She certainly can wait for another five minutes, but never five minutes and twenty seconds. There's a thin line between patience and impatience.

"Just five minutes, Kamsi," Princess Zeta adds.

"No, it's more than that!" Kamsi screams. "I just want it now! I want to activate me sapien!"

Ah, we all sense she has finally done it. The youngster is not bothered by the unnecessary response every sapien will give when called upon by unauthorized persons. The grownups subconsciously wait for it; it's basically a name that mustn't be spoken without purpose.

"You not me boss!" echoes around the room.

"Mhehehmm," Kamsi-Elle giggles with a sweet smirk on her face. At last she can get some sapien-attention.

"Kamsi-Elle, don't," says Princess Zeta, perfectly predicting the nearest unstoppable future.

"S – S – SAPIEN!" Kamsi-Elle screams mischievously.

"No, don't do that again," Princess Lotem-Zeta warns.

"You not me boss," echoes from the sapiens in the room.

The boys are now feeling distracted too. Sextine is the last to get bothered but the first to react effectively.

"Sapien! Sapien!!" Kamsi-Elle screams repeatedly, dancing to the tune of her tomfoolery and the sapiens are never tired of rebelliously rejecting the little princess' call.

"Sapien deactivate," Sextine instructs her gadget quickly, still sitting relaxed as she watches the sapien drama.

"Sugar, stop that now!" Princess Lotem-Zeta cautions the unrepentant Kamsi-Elle.

"Momxy, let's just kill her... that's the lasting solution," the frustrated Princess Zeta offers.

"No Beauty, that's too everlasting, you cannot kill your own sister."

"We'll have the guards do it instead," Princess Zeta suggests.

"No!" Princess Lotem-Zeta looks at her mean-faced first daughter and realizes she may not be joking about killing Kamsi-Elle. "Can you now go and see your guests," she whispers to Princess Zeta.

"No, the game is still on, no time now."

"Listen, if you take a spoonful of love, you have to add a litre of time," Princess Lotem-Zeta whispers more.

"Heh? Woh ah you talking about, momxy?" Princess Zeta isn't in the mood to keep her own voice down.

"Just go!" Lotem-Zeta pulls the confused Zeta out of the seat. "Kamsi?" she calls on the relentless sapien-harassing Kamsi-Elle.

"Sapien sapien," Kamsi-Elle continues chanting.

"Sapien deactivate," Princess Zeta orders her sapien as she walks towards her friends who all try to make the room more conducive by ordering their sapiens to deactivate too.

"YES!" Princess Lotem-Zeta throws her hands in the air. "Jermain are champions!"

Princess Zeta doesn't look back as she clutches her hand in a quiet celebration; a nation in the kingdom are world champions. She diverts quickly to a food-filled table in the corner of the room and brings along a tray of apple-like fruits – *shouites*.

Lexis and his friends happily take one each and Princess Zeta sits on Lexis' laps. The smile on her face as she watches Lexis take a big sticky bite of the shouite will really suggest to the fainthearted that those shouites are poisoned. Jax Lilyscent is not in a hurry, he pretentiously observes Lexis chew the fruit that has an inside of an orange, it's surely juicy and a natural source of energy.

The energy aura of the shouite is also seen in the way it harvests itself from the main plant often called *Jesse's stump*. Once the fruits are ripe and ready to be eaten, they get catapulted from the tube branches to any direction fate deems fit, with some covering as much as ten kilometres. This behaviour of the shouite prompted the warning signs around their only habitat in the *Jungle of Zion* preceding the Youlv Ocean, informing rare human visitors to the thick jungle whenever they are within the radius of the shooting fruits.

Princess Lotem-Zeta grabs the noisy Kamsi-Elle and lifts her up in excitement. "Now babe, be quiet. You making here more spoisy than it should be. We'll activate her now."

"Ha," Kamsi-Elle exhales, "finally."

"Sapien deactivate," the crown princess orders her sapien as she also turns off the intellivision.

"Sapien deactivated," her sapien brings to a close the raucous era of the room.

Princess Lotem-Zeta sits Kamsi-Elle on a chair and unpacks the sapien. Its golden colour prompts Sextine to move for a closer look. The crown princess wraps and buckles the sapien around Kamsi-Elle's left wrist.

"What next?" Kamsi-Elle asks enthusiastically.

"She's thermo-activated for the first time. We'll wait for her to feel your skin tempewature, good thing you've been hyperactive."

The sapien suddenly vibrates intensely; this startles Kamsi-Elle and she almost shakes off her hand from her forearm. She stands easy when the sapien welcomes her.

"Welcome. Speak only if you... Pwincess Kamsi-Elle of Sexat."

Princess Lotem-Zeta mouths "go on," urging Kamsi-Elle to speak.

"I am," Kamsi-Elle responds, suspecting all sorts of things both seen and unseen as she rotates her wrist to look properly at the sapien.

"You are?" the sapien asks.

Now that's unusual. Princess Lotem-Zeta is wondering if that was an acknowledgement of Kamsi-Elle's response or yet another question. Early signs of a malfunction? She signals Kamsi-Elle to say something.

"Yes?" the dumbfounded Kamsi-Elle simply says. She could read the words from her mother's eyes, 'Really? That's the something you could say'.

"Welcome," the sapien begins again. "Speak only if you... Pwincess Kamsi-Elle of Sexat."

Kamsi-Elle shrugs and her mother is visibly confused but Sextine seems to know what has to be done.

"I think..." Sextine begins.

"Shh!" mother and daughter beg her to be quiet.

"...that she..." Sextine continues and pauses again; Princess Lotem-Zeta's eyes are definitely louder and harsher than that 'Shh'.

"Can you be quiet? You not Kamsi-Elle, are you?" Kamsi-Elle asks the stubborn Sextine who has undeniably made it clear she intends to finish her statement.

"You are?" the sapien asks.

"She doesn't hear anything until you call her by the es name," Sextine says quickly.

"Oh!" Princess Lotem-Zeta's anger-building program comes crashing down with an appreciative smile. "Twue that, I forgot."

"Welcome," the sapien is going over the same sequence. "Speak only if you... Pwincess Kamsi-Elle of Sexat."

"Sapien," Kamsi-Elle calls out after getting a nod from her mother.

"Yes boss," the sapien responds, "complete the voice ownership sequence. Say sapien."

"Sapien," Kamsi-Elle responds, unaware of the lengthy sequence to come.

"Say again." instructs the sapien.

"Again?" Kamsi-Elle wonders aloud.

"Not understood boss, speak some more. Say sapien."

"Sapien."

"Say again."

"Sapien," Kamsi-Elle responds.

"Again."

"Sapien."

"Again."

"Again," the confused Kamsi-Elle responds.

"Not understood boss, speak some more. Say sapien."

"Sapien."

"Now," the sapien throws in another request, "hold your nose and say sapien."

Princess Lotem-Zeta and Sextine won't wait around for this ritual. The crown princess walks away to get a bowl of water. Undoubtedly she's unaware these modern sapiens don't ask their new wielders to put their heads underwater and say sapien. The new commands, however, include, 'cough and say sapien,' 'say sapien while coughing,' 'laugh and say sapien,' 'say sapien while laughing,' and same goes for cry, run, jump, crawl, panic, hold your breath, and hold your throat.

Sextine walks to her brother's side; she can still hear Kamsi-Elle responding impatiently to the sapien's demands. The boys are concentrating on the intense quess game.

Lexis is evidently in control; his officials are threatening the royal families of Easy and Hanson. Jax Lilyscent is a bit freer since he and Lexis are adjacent allies until the unwritten truce is broken without notification. Well, it's Jax's turn to play and he's about to do just that. He lifts up his Archbishop which has been protecting Lexis' Princess from Easy's protected Queen, one of Easy's few surviving officials. Easy is to play next after Jax and Lexis finds Jax's anticipated move not easy to accept quietly.

"No, not now... you can't leave. What are you twying to do?" Lexis asks.

"Playing quess," Jax responds coldly.

"I thought we still allies."

"No Lexis, your Pwincess has been standing dangewously in my terwitowy."

"Jax, my pwincess is sitting on my laps."

Princess Zeta, Easy and Hanson giggle.

"Lol Lexis," says Princess Zeta, "focus on the game... leave me out of this."

"You know," Jax advances with his Archbishop towards Lexis' Princess, "my Archbishop isn't actually leaving, your Pwincess is."

Jax sacks the Princess and places his Archbishop in her spot.

"Jax Lilyscent!" Princess Zeta screams, prompting Princess Lotem-Zeta to pause with the bowl of water she's carrying. "That is absolutely the worst betwayal I've seen! Backstabbing!"

"Hmm" Princess Lotem-Zeta sighs to herself. A sentence always associated to the Lilyscents, this time her daughter who knows little about them is gradually discovering Jax kind of person.

Easy picks up his Queen gently and speaks in his usual confident tone. "When an old man is dying of old age, you don't blame his enemies for being happy. But when an impatient enemy goes to stab the old man to death, the enemy is seized by the state. Old age cannot be cured but the state will succeed in purging Oh of another killer."

"What is the essence of this lecture?" Jax asks.

"To let you know that I would have given up my all important Queen to sack that Pwincess myself, and you know this," Easy sacks Jax's Archbishop, "which means you would have saved your Archbishop."

"That point is obvious, Easy. What still is the essence of saying what is known to those who know?"

"Because your move suggests you have plans to sack the living Pwincess Maywy-Zeta."

Princess Zeta splutters in surprise.

"I beg your pardon!" Jax Lilyscent is almost livid.

"Guys please let's stick to the game," Lexis urges them.

Jax Lilyscent's eyes are still fixed on Easy, filled with anger, and we can understand why... or so we do. It's more like Jax is wondering how a little quess move almost exposed a bigger plan.

Sextine walks away from the tensed game and towards Princess Lotem-Zeta who is staring at Jax Lilyscent with so much interest she doesn't even realize immediately that Kamsi-Elle is tugging her cloth.

"Yes sugar..."

"I'm done."

"Sure? But I didn't see you say her name underwater."

"She didn't ask me to."

"Well then, give her a shout." Princess Lotem-Zeta suggests.

"Watch this," Kamsi-Elle tells her mother. "Sapien," she calls out in her normal voice.

"Yes boss," the sapien responds with the same volume.

"Sapien," Kamsi-Elle whispers.

"Yes boss," the sapien whispers back.

"Whoa, that's cool!" says the approaching Sextine. "How did you do that?"

Kamsi-Elle giggles. "I'll show you." "Sapien," she calls out while giggling.

"Yes boss," the sapien responds with a similar giggle.

This makes Sextine smile even more, certainly the type of feeling she loves, but the quess game cuts everything short. The boys shout and hoot at Jax Lilyscent.

"Make your move boy! Jax your King is dead!" Easy mocks him. "And having the Pwince is of no use since you failed to keep any clergy alive."

"The Archbishop sacks the Pwincess," Hanson reminds Jax of the move he made earlier.

"And the state has come to seize the killer..."

"You should know I don't play to get cowoneted," Jax tries to pretend he made no mistake. Without the Archbishop to coronate his Prince, the death of the King is simply game over for his kingdom.

"I need to put this game on bwacketier," says the elated Lexis, "a classic lesson on ending a partnership pwematurely."

"Do your best not to enlist me in the bwackets," Jax says.

"Lol, just play first," Easy urges Jax, "it's pwactically your last move."

"Sapien," Lexis calls on his sapien. He's quite motivated to embarrass Jax on *Bracketier.*

Bracketier is the most popular social network on Oh; it will be very easy to let everyone who has ever heard of the name 'Jax Lilyscent' see and understand what mess he made of the game.

"Sapien activated," Lexis' sapien is ready to do the job. Everyone ignores Kamsi-Elle's sapien rejecting Lexis' call. Lexis waves an apology but Kamsi-Elle is too busy with Sextine looking at a list of new action games on her sapien.

"Launch Bwacketier," Lexis instructs his sapien.

The sapien quickly pops up the yellow and red themed Bracketier [B] page. The slogan 'don't be shy' is clearly visible. The sapien alerts him on 'four hug offers' – an open arms icon, 'ten replies on open conversations', and 'five whispers' – an envelope icon with a lips speaking into a fine ear.

"Ignore," Lexis instructs the sapien ignore them for now. "Upload quess game."

"State the board's location," the sapien pulls up the digitizer icon and Lexis retrieves a strand of digitizer. He lines it along the quess board and the quess game appears on his Bracketier page – (L.A. Rho) Arc/Imgr. Lexis Alpha Rho.

"Upload," he instructs the sapien.

"Quess game now live. Enlist players?"

"Skip."

"Choose bwackets."

This last request keeps Jax's eyes fixed on Lexis'. Lexis doesn't blink and with a half smile and a half grin, he picks almost all the brackets available – age brackets, school brackets, job brackets, location brackets, quess brackets, and lots more.

Princess Zeta is certainly enjoying the look on Jax's face; at last something has sobered him up a bit. Her sister

Kamsi-Elle is still hyperactive and she has infected Sextine with some noisy energy.

Sextine cheers for Kamsi-Elle as the little princess overcomes her enemy in the sapien game she's playing. Princess Lotem-Zeta is not feeling very comfortable about the game. Kamsi-Elle is completely connected with the fighter in the game after she had taken digitizers from the game and applied them randomly over her joints and muscles. The third round is over and Princess Lotem-Zeta's discomfort peaks when her daughter faces off with a fierce warrior in round four. It takes the game warrior just two swings of the arm to land a heavy punch in the face of Kamsi-Elle's fighter. The real Kamsi-Elle is thrown to ground, leaving her with a bleeding lip.

Lexis and his friends are alerted by the instant short scream of Sextine and Princess Lotem-Zeta. Princess Zeta springs up quickly and leads the rest of the boys to Kamsi-Elle who is being assessed by her mother and Sextine. Jax Lilyscent, however, lags behind. He places a hologram portal under his chair before joining the rest of his friends.

"Have you quit the game?" Princess Lotem-Zeta asks Kamsi-Elle.

"Momxy, what happened?" Princess Zeta asks.

Kamsi-Elle nods "yes" and tries lifting herself up.

"The fighter in the game punched her."

"Maybe she was playing fwom the simulation section." Easy explains.

"No," Sextine objects, "I saw her select the kiddies section."

"How did the game appear there?" Lexis asks.

"It's one of the new games."

"How did they get past the limits?"

"Why would anyone want to get past the limits? Princess Lotem-Zeta asks. "Can you find out who made the game?"

"Sure," Lexis confirms. "What's the name of the game?"

"Denzers," Kamsi-Elle tells Lexis as she stands on her feet.

Lexis quickly instructs his sapien to find the game and the makers of the game. The first name to pop up as the CEO of Denzers is unsurprisingly Sir Nnia Den.

"Sir Nnia Den?" the irate crown-princess yells. "Lexis, call your popmy now."

Lexis again quickly instructs his sapien to call Lord Omicron Rho. Once he responds, Princess Lotem-Zeta picks up the call screen from Lexis' sapien and walks into another room.

Lord Omicron goes from an excited "Hey Lexis, Howdy?" to a worrisome "Your highness? What's the matter?"

Princess Lotem-Zeta keeps mute until she's alone and then she whispers aggressively.

"Omicwon, before I do anything harsh to jeopardize the importance of Team Epsilon, you best act now."

"Calm down, your highness... what is..."

"...my daughter's life has just been endangered by one of us and I will not take it lightly."

"What happened?"

"Sir Nnia Den's game, Divers... Denzers or whatever evil he named it, had its fighter punch my Kamsi-Elle on the face!"

"These things are simulators, weality games, it is normal."

"NO! It is not! Her gadget is wegistered to her, I'm sure of that. How did she get to that game at her age? There are meant to be limitations to what she can see."

"Oh yes yes, that is corwect. How did Sir Nnia bweak thwu the limitations?"

"I don't care how he did it! You should be more concerned about why he did. I will kill that man."

"No your highness... like you wightly pwedicted, it may jeopardize our twip to the lost earth. Have you spoken to Sir Nnia about it?"

"Have I spoken to Sir Nnia?!" Princess Lotem-Zeta is utterly disgusted. "How can I bwing my lofty self to that low state of insanity? If my dear husband was still alive I'm sure he must have moved against Sir Nnia by now."

"I'm sowie your highness. I will speak to him... I will call him to come over to my house now. I'm sure he'll have a good explanation for this mistake."

"I don't want an explanation. I want you to tell him what he has done and inform him of the consequences."

"That will be done your highness. Are my kids fine?"

"I will send them home at once. Goodbye."

Lord Omicron nods coldly after the call is over. He looks at the surprised Archprofessor Elise who is still with him in the laboratory.

"You think he did it on purpose?" she asks Lord Omicron.

'It doesn't matter what I think now. Call Sir Nnia and ask him to come here immediately."

11

LEXIS and Sextine walk thru the front door with their eyes and mouths full of stories. Dame Nissi stands at once, looking very concerned. Leontine is still focused on the intellivision.

"What's going on?" Dame Nissi asks curiously.

"Wow momxy!" Sextine exclaims. "Pwincess Kamsi-Elle got punched by a simulator game fighter."

"Ohemgee, is that legal? Is she alwight?"

"She's fine. And guess who the game maker is?" Lexis asks.

"Sir Nnia Den?"

Lexis and Sextine are stunned.

"Like what?! In the whole Oh, is there none like him?"

"Lol Lexis, it's him eh? Only a western knight can afford to joke expensively with the Sigmas. Only Sir Nnia is such a knight. I've seen him just once and since then I've heard a lot about him."

"The evil genius," Sextine whispers before diving at the sad Leontine. Sextine gives her a quick peck on the cheek and realizes she's quite moody with her eyes fixed on the Earth Age movie. "What is it?" Sextine signs.

"Ben is dead," signs Leontine.

"What? NO!" Sextine screams with her first finger pointing at the screen.

We can see Morpheus and Biggy looking more dejected than Leontine.

"Momxy, why should they kill the only living monkey?" Sextine asks.

"Lol Sextine, it's just a movie; perhaps there is no living monkey."

Leontine suddenly throws her hands up in excitement. Ben has just surprisingly reunited with Morpheus and Biggy.

"Oh look, the monkey is back," says Lexis, dragging himself out of the living room.

"HAPPY!" Leontine voices out.

Sextine is completely bemused. "Momxy! Leontine just spoke." She taps and signs to Leontine, "You just spoke."

Leontine is not at all surprised. "I am deaf, not mute," she signs.

"Momxy, did you see that?"

"I am surpwised myself," Dame Nissi says ironically. She's aware before now that Leontine could speak.

"Why don't you speak?" Sextine signs to Leontine.

"I don't like the way I sound," Leontine signs.

"You can't hear you. You don't know the way you sound."

"Exactly... how can I like what I don't know?" Leontine signs.

"Sewiously? Leontine!"

"That's enough Sextine, wespect your sister's decision," Dame Nissi says.

"*Haba*! I've known this babe for ten years, and I just learnt something new about her."

"Guess you don't pay attention."

"That's not a fair assessment momxy." "Leontine," Sextine taps Leontine. "Say something," she signs.

"Say what?" Leontine signs back.

"Anything... I want to hear your voice."

"I've seen someone laugh at my voice before. I am not taking that risk again."

"It is not a risk," signs Sextine, "I am your sister."

"You can wait until you become a shouite tree, I will still not speak."

"Ah!" "Just be in hell already!" Sextine signs in frustration.

"Hey!" Dame Nissi tries cautioning Sextine.

"Get out!" Leontine signs to Sextine.

"You cwazy or something? You dare not sign to my daughter like that." Dame Nissi scolds Sextine.

"I am your daughter too," Sextine reminds Dame Nissi, "you dare not talk to me like that."

Dame Nissi's eyes at this moment say it all. Nothing more than those eyes of fury could compel Sextine to leave for her room without saying or signing any other word.

Dame Nissi looks at Leontine who is already focused on the cast of the Earth Age movie. She hears the front door giving instructions to a visitor.

"Place your hand on the scan and state the purpose of your visit," the door says.

Dame Nissi hears a young male voice say, "I've come to chat with Sextine."

"That's a lie," the door announces. "State the purpose of your visit."

We see the stranded fourteen year old, *Pharmacist Eoin Traple,* scratching his head, absolutely wondering why he's here.

"I have come to see Sextine?" Eoin practically asks the door.

"That's a lie." the door loudly proclaims. "For your age," it informs Eoin, "you have just one twy left. State the purpose of your visit after the beep."

The beep doesn't come immediately as the door is basically alerting the named member of the house that she could be in danger.

"Alert boss," Sextine's sapien alerts her. "Do you know Pharmacist Eoin Twaple? He has lied twice at the door."

"Yes," Sextine responds uninterestedly.

The door beeps and Eoin unreservedly states why he's here. "I want to copy some design ideas fwom Sextine."

"That is not a lie," the door responds before alerting Sextine again thru her sapien. This time it replays Eoin's voice.

"Let him in!" Sextine instructs the sapien as she gets up from her bed.

The front door opens up for Eoin. He walks in quietly and meets the eyes of Dame Nissi Rho.

"Little lies will only elongate the duwation of judgment day. Welcome Eoin."

"Good evening, Dame Woe."

"How is your momxy?"

"Bubbling okay... is Sextine home?"

"Of course," Sextine announces her presence. "You late, and that door is telling me you are here for something else."

"I swear, I did plan to have a chat, your door is faulty."

"Hmm, so I shouldn't expect you to ask me for design ideas?"

"No actually, I need that too. Then I will leave for today, something else needs to be taken care of."

"Hmm," Sextine nods, "and my door is faulty."

"You know architecture is not my thing."

"Yeah yeah, come and take what you need."

Sextine walks towards the dining room and decides to give her sapien a whispered call, still being tickled by the new sapien response behaviour she acquired.

The sapien whispers back, "Yes boss," and Sextine goes from giggling to laughing out loud.

Dame Nissi stares at her with an eyebrow raised. She's soon drawn into the laughter when she hears Sextine's sapien laugh like Sextine and say, "not understood boss, speak some more."

Leontine falls into Dame Nissi for her usual cuddle. Dame Nissi holds her passionately and pets her. Sextine asks her sapien for her photo gallery; she selects the architecture folder and tries getting the attention of Eoin Traple who is still busy admiring the Rhos' newly acquired Ambrosia Food Printer.

"You hungwy now too?"

"Lol, no... I'm sure your door would have insisted I say that too."

"Haha! No way. Here, which of these designs can serve?"

Eoin swipes thru a couple of the pictures; Sextine could sense he's in a hurry.

"Maybe we'll look at them pwoperly in class on Monday?"

"No, too far. Maybe I can copy these?" Eoin suggests.

Sextine's sapien is not only a smart gadget; it's not shy of letting one know it can serve as a perfect gossip machine. The sapien, obviously paying attention to keywords, quickly pops up a 'select all' and 'send' option.

"Vewy well then," Sextine accepts Eoin's proposal. She taps on the send option.

The sapien creates a ghost of the pictures in a more translucent screen. Sextine picks up the screen and begins to fold it casually into a smaller square.

"So, what else needs your attention so urgently?" Sextine asks Eoin.

"I am not sure yet... just a family emergency," Eoin says impatiently as he clicks on his sapien and pops up a receive file option.

"You can do that manually?" Sextine asks.

"Yes. I am an old boy of the School of Gadget Acupuncture."

"Cool... my popmy said he went there too. My sister Leontine will be going to one tomorwow."

"Yes, it's the ideal thing for her." Eoin's eyes are now fixed on the pictures Sextine has almost folded into a tiny shapeless cube. "We should have sent that with a digitizer."

"Well, she didn't offer me a digitizer," Sextine explains. "I would have used it, save myself this stwess."

"You didn't ask her for a digitizer."

"I don't usually ask for a digitizer," says Sextine and her sapien suddenly pops up a digitizer option. "See? She offers it by herself. Perhaps this method is quicker."

Sextine drops the cube into Eoin's sapien and it announces the new files have been received. Eoin watches Sextine smirk and the proud face suddenly turns into a wondering face. Sextine's facial expression is quickly explained by the emergence of the running footsteps she was first to hear.

As expected, Lord Omicron and Archprofessor Elise are rushing towards the front door to see the returning lilies.

"Is the lab on fire?" Sextine's loud question prompts a jumpy reaction from the confused Eoin.

Dame Nissi is caught between standing up to flee and almost throwing Leontine to the ground. Leontine's eyes are wide open.

"Who set her on fire?" Dame Nissi asks anxiously.

Lord Omicron slows Archprofessor Elise down in an attempt to read meaning into Dame Nissi's moving lips. Archprofessor Elise gets a clue of what she's saying.

"Who set she on fire?" Archprofessor Elise asks.

"Who is the whom who set who on fire?' the motionless Lord Omicron asks.

Archprofessor Elise waits restlessly for Lord Omicron to continue moving. Her knees are bent and touching each other while she whimpers and whispers, "lilies."

"Why are both of you making us panic for nothing?" Dame Nissi asks as she relaxes.

"Panicking? Not panicking, no. Don't tell me you were dweaming again?" Lord Omicron asks.

"No... so?"

"Sugar, nobody was panicking."

"I was, popmy," Sextine reveals.

"Me too, Lord Woe," says Eoin.

"Well... you were not panicking over nothing."

"What is wong with Elise?" Dame Nissi asks, feeling quite irritated by Archprofessor Elise's moaning.

Archprofessor Elise stands still immediately and grins.

"Nothing," replies Lord Omicron. "The lilies, that's all."

"The lilies!" Sextine screams like a danger notifier.

Dame Nissi shakes her head and giggles as she watches all of them run out thru the front door. Leontine looks at the time, 5:20 p.m. She understands the event and she jumps down from her mother's laps and stands beside Sextine and Eoin outside.

The first set of lilies comes in melodiously, just about eight of them sounding short bursts of harmonised whistles. The lilies are very much aware of the kind of attention they attract; they tend to sing more when they are few. The rest of the lilies move quietly because they are many; the glory of their beauty in numbers is certainly enough to create a spectacle for their numerous fans. The lilies soon settle into their usual vases around the Rhos' family house.

The show is over. Archprofessor Elise and Eoin bid the Rhos farewell. The return of the lilies means bedtime is fast approaching. For Sextine, this is a good reason to fall asleep. Lord Omicron finds it as a perfect time to work more. For evil geniuses like Sir Nnia, this is the perfect time to honour Lord Omicron's invitation.

Leontine is backing the front door, facing her mother who is fast asleep on the couch. Leontine is reading the book from Nissi's Gallery.

We are unaware of Sir Nnia's quick conversation with the door because our eyes and ears are thru Leontine's. Sir Nnia stands dangerously close to her, his intensions are still not clear, certainly not pleasant, no.

Lord Omicron is out of his lab for reasons best known to fate. He walks into the living room and on seeing Sir Nnia, his emotional state swings from fear to astonishment to disbelief to shock to anger to fury and then stuck in all of that at once. If he was out for some seafood, Sir Nnia would have been nice bait for fishing.

"Who let you into my house?" Lord Omicron's voice is caught between a roar and a whisper; he wouldn't want Dame Nissi to get involved.

"Your door did," Sir Nnia states the obvious. "I told her the twuth."

"What... no! It's meant to alert me first." Lord Omicron walks worriedly to the door. He taps on the 'contact us' button and syncs the call to his sapien. A representative of *Premium Doors* soon responds.

"Hello, Pwemium Doors. Good evening, Lord Woe."

"Your door let a stwanger into my house just now without alerting anyone," Lord Omicron complains.

"Our doors won't let in a stwanger even after alerting you, sir."

"Weally? I didn't know I'm standing with a ghost now in my house."

"But Lord Woe, the last visitor to your house is Sir Nnia Den."

"And so?"

"The doors have been pwogwammed to act accordingly if you give the same wesponse a thousand times consecutively."

"What is that supposed to mean?" Lord Omicron asks.

"It means you always let Sir Nnia Den into the house."

"Oh you stupid Stupid, you more stupid than your stupid stupid door."

"A thousand times is a whole lot sir."

"You are stupid a thousand times over!" Lord Omicron can no longer hold back his anger and Sir Nnia pats him on the back to calm him down. "Has he even been here a hundwed times?"

"Sir, the same sequence has been on for more than five years."

"I am terminating this contwact. Goodnight," Lord Omicron stresses thru gritted teeth.

Lord Omicron ends the call and shakes off Sir Nnia's 'caring' hands.

"You made the Denzers game, sure?" Lord Omicron asks Sir Nnia angrily.

"Yeah?"

"And why did you choose to supply it to the King's gwanddaughter?"

"No, she chose to play the game," argues Sir Nnia.

"She chose? You then admit you were sure she was the one."

"She identified herself, Lord Omicwon."

"And you were at hand to know all this. Don't you have workers anymore?"

"Lord Omicwon, you not saying I personally attacked her on purpose, are you?"

"Yes, that's what her momxy is saying and I'm damn with her on that."

"What are fwends for?"

"This has nothing to do with fwendship, you attacked a little girl!"

"Please, Lord Omicwon, I didn't invite her to play the game. She came on her own."

"That is absolute madness!"

Their voices begin to filter into Dame Nissi's ears; there is no doubt she soon begins to see the faces with the arguing voices. The voices are loud at first but then it fades quickly and mixes up with other voices as her awareness ascends a mountain top.

Dame Nissi is first in line. She sets her eyes upon a horned man holding a replica of the book from her gallery.

For Dame Nissi, his frightening appearance can wait; there are other serious issues to address.

"What are you doing with me book?" Dame Nissi shouts at the man.

"Your book?" the man speaks in a regular lost earth tone. "You must be a god at least."

"I am simply a Dame."

"No, you are simply dead. Now you be quiet, I will read your judgement."

"My judgement on what? Give me back me book first."

"Look behind you lady, I have a lot to do."

Dame Nissi looks behind her and she loses her balance. She has just come to understand she's standing atop a very high mountain lined by thousands of arguing men and women. Dame Nissi rightly lets out a loud scream.

"Stop screaming you woman!"

"What... Where am I?" Dame Nissi asks. "And what is wong with your tongue?"

"My tongue? You are not here to question me now, are you? If you don't mind, I will have to proceed."

"It is called 'pwoceed'," Dame Nissi corrects him.

"Haha! I am a creature way back from history."

"Cweature, Histowy! Just give me that book now, I am vewy much afwaid of heights."

"Alright woman," he begins reading from the book, "you have sinned against God, the creator of Heaven and Earth, and you have fallen short of the glory of the Lord..."

"Just give me that damn book, you certainly not the Lord!" argues Dame Nissi.

"Oh people of Oh, you think God's got time for this?"

"Yeah? He's to judge both the quick and the dead!"

"Ahahahaha! Adorable bible scholar. Woman no, God ain't got no time for the dead... you slimy slime, the quick are over there at Mount Zion sorting for lawyers... they are numerous."

Dame Nissi squints with her lips shifted to the right, causing her right cheek to swell. She dabs her tongue on her upper lip, desperately putting in all her senses to understand this man. This is sheer nonsense her tongue concludes from the taste of the man's words. She throws her hands aggressively at the man as she tries to grab the book.

"That is mine, just give her to me!"

"Woman, nobody owns the judgement book."

"There's nothing like a judgement book... it's the book of life or the book of death, stuff like that..."

"Now you keep your filthy hands away from me or I strike you with lightening."

"You just an evil demon, you surely have no access to lightening."

"Oh really?"

The mean looking 'demon' raises his little finger and points a bright white multi-branched lightening at Dame Nissi's forehead. The lightening sends her into an agonising tremor, her voice vibrating. The brightness forces her to shut her eyes and the pain drags her up from the couch in the living room. She opens her eyes, set upon Leontine reading the same book.

Dame Nissi's eyes are now wide open, short of reasoning or understanding, no, not insanity yet, but we are getting there slowly, dream after dream.

"Hi momxy," Leontine signs innocently and happily.

"Heh?" Dame Nissi whimpers and blinks twice. Certainly Leontine is the reason for her weird dream. She raises her hands swiftly with intent to land them with the best swear signs ever communicated. Her ears awaken right on time to save Leontine from taking all the blame because Sir Nnia and Lord Omicron are still arguing about the Denzers game.

"I will hire the best lawyers!" Sir Nnia boasts.

"It still doesn't mean the Sigmas don't have enough power to hang you fwom a twee in the Jungle of Zion."

"Nobody can pass such judgment, Lord Omicwon."

"For the last time Sir Nnia, how did you export that game thwu the limitations?"

"Whew!" Sir Nnia sighs. "If you weally want to know, I used the *Gadhuvi*."

"Gadhuvi? What is the Gadhuvi?" Lord Omicron asks.

"A dawn of madness, a gush of stupidity, the foolish one of our age..."

"The Gadhuvi?" Lord Omicron tries to understand Sir Nnia's confusing explanation.

"No! Your question! How on Oh don't you know what the Gadhuvi is and you be lording over the biggest jack of all twades title in the universe."

"Sir Nnia, I will not have you insult me in my own house!"

"Neither will I. We have cweated a world where evewything is possible and here we are, twying vewy hard to contwol ourselves fwom doing evewything. I cannot be in that union anymore."

"You will go against the law, and you will do evewything? Lord Omicron asks.

"Evewything will happen to the two of you if you don't stop disturbing me," Dame Nissi snaps in.

"Dame Nissi Woe," Sir Nnia offers his greetings. "How nice to..."

"Don't stwess yourself, Sir Nnia," Dame Nissi cuts him short, "just go home."

Sir Nnia raises his shoulders at Lord Omicron; he can't refuse the exit opportunity presented by Dame Nissi. "Goodnight, Lord Omicwon."

Sir Nnia leaves the house.

Lord Omicron is wary of Dame Nissi's piercing eyes as he shuts the door, thinking of the best words to pacify her, or at least her eyes.

"Babe..."

"No no," Dame Nissi rejects the attempt and stands from the couch, "I have told you people to stop doing anything awound me when I'm asleep. But you keep doing just that, now Leontine has learnt it too. You are meant to lead by example here."

"Nissi..."

"Whatever you say won't change the fact that you'll do this same thing again and again. Goodnight Omicwon."

Lord Omicron nods an apology and an acceptance of wrongdoing and Dame Nissi walks away, taking the book along with her of course.

"Did she have a dream?" Leontine signs to her father.

Lord Omicron smiles and nods 'yes', "Apparently," he signs.

"What did the book do?" Leontine signs.

"Maybe you were studying it to death."

Leontine laughs at that response.

"Who knows," signs Lord Omicron. "I've heard worse stories from her dreams." Lord Omicron walks across to Leontine and kisses her goodnight.

"How is the project going?" Leontine signs. "The heart whisperer."

"The heart whisperer?" Lord Omicron signs in confirmation. "We are close. Elise and I made reasonable progress."

Leontine gives Lord Omicron a smile as expected. She has never shown any worries about not communicating effectively. This exactly makes Dame Nissi wonder why her husband is sweating on the heart whisperer year after year.

The long night seems to be quite short for the Rhos. The frequent sleepers of the family, Sextine and Lexis, have never felt any night was long enough. Lord Omicron's work on the heart whisperer makes him unaware of how fast the night is spent.

12 UP early, Leontine is anxious about her visit to the School of Sapien Acupuncture. She's admiring her sapien in the presence of her sleeping mother, hoping she'll be up early enough too.

Dame Nissi isn't really sure if she's still fast asleep. She clearly can see Leontine pull out a digitizer and throw it at her.

"What do I do with this?" Dame Nissi asks.

"Wrap it around your waist," Leontine signs cheerfully.

"Lol, you want to fix my catwalk?"

Leontine grins and then looks on as her mother happily ties the digitizer around her waist. A live image of Dame Nissi appears on Leontine's sapien.

"So?" the thrilled Dame Nissi asks.

"I will take you for a spin," signs Leontine as she selects her manoeuvre tools on the weaponized sapien.

"Is this digitizer weaponized?" Dame Nissi asks as fear and doubt come creeping in.

"How could I have fixed your catwalk?" Leontine signs with a mischievous blink.

"No no, that was a joke, Leontine."

Dame Nissi tries to remove the innocent looking digitizer but Leontine pulls her image out of the ground and ultimately suspending the real Dame Nissi in the air.

"Relax," Leontine sarcastically tries to calm her panicking mother. "You know you can't touch the digitizer... this will only take a few seconds."

"How many seconds is this one?" Dame Nissi signs.

"The standard limit."

"No you liar, I am already up here past any standard limit of any nation. Put me down now!"

"Just a little spin, momxy."

Leontine spins Dame Nissi indiscriminately. Dame Nissi is no longer at liberty to use the sign language. She screams and pleads with Leontine nonetheless, hoping she will hear her somehow.

"Leontine stop! The standard time limit is up alweady. Please I am begging you Leontine, stop! The time is up, Leontine!"

As expected, Leontine turns a deaf ear. She pulls Dame Nissi's image towards the ground to build up momentum for the final vertical flying act. She wobbles Dame Nissi a little and swipes her finger upwards across the sapien. This flings Dame Nissi upwards with great speed. Dame Nissi wraps her hands over head anticipating to crash into the ceiling as she yells for help. She soon relaxes and realises there was never a roof overhead when she sees herself among clouds.

"Am I dead? No you pebble, you dweaming again. Wake up Nissi, wake up!" Dame Nissi says to herself as she taps her cheeks rapidly.

Dame Nissi is neither rising nor falling, she's almost carried away by the beauty of the stars before a huge false prophet flies aggressively over her. She's absolulely gobsmacked by the magnificent creature, yet tending quickly into a terrifying sight, she screams and suddenly begins to fall from the sky. Thru the same path she had ascended, Dame Nissi falls straight into her room but she sits up quickly on her bed just before she crashes into the floor.

As Leontine's luck may have it, Lord Omicron strolls casually into the room at the nick of time to take all the blame again. Leontine could read the fear and fury in her mother's eyes but she's still eager to pass her message across.

"We are late, momxy," Leontine signs. "Are we going to make it there before the school time is up?"

Leontine understands her mother has just snubbed her for something more urgent behind her. She turns around slowly and sees her father paused on one leg, his tongue bulging out his cheek, his eyes on Dame Nissi and his sapien screen hovering around his wrist with the morning news about Epsilon.

"No, Nissi," Lord Omicron quickly protests his innocence.

Leontine turns to her mother who speaks and signs at the same time.

"I will have to kill one of you so I can send a powerful message to the thwee of you."

"Sugar..."

"Eh eh!" Dame Nissi silences Lord Omicron. "This matter, you see her? She's closed."

"Don't kill anyone anyway..."

Dame Nissi comes down from the bed. She gives Leontine an affectionate smile and a kiss on the head, "I will get set now," she signs. "Go and eat."

Leontine nods and leaves the room. She gets a pat on the head from Lord Omicron by the door.

"When last did you cook?" Lord Omicron asks Dame Nissi.

"Lol, my days of being a chef are long gone."

"Not even in the gallewy kitchen?" asks Lord Omicron as he walks towards Dame Nissi in the centre of the room.

"Me've got gweat staff there. They say they are making plans to start giving pwinting services, especially here in Genia."

"That will be fantastic!" declares Lord Omicron and he exchanges pecks on both cheeks with Dame Nissi. "I'll go catch some sleep."

"It is vewy elusive these days".

Dame Nissi is never the slow type. In no time, she's ready to go. She and Leontine board her conveyor and they soon arrive at the School of Sapien Acupuncture as the students for the day are settling into their sitting spots on the floor of the classroom.

Just before they get to the classroom, Dame Nissi's sapien alerts her on the school fees – Two hundred digits for Doctor Leontine Rho SSA School Fees, which she grudgingly accepts to pay. She had keyed in her name as Doctor Leontine Rho back at the school's reception.

"Two hundwed digits is more than the pwice of a normal sapien."

"Yes boss," her sapien responds to the word 'sapien'.

All the same, Dame Nissi feels someone or something at least agrees with her. She certainly nags on.

"And to the think the bill is just for a day, it's alarming."

"Not understood boss, speak some more."

Dame Nissi giggles and sighs at the sapien. She slows down to allow Leontine advance towards the door, waiting for her to turn and say goodbye.

Leontine is still fascinated by the beauty of the school. She soon realises that Dame Nissi is not keeping up with the pace.

"Why are you slowing down?" Leontine signs.

"This is the classroom," Dame Nissi signs back.

"Oh, like I should go in there alone?"

"Yes?"

"No, momxy, I cannot go alone."

"Ah ah?" Dame Nissi wonders and then signs, "Only students can enter. I will wait for you here."

"No!" Leontine shakes her head in frustration. "No no, I am scared, I will not go in alone."

"Sugar relax, they won't kill you in there."

"They don't need to kill me... they can still eat me alive."

Dame Nissi laughs at how serious Leontine is looking.

"Alright, come on," Dame Nissi signs. "I will stand behind the class."

Leontine waits for her to go into the classroom first. Dame Nissi steps in and ushers Leontine in. Leontine stands behind the classroom filled with about fifty children, all of them quietly watching the school teacher who is positioning an extracted large sapien screen in front of the class.

Dame Nissi lets go of the door and it bangs loudly. She shivers and turns quickly to apologise to class but they surprisingly seem to be more interested in what the school teacher is up to.

"Okay," Dame Nissi says to herself, "sowie all the same."

Leontine gives her mother one last look. Dame Nissi understands that look, 'I've got my eyes on you'. Leontine walks boldly to the front of the class and sits right under the nose of the teacher who was waiting patiently for her to settle down.

"Alwighty then! Good morning! The teacher says enthusiastically. "I am Pwofessor Oxlade Z.Z, you can call me Pwoxzy, and welcome to my class. I will be teaching you how to manually opewate these beautiful gadgets in your hands. Yes, we'll call them beautiful gadgets, I'm sure you know why. I don't want them talking in my class. So, is there anyone who isn't here in person? Anyone? Or not here in the Holo-X-cube at least."

Dame Nissi throws her hand up and Professor Oxlade couldn't avoid seeing her. She's definitely not responding to his question.

"Yes please..."

"Okay," Dame Nissi tries moving forward.

"You can talk fwom there," Professor Oxlade advises her.

"Okay," Dame Nissi whispers. "Please my daughter is deaf. Hope you can sign?"

"Ohemgee, I'm sowie about that."

Dame Nissi nods and steps back.

Professor Oxlade smiles to the class, and especially to Leontine. He then signs as he speaks. "I am sowie... I forgot some of you cannot hear me."

"That's okay," the entire class signs back with a smile.

"Oh," Professor Oxlade nods, certainly only Dame Nissi heard all he had said initially. "Alright," he signs, "is there anyone who is not here in person?"

More than half of the children in the class raise their hands up.

"Hmm, Holo-X-cube maybe?"

The children nod "yes".

"Fine, because you'll do a lot of touching here." "Now," Professor Oxlade points to the sapien image on the sapien screen. He taps the screen and the image is partitioned into 16x16 tiny boxes, "this is the first line your gadget will show if you were to call its name. Each box represents a certain command, and in each command," Professor Oxlade taps one of the boxes and it opens up another set of 16x16 boxes, "gives you a chain of specific commands. These boxes are never visible anyway. We will be looking into every single box and what it does. If your BEM be ready, we'll then activate your beautiful gadgets for you."

Dame Nissi takes a sitting spot on the floor; she understands this will be a very long class. The class doesn't last as long as she thought, however. Though with everyone assimilating with their BEMs, five hours is certainly way too long to spend on learning a BEM-ready downloadable knowledge and skill.

A few minutes before 5 t.m., Dame Nissi and Leontine are back at home. Dame Nissi is now worriedly tasked with the duty of guiding the staggering Leontine who has been blinded by the excitement of tapping, swiping, and flipping thru the multiple sapien screens she popped up – basically containing pictures and videos of Oh's plants and animals, a Bracketier chat screen with her sister, Sextine, a deaf bracket alert on Bracketier, and an array of cook lessons, one would wonder if she's trying to enrol to be a chef for her third academic degree.

The house is quiet and smells deserted. This doesn't worry Leontine as much as it worries Dame Nissi. Since she has been chatting with her siblings, Leontine is aware no one is home.

"SEXTINE!" Dame Nissi calls out to her first provisional diagnosis for a quiet lonely house.

Leontine looks at Dame Nissi exactly when she calls for Sextine the second time. She taps her and signs, "She's not home."

"Oh," Dame Nissi wonders. "LEX..." she tries calling out for Lexis before Leontine taps her again.

"And Lexis is out too... on a date with Princess Zeta," Leontine signs.

"Ok, is your popmy home?" Dame Nissi signs hopefully.

"No, he said he needs to use the lab at Unmi to finish up his work."

"How do you know this and I don't?"

"We have been chatting," Leontine points at her sapien. "Not arguing..."

Dame Nissi swings her hand lightheartedly towards Leontine and she withdraws the apparent joke immediately.

"Sorry! I didn't mean that," Leontine signs with a smile.

Dame Nissi ignores the apology and the offence; she can only see food all over Leontine's sapien screens now.

"You going to be a chef too?"

"Yeah, thanks to you." Leontine is still smiling.

"A chef..." "Hmm."

"And you have to teach me some things. Can we go to the gallery kitchen today? No one is home, please?" Leontine pleads.

"Anything for you, my darling, but what else will you be combining with the chef course?" Dame Nissi signs curiously.

"I want to be a poet too," Leontine signs happily.

"A poet? A Poet?!"

"You need to sign it twice?"

"You serious?" Dame Nissi signs and giggles. "That is the funniest thing I have heard in my thirty-eight years experience on Oh."

"Then momxy, you've not been paying attention to Sextine. She's very funny."

"Haha! Adonbelivit," Dame Nissi says and then signs, "You find Sextine funny?"

"Yeah? She is. She always jokes around, doesn't she?"

"Just because people joke around and are never serious doesn't make them funny people."

"She's seriously funny to me," Leontine remains seriously adamant.

"Ha!" Dame Nissi chuckles. "A poet."

"Yes..."

"Have you published anything before?" Dame Nissi signs

"No, not exactly poetry, so yes."

"What exactly then?"

"I don't know. See for yourself," Leontine pulls up one of Sextine's posts on Bracketier dated 4th Hipnoary, 310.

"This is by Sextine..."

"No, I used her account. I just got mine today." Leontine enlarges the screen and reveals the long article.

"The circle of Nothingness," Dame Nissi reads out the title. "Sounds nice," she signs to Leontine.

"Yes? Read it then... to be sure. I need to change these cloths." Leontine walks away from the living room.

"Okay," Dame Nissi says and begins reading the note to herself. "Nothing good comes easy. Nothing good is achieved using bad methods. Nothing twue is pweserved with lies. Nothing bad is kept for a good weason. Nothing bad is worth a good name. Nothing that has been used is worth its owiginal usefulness.

Nothing big should be wendered a small meaning. Yet evewyone is claiming to know how to define life, love, likeness and loyalty.

Nothing is more pwecious to a twoubled mind than the gwace of God. Nothing is more consistent than the word of God. Nothing should belittle the Glowy of the Father and the Son.

Nothing is as sweet as honey?? Nah... Pwivacy is sweeter than honey. Too many ears will spoil the tale.

Nothing can take the place of another human being cell for cell... Supplements are not solutions; an impwovement maybe. One can't deny the comforting powers of those supplements.

As for me, I can decide that nothing in this world can make me smile. Yeah, nothing is as silly as lying to myself.

Nothing will secure you a lot of 'fwends' more than pwogwess. Nothing will show you your fwends better than sadness. Nothing will pwove your faith better than temptations. Nothing will bwing one closer to God other than twials..."

Leontine returns, still dressed in similar cloths. Dame Nissi wonders what the change is but Leontine urges her to finish up the note.

"Well, it is cool so far I guess," Dame Nissi signs and then continues reading. "Nothing will make you agwee with me if you hate me. Nothing will make you disagwee with me if you love me blindly.

Nothing 'enslaves' a man more than listening to and obeying evewy instwuction of a fellow man... the hidden desire of many such men is to be like Jesus (not to be as holy as He is, but to have followers as He did, and most falsely 'start a weligion').

Nothing helps you think more than your own bwain. No don't say BEM!

Nothing will tell you the saddest twuth other than your heart or whoever that lives in it.

Nothing will tell you the sweetest lies other than your heart or whoever that lives in it.

Hence nothing is more weasonable than listening to your heart carefully; both the twuths and lies, and the half twuths are designed to pwotect you, natuwally. Ask your heart.

Nothing is mankind's biggest problem other than loneliness. Nothing can heal such better than God himself. But if you can twust men, then it should be for love. If you love someone, nothing will pay more than telling them plainly. And when you finally hate them, nothing, not even the biggest amount of excuses, can save you the stwess of informing them you finally hate them.

Now wemember this, NOTHING can be the only thing. Yeah start again and see that Nothing is not the only thing. And that one thing cannot be the only thing."

"Hmm... nice. Lengthy, quite religious too," Dame Nissi signs.

"It is not religious... I didn't give a sermon, did I?"

"It's still good even if you did. Can we go now?"

"Yeah? Been waiting for you."

"Seemesh." Dame Nissi shakes her head.

That has been Leontine's little manifesto to convince her mother to trust her choice of being a chef and a poet as her next set of professions. Dame Nissi and Leontine spend the rest of the day at the gallery kitchen cementing their love for cooking.

13 BACK to the house at night, they are both very exhausted and sleepy and Dame Nissi joins Leontine to lazily fall into her bed. This will be a much needed sleep, or so we think.

Moments later, Dame Nissi is still lying restless on the bed. She sits up and realises Leontine is no longer beside her. Well, that's strange she thinks to herself, she certainly didn't hear her leave. Leontine is probably also restless.

Dame Nissi walks out of the room slowly and heads straight to the living room – one of Leontine's favourite spots, but she's not here. Dame Nissi looks at the dining room, there's no sign that anyone has been there this night; everything is rather too neat and tidy. She hears the wind come into the house thru the front door that is barely a crack open.

She walks to the door and opens it, letting in a strong wind that blows across her face. Her brain and BEM are finally interpreting what her eyes are looking upon but she's yet to comprehend it all. This is certainly not the front of our house Dame Nissi thinks to herself. She looks back at the house, it is still the same gorgeous house we've all known. She hears Lord Omicron's voice laughing in excitement. She looks ahead, thru the arid expanse of dark brown land, and sees Lord Omicron putting the heart whisperer on Leontine. She ignores the weirdness of her environment; she's glad to see familiar faces.

"Omicwon, what's going on?" she asks as she walks towards them.

"Hey sugar, the heart whispewer works!"

"Is that so?" Dame Nissi asks sceptically.

"Yeah, come listen and watch this," Lord Omicron tells her as he switches on the small gadget he placed on Leontine's chest. "Okay sugar, you can hear me, yes?"

Leontine started smiling once she heard "Okay", she nods "yes".

"Put up your left hand," Lord Omicron instructs her.

Leontine raises her left hand and Lord Omicron punches the air in celebration.

"Weird," begins the sceptical Dame Nissi. "How does she know those words if she has never heard them before?"

"Leontine can say those words *bae*, she knows how they sound. Perhaps it's connected to the BEM," Lord Omicron responds excitedly as he watches Leontine spin and skip joyfully.

"How come these BEMs don't listen to conversations and tell the bwain what has been said?"

"That's the next pwoject I'm working on. The issue is that the bwain will actually act deaf to anything owiginating fwom sounds, so..."

"She can't hear me, sure?" Dame Nissi throws in another question as Leontine wonders away in happiness.

"No, you have to speak thwu this mouthpiece," Lord Omicron reveals a tiny mouthpiece on his collar. "Stop moving, baby," he tells Leontine.

Leontine stops at once and Lord Omicron giggles.

"This is certainly a mouth talker not a heart whispewer."

"Oh Nissi, can you optimistic for once?"

"What now, I'm not being pessimistic. I simply said what it is. There is no heart here speaking in hush tunes, you simply talking with your mouth."

Dame Nissi's eyes have been reacting fearfully to what she's seeing just before she finishes her mouth-talker remark. She has just realised the space beside them is a dead end expanding into an endless darkness. 'We are certainly on a cliff', she wonders.

"Okay, hop on now," Lord Omicron instructs Leontine.

"No no Omicwon, we on a cliff!" screams Dame Nissi but that revelation ends with the fall of Leontine.

Lord Omicron is yet to understand what his wife has just said when he sees Leontine fall off the cliff unceremoniously.

"LEONTINE! Sweet Jesus, please, me baby!" Dame Nissi rightly panics as she dashes towards the edge of the cliff.

She and Lord Omicron slow down instinctively and lean over quickly to peep, still very much hopeful of seeing Leontine hopping in the darkness. Their heads, bending over into the darkness, are suddenly lifted by the awe and strength of a false prophet. Dame Nissi lets out a sorrowful scream and even more screams when she realises that Leontine is sandwiched between the hind limbs of the folf.

"No! Give me back me baby!" Dame Nissi pleads agonisingly.

"Come on," Lord Omicron tries to pull her out to relative safety.

"Leave me alone!" Dame Nissi yells as she pushes Lord Omicron away. "Just get out!"

"Come on Nissi, it's dangewous here."

"Just get out! Don't you dare talk to me!"

"Let's go get help Nissi, come on, a PES too can help, come on," Lord Omicron offers to take her hand but she stamps her foot on the ground aggressively.

"Just get lost! This is all your fault!"

Dame Nissi foot presses harder on the ground and it rapidly breaks off and drags her along into the darkness.

Dame Nissi keeps her right arm up as long as she could, waiting and hoping for Lord Omicron to grab her to safety, she'll certainly agree this time. No, Lord Omicron is not fast enough.

Amid the tears and fears and deafening scream, Dame Nissi fades away quickly and she noisily sits up from her sleep on Leontine's bed.

Her eyes are still red and teary; she still can't believe what they are seeing. Lord Omicron is standing with Leontine, kitting her up with the completed version of his heart whisperer. The enthusiasm on their faces quickly turns into a worrisome fear, the tears still gathering in Dame Nissi's eyes cannot be overlooked

Leontine feels sorry for her mother; she need not be told over again that they must have made her have another bad dream. She looks quietly at her father, her eyes urging him to break the silence. Lord Omicron is struggling to break free from the accusing eyes of Dame Nissi; he could even hear the anger and fury boiling out from the tears. Sometimes he wishes this was the dream and something else will wake them up to reality, all smiling and laughing.

"Baby..." Lord Omicron stutters.

"GET OUT!" Dame Nissi has never yelled this loud. Since Lord Omicron failed to hear her scream in her dream a while ago, then she certainly needs to up her scream-game.

Her voice echoes around the quiet house, most of which filters into Sextine's room. Nothing on Oh or even from the lost earth could have succeeded in waking Sextine up against her will, especially when it's still just past 10 a.m. in the middle of the night.

The shock, the timing, the get-out words, and the fact her BEM is not activated, leaves her natural brain and lips with only one conclusion: "Intwuders!" She flies out of the bed and whispers a call to her sapien.

"Yes boss," the sapien whispers back.

"Bwing my PES."

"PES on the way, boss."

A neatly camouflaged wardrobe opens on the wall beside Sextine's bed and a lighted hanger carrying a green PES floats swiftly to Sextine. Sextine unburdens the hanger and puts on the performance enhancing suit as fast as possible with her speed going higher when she hears Dame Nissi scream 'get out' for the second time.

Back in Leontine's room, Dame Nissi is crying bitterly, her voice drowned in sorrow and refusing to listen to anyone.

"I have warned you many times Omicwon, just leave please, just get out, and you leave Leontine alone, enough of this madness!"

"Listen, Nissi," Lord Omicron seems to have given up on begging, "if this is about Leontine..."

"It is about you and the amount of danger you subject me to."

"Then stop being against Leontine and I."

"What's that supposed to mean?!"

"She is my daughter too."

"Omicwon Woe son of Alpha, you will leave this place wight now or I will do something that will be vewy hard for you to digest."

Lord Omicron raises a finger in anger, still short of words to express his frustration. "Damn you, Nissi!"

"Oh be damned too!" Dame Nissi yells back at him. "Get the hell out of here!"

Lord Omicron walks away furiously; the aggressive speed of his movement could nearly leave marks on the floor. He bursts out thru the front door and goes straight to the garage.

Sextine runs into Leontine's room feeling fight-ready. Dame Nissi's heart skips before she recognises Sextine.

"What's going on?" Sextine asks with her last strength as she breaths heavily, certainly not enough fuel to fight anymore.

"Why you dressed up like that?" Leontine signs.

"How can you be in that suit and still look this tired?" Dame Nissi asks.

"*Amam*? Do I know for this suit?" Sextine responds with a question of hers too. "What happened here?" she signs to Leontine. "I heard someone scream 'get out'."

"That was me young lady, and I wasn't scweaming."

"Eh? Wailing then? Your voice shook me out of bed!"

"She had a bad dream," Leontine signs.

"Aw," Sextine sits beside Dame Nissi and pats her on the back.

Lord Omicron is having an argument with his conveyor in the garage, the car has apparently refused to move. Lord Omicron is not in the mood to obey any instructions, perhaps rebelling against all sorts of rules now, an indirect protest against Dame Nissi's 'do-nothing-around-me rule'.

"You have to activate the safety measures," the car insists.

"And who asked for that intelligent suggestion? Just move damn it. I get a complainer by marwiage and I also buy one with my digits."

Lord Omicron punches on the buttons randomly and aggressively, trying his worst to force the car to move forward. As luck may have it, the car responds to an unknown combination and zooms out of the garage at top speed. The car warns Lord Omicron desperately. With too many warnings at once, it would have been difficult to obey any at all.

"Warning, unsafe movement... warning I am under attack... warning, mind scanner is inactive... warning, oncoming conveyor..."

The last warning almost gets Lord Omicron's clouded attention, maybe just a tad too late. Once the bonnet of the car emerges into the seemingly empty street, another fast approaching car clips it and spins the car upwards and bouncing away on the street. The car finally brings itself to a halt; the driver's door is completely detached from the damaged car.

Lord Omicron lies on the road with his right foot still stuck inside the car. He groans agonisingly seconds before his eyes shut, everywhere is as quiet as the grave. His BEM and sapien come on simultaneously, they did survive the crash and they seem to be aware of what has just happened. The BEM beeps and the sapien gives its traditional 'yes boss' response, it must have read that to be Lord Omicron himself, or at least a program he approved.

"Your vital signs are low," the sapien reveals as it pops up multiple screens placing emergency calls to Saint Adaora's Hospital and Lord Omicron's list of next of kin.

Dame Nissi's name is more conspicuous, overshadowing that of Lexis, Sextine, Leontine, Sir Louis, Princess Lotem-Zeta, Archprofessor Elise Leo Elise, Sir Luminescence Wellington, Saint Ose Neo and Archprofessor Lux Eden.

Dame Nissi is still sitting on Leontine's bed, watching her daughters trying to switch on the heart whisperer. She becomes a bit worried when she hears her sapien reactivate itself and announce an incoming emergency call.

The call overrides the 'accept/reject call' dialogue box and quickly delivers the message.

"Lord Omicwon Woe has been involved in an accident," the sapien announces calmly.

Dame Nissi almost faints in shock but considering her recent experiences, she taps her cheeks rapidly in a bid to wake herself up from yet another bad dream.

"Wake up Nissi... I will wake up... I will wake up," she proclaims frantically.

Leontine is yet to understand why her mother is slapping herself and why Sextine has her hands on her owm head. Sextine is certainly waiting for Dame Nissi to announce a scientific breakthrough in converting reality into a dream. She quickly runs her hands from her head down to her hips. Just as she begins to believe she's actually real, her own sapien informs her of the accident.

"No!" Sextine jumps to her feet. "This is not a dweam, momxy."

Sextine is next seen on the ceiling, then by the wall and zooming out of the door. The PES is completely in control.

Leontine's sapien vibrates and she takes her eyes off Dame Nissi to behold the bad news spelt out on her screen.

She covers her mouth immediately with tears gathering in her eyes as she looks on at her mother.

Dame Nissi is completely traumatised beyond making any intelligent move. Both BEM and brain alike could not generate any response to this shock. We could argue they are very busy singing a sweet chorus to whatever that is left of her senses – 'it's all your fault, Nissi, it is all your fault. That was the dweam a while ago but you will never wake up now'. No, we still don't hear what the lead soprano singer has to sing, it's just a high pitch sound aimed at chattering expensive glasses.

Dame Nissi puts her hands over her ears, not to confirm she's being fed any silly song, she's simply very disappointed with everything. 'But I warned them, I did warn them all' is the truest thing she could think of.

Sextine lands strongly beside Lord Omicron, her feet almost breaking open the hard floor. Lord Omicron is now soaked in a pool of blood; it takes Sextine extra quick breaths to keep her emotions in check. She basically dances around in fear and panic for a couple of seconds before accepting that she has to act. She pulls her father easily away from the car, she can't help but notice his right foot is not at all normal – it is flatter than it should be. His right leg is also visibly fractured with a part of the bone sticking out of the flesh.

Sextine quickly kneels and bends over to his chest to confirm if he's still alive. Lord Omicron groans.

"I am alive, Sextine," he says inaudibly.

"Popmy! Yes, I... I have to get you to my clinic. We need to stop this bleeding before the ambulance comes."

"I cannot feel my wight leg," Lord Omicron informs Sextine.

"It looks bad popmy..."

"How do we get to your clinic, did you bwing help?"

"I'm putting on my PES, I can lift you. We have to go now."

Sextine lifts Lord Omicron easily in her arms and carries him swiftly back to the house and into her personal clinic, just adjacent Lord Omicron's home lab. She took extra care not to be disrupted by the panicking Leontine and Dame Nissi who caught up with her just before she got to the house.

"Have you called for an ambulance?"

"His gadgets must have done that."

"How can you be so sure?" Dame Nissi shouts as Sextine's PES speed eludes them.

"She called you, didn't she?" Sextine's voice echoes back.

Seconds later, Dame Nissi and Leontine arrive outside Sextine's clinic. The door is locked and Dame Nissi bangs desperately on the door.

"Sextine?"

"Just hang awound," Sextine's voice filters thru the door, "I'll be out in a moment."

"What do you mean in a moment? Open this door this second."

"Momxy, it's standard hospital pwocedure, give me one second."

"I thought the standard means you don't get to work on your family..."

"So what now, I should watch him bleed to death?"

"Just let me in damn it, your one sec is up."

"Yeah give me a thousand more, my hands be tied."

"Wonder what hands you using in there," Dame Nissi grumbles.

"Will he be okay?" Leontine signs to Dame Nissi.

"What?"

"What's what? You can see my hands or do I get to sign louder too?"

Dame Nissi's fear and frustration is caught up with an urge to laugh at Leontine's naughtiness, the perfect mixed feeling. She stamps her foot and flaps her hands for a couple of seconds before signing to Leontine.

"Sextine can really be mean and annoying sometimes, I wonder how you find her funny."

"Yeah, see what's she making you do," Leontine signs back. "That's funny to me."

They both share a brief consoling smile before their fears cripple back into their minds. The ladies can't stand alone anymore. Leontine quickly falls into Dame Nissi's open arms and her mother pins a kiss on her head as long as she could endure before relaxing her lips.

"We'll just shake it off soon," Dame Nissi mutters to herself.

A few minutes later, paramedics storm into the house, tracing Lord Omicron to Sextine's clinic with the help of location signals sent from his sapien. The front door seem to have let in the five man team; Dame Nissi pays no attention to how exactly they got into the house. Their white apparels reassure her that they are here at least to rescue Lord Omicron from Sextine.

"We've come for the accident victim, Lord Omicwon Woe," announces one of the paramedics.

"He's in there," Dame Nissi points at the locked door.

The team leader pushes the door before realising it is locked. He turns to Dame Nissi and she raises her shoulders, "Standard pwocedure."

"Is there a doctor or a nurse in there?"

"Yes, my daughter, she's twying to stop the bleeding."

"I am coming out now!" Sextine's voice resonates from her clinic.

Everybody is yet to react to that vital information when the door opens up and a trolley carrying the unconscious Lord Omicron emerges. He has been placed on oxygen and a hanging fluid bag drips fluid thru tubes into his blood vessels. He's heavily padded with blood stained bandages especially around his right leg. We, just like everyone else, are completely perplexed by the incompleteness of Lord Omicron's right leg. Sextine pushes out the trolley feeling less worried about the missing distal leg and foot.

Dame Nissi wags her finger bewilderedly at the amputated leg. "What happened, Sextine?!"

"I had to take it off, it was distorting my efforts and it was never going to be saved."

"What do you mean never? Sextine!"

"Momxy chillax! This will only take a few digits to fix. His foot was cwushed."

"Adonbelivit! And you took that decision alone?" Dame Nissi asks as they chase after the paramedics team who are moving quickly out of the house with the trolley.

"Momxy, he was awake and he asked me to do it, it's an inevitable outcome. When they get to the hospital they'll clone him another leg, it will only take a few hours."

"It still doesn't mean you should subject him to this amount of pain," insists Dame Nissi.

"Look at him, momxy, I took the pain away. Stop undermining my work."

"Yeah, you took his leg away..."

The Rhos look on as Lord Omicron is taken into the ambulance and the conveyor speeds off.

"Which hospital are they taking him to?" Dame Nissi asks.

"Saint Adaowa's Hospital, it was witten on the ambulance."

Dame Nissi nods and returns towards the teleport system. Lexis stumbles out of the house; it is evident he's been battling with sleep.

"What's going on?"

"Lexis," Dame Nissi quickly reminds herself of her son. "Your popmy had a car accident. I'm going to the hospital now." She steps into the teleport system quickly.

"Who will stay with me?" Leontine signs.

"Why don't we use your car?" Lexis asks Dame Nissi.

"Um," Dame Nissi steps out of the teleport system, "I am scared of using that thing wight now. Lexis, you should stay home with Leontine."

"Me?"

"Yes..."

"I want Sextine to stay," Leontine signs.

"That's more like it," Lexis agrees.

"You so ain't sewious," Sextine grumbles.

"Lexis, you still have to stay home," says Dame Nissi. "You all can come over by morning."

"I need to go there," Sextine insists and then signs to Leontine too. "At least to tell the doctors where I stopped."

"Can't they figure that out themselves?" Lexis asks.

"Aideekay! I doubt."

"You only took his leg off, what else are you going to tell them?" Leontine signs.

"You took his leg off?!" Lexis wonders aloud. "He's going to kill you."

"He alweady knows I did it..."

"No point wasting time," says Dame Nissi. "Lexis, please stay home with Leontine. Sextine will be back to join her in a matter of minutes. By morning I'll come home to take Leontine with the car, okay?"

"Sure momxy," Lexis agrees, placing his hand on Leontine's shoulder.

Leontine, however, is far from satisfied with this arrangement. She give Sextine a stern look and signs, "You should better be back in two minutes."

"She will!" Dame Nissi reassures her. "And Lexis, watch this door closely, it seems to open up without questions these days."

Dame Nissi arrives first at Saint Adaora's Hospital's teleport system; Sextine comes in almost immediately. They recognise the ambulance parked near the front door and they race over to it immediately. They find the driver cleaning up the inside.

"Where is my hubby?" Dame Nissi asks the driver.

"ER 16."

"Thank you."

Dame Nissi follows Sextine closely as they scurry in search of the ER 16. Sextine seems to know her way around the hospital. They soon have their sights on the room and a doctor is about to shut the door.

"Hey!" Sextine tries to alert the doctor.

"HEY!" Dame Nissi eagerly amplifies. "Is that the place?" she asks Sextine.

"Yes, but you *heyed* too."

"What then, we can go faster."

"Sure..."

Dame Nissi has barely blinked when she sees Sextine speaking with the doctor already. She shakes her head. Certainly Sextine has been suppressing the PES to allow her mother keep up with the pace.

"That is my popmy in there," Sextine informs the doctor. "I'm Doctor Sextine Woe."

"Nice to meet you, I'm *Pwofessor Ujay*."

"Yes, I'd like to bwief you on what I've done alweady before he was bwought here."

"We got that fwom his gadget," Professor Ujay points at his own sapien. "You saved evewything there."

"Oh yes, that is twue," Sextine reckons.

"What is happening now?" Dame Nissi asks as soon as she's within whispering distance.

"He's quite stable now. The next major thing is to fix his leg... so, just be calm... we'll be out as soon as we are done."

"Can't I come in?" Dame Nissi asks.

"No my dear, it's standard pwocedure."

Professor Ujay shuts the door and Sextine grins mischievously at Dame Nissi, it has 'I told you so' written all over it.

"Why you gwinning now?"

"I'm not..."

"Pfft! Just go home before Leontine goes cwazy."

Sextine gives Dame Nissi a long hug. "Popmy will be fine."

"I know dear. I will be with you guys soon, go on."

Sextine leaves Dame Nissi lonely and cold. She soon begins to walk slowly up and down the hallway. The seconds turn into minutes and minutes into hours. Dame Nissi ignores the seat and squats on the floor, resting her back on the wall. Her hands are over her head with her face buried between her knees. She's motionless for a while; we can all sense she has fallen asleep.

A young nurse walks by and deliberately runs her knee into Dame Nissi, clearly determined to pass thru the exhausted dame.

"What now," Dame Nissi flares up, "do you guys come in blind formats?"

"Ohemgee... lol! I am so vewy sowie, I thought you were a hologwam!"

"Sweet shouites, I have smarter kids. What hologwam squats to take a nap?"

"I haven't seen anyone sit here waiting for anything."

"Me hubby is in there..."

"Once they are thwu they'll alert you, you can teleport over... takes just a few seconds."

"Yes I know that. You should know living people when you see one," Dame Nissi begins to gibber. "It's my husband in there... yes, in times of difficulty, I got a husband..."

"Ma'am," the nurse can barely understand Dame Nissi, "I think you should go home, take a bweak. It will soon be five o'clock."

"They've been in there for five hours?!"

"What happened to him?"

"An accident... he lost his leg too."

"Well, cloning takes a minimum of thwee hours, then some more to do the fixing and alignment and stuff."

"Hmm," Dame Nissi sighs, "yes, I know that."

"And..."

"...You know I'm going home alweady."

Dame Nissi stands immediately. She wouldn't enjoy having a bad dream in this hospital; the reality of being disturbed by this nurse is terrifying already.

She arrives home in a matter of seconds. She draws a little comfort from the front door which takes its time to analyse her print. She walks slowly thru the empty living room and to the dining room where Lexis is having a laugh with Princess Mary-Zeta. They seem to be discussing Jax Lilyscent's angry reaction to the Bracketier quess post by Lexis.

"Lexis," Dame Nissi subtly announces her presence.

"Mommxy!" Lexis stands quickly and goes to her. "How is he?"

"He'll be fine. They are still in the theatre... they'll call when the pwocedure is over."

"Sowie about what happened," Princess Zeta offers her condolences.

"Thank you, your highness. When did you come? I can't see any of your guards awound."

"No, I'm not here in person... holo. Came in as soon as I heard."

"Quite thoughtful of you. Lexis, I'll be inside."

"Sure," Lexis nods.

Dame Nissi walks to her room. She lies on the bed with her eyes wide open. Another dream wouldn't help, especially the reaction that will follow. She twists and turns restlessly as the minutes go by. Her sapien suddenly pops up a message, rousing her up from the bed immediately. She's maximally disappointed to realise it's the weekly Sunday home gospel messages, the *vSHOG*.

"Boss, voice SHOG has been delivered," her sapien announces.

"Six o'clock alweady?" she says to herself. "Play messages," she instructs the sapien.

She pulls up the audio screen as the voice of the first enthusiastic saint reverberates. She is lucky to meet the greetings.

"Good morning and pwaise the Lord! Today is Sunday and I'm glad to send you this SHOG. Be sure to spend time to study the sermon she contains. You can pay your tithes and donations to our Vault account name 'MARCH ON CHURCH OF THE MOST HIGHLY HIGH', thank you. I am pwaying for you now. Yours in the Lord, *Saint Luxian Ladi.*"

Dame Nissi can't hide her disappointment. She had subscribed for voice messages, not typed sermons. She swipes the screen for the next channel, this happens to be playing a song. We surely can recognise this song; it sounds a lot like *Carl Orff's 'Carmina Burana'*, clearly with lyrics we just cannot fix into place. Something about *Apostle Paul giving salt from the deeper cities to other Pauls, he sent them crunches, oystered crunches, whipped up their pairs [of] salty leaves... looked up too much, edge to cool much, look though mentis are chilling... aged something, hopeless something, give soup it could not chill it... saucy momxies, earthly momxies, rocked up too voluminous... Sanctus Magnus, fowl nut sinus, secretary sewed new minis... Rockum-raka, get them locked up, milking Book-amine cherries... book them noodle, dog soup noodle, failure to eat che-le-rries...* and they murmur on and on.

The murmuring promptly reminds Dame Nissi of how hungry she is. She gets down from the bed and has a small fight with the sapien audio screen; it doesn't want to be left behind. Dame Nissi pushes it back over the bed twice and moves out of the room quickly. She continues pompously to the empty dining room in a 'tea-tea-tea' rhythm.

Dame Nissi knows better than burning up her tea cup. She picks the right milk and the right water and some biscuits and heads back to her room. She places the plate of biscuits on her tea cup, allowing her to open the door with her right hand.

She's completely startled by the voice of a man screaming from the sapien screen dangling just at the entrance. She can't help but scream along.

"Aaarhhh!!!"

She's surprised to realise that this is just an energetic preacher pumping out a very loud hallelujah. She splutters when she hears him finish up with '...lelujah'.

"Sweet Jesus!" she exclaims softly. "This man can kill."

She swipes the screen to the next channel and we hear the voice of a gentle female preacher. Dame Nissi walks to the bed and the sapien screen floats along.

"...and when it seems all is not well, it is good to believe that we are, yet, evermore abundantly blessed by God, blessings so huge that we have many to spare, and with faith it is passed on to you, my fwends. God bless you today and always, may He..."

Dame Nissi swipes for the next preacher as she munches her biscuits.

"...Yes, yes, of course... he that finds a good wife finds a good thing. I'm sowie this is not the message for those of us here that are gay, but I'll see what I can do to fill you in. No man can ever find a good wife without finding Jesus first, because her heart obviously has to be hidden in Chwist. Marwiage is an institution by God, and when two don't have Chwist in common, it will eventually become hard to stay united. Seek first the kingdom of God. Yes..."

To the next channel... we are confronted by an aggressive preacher.

"May God forgive you for being a church when you not one. May God forgive the church for cweating diffewent vawiations of God such that you only feel safe in your own denomination... Deutewonomy six verse four. May God forgive the church for taking away the salt in the word. May God forgive the church for not being able to impact spiwituality. May God forgive you for being a part of church and may he forgive you for decaying with it. May God still forgive you for fleeing fwom the church instead of staying to heal it!"

Dame Nissi shakes her head and swipes for the next channel.

"Now God and digits are two masters, Mathew six twenty-four. So why should you tweat God way less than you tweat digits? You have to plan ahead. You cannot spend the digits you didn't save in the first place; likewise you can't utilize the faith you don't have. If you don't build a communion with God, you cannot just walk up to him and demand answers to pwayers."

Dame Nissi is not quite warming up to the messages yet. The next one had better be good enough.

"Without the times of twouble and distwess, there will be no need for these words, 'I'll never leave you nor forsake you; no weapon forged against you will pwevail; consider it pure joy, my fellow humans, whenever you face attacks of many kinds."

No, not this either. She doesn't withdraw her hand from the screen this time. The next channel has just a few seconds to impress her. A calm male preacher speaks.

"Heaven and earth passed away but his word is here the same. For long we doubted this until the team on Epsilon came back with good news that there was indeed a lost earth. A lost earth that has passed away, to a point that nothing meaningful was seen to be collected as evidence. We thank God for using Saint Ose Neo to bwing us this message..."

The last remark prompts Dame Nissi to swipe for the next channel. She's not in the mood for the little politics. She inevitably runs into Saint Ose Neo's vSHOG channel. Her voice is even calmer than that of her John-the-Baptist.

"Genesis one verse one... In the beginning God made Heaven, Moffat, and Oh. That change in the bible was a delibewate act by the church to be at peace with the blind belief of many members of this genewation that there was never a lost earth. Team Epsilon will, on Tuesday..."

NEXT!!! And it is yet another Neo-like preacher.

"Man and God can never be the same. Annoy a man and learn how you can never be forgiven. Annoy a man and discover how much hate he has been pwetending not to have for you. Say NO to it! If they choose to have you godded once you die, here's your chance to shout NO! They will come to you and say that the bible says that ye be gods..."

Dame Nissi swipes thru five channels nonstop. She decides to give a young voice a chance, with her breakfast still only halfway gone.

"Some people imagine Jesus dead on the cwoss while for others he is alive on the thwone. We have even divided beyond that. Some don't even agwee he died at all not to talk of being on any cwoss for a moment. In fact, the only similarity many Chwistian bodies share is not the God they serve but the pwetences they observe."

"Hmm," Dame Nissi sighs as she swipes for the next channel.

"You won't imagine the pomposity in his voice," a female saint says. "Do you know what this... this lawyer said to me? That it is because of man's pure love for animals that the law has awarded them permanent human pwonouns. Dogs cannot for any weason be called an 'it', just he or she and as a matter of law it has extended to doors, cars, objects, even our feelings, she no longer can be called 'it' legally. Humans, especially women, have lost value. Saint Ose Neo once said ..."

Dame Nissi wags her head, 'blah blah blah'. Next, she swipes, slowly giving up on hearing anything meaningful.

"When you've dweamt too large, you'll begin to see the hopelessness in others!" a male preacher yells arrogantly.

Dame Nissi swipes for the next channel. She walks to the bathroom to wash her face and the screen follows her, playing the voice of another male preacher.

"You know the Bible says that man shall not live by bwead alone... but that doesn't mean man shouldn't live by bwead at all! So yes, we need your tithes to keep coming in.

The Lord indeed shall multiply especially for us, but nil times a million is still nil. We need to add in something first..."

Dame Nissi's face is still soaked in water when she follows the screen sound and squeezes off the audio message; that's enough for one Sunday. She dabs her face with a towel and picks up the empty tea cup and plate. She opens the room door and she's startled by Sextine who is just about to knock on the door.

"Me Gee, Sextine! Did they send you?"

"Lol," Sextine shrugs off the fact that she too was startled by Dame Nissi. "Depends on who you fear the most, I do work for all of them."

"I am not surpwised," Dame Nissi concludes as she leaves for the dining room.

"You not coming? Popmy is awake..."

"He's awake? They done? Did they call you?"

"Yes, yes, and no," Sextine answers all her questions. "They called Leontine... he called Leontine..."

"Oh," Dame Nissi smiles disappointedly, it is a sign he does blame her for the accident. "We better get going. Where is Lexis and Leontine?"

"Waiting in the car..."

14

IT'S only a matter of minutes before the Rhos flock into Lord Omicron's room in Saint Adaora's Hospital. They find him flanked by a sad faced Archprofessor Lux Eden and a comical Archprofessor Elise Leo Elise. The almost voiceless wall intellivision is showing a news broadcast on Jermain's kickers world cup triumph.

Leontine and Sextine are way too glad to see their father awake and smiling. They jog quickly to his bedside while Archprofessors Lux Eden and Elise have a quick eye contact argument just before Lexis and Dame Nissi stroll over.

"We have to leave," communicates Archprofessor Lux Eden's eyes.

"No."

"Come, we have to, now!"

"Mm mm, no, I'm family too."

"Woman, I will kill you!"

"Okay, let's go." Archprofessor Elise reluctantly follows Archprofessor Lux Eden out of the room.

Archprofessor Lux Eden waves at Dame Nissi while Elise calls her by name.

"Dame Nissi Woe..."

"Elise, Leo, Elise, Elise Leo Elise," Dame Nissi isn't quite sure what to call her in return. Elise or Leo or Elise or three of them at once.

Archprofessor Elise... Leo Elise gives her a Sextinesque smirk. We aren't sure what to call her or that either. Dame Nissi manages a mild giggle.

Leontine and Lord Omicron are happy to sign in reunion. When he's coming home is the most important thing Leontine wants to know. Lord Omicron realises she's still with the heart whisperer.

"That... did it work?"

"No, it gave me a headache, I turned it off," Leontine signs.

Lord Omicron tries switching on the device but the marvelousness of Dame Nissi's presence makes her too around to be ignored. He looks at her and his eyes lock into hers. Neither twitch nor blink, and Lexis is certain it's time for the kids to move away.

Lexis takes his sisters to the seat beside the wall and they all pretend to be watching the news – now showing Jermain's fans reaction to the world cup victory.

Dame Nissi and Lord Omicron are still eye-locked. To blame her or not to blame her, to accept blame or not to accept blame. Definitely sorry for what happened but if they needed a middle ground, they'll blame the car for malfunctioning, or even the front door for letting Lord Omicron out in the first place! If the 'blame god' requires something with blood, it is easy to accuse Sir Nnia Den for tampering with Lord Omicron's car... or maybe he did. Who knows?

Crown Princess Lotem-Zeta storms nosily into the room, leading an entourage of familiar faces. Most notably is the delighted Archprofessor Elise swaying alongside Sir Luminescence. Others are Princess Zeta and the returning Archprofessor Lux Eden.

"How did this happen?!" Princess Lotem-Zeta asks loudly.

"Lol, your highness," Lord Omicron giggles a welcome note.

"Hello," the princess greets Dame Nissi who nods a response.

Well, Dame Nissi is glad she's been saved from the awkward situation. Princess Lotem-Zeta realises this too so she doesn't mind continuing her rising conversation with Lord Omicron.

Dame Nissi points to the door with her eyebrows and her children understand the order – vacate the room before we get ignored by friendship.

The visitors give a few seconds silence for the demise of the blame game as the Rhos leave the room. They are optimistic a better husband-wife reunion is on the cards for the future. Princess Zeta has a shoulder brush from Lexis as she walks unnoticed towards the intellivision screen.

"Well, what happened?" Princess Lotem-Zeta asks again as soon as the door is shut.

"Manual floating," Lord Omicron reveals as he tries to regain his happy face.

"Manual what?" the princess is surprised. "You know if you did that today, you'll be doing something illegal."

"It is not illegal," argues Lord Omicron.

"I am telling you, it is now illegal to float the conveyor manually," Princess Lotem-Zeta insists.

"How can that even be twue?"

"It is twue Lord Woe," Princess Zeta chips in. "It is still on the news now." She turns up the volume of the *IV* and they all fix their eyes on the screen. They catch a glimpse of the headline just before the newscaster moves on to the next story.

'THE STATE OF GENIA CRIMINALISES MANUAL FLOATING'

"Let's hope you won't be the first to disobey this. Talking of new laws," the newscaster continues, "the nations of the Mid Mowal World have signed into law a bill that bans bestialists fwom adopting human childwen. In a statement gaining much cwiticism as the worst discwimination against animals in decades, a leading minister fwom Pena said and I quote, 'If I come of age and get to know that my popmy isn't actually my popmy, I'll pass. But when my foster momxy isn't even human, that alone will make me kill myself. It is even awkward that a couple of centuwies ago, our people allowed gays who can't make babies to adopt and enjoy what others enjoy in having a family with kids, how do you explain to a child that her pet in the house is actually one of her pawents?' Western leaders however have condemned the new anti-adoption bill saying it is a huge step backwards and a violation of human and animal wights. Still to come... Acanthian leaders are set to visit Sexat on Monday, and Team Epsilon to fly to the lost earth again. Stay with us."

Princess Lotem-Zeta will surely stay tuned. She has subconsciously walked to the front of the screen anticipating what will be said about Acanthia and Epsilon.

Archprofessor Lux Eden clears his throat, reminding everyone why they are here.

"Just give me a moment," Princess Lotem-Zeta requests as she turns down the volume of the intellivision to her hearing alone. She listens eagerly to the news.

"You still haven't said what happened," Archprofessor Lux Eden reminds Lord Omicron.

"Lol, but I did."

"No," Sir Luminescence objects, "we meant how it happened."

"I am not sure, another car hit mine, so, my daughter pulled me out and took me home."

"Where were you going to?" Archprofessor Lux Eden asks.

"Nowhere... just nowhere..."

"I've never heard of that place," says Archprofessor Elise.

"Where? Nowhere?"

"Mhm?"

"You must be joking... well, I was going nowhere."

"Why were you going nowhere?" Archprofessor Lux Eden asks.

Lord Omicron giggles, "Fwom what to how to where to why. Well, I was upset."

"Who upset you?" Archprofessor Lux Eden asks.

"Um... who now..."

"Your wife did, Omicwon," Princess Lotem-Zeta chips in from her newsstand, her eyes still fixed on the screen showing videos of previous meetings between Acanthia and Sexat.

"Ha!" Lord Omicron exclaims. "Well, yes, no point hiding anything. These things happen."

"Women! I will divorce me wife if this happens to me," says Archprofessor Lux Eden.

"Oh please, don't go there," Archprofessor Elise defends accident-prone relationships.

"Well, Lux, I am not you. Perhaps I'm fine."

"Lol, will one be dead before the divorce? Funny."

"Hmm... my own wife is twoublesome," Sir Luminescence reveals.

"Then my fwend, you are a lucky man," Lord Omicron says. "In one lifetime you've been able to understand a woman so perfectly that you can descwibe her in one word – 'twoublesome'. I don't know who my wife is exactly but I'm sure I'll be lost without her."

"Then my fwend," Sir Luminescence mimics Lord Omicron, "you've been able to love one woman so perfectly that you understand what she means to you."

"I am twying to understand what my wife means most of the time," Archprofessor Lux Eden laments.

Archprofessor Elise, Lord Omicron and Sir Luminescence burst into laughter and this attracts Princess Lotem-Zeta's attention again.

"No but I'm sewious," Archprofessor Lux Eden continues. "Sometimes I feel she's a liar. Though all the lies she tells me are exactly what my ears want to hear. I blame her, since I cannot effectively blame my own self. What is confusing now is, I don't know, is she lying to me or am I lying to myself?"

"What are you saying? Archprofessor Elise is rightly confused.

"Now now now..." Princess Lotem-Zeta calls for their attention as she rejoins them. "You men wouldn't be Zophar and Bildad condoling and comforting Job here in his sickbed."

"Haha!" Archprofessor Lux Eden laughs sarcastically. "I'm sure if his wife had no hand in this, she would have urged him to curse God and die! Eh?"

Lord Omicron joins the rest in laughing at the harsh joke, each with a disapproving happy face.

"Oh that's so evil of you Lux Eden," says the princess. "If any of you men say another word against women, I will make sure your names become a symbol of womanhood when I become queen."

"Lol, your highness, that will be mean," admits Archprofessor Lux Eden.

Princess Lotem-Zeta pats Lord Omicron on the shoulder, "Whoever you want to blame she or yourself or God, just don't. You should let it go. Our abilities to let things go define our level of kindness..."

"...and meanness..." Sir Luminescence chips in."

"Yeah... both," Princess Lotem-Zeta agrees. "It depends on how you descwibe yourself... kind or mean."

"No, it depends on who you are actually. You kind or mean?" Sir Luminescence asks Lord Omicron.

"I am a husband," Lord Omicron replies.

"Haha! How lame!" exclaims Archprofessor Lux Eden. "It doesn't mean she won't still misunderstand you and hate you."

"Does misunderstanding cause hate?" Archprofessor Elise asks.

"Is having understanding the cause of love, you mean?" Sir Luminescence rephrases the question.

"Whichever..."

"Yes, certainly!" Archprofessor Lux Eden proclaims. "Nothing will make you agwee with me if you hate me. Nothing will make you disagwee with me if you love me blindly. Lord Omicwon's daughter, Sextine, published that."

"I believe that's Leontine's handwork. Sextine doesn't make such intelligent guesses."

"But that doesn't answer me question," Archprofessor Elise protests to Archprofessor Lux Eden. "You simply implied that I will have to love you in order to understand you."

"Absolutely!"

"But you said understanding causes love."

"Did I now?"

"Oh you confused too?"

"It is my wife's fault."

"Spot on!" yells Sir Luminescence in agreement to Archprofessor Lux Eden.

"I will kill you both soon!" Princess Lotem-Zeta informs them.

"But what's your take on the issue, pwincess?" Archprofessor Lux Eden asks.

"Um," Princess Lotem-Zeta thinks for a second. "Well... people can hate you for two weasons. First, because they actually misunderstand you, and secondly, because they actually do understand you perfectly but they don't just like what they understand."

"Hmm..." No one speaks for a few seconds.

"For none of those, my wife still hates me!" declares Archprofessor Lux Eden.

"The way you speak of your wife, you divorced?" Princess Lotem-Zeta asks him.

"No, still sadly marwied. This is the only time I'm psychologically able to speak about it."

"It can't be that bad!"

"Actually it's not bad... it's a mistake, the marwiage, you know, lame love at first sight and I went all poetic. I shouldn't have confessed I 'loved' her."

"Lahmao! Love at first sight," Sir Luminescence mocks the situation.

"No Lux," says Lord Omicron, "if you don't confess your love at first sight, your tongue will deny it next while your eyes will weep for your heart."

"What does that even mean?"

Lord Omicron waits for someone else to help him explain his own words. Nobody speaks.

"Nobody? Nobody knows what that means?"

"Okay," the young Princess Zeta speaks up from her seat, "what he meant was..."

She can't speak on. The awe in the manner at which everyone is looking at her, she goes from feeling shy to feeling incompetent to feeling stupid. She joins the rest of them trying so hard to hold back the laughter.

A few breaths later, it's Archprofessor Elise who leads them all into laughter. Princess Zeta laughs with her hand covering her face, still waiting to be told why she's laughing along.

"To think she was even listening to us," says Archprofessor Lux Eden.

"And opting to give an explanation," adds Archprofessor Lux Eden.

"Please, leave my daughter alone. She's knows about these things... an expert!" jokes Princess Lotem-Zeta.

"What did I do?" Princess Zeta asks.

"What you were about to say, not do."

Lord Omicron seemingly can't remember the laughter fade away nor his friends go away. He's just up from a long sleep and he finds his family sleeping around him in the hospital room. He smiles sympathetically and checks the time – 8:10 p.m. He quietly puts his head back on the pillow, almost certain that any recorded activity now will be interpreted into a bad dream by his sleeping wife. He shuts his eyes, sleep is inevitable.

15 THE next morning comes quickly and so do Princess Lotem-Zeta and a few guards. This time she's with the little Princess Kamsi-Elle who is still obsessed with her new sapien. She's looking at a couple of screens and a few others float around her; a guard has to secretly squeeze off a screen that is lagging behind.

Leontine is already awake, watching over her sleeping family.

"Good morning evewybody!" shouts the vibrant Princess Lotem-Zeta.

Dame Nissi opens her eyes immediately. She's relatively calm after realising it's the princess' voice. Princess Lotem-Zeta proceeds to Leontine and fondles her cheeks briefly.

Dame Nissi seats up slowly and taps up the dozing Sextine. "Good morning, your highness," she greets the crown princess.

"Good morn..." Sextine attempts to lap up the greeting. She's certainly not high enough to chance the real highness.

"Good morning Dame Nissi. Has Omicwon gotten up this morning?"

Dame Nissi points at the motionless Lord Omicron... she wouldn't know.

"How are you feeling?" Princess Lotem-Zeta asks.

"I feel dirty," Lord Omicron awakens.

"Lol, momxy bwought you fwesh cloths," Lexis reveals. "You can shower here."

"Good morning Dame Woe, good morning Lord Woe," greets the inattentive Kamsi-Elle.

"Good morning little pwincess, how are you?" Lord Omicron asks.

"The little pwincess is fantastic!" Kamsi-Elle's sapien proclaims. "She's ..."

"McAirdo, be quiet," Kamsi-Elle orders her sapien.

"Yes boss," the sapien becomes mute.

"I am vewy fine Lord Woe," Kamsi-Elle tells Lord Omicron.

"McAirdo?" Lord Omicron mouths the name to Princess Lotem-Zeta.

"Don't ask me... I don't where and why she picked that name, but with the way she's always calling on that thing, I believe it saves us the noise at home."

"Certainly..."

"I'm thinking you might want to get some air."

"Why?" Lord Omicron asks quickly.

"Dunno... I don't want you and Nissi feeling awkward about what happened."

"We... oh well," Dame Nissi is short of words.

"Yeah, well," the princess continues, "just for a few minutes. I will bwing him back home."

"Where will we go?" Lord Omicron asks sceptically.

"Um, the diplomatic meeting with Acanthia, you can help us tell Pwesident Aminu how dangewous weaponized digitizers can be."

"I'm not sure the cloths I bwought for him will fit in for the meeting," says Dame Nissi in an indirect objection to the idea.

"Any cloth is allowed," claims Princess Lotem-Zeta.

Dame Nissi avoids making any eye contact with Lord Omicron. She wants him to suit himself whichever way he wants it – home or meeting.

"I'll go shower," Lord Omicron concludes.

"We'll be at home," Dame Nissi stands gracefully to her feet and looks on as her kids kiss their father goodbye. She gives him a short unemotional wave and leads Sextine and Lexis out of the room.

Leontine follows them reluctantly, not quite sure why they are leaving without Lord Omicron. She tugs on Sextine's cloths once they are out of the room.

"What is it?" Sextine signs.

"Is he not coming?" Leontine signs.

"He is coming... in slow motion," Sextine speaks as she signs.

Lexis giggles briefly after Leontine slaps Sextine's shoulder. Dame Nissi looks sternly at Sextine.

"What now... she hit me and you be looking at me that way, bet I'll be damned if I hit her back."

"You can bet on that you bundle of mischief."

"Popmy is going for a meeting," Lexis signs to Leontine.

Leontine appreciates the info with a nod and then pokes Sextine hard on the back. Sextine knows a playtime invitation when she gets one, she can do with some exercise.

Leontine instinctively runs ahead of Sextine thru the hospital hallway. Sextine begins the chase... Dame Nissi's piercing eyes can't stop this.

"Be sure you bwing her to the car in the next minute," Dame Nissi yells at Sextine.

"Dead or Alive?" Sextine shouts back.

"ALIVE! You scallywag."

Lexis' laughter forces Dame Nissi to giggle.

"Please go and make sure they are heading to the car."

"Sure."

Lexis opts to move slowly though, he's confident his sisters are heading to the car. Princess Lotem-Zeta certainly did hope their father would opt to move faster than normal. His bath and preparation takes the spare time off the princess' clock and they find themselves coming in late for the meeting at the capitol in Genia.

"You bath like a woman," Princess Lotem-Zeta nags as they make their way towards the meeting room.

"Sowie sowie, I thought we had time," says Lord Omicron.

"Yes, time to get here, not time to get set."

"Sowie. Now do smile... you'll need that charm to win any battle today."

Princess Lotem-Zeta looks meanly at Lord Omicron.

"Alwight, you don't have to smile if don't mean to."

"*Cha-cha!* Not at all."

Princess Lotem-Zeta gets to the door with Lord Omicron and four guards right behind her. The door slides open and they find six men sitting restless in the meeting room. It is easy to spot the well structured moustached President Aminu of Acanthia. He is flanked by two of his cabinet members. The other three young men are ministers from Sexat. They are relieved to see Princess Lotem-Zeta.

"I have been twying to contact you," President Aminu laments, "I couldn't find you. Is the name not Lotem-Zeta?"

"Pwincess Lotem-Zeta..."

"Yes, with the pwincess, still didn't find you," insists President Aminu.

"It is just pwivacy settings. You don't expect me to leave myself findable for evewybody to place a call to the pwincees... that will be huge work, wouldn't it?"

"Yes certainly, but at least not when you have important people twying to contact you."

"I'll twy and see what I can do about important people... why hasn't the meeting started?" the princess asks.

"The Pwesident asked that you should stand in for him," says one the three Sexatians present.

"He said? I didn't hear that."

"No one was able to get thwu to you. Without the pwesident or the king, we can't convene."

"Oh dear, I sincerely apologise. Seems the pwivacy settings on my gadget are a bit extweme. Pwesident Aminu, I had no idea I'm meant to stand in for my pwesident otherwise I would have been here earlier for the pwesident's sake at least, he's known for keeping to time. I hope you understand."

"Oh sure, certainly, your highness. What about your popmy, is he on his way yet?"

"No, I am standing in for him as well."

"Ah yes, yes, I was told. Forgive my forgetfulness."

"I have forgotten it alweady," jokes Princess Lotem-Zeta.

Princess Lotem-Zeta and President Aminu smile broadly as they shake hands. Princess Lotem-Zeta offers handshakes to others in the room before taking her seat. She signals the motionless Lord Omicron to come sit beside her.

Lord Omicron switches back on and begins to move quickly to the seat beside Princess Lotem-Zeta who introduces him as fast as he moves.

"Gentlemen, this is Lord Omicwon Woe. He's the owner of the jack of twades company Woediculous; he's my vewy good fwend. As you all know, I'm Cwown Pwincess Lotem-Zeta, I'm here in my capacity as the chairlady of the House Committee on International Secuwity and Co-living. I am also sitting in for my popmy, King Sigma the third, the head of all western nations, and for my pwesident, Leonard Eddy-Tome Junior, the pwesident of Sexat. I'm sure you all know the Acanthian pwesident... others should kindly intwoduce themselves... wouldn't want anyone shushing evewyone in the heat of the meeting."

"I am *Effendi Khalid Mede,*" says one Acanthian, "Acanthia's Minister of Defence and Offence."

"And I," says the other Acanthian, "*Pasha Nenadi N'miji*, Acanthia's Minister of Technology.

Princess Lotem-Zeta nods along as the rest in the room introduce themselves, a lot of familiar surnames. One is *Prince Jordan Sigma*, a distant cousin of hers and Sexat's Minister of Defence. The second Sexatian is *Archlord Jade Eddy-Tome*, Sexat's Minister of Weapons Survey and Regulations, and the third man is *Lord Captain Cello Onward*, Sexat's Minister of Gadgets and Technology.

"Okay," says Princess Lotem-Zeta. "You all welcomed. Pwesident Aminu, what's the first thing you'll like us to discuss?"

"Thank you, your highness," President Aminu begins. "There are just a few things I have come to discuss with Sexat in person. In totality, they are about the weaponized digitizers, collabowation on Space journeys, with emphasis on the lost earth, and curbing the menace of international teleport systems."

"What about the international teleport system?" Princess Lotem-Zeta snaps in. "You want to bwing back the airports?"

"The airports are still functional in a few nations and still vital to their economy... but that's not the first thing I'll like us to discuss."

"I doubt we'll discuss it at all..."

"Your highness, it is too early to disagwee on something."

"No, Pwesident Aminu, I'm just saying what I feel. I am not disagweeing with you yet."

"Of course, we'll begin then. Let's talk about the weaponized digitizers."

"What about them?"

"Boss, you on the news," the princess' sapien announces.

"Ignore that," she commands the sapien. She's sure it's the meeting they must be ranting about on the news. She signals President Aminu to carry on.

"I know Sexat must have a clue why we intend to upgwade the value of WGDs."

"Hmm... we have no clue you intend to do that, and certainly we don't know why."

"Nobody is allowed to do that," Archlord Jade says.

"Yes, that is why we are discussing it now," President Aminu says.

"Do you have an idea what other nations will do if they learn you intend to upgwade your WGDs?" Prince Jordan asks.

"They've done nothing all these while... they've done nothing to you surely... and they know what we intend to do."

"We didn't upgwade our WGDs... you can't expect them to do anything to us 'surely' now, wight Mr Pwesident?"

"Pwince Jordan, was Sexat found with five seconds weapons gwade digitizers existing naturwally under Oh's surface? Somebody made them obviously..."

"Somebody had to make them and Oh need only one nation to do so."

"Is that a commandment fwom God?" Effendi Khalid asks.

"I don't get you, Effendi Khalid."

"You said Oh needed only one nation to do so. Who gave us that guideline, God?"

"Which of the gods are you asking of now?"

"Cousin, forget about that," Princess Lotem-Zeta calls the gentlemen to order. "Let's talk about the digitizers, not the gods. But before we continue, we must wemember the sacwifise of Saint K.K Jamima to cleanse the nations of weapons, and the ongoing efforts of the head of Universal Church, Saint Maywy-Jane the third. We, that is Sexat, are vewy unlikely to deviate fwom the pwinciples of these two women."

"You have weapons well above other nations, your highness."

"Pwesident Aminu, someone has to keep others in check."

"Yes, that is why we are not asking to make five seconds WGDs."

"How many then? You alweady make thwee seconds, which is second to us alone."

"And Jermain..."

"Jermain make thwee seconds WGDs, not higher."

"But they have the licence to make four point five seconds."

"Which they've never done... it's called twust."

"You don't twust us then, I suppose."

"I suppose you can say that again," says Princess Lotem-Zeta.

"I understand your scepticism about this..."

"Scepticism? We understand the danger in it."

"Please, let me explain why we need this," says President Aminu.

"There is only one use for weapons, and it is to cause harm on other people."

"Your highness, may I wemind you that Sexat owns these weapons. How many people have you harmed with it? Acanthia is not at war with anyone, so you need not to fear. We..."

"...You... okay, go on..."

"...We want to make these things for domestic use."

"Domestic?"

"Sowie, domestic... like, within your nation or is it within the homes of normal people?" Lord Omicron asks.

"Yes, within the homes of normal people..."

"This is sewious. You intend to equip your households with weapons?"

"This will not be weapons... can't even be any more of a weapon than the PES," President Aminu explains. "The WGDs will only serve as a helping hand especially for our busy women. They can use the WGDs, for example, to fix a scattered kitchen. Just imagine doing all that work in one click."

"Lol, she will need many WGDs to get attached to all her twoubles before solving them in one click," says the princess.

"Yes, we can achieve that with a missile digitizer. It explodes over evewything and alignment buttons can fix them back as weasonably normal as possible."

"Am I the only one listening to you? Can you hear yourself? I mean no diswespect but Jeez, who delibewately sells weaponized missile digitizers to civilians?"

"Pwincess, they'll be labelled domestic digitizers," says President Aminu.

"It doesn't take away the evil potential of the digitizers. To fix a bwoken marwiage for example, just imagine killing all those people in one click. Don't cweate what you can't contwol."

"What about incweasing the number of thwee seconds WGDs we pwoduce?" Effendi Khalid asks.

"Your entire police use those thwee seconds WGDs," says Prince Jordan. "Incweasing the number will only make it commercial."

"What about incweasing the value to thwee point five seconds?" asks President Aminu.

"No, you want other nations to demand an incwease too?"

"What of thwee point two seconds then?"

"No!" Princess Lotem-Zeta insists.

"It is vewy little, what diffewence does it make?"

"If it makes no diffewence then why do you want it?"

Lord Omicron is totally bored now. He could sense this meeting will drag on for a very long time. The whole day is certainly not enough for the Sexatians to agree adequately with the Acanthians. The meeting extends deep into the night with Lord Omicron thinking mainly of his family and his house, especially the meals he's missing out on; the meeting's brunch and lunch are not very satisfying.

Lord Omicron emerges from the teleport system in his house at about nine o'clock in the night. He slides his hand across his right leg, just to be sure the new limb did arrive with him; he has been hearing some disturbing rumours.

He looks tired and sorry, at least for staying out all day and night. He's beginning to trust his front door to open up for him without any questions, he'll be mad to learn his door is beginning to trust everyone else too. It will be nice to meet someone awake, but he isn't sure if any of them will approve of the timing. Just as he feared, his wife is sitting right here in the living room, on the very seat facing the door, targeting the first impression portrayed by any intruder.

Lord Omicron comports himself quickly, stuck between a generous smile and a mean look, Dame Nissi has to help him choose. But she's not moved by his presence. Her eyes are steady, her hands resting on her knees and there is no sign she's angry or happy or indifferent, there's no sign she's breathing at all.

Lord Omicron maintains the straight line leading to the seat. He reaches out for Dame Nissi's cheek with his right hand, earnestly hoping to feel the warmth again. He's ready to forget about the accident but he is left in a state of disappointment and amusement when his hand dips into

Dame Nissi's face. Yes, it is what he's thinking. He slides his hand thru the face and giggles inwardly.

"Hologwam," he says to himself.

To him, this is a clear indication that his wife tried staying up by every means possible. Since she's obviously sleeping somewhere in the house, the hologram is practically on hibernation. It's exhaustively too difficult to stay up all morning and afternoon and not fall into a deep sleep at night. Lord Omicron understands these facts, coupled with his wife likely to wake up from a bad dream if he walks around her real self, and how exhausted he is from the inconclusive meeting with the Acanthians, he staggers into an empty bedroom and falls into the bed.

16 THE next day comes quickly as usual, a very important Tuesday for Lord Omicron; he'll be flying Epsilon back to the lost earth.

Lord Omicron bursts out of the room, all dressed up, feeling he's already late. It is just 8:35 a.m. He does need time to put things in place before the team arrives at the station at 1 t.m.

He stops at Leontine's room and opens the door gradually, there's no telling where exactly Dame Nissi could be. He finds Leontine, all dressed up, standing in front of the mirror, trying to put on the heart whisperer. Leontine looks at him and smiles broadly, not overly excited.

"Hi! You home," she signs.

"Yes," Lord Omicron nods. "You going out?" he signs.

"Yes, to the lost earth... with you."

"The lost earth?"

"Yes popmy. Like you said you'll see what you can do. Lexis said you've seen what you've done."

"Oh he did? What did he say I saw I did?"

"You know... that I can come too... that I can go too, whichever."

"And what did your momxy say about that?"

"She said I can go with you," Leontine signs. "She said she doesn't like you having the impression that she's keeping me away from you."

"No..."

"Yes!"

"No, I don't mean that... meant she shouldn't have said that, or you shouldn't have told me anyway."

"We are late, popmy."

"Yes we are... I'll go get Lexis."

"I'll go wake momxy."

"No! Best you don't walk in there."

Leontine notices Lord Omicron moulding up a fist with his right hand before turning slowly towards the door, he must have heard an unusual noise. She tries looking thru the side of his muscular arm; she's certainly not tall or stupid enough to try looking over his broad shoulders but her raised heels suggest otherwise. We notice the father and child relax when they see Sextine's head popping quietly thru the door. She can sense they were tensed and she withdraws her head to make a proper entrance. She's certainly not alone; Lexis makes a quick enquiry as she pulls her head out of the room.

"Is she still sleeping?" Lexis asks.

"Awake. Popmy is even here," Sextine replies before opening the door.

"Why were you sneaking up on her?" Lord Omicron asks Sextine.

"Nobody is sure where momxy slept," Sextine responds. "So, I don't want twouble."

Lord Omicron giggles.

"Set to go?" Lexis asks him.

"Yeah, you?"

"Yes. Leontine is coming, yes?"

"Yep, you alweady saw what I've done."

"Lol, she loves all the lost earth tales, she'll love it too."

"I know," Lord Omicron smiles with his arm across Leontine's shoulders.

"You guys should get going," says Sextine, "I need to get to school."

"Tell momxy we've gone," Lord Omicron tells Sextine. "We'll be back hopefully before Thursday night or Fwiday or just as soon as possible."

"Sure."

It takes Lord Omicron about fifteen minutes with his wife's car at top speed to arrive the *Genia Spaceport* without Lexis and Leontine losing their minds in the quick ride. Quite expeditious, far from hasty and nasty, especially with all the car's instructions being obeyed.

Back in the house, Sextine is holding up a bowl plate, receiving extra drops of milk. We are surprised to see Dame Nissi standing beside her.

"Isn't that enough?" Dame Nissi asks, sending Sextine into a quick burst of panic.

The bowl plate falls out of her hands as she assumes her best self-defence posture.

"Holy ...!" Sextine fidgets as she spins with her fist. "Momxy?" she is quick to withdraw the pumped up punch. "Momxy!" she reconfirms.

"What is wong with you?" Dame Nissi wonders.

"With me?! Ha! Like how did you get here? When did you get out of bed?" Sextine asks quickly and anxiously.

Dame Nissi smiles and pushes her finger thru Sextine's chest. "I am still in bed *yunlade*."

"We just lost a plate for that."

"Fate. Get me something to eat, I'm starving. Has Leontine woken up? Lexis... has your popmy eaten? Is he even back?"

"They've left for the lost earth," Sextine informs Dame Nissi.

"All of them?" Dame Nissi mutters with deep sadness overtaking her countenance. "He left without saying goodbye?"

"He said goodbye to me... and he'll be back soon obviously. Momxy, come on, you sad?"

"No no, I kept the hologwam up all night," Dame Nissi's voice begins to break, "it's losing energy."

Sextine doesn't buy that. She can sense her mother is about to cry. She walks thru the hologram as she hurries out of the dining room, heading to Dame Nissi's room where someone surely needs some pampering.

At Genia Spaceport, thru the numerous hallways and open spaces, Lord Omicron and his two children arrive at the launch park of the giant Epsilon space shuttle. Looking thru the thick glass doors, Leontine and Lexis are completely amazed by the fascinating Epsilon. They realise they've actually never seen it before now.

A man in uniform – *Captain Chuddy Desea,* slides a screen to Lord Omicron thru the space where the two doors meet.

"Good morning, Lord Woe," the captain greets.

"Captain Desea, how have you been?" Lord Omicron asks as he receives the screen, turning it over and letting it hang on the door, just above the level of his chest.

This appears to be a routine. The screen comes on, displaying the names of Lord Omicron's team members. The new additions, 'Imgr. Lexis Rho' and 'Archprofessor Elise Leo Elise' are already on the list. There's a smile on Lord Omicron's face when he sees that Sir Nnia Den, and Archprofessors Lux Eden and Elise Leo Elise have already been checked in by the screen.

"I'm bubbling ok, Lord Woe," Captain Desea replies.

"They are here alweady?"

"And eager too," hints Captain Desea.

Lord Omicron taps his name and the screen verifies his finger print. He looks at Saint Ose Neo's name, "Take her name off, Saint Ose Neo... she's not coming."

"Yes, Sir Den said the same thing. I was waiting to confirm from you."

"Yes, she's not available for this journey," Lord Omicron confirms.

He points Lexis to the screen and Lexis taps on his own name immediately. The screen displays a clear message, 'TAP SCREEN AND SAY YOUR NAME'.

Lord Omicron nods. "For first timers."

Lexis responds with a double nod and a tap on the screen. "Lexis Woe."

'VOICE RECOGNISED. IMGR. LEXIS RHO'.

With the screen having the same application logo as the sapien, there's no point wondering how it recognised his voice. Lexis joins his father in anticipating the doors to open up.

"Is the door jammed?" Lord Omicron asks.

"No, Lord Woe," Captain Desea says and then points at Leontine. "She's in the vewification zone. She has to clear the zone or get vewified."

"No, she's my daughter. She's coming with us... just to see Epsilon."

"You have to get her vewified then."

"Her name is not on the list," Lord Omicron reminds the captain.

"Yes, those names were appwoved by the ministwy. But you are Epsilon's captain, your pwint is authowized to cweate a new pwofile."

"How do I do that?"

"There, bottom of the scween... click on 'new'."

"New... okay." Lord Omicron squints as he tries spotting the 'new' option at the bottom of the screen.

There's only one box visible, he clicks it all the same.

'TAP SCREEN AND SAY YOUR NAME' is the message on the screen.

"Um," Lord Omicron is concerned. "My daughter is actually deaf," he says to Captain Desea.

"Okay, I'm sure that won't be a pwoblem for a deaf person. She can just say her name."

"Oh, yes... pwoblem is, she doesn't talk too... never heard her speak."

"I don't know... maybe she can tap the scween to get her pwints taken, then you can speak her name... since she's just here to visit."

Lord Omicron agrees. He points Leontine to the screen and she taps it. She has been doing her best in reading Captain Desea's lips so she turns quickly to Lord Omicron to say her name as the captain suggested.

Lord Omicron says her name but the screen rejects it outrightly, identifying the voice as Lord Omicron's. Lord Omicron tucks in his lips in disappointment. Lexis and Leontine look briefly at each other, Lexis' eyes still beaming with hope, no point giving up on the journey just yet.

Captain Desea understands the screen has rejected the voice so he offers a more futile advice. "Maybe you can whisper the name, or talk like a girl or something."

"Sure..."

Lord Omicron taps on 'new' again and points Leontine to the screen. Leontine obliges immediately and taps the screen.

"Leontine Woe," Lord Omicron says in a shy girly voice.

The response from the screen this time is quite quick and bold, and accompanied by two mild notes of siren. 'REJECTED! VOICE OF LORD OMICRON RHO'.

Lexis looks back warily, very much expecting security men to be closing in on them, or even worse, they might release a poisonous gas of some sort to get rid of the 'intruders'. Waiting for Captain Desea to grab a mask, Lexis could be dead before inhaling the gas at all.

"There has got to be another way now," Lord Omicron says.

"Maybe your son can twy," Captain Desea suggests again.

"No," Lexis recollects himself. "It should have pwovisions for mute people." He double-clicks the screen and two relieving options pop up.

'VOICE ONLY' and 'PRINT ONLY'.

"Go ahead," Lexis signs to Leontine.

Leontine taps the 'PRINT ONLY' option optimistically. The screen offers a keyboard to type in her name. Without a blink, she pokes the right keys and 'Leontine Rho' gets an entry verification within seconds.

The door opens up and Captain Desea grabs the screen and welcomes the three Rhos. Leontine is particularly wondering why the room is empty. Thru the glass just half a moment ago she could see Epsilon. Lexis quietly nods with a one-cheek smile; he did fall for that optical illusion.

Lord Omicron pretends he's not aware of their expectations to see Epsilon inside this very room. He leads them quickly towards a small door and slows down just before he grabs the door handle. He takes a deep breath and smiles at Lexis and Leontine.

"What, like you keep the entire ship inside an office?" Leontine signs impatiently. She's certainly not in the mood to see anything else but Epsilon and the small size of the door isn't helping.

"Seemesh," Lord Omicron giggles with a shake of the head.

Lord Omicron opens up the door into a large hall. We all see Epsilon sitting in the middle of the highly digital room. The walls and ceiling are oozing of unreality; one can't blame Leontine for taking ten seconds to believe her eyes. Lexis taps her on the shoulder, urging her to follow Lord Omicron who is already near the magnanimous spaceship.

Leontine switches back on. She grabs Lexis' hand and they jog to their father.

"This is it," Lord Omicron says to them. "Epsilon..."

"It is huge," Lexis responds.

Archprofessor Elise suddenly jumps out from the back of Epsilon, her voice bellowing at its peak, saying nothing in particular; a roar maybe, we can't really say of this mischief. Lexis and Lord Omicron raise their eyebrows as they stare back at her. Leontine is too busy looking at Epsilon she didn't notice Archprofessor Elise's grand scare-them-all entrance.

Archprofessor Lux Eden and Sir Nnia reluctantly reveal themselves too.

"You werwen't even moved?" Archprofessor Lux Eden asks.

"I told you it was a lame idea," says Sir Nnia. "You had a joke of a lady come yelling like a baby folf, attempting to scare the owner of the shuttle, his don't-give-a-shit son, and his deaf daughter."

"Don't ever wefer to my daughter like that," Lord Omicron warns.

Sir Nnia raises his hand in a sarcastic apology.

"Is she coming too?" Archprofessor Elise asks about Leontine.

"Yes," Lord Omicron nods.

"She is coming too?" Sir Nnia asks loudly. "What sort of unofficial expedition is this?"

"Unofficial enough to have you in it."

"I am..."

The entrance door to the room swings open just in time to shut Sir Nnia up. They all turn towards the door and watch Princess Lotem-Zeta walk in.

The princess stops moving, her eyes searching the faces of the people standing up ahead. She squints; she has seen him – the basic reason why she's early. Lord Omicron tries to wonder along about the princess' earliness when she walks robotically towards Sir Nnia.

It has to be Sir Nnia, Lord Omicron finally decodes. He's yet to get the meaning of the word 'Gadhuvi' and there's no more time to find out peacefully.

"You here alweady," Lord Omicron attempts to slow the princess down.

Princess Lotem-Zeta snubs him and everyone else keep their greetings to themselves.

The unsuspecting, or rather, the fearless-near-proud Sir Nnia receives a resounding ear-shutting slap from the furious princess. Her decades of training to act gracefully perfectly concealed the extent of her anger. Sir Nnia stumbles to the floor; the weight of the slap need not be understood let alone withstood. Her highness is highly irate.

"Holy cwappers! Woman, you meant to be woyalty," laments Sir Nnia as tries to feel the texture of his battered cheek.

There is no one holding back the princess yet, they all secretly enjoyed that slap. Leontine stands with her mouth wide open.

"If you for one day think that you can endanger my daughter's life and go scot fwee..."

"I know, I know, you'll slap me to death, hey?"

The infuriated princess charges towards Sir Nnia but Lord Omicron holds back.

"Your highness, please no, calm down," Lord Omicron pleads.

"Get your limbs off me body!" Princess Lotem-Zeta pushes away Lord Omicron who has successfully diverted her attention himself. "I asked you to find out why he chose to attack my daughter."

"I didn't attack..." Sir Nnia snaps in.

"Shut up!" Princess Lotem-Zeta orders. She turns back to Lord Omicron. "And you ignored what he did?"

"I didn't ignore what he did. He said it was a Gadhuvi... I was getting to find out more but it was late in the night and my wife's sleep was being disturbed."

"And afterwards?"

"You met me afterwards... in the hospital."

"No, Lord Omicwon. You had the whole of Saturday to find something out. What is the Gadumvi?"

"Gadhuvi," Sir Nnia corrects the princess.

"And what is Gadhuvi or do I need to *unteeth* your jaw?"

"You can even completely *unjaw* my face," Sir Nnia staggers up, "but I will speak at my pace."

This is sure an all new height of arrogance from Sir Nnia. Archprofessor Lux Eden feels so embarrassed he walks away to the other side of Epsilon.

Lord Omicron signals the piercing-eyes armed princess to hear Sir Nnia first. Her eyes are not disarmed that easily.

"You see, the Gadhuvi," Sir Nnia is suddenly acting a-bit-drunk, "is something special. It is... just a portmanteau fwom Gadget-Human Viwus."

"A viwus?"

"Gadget-Human Viwus," Sir Nnia reiterates.

"You infected my daughter with a viwus?"

"No, your highness, I put a viwus in her gadget to make it act unusual towards her. What happened was just an illusion."

"You mad? Kamsi-Elle was *illusionally* knocked to the floor? I have witnesses you *cwapid* man!"

"Vewy illusionawy isn't it? I'm neither cwazy nor stupid."

"You behave nonchalantly online, you lack common netiquette and for this I shall fight you until you have nothing left to cause anymore twouble."

"Now is that the kind of queen you'll be?"

"You dare not play mind games with me! Queen or no queen, you deserve to be spanked..."

Lord Omicron again holds back the advancing princess. "Let's stay calm your highness. This hasn't escalated yet."

"Escalated? He alweady got to me daughter! Is it until it is news on the intellivision before I can do something about it?"

"I understand how you feel," says Lord Omicron.

"Then you should be punching Sir Nnia. Please open up Epsilon, let's go." She turns again to Sir Nnia, "Once we get back, I will have you detained."

Lord Omicron takes the princess to the door of the spaceship. The screen keys appear and Lord Omicron begins punching in the codes with his middle finger.

"I shouldn't be here while you do this," says the princess.

"You plan on stealing my finger? Knowing the code isn't enough."

"I know what I'm saying... things can easily change. You can see Sir Nnia for example..."

"No, don't let him kill your faith in the system. Sir Nnia has certainly been evil fwom birth."

The shuttle doors open gradually and Archprofessor Elise, Lexis and Leontine move quickly to see for themselves.

Archprofessor Lux Eden speaks quietly to Sir Nnia. He's quite sceptical about the Gadget-Human Virus.

"The Gadhuvi hmm?"

"What about it?" Sir Nnia asks.

"Does the ministwy know?"

"Which of them?"

"Anyone... defence, gadgets, or even space, Archpwofessor Nightingale at least."

"Hmm," Sir Nnia smiles wickedly, "they will get my message before we touch down on the lost earth."

"Yeah, you may end up staying there on exile."

"Nah, I shall come back a king... the King of Oh."

Archprofessor Lux Eden stands speechless as Sir Nnia walks into Epsilon. He hears the room door open and he looks over his shoulder; he's quite glad to see Sir Luminescence Wellington walking in.

"You are late Sir Luminescence," announces Archprofessor Lux Eden.

"It is many hours to one o'clock."

"Lol... it is almost ten o'clock..."

"Then I am not late."

"No, you missed a showdown."

"What? Who? Is he dead?"

"I am vewy much alive," Sir Nnia speaks with his head popping thru Epsilon's exit. "Both of you should come inside, we about to leave."

They nod and Sir Nnia goes back inside.

"Was it about him?" asks Sir Luminescence.

"Yeah... with the pwincess."

"Whoa..."

"He attacked her daughter via a Gadhuvi, whatever that is."

"A Gadhuvi?" Sir Luminescence whispers. "Is it what I think it is?"

"I doubt."

"A viwus?"

"Yes... heard of it?"

"Yes. It is just like cloning... such things are better left undone."

"I have never heard of it," says Archprofessor Lux Eden.

"No one speaks of it. It was last made in the lost earth according to some scholars. With no evidence of the lost earth, nobody believed them."

"Well, Sir Nnia has the Gadhuvi, and I believe him."

"And I believe the fear in your eyes, Lux."

"I am not afwaid."

"An evil weapon with an evil genius? You should be."

"If it is that evil... if it's a thing to fear, why is nobody acting against it?"

"We must not be loud to make a plan, Lux. I don't need a month to make a plan. I just heard you and I know what I intend to do."

"What do you intend to do Sir?" Archprofessor Lux Eden whispers.

"If you must know," Sir Luminescence whispers back, "it is my intention we forget Sir Nnia on the lost earth."

"Forget?"

"La yeah? In the gwound, if we be noble enough; or just hanging over any object we find."

"Sir Luminescence, that fellow boasts of coming back a king, it will be quite hard to 'forget' him on the lost earth."

"I may speak with the others. Enough said for now."

They enter Epsilon with the reserve boldness in their attitudes. Archprofessor Elise pops out from the corner and unintentionally startles the two men. She's too happy with her Epsilon uniform to notice their reaction.

"You two should go change," she says excitedly.

"Yes newbie, we know that," Archprofessor Lux Eden responds.

"What, if you don't love it, Leontine can use your uniforms."

"You should go and ask Lord Omicwon where you meant to sit down, your head is in the cloud alweady."

"Lol," Archprofessor Elise giggles, "I'll let you know when I get to the cloud."

Lord Omicron is sitting on the pilot's seat with the princess seated as the co-pilot. Lexis is standing behind him, still trying to make sense of the unexplained details within the shuttle.

"Our school work was just too mediocre," Lexis confesses.

"Lol... at least you are here now," Lord Omicron responds. "Epsilon," he calls out to the spaceship.

"Epsilon activated," the machine responds with the pilot screen lights coming on.

"Power on engine," Lord Omicron says.

"Epsilon powered on," the machine informs Lord Omicron as soon as it has powered on the engine.

The entire cabin is lighted magnificently and it all makes a little more sense now to Lexis. The controls are clearly outlined, the seats for other crew members are easier to locate and more importantly is the small corridor leading to the kitchen. With brunch time fast approaching, a *nutriphile* like Lexis will not be denied food.

"Epsilon, align takeoff pathway," Lord Omicron instructs the machine.

"Yes captain," Epsilon responds gracefully.

"Go get Leontine to see this," Lord Omicron tells Lexis.

Lexis suddenly finds himself on the floor as he turns to go fetch Leontine. He sees Sir Nnia standing over him and realises he had just bumped into the irritated evil genius who reacted by pushing him away.

"You alwight?" asks the concerned Princess Lotem-Zeta.

"Watch where you going young man," Sir Nnia says to him.

"What happened?" Lord Omicron asks, looking curiously at Sir Nnia.

Lexis sees Leontine coming; that's all that matters to him now. He picks himself up quickly and urges Leontine to come quickly. Leontine senses there's an activity she's missing. She obliges to Lexis' gestures and whisks thru the side of Sir Nnia who is arrogantly resisting arrest by Lord Omicron's eyes for allegedly 'assaulting' Lexis.

Leontine leans forward on Lord Omicron's seat and calmly turns his head away from Sir Nnia and towards to screen. She too already has her own opinion of Sir Nnia – he doesn't deserve the attention, especially when there's a beauty of stage reconstruction going on outside.

Epsilon has just initiated the alignment of the shuttle's takeoff pathway. The entire roof of the building opens up and the wall appear to be floating out of position. It is like solving a mysterious puzzle, the only thing still in its place outside Epsilon is the small entrance door. The materials making up the walls and the roof link up with one another to form a broad ascending spiral runway.

Leontine, Lexis, and Archprofessor Elise unconsciously keep their mouths open during the pathway creation.

"If the things on Oh amaze you this much," Sir Nnia mocks them, "I hope we find nothing on the lost earth."

"Take a seat Sir Nnia... and you guys too, show is over. Time for takeoff."

Everyone aboard obeys the captain as they move quickly to their seats and buckle up. The space minister pops up from the communication screen.

"I see you are set to leave," says Archprofessor Knight.

"Archpwofessor..." Lord Omicron is about to respond before the princess addresses the minister more appropriately.

"...Dame, Knight Nightingale, yes we are. It's good to see you."

"Dame?" Lord Omicron asks. "Why doesn't anyone celebwate these achievements?"

"When you got to be a lord before me, what's there to celebwate?"

"I am older than you Nightingale... way smarter too," Lord Omicron boasts.

"Egomaniac, be sure to come back with evidence this time... I don't mind joining the league of Archdames afterwards."

"Will do, Dame Nightingale. See you when we get back."

Dame Knight terminates the communication and Lord Omicron takes a last look at his crew members.

Archprofessor Elise is sitting beside Leontine with Lexis at the opposite side. Archprofessor Lux Eden and Sir Luminescence are sitting side by side, same row as Lexis with Sir Nnia sitting directly opposite and alone as expected.

"Epsilon..."

"Yes captain..."

"Save pwesent location."

"Location saved," Epsilon confirms.

"Takeoff, manual destination."

"Taking off... You'll be in charge in ten minutes."

Lord Omicron chuckles at that, he's already feeling in charge, but he has little to do about the takeoff.

Epsilon moves slowly into the runway before accelerating to a great speed.

Leontine begins to vomit.

"Ha!" Sir Nnia is first to make an audible reaction. "First timers. Good thing you not putting on the uniform."

"None would have sized her, you!" Archprofessor Elise responds as she rubs Leontine on the back.

"My point exactly," says Sir Nnia.

"Just be quiet Sir Nnia," Sir Luminescence rebukes him.

"Elise, is she alwight?" Lord Omicron asks.

"Yes, vomiting has stopped."

"Clean her up when we get into the air."

"Will do..."

And into the air they get in a blink of an eye as Epsilon darts thru the runway and smoothly ascending thru the almost-green clouds.

Archprofessor Elise raises her eyebrows at Archprofessor Lux Eden and Sir Luminescence. "My head is in the cloud now."

The two men shake their heads.

The crew soon realise they are out of Oh's atmosphere. Lord Omicron keys in the flight coordinates for Epsilon and unbuckles his seatbelt. This spells freedom for the rest of the team. Archprofessor Elise is first to unbuckle herself. She stretches her back and then helps Leontine release her seatbelt.

"Are there spare clothes here?" Leontine signs.

"I don't know, but I saw a washing machine," Archprofessor Elise signs.

"You don't expect her to sit naked waiting for the clothes to get washed," the attentive princess chips in.

"She can use my shirt," Lexis says. "It's in my cabinet... I need food..."

"It is not even bwunch time yet," says Archprofessor Lux Eden.

"I will skip that, but not this."

"The kitchen is over there... pwint whatever you like."

Lexis quickly stands to his feet. He accompanies Leontine and Archprofessor Elise to his cabinet. He shows them the shirt and walks straight to the food printer in the kitchen.

It is quite hard to understand how much time is required to get to the lost earth. The brunch is eaten, Leontine's clothes are clean, lunch has also come and gone, and the crew wait earnestly for a glimpse of the lost earth. Lord Omicron is sure of his coordinates, but Sir Nnia doesn't trust him, and he certainly doesn't trust Leontine and Lexis who are laughing quietly while stealing glances at him.

Sir Nnia is quite sure they've been chatting thru the sapien and now he curiously wants to know why they've been laughing, or rather, what has been said about him.

"What *thawef* you laughing at?" he asks as he struggles to grab Leontine's arm.

Leontine hits his hand away.

"Sir Nnia!" Princess Lotem-Zeta tries to call him to order.

"HEY!" Lord Omicron voices bellows.

"They were talking about me," Sir Nnia laments furiously.

"You don't know that," says Lord Omicron.

"Whatever happened to the children of lords being honest people?"

"That is archaic," Sir Luminescence responds to Sir Nnia.

"I don't care! Show me what was said now."

"Sir Nnia, there is nothing to hide," Lexis claims.

"Then let me see what you sent her... you two were laughing at me."

"She sent it to me, it's just a joke."

"I want to see..."

"And if you don't?" Lord Omicron asks.

"It's cool popmy, I'll show him. At least we all can laugh together."

Lexis pulls out the text screen and Sir Luminescence snatches it from him.

"I will do justice to that," he offers to read it out, "thank you."

Sir Luminescence enlarges the screen and reads out the text. "It says, 'Why is this man *annoffewent*?' that is annoyingly diffewent..."

"I know what it is, Sir Luminescence," says Sir Nnia, "I wasn't born today."

"Alwight... 'Why is this man annoffewent? He indeed acts funny at times.' Then Lexis sends, 'I wouldn't have an idea why. People differ.' Then Leontine replies, 'I think I have an idea. Evewybody here has an element of L in their names.' 'How?' Lexis asks, and Leontine replies, 'See popmy is Lord Omicwon, the pwincess is Lotem-Zeta, and I am sitting with Leo Elise. We have Lux Eden and Luminescence Wellington. You are Lexis and I am Leontine. Me've been thinking why not *bapt* him Lunatic Den?'... That's it!"

Sir Luminescence and the rest of the crew burst into laughter. Sir Nnia feels insulted, maybe rightly so. He succeeds in grabbing Leontine by the arm and puts up his hand to hit her.

"Don't you dare!" Lord Omicron flares up with both hands fisted. "All hell will let loose if you dare... I will dump you wight into space."

Sir Nnia thinks deeply about that counter threat. He can't recall Lord Omicron bluffing about anything. He looks at Sir Luminescence who is bent halfway thru rising from his seat; quite certain he'll join Lord Omicron to throw him off the spaceship.

"Your daughter insulted me!" Sir Nnia roars.

"That is because I'm here. If you can't deal with me then I suggest you don't start what you can't finish," Lord Omicron warns.

"But your daughter insulted me!" Sir Nnia reiterates aggressively.

"Watch it Sir Nnia, your gwip is getting tight... that was a pwivate message to her bwother..."

"Sir Nnia, leave her alone," Princess Lotem-Zeta orders.

"What kind of system is this? You'll ask me to leave her alone?"

"Sir Nnia, wight now you not solving this pwoblem. Just leave her alone."

Sir Nnia pushes Leontine's arm to her as he lets go.

"Apologise to him," the princess signs to Leontine.

"No vex," Leontine signs immediately.

"Whatever that means," Sir Nnia mutters as he takes his seat.

Sir Luminescence is visibly disappointed, shaking his head as he collapses back into his seat. He would have loved to toss Sir Nnia into space.

"You look uncomfortable," Archprofessor Lux Eden says to him.

"This would have been our moment," Sir Luminescence whispers.

"Is there something you are not telling me, Sir Wellington?" Archprofessor Lux Eden ponders on his desperation.

"I know the Gadhuvi. I have seen it. I was making one myself; yes just for the fun of it... no evil intentions. It went missing. I know he stole it fwom me. I couldn't alert anyone because I knew I was doing something many people consider unethical, and quite illegal too."

"Sir Luminescence, I am surpwised that you guys know the danger in this ish and you guys sit here in peace with him."

"I said I will take care of him before we leave the lost earth."

"What about Lord Omicwon? What about the Pwincess? They heard him say it to their faces that he owns the Gadhuvi, and they did nothing. What if they are in it together?"

"No... Don't... they can't be. They are simply unaware of what Sir Nnia can do with the power of that viwus."

"It means if they see you attacking Sir Nnia, they may not understand why. They could stand in and defend him."

"I can only hope he'll be dead before they do."

Archprofessor Elise walks over to a juice printer after a brief consultation with Leontine and Lexis. They all seem to want a drink.

"What's your *flavouwite*?" Archprofessor Elise asks Lexis. "Shouites or peachewine flavour?"

"Just between the two?"

"Yes... sadly."

"Shouites then..."

"Me too," says Lord Omicron.

"Me too," echoes the princess.

"And me," adds Archprofessor Lux Eden.

"Peachewine please," Sir Luminescence concludes the sudden orders for a cup of juice.

17 IT'S just a regular afternoon back in Sexat. With the clock ticking towards 9:00 t.m., Sextine and Dame Nissi are happy to arrive at the African pot shaped Nissi's Gallery Kitchen. It's way past their lunch time.

There are a lot of food tourists here in the restaurant. Some have come to eat something new, some to look at the wonderful food pictures on the wall, and some have simply come to argue the origin of the pictures.

Dame Nissi takes Sextine to a less populated corner and a waitress hands them a menu-screen.

"Welcome boss," the waitress greets Dame Nissi.

"Thank you."

The waitress walks away.

Dame Nissi scrolls thru the screen. She's just sane enough to ignore the growing distraction from a noisy wealthy family sitting next table. The unbearable noise comes from the main noisemakers – the sapien. The family's dog apparently owns a sapien and he's quite glad to torture it.

The dog barks once every four seconds, leaving the sapien in a noisy episode amidst the laughter and argument within the family of six.

"Yes dog... not understood dog... dog, bark some more," the dog's sapien keeps reciting.

"Let's be fast please," Dame Nissi says in discomfort.

"Why? No food here yet," Sextine responds.

"I need to get back home."

"I can't be fast eating the air."

"Yes, I know that. Just saying you should place your order quickly."

"You with the menu, momxy."

"And it's a law I click on it alone? Come on, tap tap..."

"What are you even going home to do?" Sextine asks. "I thought your days as a sahmxist are over."

"Oh hell no. Being a sahmxist is super awesome. Which momxy on the entire Oh wouldn't love to stay at home and earn digits?"

"But you need... just click on wegular, it should know what we want." Sextine is tired of watching her mother scroll aimlessly thru the menu-screen.

The two ladies quickly click on 'regular' and the menu-screen fades away.

"You said I need what?" Dame Nissi brings back the conversation.

"Yes, you've always told me about bubbling with people. But you too need fwends, lots of them too."

"Ha! Look who's talking..." "...Can you shut that thing up?" Dame Nissi complains about the dog's sapien. "And how many fwends exactly do you have?" she asks Sextine.

"Me?"

"No, the dog over there..."

"Dog, barks some more," Sextine mimics the dog's sapien.

"Stop that... seemesh."

"Well, I can still make fwends, but you getting old. I'm young... I have my entire life ahead of me."

"Oh sugar, I have eternal life ahead of me after I die of old age... I'll have plenty of time by then."

Sextine laughs quietly and shakes her head.

"What?" asks Dame Nissi just about when Sextine stops laughing.

Sextine looks at her and starts laughing again. Dame Nissi ignores her; the approaching waitress is a more promising sight. She's carrying a tray of covered dishes – we aren't sure what the ladies' regular is.

But we are certainly sure of what has sent the entire Epsilon crew to sleep – cups of juice too many. And as for Sir Nnia who had none, sleep is contagious and we are way too glad he's not awake outthinking the rest.

Lord Omicron does a Nissiesque awakening, he's been learning from the masters of Sudden Life. His wide open eyes are oozing of terror and fright. He must have seen the worse; he must be thinking the worst. He takes a quick look at everybody, his worrisome look intensifies.

"Oh no no," he laments as he scrambles towards Princess Lotem-Zeta. He places both hands on her chest immediately and tries to resuscitate her.

Princess Lotem-Zeta wakes up at once, looking a bit frightened and confused as she pushes Lord Omicron away.

"What are you doing? What's going on?" she asks in quick succession.

"You alive!"

"La duh? I was sleeping!"

"It must be a bad dweam, jeez, wake up all of you! Go to your beds if you want to sleep. You can't just be sleeping off here."

"You slept first..."

Lord Omicron ignores the princess and taps everybody up. "Come on, wake up."

"Are we at war?" Archprofessor Lux Eden stretches himself up.

"Have you ever been to war?" Lord Omicron asks.

"It starts with one alarm like yours."

Epsilon shakes briefly; it seems to have bumped into a rough atmosphere.

"Alert, manual contwol is inactive," Epsilon informs the crew.

"Are you not meant to be flying this thing?" Sir Nnia asks.

"I think we just entered the lost earth's atmosphere," Lord Omicron informs them as he walks quickly to the pilot's seat and buckles himself up.

He places his hand on the shuttle's steering and the alert message on the screen disappears.

"Welcome back, captain," Epsilon says.

Archprofessor Elise wakes Leontine up. "Earth!" she mouths to her.

Leontine quickly tries to unbuckle her seatbelt.

"No," Archprofessor Elise holds her back. "We have not landed yet," she signs.

"But I want to see," Leontine signs.

"You will see thru the window."

The spaceship gallops more than usual until they are now gliding thru clouds. This is certainly earth, and the sun is just about to rise here.

Lord Omicron lands the ship in an open space, a few meters away from a big dilapidated building; hopefully it will contain all the evidence the people back on Oh are dying to see.

Leontine unbuckles her seatbelt and looks properly thru the window, admiring the building. She confirms what we feel about the building as her eyes are set upon the old building signboard. The 'A' name of the bank has been washed away and 'BANK' and 'NIGERIA' have almost faded away.

Leontine feels the wind brush thru her back. She turns quickly and sees Epsilon's exit completing its slow opening. She skips off the shuttle immediately and Lexis and Archprofessor Elise converge on the spot where she was.

Archprofessor Elise looks at the building and thinks for a while. They could hear the footsteps of the others getting off Epsilon.

"The Afwica?" she mumbles.

"I wouldn't know. It says 'A... Bank, Nigewia'," Lexis responds.

"The Nigewia was in the Afwica."

"What is the Afwica?"

"Folktales... me's not exactly sure. You should visit your momxy's gallewy more often."

"Hmm..."

"Come on, evewybody is going down."

"Is it safe?" Lexis asks.

"Look..." Archprofessor Elise points at the happy Leontine spinning around the empty breezy space. "Does she look unsafe?"

"What if a gas is making her do that?"

"A happy gas then. Come on!" Archprofessor Elise rushes towards the exit.

"But popmy told them years ago that this planet may not be safe."

"Lexis, look awound... they've all gone down. They were only making excuses for not bwinging home any evidence."

"Wait, let me put on my boots."

Lexis' plea falls on straying ears as Archprofessor Elise alights the shuttle and joins the rest of the crew matching towards the bank.

Lexis hurries down with his boots in his hand. He steps on the sand, it feels quite different under his feet. Of course there's sand on Oh, but for a boy of his class who knows only hard floors, this is the first time he's stepping on sand. He presses his toes into the sand and wiggles them briefly. He's just about to smile before he recalls, 'it's not safe'; maybe the smile or the sand or both, we don't know. He sits on the exit steps of the spaceship and sinks his feet quickly into his boots. Firmly strapped, he runs towards the crew being led by the jovial Leontine.

"We should check that building out," Sir Nnia suggests. "We need to wander with purpose."

"I hate to imagine we'll jump over the building after we walk to it," Lord Omicron responds.

"I am just being sure your daughter knows too."

"Glad she didn't hear you, you'd kill her vibe."

"She cannot hear me," Sir Nnia stresses.

Lord Omicron looks sternly at him, still wearing a fading smile.

"Maybe we should split up," Sir Luminescence suggests. "I and um... Sir Nnia will go thwu the back of the building."

"Unwell dude, I am not going anywhere with you," Sir Nnia says as he moves closer to Leontine who is peeping thru the broken glass door.

"I can go with you," Archprofessor Elise tells Sir Luminescence.

"Maybe we shouldn't split up yet," Sir Luminescence responds disappointedly as he snaps at Archprofessor Lux Eden.

Lord Omicron walks into the bank and the rest of the crew follow him closely. The huge banking hall is covered in thick dust and a number of rusty chairs lying around; with damaged bulbs hanging from the ceiling and broken photographs dangling on the wall, a few of those shattered on the floor.

Lexis sneezes and this startles everyone. Leontine joins them in looking at Lexis.

"Sowie," Lexis calms them down and they all keep moving.

"What..." Leontine signs to him.

"I sneezed," Lexis signs back.

"I thought they saw a folf or something."

Lexis raises his shoulders.

Archprofessor Elise is now behind the counters. She picks up an old book and dusts it. She raises it for the rest to see.

"What is that?" asks Sir Luminescence.

"A book," Archprofessor Elise responds. "For noting down things... with a pen."

"I thought the pen is used to wyte in the book?" Sir Nnia asks.

"That's what she said, that is what it is," says Lord Omicron.

"Well it sounded diffewent."

"We go with the book?" asks Archprofessor Elise.

"Where... Oh?" Sir Nnia wonders.

"La duh?" exclaims Princess Lotem-Zeta and Sir Luminescence.

Archprofessor Lux Eden looks at a desk. A small calendar on the table suggests it was last used in October 2680. He reads a notice glued to the table. "This bank complies with cashless policy. You cannot take more than en one thousand or es ten."

"What is en one thousand and es ten?" Sir Nnia asks.

"This was a bank no doubt, perhaps a method of exchange back then. That N and S are not alphabets."

"Paper digits?"

"Money, paper money. That kind?" Sir Luminescence asks of the notice paper.

"That looks too big, not fanciful too."

"What of that book?"

"It is for diagwams... ok signatures, a witten password I guess," Archprofessor Elise says as she flips thru the book. "It has time in and time out."

"The book moves?" Sir Luminescence wonders.

"No it doesn't... the people who use it move."

Lexis helps Leontine to force a small metal cabinet open. There are several of them kept beside each banker's desk. The box contains few bundles of the Nigerian Naira and the US Dollars, another notebook, and several sheets of plain paper.

"Come see this," says Lexis as he pulls out a few cash.

Leontine picks up the notebook and a couple of plain sheets.

"Are we going with that too?" asks the pensive Sir Luminescence. "We don't need too many unsafe things on Epsilon."

"Nothing is unsafe," Lord Omicron assures them.

"But those papers are small. Best we go with the book Leontine is holding, "Princess Lotem-Zeta suggests.

"I think this is paper digits," says Lexis as he reads the notes. "Here, N one thousand, S ten."

"We'll take a few then," says Lord Omicron.

"No," Sir Nnia objects, "we should take all of them."

Some members of the crew suddenly look upwards; they must have heard a thud on the roof. Sir Nnia, Archprofessor Elise and the Rhos obviously heard nothing.

"Did you hear that?" asks Archprofessor Lux Eden.

"Hear what?" Lord Omicron wonders.

"I heard it too," the princess confirms.

"I heard nothing," says Sir Nnia.

Archprofessor Elise shakes her head, she heard nothing.

"I heard something too," Sir Luminescence declares.

"Maybe this isn't safe. Let's take one book and leave," Princess Lotem-Zeta suggests.

"No, we take evewything," Sir Nnia insists.

"Okay sir," Princess Lotem-Zeta agrees, to the surprise of Archprofessor Elise and Lord Omicron.

Sir Nnia could sense something has gone in his favour. The princess has never addressed him with so much respect. He stands tall, clears his throat and points at the crew members.

"All of you... kneel down," he commands.

"What's going on?" Archprofessor Elise asks quickly.

"It's just an order."

Lord Omicron is just about to giggle when he realises the rest of the crew are going on their knees.

Lexis is quick to understand the situation and he joins the rest in kneeling down. Perhaps the Gadhuvi is fully at work he thinks to himself.

"What are you doing, Sir Nnia?" asks the confused Lord Omicron.

"What am I doing? Or what have I done?"

"What is the meaning of this?"

"Shame even your son uses the Fahwenheit BEM. And yes, get it wight, I am in contwol now."

Archprofessor Elise walks slowly towards Lord Omicron.

"Is something coming?" Leontine signs at one in particular.

"Nothing me dear, we safe," Lord Omicron signs to her.

"Your daughter..."

"Leave her out of this," Lord Omicron interrupts Sir Nnia, cleverly hiding his mouth from Leontine. "She cannot hear us. Just cover your lips and leave her out of this, Sir Nnia. She is not twained in any combat skills either, so she won't pose any danger to you."

Sir Nnia obliges and covers his mouth while he speaks. Leontine suspects all sorts of things.

"I am doing this... concealing my mouth ish because I need you to focus here. Unless you pwefer we kill her first."

"Don't you dare!" Lord Omicron is about to charge at Sir Nnia.

"Better stand there... are you willing to kill your fwends too? Your son? Look at them. They will defend me, their king. THE KING OF OH. Say it!"

"The King of Oh," the kneeling crew proclaims.

Leontine need not be told again, she gets the idea.

"This is insane!" says Lord Omicron.

"Yes, sad as it is, welcome to my world, Omicwon Woe."

"Whatever you have done, it is demonic."

"No please, don't give thanks to the devil... this is just technology. The power one can get thwu the Gadhuvi is unimaginable. You and Elise are wenowned imagineers, bet you didn't see this coming."

"You bet wongly," says Archprofessor Elise. "Why are we not under your spell yet? Is Vexim beyond you?"

"We will come to that yunlade, we will. The last wall is locked with Dame Nissi Woe's thumb pwint, I am not even sure she knows about it."

"You don't know what you talking about," says Lord Omicron. "You have to do the hacking within the walls of Vexim HQ."

"Oh yes I do. I have been visiting Vexim. I have been hacking thwu it, quietly. At least now I know whose finger I need to chop off."

"You will not go close to my wife..."

"Listen Lord Omicwon, as these ones kneel before me, I can command them to jump to their deaths."

"Not if you are dead first..."

"And the whole of Oh will mourn me forwever. Can you comfort them? They will avenge my death against all Vexim users until I tell them to stop. How can I tell them to stop if I'm dead? How many are you willing to kill to get to the Fahwenheit HQ if you wish to hack back what I've done? Economically speaking, I doubt your Vexim customers have the numbers to defend themselves fwom my people."

Lord Omicron chuckles, "Your people."

"This is no time to share jokes anyway. I need you to fly Epsilon peacefully back to Oh, if you still love your family and your fwends. If you do anything stupid along the line, I will make your son fight you to the death. Don't exalt your importance, I only need you to fly us back to Oh, afterwards you can bwing your wife quietly to my HQ or I take her thumb myself."

"My wife uses Fahwenheit."

"Oh, that makes it perfect..."

"It doesn't mean you'll take Vexim. I will kill you myself and you will give up Fahwenheit before you die."

"I love how we thweaten each other peacefully. You are one lucky bastard though, a pwoduct of monopoly. If the knowledge of how to fly Epsilon is available on the BEM servers, you'd be dead by now... and for other weasons too, yes, I will love you to see what I want to do... I will let you watch and I will let you wish you can do anything about it. Do what you can do for now... which is flying us back to Oh, or you can choose between killing your son and letting him kill you. And you Elise, you should know you are of no use to me. Don't walk or bweathe funny or I'll hurl you off the shuttle personally."

"Can we get going?" Lord Omicron asks.

"Lol... of course. I am more eager than you are." Sir Nnia smiles and signals the rest of the crew to stand. "Quickly now, take all the evidence we need. Take the book, those little papers and get that weird clock too..." Sir Nnia points at the non-ticking 12-hour clock hanging on the wall.

Archprofessor Elise joins the rest in moving things back to Epsilon. Lord Omicron stands on the same spot, maintaining eye contact with Sir Nnia. Sir Nnia spots Leontine again and giggles.

"You know your daughter made an important observation back then, about the 'L' in your names..."

"Is that what this is all about?"

"Oh don't be silly. I set up the takeover sequence hours before we left Oh. I didn't know how long it will take, so, nothing new could have changed my decision to govern the entire people of Oh. If your daughter had more knowledge, maybe she would have guessed I'm a Lilyscent."

"You?" Lord Omicron spoofs. "A Lilyscent? Is that what this is all about? You don't even look like a Lilyscent. You are either deluded or you must be a bastard of the bastard of the bastard of the gwand bastard Lilyscent himself."

"He was the King of the Western Nations!"

"He was a bastard son of the king. He was not only a fake heir to the thwone but also unfit mentally to be king."

"When a man putting on an iron shoe stamps on your foot, it is the shoe that inflicts the pain, not just the stwength of the man. I am a Lilyscent and I am that man with iron shoes and iron gloves. I am equipped to govern Oh... I must not be fit to do it. Now Lord Omicwon, you will do well not to push me again or you'll feel the weight of my power. I still wish you'll survive this first phase of my takeover. I'll let you lead a small opposition party... Vexim party or something. Without opposition I'm sure I'd get way too bored being king."

"You not even king yet."

"Oh yes, King Sigma? Shame he and the palace guards use the special Gobbet BEMs... it is a waste of time to hack that little company just to gain a handful of the King's household."

"What do you intend to do?"

"Stop questioning me like I'm your child!" Sir Nnia roars. "I speak, you listen, no more questions."

"You don't have to keep emphasizing that you are now in charge, otherwise you are not in charge..."

"Go and power up Epsilon," Sir Nnia instructs Lord Omicron.

"Sure," Lord Omicron resigns towards the spaceship.

"We are leaving!" Sir Nnia announces to the crew.

Sir Nnia takes a last look of the vast empty land and nods before joining the rest of the crew inside the spaceship. The door closes and the shuttle is powered on at Lord Omicron's command. Sir Nnia sits as the co-pilot this time, exchanging seats with Princess Lotem-Zeta.

Epsilon floats a few meters above the ground and Lord Omicron flies the ship slowly.

"What are you doing?" Sir Nnia asks immediately.

"Cwuising awound town."

"This isn't a town. Just launch this thing out of this lifeless planet. I don't have time for this."

"Sure," Lord Omicron agrees. "Epsilon," he calls to the machine.

"Yes captain?" Epsilon responds.

"Launch shuttle."

"Launching in fifteen seconds," Epsilon begins a launch countdown.

The shuttle stops moving and the much needed rocket boosters, four in all, open up from underneath the spaceship. The rocket boosters begin to burn their propellants quickly and aggressively, generating the liftoff thrust required to propel Epsilon into space. The fire and dust from underneath the shuttle engulfs the dilapidated building and beyond. The shuttle is soon in space and Lord Omicron keys in the travel coordinates.

"What is the final destination?" Sir Nnia demands to know.

"Oh of course."

"Where exactly in Oh?"

"Genia... the spaceport?"

"Land anywhere but the spaceport... land miles away from it. Folks there use Vexim, thanks to you. You know the consequences of disobeying me... someone's gonna die. Don't twy any stupid manoeuvre of this ship, don't even land in any neighbourhood or close by, do you understand me, Lord Omicwon?"

"I do."

"Lotem-Zeta," Sir Nnia calls on the princess.

"Sir?" she responds.

"Get me a glass of water."

Lord Omicron shakes his head in humiliation as Princess Lotem-Zeta goes about getting Sir Nnia a glass of water. There is nothing more in his mind other than how best to reverse the effect of the Gadhuvi. He's aggressively blocking the thoughts of his dear wife serving Sir Nnia in this manner. Dame Nissi and Sextine still use the Fahrenheit no doubt, but he's wondering why Lexis is being controlled by Sir Nnia. He looks at Leontine and Archprofessor Elise, quite glad to have them on his side of people with free will. Turning towards Lexis with his eyes full of pity, he gets a bit confused why Lexis just winked at him. To Lord Omicron, that's Sir Nnia winking thru his eyes, horribly disgusting. But that's Lexis first try to let his father know he's not being controlled.

18 BACK in the Rhos' Mansion, Dame Nissi and Sextine are naturally not aware their BEMs are poised to obey and defend 'King Nnia Den-Lilyscent' as it interprets it to their brains. In Dame Nissi's room, Sextine is patiently trying to talk her mother to bed, both ignoring the plate of brown cookies between them. We could sense both ladies have been having a good time. Both lying on their backs, Dame Nissi, however, couldn't stop thinking about Leontine, she wouldn't stop talking about her either and surely Sextine shouldn't be willing to hear more.

The name "Leontine" from Dame Nissi is followed by a frustrating bang on the bed by Sextine.

"What now?" Dame Nissi asks her.

"If people age each time you call them for nothing, Leontine will surpass the twenty-four years that machine estimated she'll live."

"That's not a nice to say!"

"No momxy, I don't mean it that way..."

"Whatever you meant..."

"Just saying I wished talking about her will make her stay longer... I do love Leontine."

"I know babe... and I know God is with Leontine."

Sextine sits up quickly with a half smile, staring funny at Dame Nissi.

"What is it now again?" Dame Nissi asks Sextine who sniggers in response. "What, God is with Leontine. Did I say something out of place?" Dame Nissi asks, now wondering if she said something *religulous* enough to warrant the look on Sextine's face.

"God cannot change what the Baby Scanner has said," says Sextine.

"You kidding me or what?" Dame Nissi sits up quickly, pushing Sextine back to the bed.

"Is there even God?" Sextine asks as she relaxes on her back.

Dame Nissi stretches her neck to look properly into Sextine's eyes. "Sextine? How can you... do you even listen to your Sunday messages?"

"Half of the time? Not at all... it's all just job opportunities for the saints. There's no God," Sextine declares.

"Why would you say that? So who cweated you?"

"Momxy... we all just pop out, don't we?"

"No, big head. We don't just pop out. We come thwu God's plan."

"We came via evolution."

"Oh don't start that ish with me. You evolved fwom what now... a Ben?"

"That thing is a monkey, and no, we came fwom something way smaller than that."

"Okay Sextine, you are an Auto Imagineer, you made a car sometime ago..."

"Yes..."

"So how will you feel if I believe you actually didn't make the car... that the car just popped out of a pwoton of irons and plastics?"

"Are we talking about God's feelings now? Let him exist first."

"That is where I'm heading to... I don't know your terminologies as an engineer but sure you made that car engine? You set the things in place to function the way they do... the gear, the steerwing, the gwavity details for its floatability, all the connections in the car... the car didn't just evolve and thought to itself, 'I'll have seats in me because a human may want to float me, I'll have a speedometer on display because humans may love that information, I'll have bweaks, wipers and solar energy optimizers'... no the car didn't think of all that, you thought of all that."

"Yes momxy, all imagineers and engineers do. People see us make these things."

"Just because you don't get to watch cweation doesn't mean nobody is cweating things. Then you are a doctor too. You must have seen the body. Placing it side by side with a car you still think something as complex as the human body just decided to evolve out of something 'way smaller'. So these things said to themselves, 'let's become the heart, then we beat, we'll pump blood whenever blood evolves fwom wherever it will come. Let's have an intestine... no see, best we come together and form systems, let the intestines not stay on their own and just feed on food... what is food? Don't bother, foods are yet to evolve. When they do, the new systems we'll form will love to earn energy fwom food. Oh let's become male and female, then let something in the male of us evolve to something that will pwoduce something we'll call sperm. This sperm should house info on how to form another of us which it will take to the female of us who should have some info in the ova. Let's have eyes to see. To see? What is see? To see what? When we evolve into eyes, you'll see. Let us..."

"Okay okay momxy... yes, maybe just yes... someone, God, does make humans and stuff, but why should I believe he's higher than us? Or even smarter?"

"Dummy! At least your cars can't sleep with each other and give birth to other cars."

"Aha-ha! Momxy!" Sextine laughs.

"Let no one deceive you my fwend. There is God and that God is surely with Leontine."

"Then He isn't with you..."

"Oh Sextine, where are you fwom?"

"You and popmy had sex, ain't it?"

"Oh shatap!" Dame Nissi falls back into the bed, shaking her head as Sextine laughs hysterically.

Back in the quiet spaceship, Sir Nnla still has things under control, keeping a close eye on Lord Omicron. Archprofessors Lux Eden and Elise Leo Elise are sleeping on their seats. Lord Omicron stands on his feet.

"What is it?" asks Sir Nnia.

"I am thirsty."

"You just had water five minutes ago."

"I had juice five minutes ago. Now, I want water."

Lord Omicron takes a step forward but he's halted by the excruciating voice of Lexis. Confused and in pain, he naturally blames Sir Nnia.

"We need to talk," the voice says to him.

Lord Omicron clutches his ears and bends in agony.

"Popmy, it's me," the voice says again.

"No!" Lord Omicron screams. "Stop it, you killing me!"

"I am not doing anything to you," Sir Nnia protests his innocence, quite acknowledging that Lord Omicron isn't pretending about the pain he's feeling.

"Just make it stop!" Lord Omicron yells, forcing Elise and Lux Eden up from their sleep.

"I just want to talk to you popmy... focus, you can coordinate this thing."

Lord Omicron shakes his head vigorously and groans.

"Popmy, don't let him know it's me... only you can hear me."

"Just stop it, damn it!"

"What is this madness?" Sir Nnia wonders.

"Get me out of here!" Lord Omicron roars.

"Get you to where? We in the middle of nowhere," Sir Nnia reminds him.

"Popmy please, listen to me," Lexis' voice pleads again.

"What are you doing to me?"

"Dude, I'm not doing anything to you," says Sir Nnia.

"Popmy, it is my new work, the bwain whispewer... I can speak diwectly to your bwain thwu the BEM," Lexis explains.

"The hell? Have you ever heard things this way before? Just stop!" Lord Omicron then turns to Sir Nnia and screams, "Just get me out of here now!"

Sir Nnia giggles and shakes his head. "You can't play a fast one on me Omicwon."

"Popmy okay, twy and think of a song, it might help," Lexis advises.

"NO!" Lord Omicron roars again. "JUST STOP IT NOW!"

Lord Omicron suddenly feels a bit better. He looks up at Lexis cunningly and sees him looking lifeless on his seat. Those last words Lord Omicron roared were only heard by Lexis. He had successfully responded thru the brain whisperer Lexis launched. Lexis barely had a second to process those words before passing out. He certainly doesn't have a good threshold for pain as Lord Omicron does.

"Lexis?" Lord Omicron mutters and dashes towards him.

"Mad man!" Sir Nnia exclaims. "He's only sleeping!"

"Get me some water!" Lord Omicron orders Sir Nnia as he unbuckles Lexis' seatbelt and taps his cheeks.

"Um," Sir Nnia is unmoved, "I'm the king here... help me out."

Archprofessor Elise tries to get up but Sir Nnia shakes his finger at her and she sits back down, looking worriedly at Lexis.

Sir Nnia reluctantly signals Princess Lotem-Zeta to get water for Lord Omicron. She moves quickly towards the water filter.

"Is any of you a medical doctor?" Sir Nnia asks.

"I am," Archprofessor Lux Eden reveals.

"Go help the kid."

Archprofessor Lux Eden moves quickly to Lexis and shoves Lord Omicron out of the way. He checks for pulse on Lexis' neck and puts him on the floor before proceeding to perform a cardiopulmonary resuscitation. Everyone ignores the princess when she arrives with the cup of water.

"What happened to him?" Lord Omicron asks.

"I wouldn't know by just looking at him," Archprofessor Lux Eden responds.

"What kinda doc are you?"

"Let him do his job!" Sir Nnia tells Lord Omicron.

"Get the twauma kit," Archprofessor Lux Eden instructs no one in particular.

Archprofessor Elise reacts first.

A couple more pumps on Lexis' chest by Archprofessor Lux Eden and he suddenly responds with a cough and a soft moan.

"What happened to him?" Sir Nnia asks this time.

"Exhaustion... maybe," responds Archprofessor Lux Eden, handing Lexis the cup of water the princess is carrying.

Lexis sits up and sips a little water.

"Alert, manual contwol is inactive," Epsilon announces.

"Alwighty then... buckle up!" Sir Nnia orders the crew. "We home?" he asks Lord Omicron as they all strap themselves back on their seats.

"Maybe," Lord Omicron responds. "No sign of it yet."

"I want to see where we are on the map," Sir Nnia requests.

"Space is not on the map."

"Put up the map, I want to see us once we enter Oh's atmosphere."

"Will do..."

"Do it now... don't forget you can't get close to the spaceport in Genia."

"How about we land outside Sexat entirely?"

"No Omicwon... we land in Genia."

"Evewywhere is close to the spaceport."

"No, stupid, your house is not close to the spaceport."

"There is no space there to land this thing. How about the space before the Jungle of Zion?"

"Fair enough, far enough. I want to see it on the map."

"You will see it."

Sir Nnia keeps his eyes on Lord Omicron as he punches in a set of commands into Epsilon's screen. The spaceship wobbles briefly and Sir Nnia can't hide his anxiousness to stay in control.

"What was that?" he asks Lord Omicron.

"Change in density... we just entered Oh."

"On the map, captain... I want to see it now."

Lord Omicron taps a button and a map pops up on Sir Nnia's side of the screen.

"Where are we?"

"Still out of scope... but shortly, any moment now."

Sir Nnia's eyes find a right strategy monitoring Lord Omicron's fingers and the map simultaneously.

"Ticking eyes syndwome," Lord Omicron mutters.

"Say what?"

"Your eyes... ticking eyes syndwome."

Sir Nnia hisses. "Move this thing faster."

"It is fast... unless you want us to catch fire."

A red dot suddenly appears on the map, covering a lot of distance swiftly.

"There!" Lord Omicron points at the dot.

"I can see it. We appwoaching Sexat now, yes?"

"Yeah..."

The map zooms in and Sir Nnia points fanatically at the screen. "There is Zion! That's the space before the jungle."

"I can see it," Lord Omicron responds calmly this time.

"Yeah yeah, land it alwcady."

The night sky in Oh is a bit brighter this time. The environment is glowing from the rays of light emitted from above, though it's only enough to cast a dull green illumination of objects. There's a region of the jungle reflecting light back into the sky – the Youlv Ocean is hence easily located, and avoided.

Epsilon hovers for some seconds before descending gradually midway between the Jungle of Zion and a highway. Each tree in the jungle is almost four times the size of Epsilon; remarkably tall. It is a waste of time trying to see the treetop, the mind normally loses concentration.

The entire crew are outside now. Archprofessor Elise stands closely behind Lord Omicron, rubbing her arms with her palms. No doubt Youlv is chilling the air as it comes thru the jungle.

The rest of the crew stand with Sir Nnia, each carrying a small black bag probably containing the evidences from the lost earth, and Lexis is still theatrically pretending to be controlled by Sir Nnia Den.

Leontine is carefree. For one, the trees and the jungle seem to catch her attention. She moves cautiously towards the thick Jungle of Zion.

"We'll go this way," Sir Nnia points towards the highway. "We'll walk while we wait for my car to come."

"Where are we heading to?" Lord Omicron asks.

"That's none of your business. As a matter of fact, you and Elise should join your little miss and head that way," Sir Nnia points to the jungle and then collects the bag Lexis is holding. "And Lexis will make sure you all head that way," he adds.

Lexis nods and steps forward, ushering Lord Omicron to turn towards the jungle.

"What will we be doing in there?" Lord Omicron asks.

"Who cares? Declare war against me or something... begin your own tale of fierce opposition... now get going. Don't forget, your son will defend me until he dies. Is that not so, Lexis?"

"Yes sir!" Lexis shouts.

"Don't disappoint me Omicwon. See this as an opportunity to be my political enemy, at least before the fall of Vexim. I'd advise you also take your BEM off. I don't want to get bored by you begging to please me. It is time to unite Oh under one King. If your face is seen anywhere in the city, you'll be seized by the Fahwenheit citizens, unless you plan to shed the blood of innocent people."

"How can I be your main opposition if you are sending me on exile this way?"

"What, you want a farewell party?"

"No, if you desire a challenge, I can't do anything fwom the jungle."

"This man, should I now hug you and walk you into my palace? The last time I checked, the Sigmas exiled the Lilyscents. How come I've made it to the top yet again?" Sir Nnia taps his head, proudly smart.

"The Sigmas took away your name fwom the line of succession. They didn't banish you fwom any city or state."

"Call it whatever you please. Take your followers and leave."

Lord Omicron quietly looks on as the Sir Nnia-led team walk towards the highway, vanishing gradually from his sights. He is far from confused or dejected, simply waiting for them to go far enough.

"Popmy, let's go towards the jungle," says Lexis, "don't know what Leontine is doing over there."

Lord Omicron and Archprofessor Elise look at Leontine, they couldn't agree any better with that suggestion. Leontine is almost stepping into the thick of things, her feet already sinking into green shrubs.

"Leontine!" Lord Omicron calls out to her.

"She can't hear you," Lexis reminds Lord Omicron.

Lord Omicron leads the way as they jog to Leontine. He pulls her back from the edge of the jungle and she turns, smiling at them.

"This place is so nice," she signs. "Should we go in?"

"Not now," Lord Omicron signs back.

Leontine dims her eyes in disappointment.

"What do we do about him?" Archprofessor Elise whispers to Lord Omicron.

"Who? Lexis?"

"Shh..."

"He's with us..."

"I was only acting," Lexis adds.

"Oh... I wouldn't have guessed that."

"Yes, that shows the lapses on the whole Gadhuvi stuff."

"How?" Lord Omicron and Archprofessor Elise ask.

"Sir Nnia is only aware of those he contwols simply by them obeying his commands. There is no confirmation whatsoever or a sign or something. It means anyone can go on pwetending to be his subject, all you need do is to be convincing in your act."

"As long as he doesn't know you use Vexim," Archprofessor Elise chips in.

"Exactly."

"It still means he'll attempt to contwol Vexim," says Lord Omicron.

"No popmy, I know about Gadhuvi, I did a lot of things to pwotect our clients against it. Intwoducing that viwus to the system will only make the BEMs initiate the self-destwuct pwogwam I made."

"So he can't takeover Vexim?"

"Yes, I'm confident he can't. We shouldn't bother about that. Even if he gets momxy's thumb for the last password and stuff, it wouldn't work."

"It doesn't mean I'd leave my wife at his mercy."

"She'll be loyal to him, momxy uses Fahwenheit."

"Somebody is contwolling BEM users?" Leontine signs in confusion.

Well, this slightly surprises everyone.

"Yes," Archprofessor Elise and Lexis sign back.

"Just Fahrenheit users," Lord Omicron signs. "Listen Lexis, stay here. The day will soon be bwight, I have to go and get your momxy and Sextine."

"We can't stay here!"

"I can't take you all along, it's dangewous. I'll be back as soon as I have your momxy and Sextine. You can bwing your PES over."

"That will take some time... something must have eaten us before it gets here."

"There is nothing but plants in this jungle."

"Can't exempt them either..."

"I have to go. There's a teleport system nearby. I saw it on the map. I'll fly over there."

"You fly?" Lexis wonders.

"I'll use weaponized digitizers."

"That is insane. You'll fall off the sky," says Archprofessor Elise.

"Not when you have many of them."

"How many minutes can you make?"

"I have enough to make an hour."

"You'll keep activated one evewy thwee seconds?"

"Ten seconds. I'm a Sexatian official... top secwet weapons."

There's absolute silence, searching eyes trying to encourage one another. Lord Omicron places his hands on his children's shoulders.

"I will be fine."

"What are you going to do?" Leontine signs.

"Something dangerous," Lord Omicron signs. "Need to go and get your momxy and your sister."

"Nothing will be more dangerous than being near her when she wakes up from a bad dream," Leontine signs.

They all manage to giggle briefly before the tense mood sets in again.

"Sapien," Lord Omicron reactivates his sapien.

"Sapien activated," the sapien responds.

"Weapons mode."

"Say again boss."

"Weapons mode," Lord Omicron reiterates.

"Weapons mode activated," the sapien responds, quickly popping up two black screens. One contains hundreds of small red circles and the other requesting for a password.

Lord Omicron picks out one red circle and stretches it into a thin line of thirty centimetres. He places the line across his stomach and picks out another circle from the sapien. After placing six lines, Lord Omicron looks at the expectant faces of his children and Archprofessor Elise.

"Set to go."

"Just six?" Lexis asks.

"Yeah, that's one minute. The teleport system is just over there. I can get there in thirty seconds," Lord Omicron explains.

"Just add more... benefit of doubt," Archprofessor Elise suggests.

"I have thirty seconds benefitting any doubt..."

"I doubt that will be beneficial. Please, just add more," Archprofessor Elise pleads.

"I can... alwight... there..." Lord Omicron decides to pick out one more digitizer. He stretches it and grins at them as he places it on his chest.

Lord Omicron types in a four-lettered password on the second screen and it reveals a schematic image of himself and his environment. He looks at Lexis one more time and nods. "Get your PES down here... maybe you too Elise."

Lord Omicron puts his finger on one of the digitizers' image on the second screen and a ten seconds countdown is initiated. He drags his image up from the ground and his real self is lifted from the ground simultaneously, so high into the night sky he could barely see those he's leaving behind. He swipes the image forward and his flight begins. The next ten seconds weaponized digitizer is activated once the current one expires. The quick flight is quite smooth, save for the transitions from one WGD to another. He's unto the teleport system within forty-five seconds and his next destination will be his mansion, to rescue Sextine and of course his wife, Dame Nissi.

19 DAME Nissi is apparently unaware of any danger coming her way. She's sitting relaxed outside her home, though she's a bit surprised to see a table before her and indistinct murmurings getting closer behind her. She turns quickly to see a crowd of people sitting and chatting on similar tables, munching and swallowing whatever it is they are munching and swallowing.

She stands up slowly and when she's just about to take a closer look at the crowd, she's startled by the sound of a man simply clearing his throat. She turns to the man and finds him covered in darkness and pointing an empty plate at her. She takes a second look at the plate, there's no doubt this is the exact plate she had on her bed a while ago.

"That's me plate, isn't it?"

"But of course, your own plate of yummy worms!"

Dame Nissi looks at the plate again and sees it's indeed filled with living worms. That's far from anything yummy.

The man reveals himself, a familiar face to her, probably the same man who had her book, and he's beginning to look like Sir Nnia more and more.

"You again?!" exclaims Dame Nissi.

"I can see you keep record of evil," the man says.

"Who dash you evil? You just a common thief..."

"...but that's evil..."

"...and that word is wecord! I don't have time to keep telling you. Why is evewybody eating worms?"

"They asked for a plate... the same way you did."

"No no, you gave it to them. They don't know, do they?"

"Do you?"

"What... do me what?"

"Take your plate, Madam Legacy, and chew!"

"Me name is Dame Nissi, not Madam Legacy."

"Alright Legacy, Nissi whatever... eat now."

"I am not touching that thing..."

"Oh yeah?" the man says with his eyebrows raised, lifting up his cheeks for a broad smile. A smile that spells nothing but success.

Dame Nissi wonders as she looks at her heavy left hand to behold it carrying the plate of worms.

"NO!" she screams. "GET THIS OFF!" She flaps her hand vigorously but neither plate nor the worms in it fall out of place.

Dame Nissi's look goes from 'utterly surprised' to 'totally impossible' when she watches her own right hand grab a spoonful of worms.

"Mm," she shakes her head, tight lipped, imagining the worse. "No no please!" she pleads. "I cannot eat this!" she adds after realising her voice slows down her moving hands.

"But why?" the man asks her calmly.

"My teeth, these two in fwont... they normally shut on their own. It... it may... it won't let it pass, see?" Dame Nissi grins anxiously, her eyeballs bouncing from her left hand to her right hand to the man's eyes as she shows him evidence of her acclaimed self-protective tightly locked teeth.

"Maybe we should just pull them off," the man suggests.

He reaches swiftly for Dame Nissi's upper central incisors before she could finish shaking her head in objection to his suggestion. He places two fingers on both teeth and we could feel them sticking together.

Dame Nissi groans in pain as the man pulls the teeth to himself. But this is taking longer than expected. The teeth elongates to about five centimetres before exposing its worm-roots. The awful sight is just about too much for Dame Nissi to comprehend quietly, and the huge decibels come ringing in. If this is the measure of comprehension, Dame Nissi's scream will provide wisdom for all mankind.

Dame Nissi sits up at once on her bed, her eyes totally petrified, but her mouth eager to continue the scream she started in her dream. Her voice filters thru the front door and alerts Lord Ōmicron who has just received his metallic PES from a hanger drone. He comprehends that scream to be Sir Nnia attacking his wife. Quickly now, he begins to put on his PES.

Dame Nissi is still sitting on the bed, now with teary eyes; she thumps her hands on the bed in frustration. She now wags her finger at the plate of cookies on her bed. "This is your fault," she whimpers, trying hard not to sob any further.

"Alert boss," Dame Nissi's sapien speaks up, "nobody is at the door."

Dame Nissi looks bamboozled, sucking briefly on the inside of her lower lip, she could taste the faultiness of that report.

"Thanks for the heads-up," She says. "And bwing my PES."

"PES on the way, boss," the sapien confirms.

Dame Nissi pats her eyes dry as she watches a section of her ceiling slide open, making way for her latex performance enhancing suit to descend into the room. She's up on her feet at once and puts on the PES, leaving no part of her body visible.

Dame Nissi hears a thud outside her room just as she's about to open the door. 'The intruder must be coming for me' she thinks to herself before standing beside the door, waiting for the intruder to swing the door open and hide her properly. This intruder, of course, is Lord Omicron.

The door swings open and it stops when it rests upon Dame Nissi's busty chest. The PES certainly made them appear incredibly more than normal. Lord Omicron is obviously tiptoeing but Dame Nissi's PES aids her in listening to his *toesteps*. It seems to have stopped, best time to attack!

Dame Nissi emerges from the back of the door, walking quietly and swiftly towards Lord Omicron, and if she had any serious plans of attacking this intruder from behind, those plans fizzle out when Lord Omicron suddenly turns around. His PES is certainly more intimidating when those green eyes are set upon his enemy. Those eyes quickly turn red with Lord Omicron assuming a boxing combat posture.

Dame Nissi wouldn't surrender easily. She musters her own intimidating moves. She moulds her hands into fists, raising them beside her chest. She swings her hands down and her PES is lighted up by fire. Lord Omicron is rather impressed by her equipment.

"Inferno-PES," Lord Omicron nods. "My wife has one of those..."

"I didn't know a petty thief can maintain a wife," Dame Nissi responds.

"I'm not a petty thief! How sure am I you didn't steal that PES fwom my wife?"

"These are mine!" Dame Nissi proclaims as she charges towards Lord Omicron with her fire-lighted fists.

"Wait," Lord Omicron attempts to dialogue more. He wants to know what and who he's fighting against.

Dame Nissi's momentum now is all out for action, enough said. She throws in a couple of punches but Lord Omicron's PES effectively swerves him out of the way. These suits are smart enough to know when they are needed, and Dame Nissi's is no different. A swift punch is on the way and she's certain she didn't engineer this one. Like a spectator in a boxing match, Dame Nissi watches her own fist move across to Lord Omicron and lands a staggering punch on his chin. The slightly dazed Lord Omicron leans backwards but his right leg reacts quickly with a low kick between Dame Nissi's thighs.

She or her PES, we can't tell who is more embarrassed by that move. The inferno-Nissi team responds with a feminine slap on Lord Omicron's heavily protected cheek. This switches off his red eyes for a second. Dame Nissi rolls in a six-combo punch to his chin and elbows him down into the bed. She bends over to pick him up but Lord Omicron shatters the plate of cookies on her head and pushes her away. Dame Nissi calmly flicks fire at Lord Omicron who rolls out of the way, leaving the bed engulfed by the increasing fire.

Lord Omicron's PES surely loves to get into the fight but Lord Omicron can make it flee, he doesn't like playing with fire. The aggression from Dame Nissi cannot be overemphasized. It will take great courage from both man and PES to stand an angry pack of fire.

The fire alarm in the house sounds and the sprinklers pour water on just the burning bed and the inflamed Dame Nissi. The water following her from above causes her to lose concentration and she runs into the fist of Lord Omicron, forcing her PES to turn off the fire.

Dame Nissi crawls up the wall to recollect herself with Lord Omicron standing still and waiting patiently. Lord Omicron could swear he can recognise his own wife's backside. Those curves cannot be mistaken, not even inside those latex suits.

"Nissi?" voices Lord Omicron as he pulls out a weaponized digitizer.

"Oh don't give me that!" Dame Nissi responds angrily. "You came into my house... did you come to attack Adonai?"

Lord Omicron throws the digitizer on the unsuspecting Dame Nissi and uses the image on his screen to pull her mask off.

"I didn't come to attack you, it's me!"

"It's who?"

"Me..." Lord Omicron slides open his own mask, revealing his troubled face.

Dame Nissi's anger gets a little more emotional. She bites on her teeth with her eyes almost shut in vexation as she crawls down slowly from the wall.

Lord Omicron walks over to her to receive her from the wall, and give her a kiss? Well, that doesn't happen. Dame Nissi is not having the same sense of urgency as Lord Omicron who is on a mission to save Oh from Sir Nnia.

Dame Nissi bites him on the lip and throws in four punches into his stomach in quick succession, following it up with a massive head butt. Lord Omicron falls on his knees, his hand clutching on his forehead. Dame Nissi manages to stand over him, caressing her own forehead – more like a congratulatory pat on her forehead.

"You left without saying goodbye!" Dame Nissi complains emotionally.

"I don't think your BEM is okay," Lord Omicron whispers.

"Is that... that's what you have to say?" Dame Nissi grinds thru her teeth.

Lord Omicron crawls quickly and stands behind Dame Nissi. He sticks a WGD on her BEM and tumbles away to avoid her swinging arm as she turns to hit him off. Lord Omicron's sapien pops up a screen containing Dame Nissi's image and he pulls off the BEM from her head.

"Vous cet homme fou!" Dame Nissi exclaims in French, all to the awe of Lord Omicron. *"Est-ce la façon de dire désole?"*

Dame Nissi is basically demanding an apology. Lord Omicron takes another look at the BEM in his hand, hoping to see an explanation why his wife's natural language is suddenly French.

"Holy gates of Heaven," Lord Omicron mutters, "woman, are you Fwench?"

"No baldy, I'm Nissi, I'm not Fwench. My family happen to speak Fwench for many genewations before I met you."

"You were not alive many genewations ago... and you know I'm your husband, wight?"

"Of course I know you!"

"So you go awound calling me baldy?"

"No, I don't go awound calling you baldy," protests Dame Nissi as she turns in circles before she stands still again and adds, "I was standing exactly here calling you a baldy, baldy!"

"Hmm... I am not even bald."

"Exactly! You stay complaining about something that is not, while I'm complaining about something that is, something that was, something you did, something you will still do!"

"Ok, just calm down Nissi..."

"Omicwon stop telling me to calm down! *Vous aimez conduite moi fou!" {You love driving me crazy}.*

"Okay, yes. But I have something to tell you..."

"Yes?" Dame Nissi is all ears.

"Leontine..."

"Where's me baby?" Dame Nissi asks immediately.

"She's fine... she's in Zion."

"ZION! The bloody jungle!" Dame Nissi flares up.

"She's safe... she's with Lexis," Lord Omicron informs her.

"You left Leontine with Lexis and you think she's safe? Leontine contwols Lexis, she'll endanger him too. She must be leading them into the shadow of death as we speak."

"Elise is with them though..."

"Aha-ha! Elise... is there a human version of her now or is it the clown that you musing about?"

"We need to go and get them, although they are not in any danger as we speak. Sir Nnia has taken over the BEMs of all Fahwenheit users. He'll be coming for you."

"Me? What for?"

"I locked the last stage of Vexim's password with your fingerpwint."

"My... my own? My fingerpwint? He should get it however you got it because I know I didn't give it you. It's cute how you've just quietly informed me that you may have singlehandedly put my life in danger..."

"It's not like that Nissi..."

"I need my BEM back because clearly I've forgotten how to walk out on you."

"Lol... you've never walked out on me... you do walk me out."

"I'll learn that..."

Lord Omicron smiles. "Tell me something, have you, since you were born, seen any lady as beautiful as yourself? Then maybe I'll conclude I'm being biased with my assessment."

"Yes, I have. Leontine and Sextine."

"Sextine..." Lord Omicron has just been reminded of the other half of his mission. He won't dump the chance of reconciling with Dame Nissi anyway. "Yes," he continues, "but your voice, your hair, your eyes..."

"You don't love me anymore I guess."

"Nissi, how can you say that?"

"Avec ma bouche," {with my mouth}, Dame Nissi responds sarcastically. "Do I need to explain how people say things again?"

"You know I love you..."

"Then leave the damn eyes and hair alone and talk about me, talk to me..."

"Why are you like this?" Lord Omicron asks with a smile.

"Why is who like how?" Dame Nissi raises her shoulders.

"You. Even twying to tell you how much I love you..."

"...and how I love you too..."

"...yes, it has to be an argument..."

"I don't want to hear the love talk."

"What do you want me to say?" Lord Omicron wonders.

"Oh son of Woe..."

"Okay, I'm sowie..."

"Are you?" Dame Nissi asks as she gives Lord Omicron a soft push towards the wall. "Or you just saying it because you have to. So what are you sowie about?"

"Evewything."

"What is evewything?" Dame Nissi asks, placing her hand on Lord Omicron's stomach.

"I'm sowie I left for the lost earth without saying goodbye."

"That's not even where it all started!"

"Why? We need to get as far as you waking up fwom a bad dweam?"

"Of course! That's the closest starting point. I know I've complained about you guys standing awound me when I'm sleeping... it gives me nightmares."

"I am vewy sowie, honestly, forgive me. You will forgive me, wight?"

"Hmm," Dame Nissi tries to smother the smile invading her face. She drags her hand from her husband's stomach to his face and squeezes his arm with her other hand, pressing him hard against the wall.

"Slow down girl," Lord Omicron mutters.

"*Oui capitaine*," Dame Nissi whispers.

"I have missed you badly."

"Hmm," Dame Nissi sighs again, "now I don't know if I should let you kiss me."

"I'd love to," Lord Omicron says softly as he moves his head towards Dame Nissi.

The time apparently stands still for the couple to have their passionate makeup kiss.

"Sweet baby Jesus!" Lord Omicron exclaims as he breaks the kiss. "We have to get Sextine."

"Why? Is she important now?"

"Yes," he replies, leading Dame Nissi towards the door. "She uses Fahwenheit. Sir Nnia might take her hostage."

"And you've been here kissing," Dame Nissi nags.

Lord Omicron pulls the door open and Dame Nissi goes back to pick up her PES mask. Lord Omicron steps outside the room and stands on the spot when he sees Sextine standing in the hallway with her eyes innocently fixed on him.

Dame Nissi comes running out of the room, trying to put on her mask at the same time. She barges into Lord Omicron who is standing right in front of the room and the couple go crashing into the opposite door.

"What are you doing?" Lord Omicron asks as he helps Dame Nissi push herself up from him.

"Was putting on my mask, sowie."

"Why would you want to do that?"

"What... I'm all PESed up," Dame Nissi responds as she fits in her mask properly. "I alweady said sowie too."

"Sextine is just standing out there in the hallway," Lord Omicron informs his wife as he stands to his feet.

"Well, let's go get her."

"Didn't you hear me? I said she's just standing out there."

"I don't get... I said we should go and get her then... wasn't that the plan?"

"She's just standing still, motionless, emotionless, looking cwazy at me."

"Me Gee, is Sir Nnia contwolling her?" Dame Nissi whispers.

"Yes, maybe," Lord Omicron responds as he pulls out a weaponized digitizer.

"No no, you won't use that thing on her."

"What now... we should go give her a kiss?"

"We don't know for sure she's being contwolled."

"Nissi, she uses Fahwenheit."

"She's our daughter!" Dame Nissi whispers strongly.

"With Sir Nnia's thinking. Just imagine her to be that evil genius Sir Nnia."

"She's not even as tall as Sir Nnia!" Dame Nissi argues, standing behind Lord Omicron who is already coming out to the hallway.

Well, we are not surprised; Sextine is still standing there, same posture, same eyeball location. Dame Nissi has a bad feeling about this. A good reason is that she trusts Sextine to act weirdly even with her normal senses. She holds Lord Omicron's arm strongly to prevent him from throwing the digitizer at Sextine.

"Sextine?" Dame Nissi calls out to her. "Is something wong?"

"Nothing's wong. You? That's you momxy, wight?" Sextine asks.

"Yes, it's me. I'm fine. This is popmy as you can see. He's back fwom the lost earth."

"Yeah..."

"Why are you standing there looking at us?" Dame Nissi asks.

"What now... I should lie down and close my eyes while you pass?"

"Are you twying not to let us pass?" Lord Omicron snaps in.

"...then let us pass," Dame Nissi says simultaneously.

"I'm not blocking your way, am I?" Sextine asks.

"I've never always understood this girl," Dame Nissi says to Lord Omicron.

"Alwight," Sextine says, "before this gets out of hand, I've memowized this sentence to let you know that my BEM is damaged."

Sextine does her trademark grin and Dame Nissi takes off her mask immediately, revealing her happy face. They must have forgotten a Vexim employee did some checks on Sextine's BEM many years ago. That would have helped them believe Sextine's story easily.

"Me baby," says Dame Nissi as she takes a step towards Sextine.

"Hey," Lord Omicron holds back Dame Nissi.

"What, she's fine," Dame Nissi assures him. "Ever seen anyone gwin this stupidly?"

"Hey, I heard that!" shouts Sextine.

"Of course sugar, I was talking to you," claims Dame Nissi as she leads the reluctant Lord Omicron towards her.

Dame Nissi gives Sextine a hug.

"Jeez momxy," Sextine complains about the warm hug, "I was with you last night."

Dame Nissi suddenly grips the back of Sextine's head tightly and pulls out her BEM and throws it to the ground. The sound of the BEM hitting the ground is accompanied with the sound of a knife dropping to the floor; the knife apparently dropped from Sextine' hand. Sextine gasps for air for some seconds before Dame Nissi gives her another hug to help her recollect herself.

"How did you know?" Lord Omicron asks, still looking shocked.

"I can't wemember anything fwom last night... wonder how she could do it with a damaged BEM. Fahwenheit usually never conveys info to the bwain for permanent keeps until 10-20 hours."

"That was close," says Lord Omicron who is now patting Sextine on the head. "You okay now?"

Sextine nods, "yes." "They came here."

"Sir Nnia?"

"Yes. They said I should stab you two, then come and meet them at the palace."

"I'm so sowie," Lord Omicron apologises, "I shouldn't have let him come close to you."

"Your PES was something else. My own bwain wasn't willing to go against you guys suited up like this."

"Lol, the importance of fear. Come on, we need to go and get your siblings and Elise. Nissi, we'll take your car."

"No," Dame Nissi objects. "You teleport to them. I'll come with Sextine in the conveyor."

"The major danger is Sir Nnia. He's not in the jungle. I have to be with you guys, please, let's go together. Come on..."

Lord Omicron sounds more convincing, at least in proving that Sir Nnia alone is more dangerous than the legendary Jungle of Zion, the feared home of the folf and the violent Youlv Ocean. The three Rhos board their floating conveyor and head to the jungle where Leontine has led Lexis and Archprofessor Elise to the peaceful region of Youlv.

20 LEXIS and Archprofessor Elise are walking along the calm river which stretches a few meters before reaching the Water Steps and descending into the main ocean at the other side of the stairs.

The river looks white with numerous green crystals scattered on it. It's just the river's unique way of reflecting the night sky. Beautiful as it may appear, Lexis and Archprofessor Elise in particular are cautious not to step into the shallow river. Lexis concentrates more on looking back and up for any incoming danger. Archprofessor Elise notices Leontine is now a few steps ahead, walking excitedly in the river.

"Isn't this Youlv?" Archprofessor Elise asks Lexis.

"Yes?" he wonders before looking up to see Leontine hopping in the water. "LEOTINE!"

"She can't hear you, you know," Archprofessor Elise reminds him.

"Yes," Lexis ignores Archprofessor Elise and begins to jog towards Leontine.

"Lexis wait!" Archprofessor Elise screams in panic when Lexis is just about to step into the water.

"O-si-m-chelu!" Lexis exclaims with his hands in the air. "Why the wait now? I have to go get her."

"Just call her out fwom here..."

"She can't hear me, you know?"

Lexis takes a step into the river; he could hear Archprofessor Elise whimpering behind him.

"Look, it doesn't kill! I'll just go and get her out, that's all. You don't need to come too."

"No, don't bwing up that idea... just go... do fast, she's going farther."

Lexis steps fully into river and races down towards Leontine. The water splashing on his hand reminds him of his sapien and he calls out to it immediately.

"Yes boss," the sapien responds.

"Call Leontine," Lexis orders it as he slows down and finally stops moving.

"Placing a video call," the sapien informs Lexis.

Leontine's sapien vibrates immediately and it forces the excited Leontine to pause for a while. With the look on her face, she's certainly trying to comprehend something else on the sapien screen other than an incoming video call from Lexis. She turns quickly to Lexis and waves at him. Snubbing Lexis' desperate attempts to urge her to come back, her attention is back to the tiny message on her sapien screen. The message enlarges when she rejects the video call.

'HEART WHISPERER-BEM-SAPIEN SYNCHRONIZATION COMPLETED. TAP HERE TO LISTEN' is the message on the screen. Leontine takes a quick glance at the heart whisperer she's wearing and realises it's switched on. She taps on the sapien screen curiously. This gives her the same headache she had earlier but Lexis could hear something pinging every two seconds, it seems to have the sound of an African gong. Leontine turns the heart whisperer off and the pinging stops.

"What was that sound?" Lexis signs as Leontine finally pays attention to him.

"I was having a headache," Leontine signs before she actually understands Lexis' question. "Wait!" she signs. "You could hear my headache?"

"Was the heart whisperer on?" Lexis signs and Leontine nods "yes". "Maybe it's working!" Lexis continues. "It wasn't a headache, you were probably hearing sounds. Turn it back on."

Leontine obliges. Lexis seems to have forgotten he wants her out of the water. The pinging from the heart whisperer resumes again and Leontine takes a few seconds to agree she's not actually having a headache.

"It should have a decode option?" Lexis signs. "I've seen it before when popmy was testing it."

Leontine clicks on an unlabelled button on the heart whisperer and pinging stops. We could hear another strange language rising gradually. It has echoes of Lexis' voice in it. The words filtering in are those of a concerned son, Lexis, saying of his mother, *"Emexei seveldi diei o fy."*

Leontine begins to hear those words even clearer but she's yet to understand them. The language is the slowest manner of speech we've heard. *"Emexei seveldi ditweto o eify!"*

"Is it talking?" Lexis signs.

"I can hear something," Leontine signs back. "I don't know, it sounds so not English."

"Just say what you hear," Lexis urges Leontine to speak the words.

Leontine listens to the words again and repeats them after the voice. *"Emexei seveldi diei o fy."*

"Is your sapien not offering translations?" Lexis signs. "Did it synchronize initially?"

"Yes it did," Leontine signs back, still hearing those words again.

"Then I think it works perfectly now. Ask it to translate."

Leontine swipes thru her sapien quickly and brings up the heart whisperer icon. She opens the application and taps on 'translate'. "I've tapped it," she signs to Lexis.

"Say the words again, can you still hear them?" Lexis signs.

Leontine nods "yes".

"You can make it translate directly into your BEM... was your BEM included in the sync list?" Lexis signs.

Leontine nods "yes" as the voice in the heart whisperer increases intensity. She taps on the translator again and smiles immediately.

"It worked?" Lexis signs.

"Yes... this does sound like you worrying about me," Leontine signs.

"What does it say?"

"Momxy would die for you... momxy would die because of you."

"Yes please, let's leave the water," Lexis signs hurriedly.

Leontine stands her ground as she tries to understand the second voice in her head chanting, "Éf, éf, éf, éf," with the first voice now saying *"Eshtoél bi harsi biarken."* She adjusts the heart whisperer setting and the second voice fades away while the first voice translates to English, chanting *'You will break momxy's heart.'*

Lexis waves his hand anxiously at Leontine as he tries to regain her attention.

Leontine looks happily at him and screams, *"Efoélfosev!"*

"What does that mean?" Lexis signs and speaks too.

"We follow the water! And stop worrying about momxy," Leontine signs quickly before turning away from Lexis to continue her journey towards the Water Steps which coincidentally just became visible ahead of her.

"Leontine!" Lexis calls her aggressively before recalling she won't hear him. He takes a step forward to chase after her but he's halted by Archprofessor Elise's panicking voice.

"Lexis! What are you doing?" Archprofessor Elise asks.

"I am dancing with the water... can't you see her going? It's not me doing anything."

"Lexis, come on... leave the water. It's dangewous."

Lexis ignores her and goes after Leontine who is now very close to the Water Steps where the current of the river is increasing every inch ahead.

"Lexis?" Archprofessor Elise mutters before she reluctantly steps into the water. Out of frustration and fear, she bounces on her feet three times and says nothing in particular. Her own way of finding courage, maybe. She races towards Lexis who is trying to get to Leontine.

Excitement and enthusiasm propels Leontine to the foot of the Water Steps. She stands in awe, gazing at the tall stairs of water. The pyramidal stairs could contain a hundred steps on each side, or whatever the numbers they are. To Leontine, they are far from challenging, they are simply tempting and irresistible. Lexis seems to be calm when he sees that the Water Steps has finally stopped Leontine from moving any further. Still worried about the rising current, he anxiously calls out to her again.

"Leontine!"

"She can't hear you!" Archprofessor Elise arrives behind Lexis, her mouth left ajar at the proximity of the famous Water Steps. "What on Oh are we doing here?'

The excited Leontine is not short of courage or energy. Like a robot controlled by nature, she suddenly begins jogging up the stairs, leaving Lexis breathless and almost speechless.

"Jesus," the only word Lexis could mumble out.

"Emmanuella," Archprofessor Elise echoes after him.

"His name is Emmanuel," Lexis finds some comportment to correct Archprofessor Elise's choice of *awexpression*.

"No, she's a girl," Archprofessor Elise speaks softly of Leontine. "Can't you see she's walking on water?"

"This is the Water Steps," Lexis reminds her. "There are steps just underneath the shallow water."

"No young man, there are no steps underneath the water. That is just how the water chooses to flow. Haven't you studied about the Youlv before?"

"I'm not an Archpwofessor," says Lexis as he quickly shuns the topic, moving to the foot of the Water Steps.

Leontine is now at the flat top of the stairs and she looks down to Lexis and screams, "COME!"

Lexis shakes his head furiously and signs aggressively. "Come down here now!"

He waits hopefully for a positive response but Leontine surprisingly sinks into the Water Steps in a flash.

"Leontine!" Archprofessor Elise and Lexis scream in shock.

Lexis quickly jogs thru the first three steps of water and turns to Archprofessor Elise with his hand raised.

"See?" he says, stamping on the stairs. "Come on... I told you they were..."

Of course he was going to say 'steps' but he suddenly sinks swiftly into the water. Archprofessor Elise dives instinctively towards the vanishing Lexis. She succeeds in grabbing his hand and she could hear his voice panicking from the water.

"Elise! Don't let me go please!" Lexis pleads.

"Bae, don't dwag me in either," Archprofessor Elise panics as she's unable to do much for the falling Lexis. "Felix..." she whimpers.

"Me name is Lexis..."

"What?" Archprofessor Elise can barely hear Lexis now.

"Lexis, not Felix!"

"Does she matter now?" Archprofessor Elise wonders. She looks at herself and realises she's lying on the steps. She takes quick breaths anticipating the obvious – a fall thru the Water Steps.

That doesn't take long. Archprofessor Elise and Lexis are enclosed in big water bubbles as they fall thru a few meters to the fluffy grass floor inside the Water Steps, backing the entire space. The grasses are short, white, and surprisingly dry.

Archprofessor Elise and Lexis can hear something breathing peacefully behind them, definitely in a deep sleep but still sounding dangerous. They turn slowly towards the centre of the space, their eyes gaping in fear before they even see anything. The fear is finally worth it. It's the notorious flying wolf sleeping graciously, and to cap it all, literally, Leontine is lying face down on the folf's back with her head resting on the creature's neck.

Archprofessor Elise bows aggressively and spins in a show of fear, anger and regret. "I shouldn't be here."

"Shh!" Lexis hushes her and pulls her away from the front of the folf. "We need to find a way out."

"Are we leaving Leontine behind?"

"No... When we find our way out, it will then be worth it to twy getting her down fwom that thing."

"Bad news," Archprofessor Elise whispers, pointing at the waking Leontine.

Leontine raises her head and soon realises what her hands are feeling – the woolly back of the mighty folf. Archprofessor Elise and Lexis wave desperately at her but they can't win the magnificent false prophet in a race for gaining attention. Their own eyes are fixed on the sleeping folf as they try to make Leontine see them.

Leontine could hear the folf's heart beating in her head. She could hear her own heart rising gradually and full of praise for the creature. She's lost in its beauty and she soon utters the words from the bottom of her heart.

"Hwasi foef htowársi," Leontine whispers. *"Emei foseven, emei fohen, emei foento, emei foenelei, emeien siawelei, emtwénto."* {My heart of hearts, my own, my one and only, mine truly}.

The folf opens its eyes gracefully, instantly petrifying Archprofessor Elise and Lexis. They both stand motionless and almost breathless. The folf roars loudly but Leontine can only hear his heart speaking back to her. The proud heart has long been melted by the love Leontine has for it.

"Who is this that adores me like she knows exactly how I was born?" the heart whisperer interprets the folf's heart to Leontine's hearing. "For I was magnificent, yes, I alone."

"Enfo," Leontine says to the folf. *"O twe seves é."* {No, I was [magnificent] too}.

The folf roars again and sits up this time, spreading its huge wings. Leontine lies on her back, digging her feet into the folf's wool to stabilize herself.

"Do you have wings this huge?" boasts the folf's heart.

Leontine giggles quietly. She certainly has no wings.

"Come down here let me see you." The folf's heart demands.

Leontine climbs down thru the folf's forelimb and lands on her feet right under the folf's nose. Lexis and Archprofessor Elise shake their heads in fear and disapproval.

"Where is your PES?" Archprofessor Elise speaks quietly to Lexis.

"Two minutes away. Maybe here alweady," Lexis tells her.

The folf grunts as it stares at the jovial Leontine. Her eyes are still calm; she can only see love where Archprofessor Elise and Lexis are seeing a fierce and brutal anger. I fear we are with them on this.

"You are aware you are just food to me," Leontine hears thru the heart whisperer, "simply food. Yet you come to me. Tell, are you poisoned? Are you edible? Are you as sweet as you look? Tell."

Leontine spins at that; she seems to be blushing. *"Twém gielwadi fy eftwéndi emto dieleisiefel."* {I am glad you find me delightful}.

"But I haven't tasted you yet... only food delights me. Not by sight, but by taste. Good food flees as fast as it tastes good."

"Twé sevtwél ensi awfyen," Leontine says boldly. {I will not run}.

"You be food all the same," the folf declares with a loud roar that sends a *spinequake* down the backsides of Archprofessor Elise and Lexis.

"Twém ensi efẏdi!" Leontine responds in a stronger voice. *"Biartwesi e cielfoesto fy emwaei ditweto tovien."* {I am not food! You may even die if you breathe too close to me}.

"Liar liar," the folf's heart replies, "I have eaten you before..."

"*Eisi twém htwewa?*" {Yet I am here?}

"You never learn, do you? I have eaten you many times before and yet you keep coming back. Little wonder you turned up deaf this time."

"*Fy kénfosev?*" {You know I'm deaf?}

"Why not? You surely cannot hear my loud burst of sound, my only potent test for food. But you are here, fearless, because you are listening to my heart alone..."

"...*En emeien e.*" {And mine too}.

"I have never spoken to a human before... and I've eaten just four since I was born."

Leontine points to the heart whisperer.

"A tool, I see. Well I don't need such to filter what I have to say. You humans definitely have a way of feeling something and thinking something else entirely."

"*Hwasi en biartoen ditwéfwa.*" {The heart and brain differ}.

"You are lucky to have this tool working. At least you won't be a meal today."

"*Wa sifocih*?" Leontine smiles, moving her hand towards the folf's head. {Can I touch you?}

"No," the folf withdraws itself, "don't touch my white."

Leontine giggles. "*Fy wár waél seveisi.*" {You are all white}.

"No touching," the folf insists as it lowers its back to Leontine. "Climb on; I will take you to the sky."

Leontine manages to contain her joy as she hops quickly on the folf's back.

"He's taking her out? This girl is mad," Lexis mumbles.

"I'm not sure he wants to eat her," says Archprofessor Elise.

The folf stands tall, spreading out its intimidating wings. It turns to the fiercely flowing side of the steps and readies itself for takeoff.

"We should call your popmy now Lexis," Archprofessor Elise panics.

"What will he do to the false pwophet?" Lexis asks quickly.

"Where is your PES? You said it was two minutes away."

"Guess it wouldn't wisk swimming the Youlv."

"Oh Lexis, what do we do?"

"Jeez! You panic more than my momxy, *haba*! You just said the folf won't eat her."

"I said I'm not sure," Archprofessor Elise reminds Lexis as they stay clear of the flapping wings of the folf.

"Pieles elsi emei biarfo ciem," Leontine pleads with the folf, asking if her brother can join them.

"He stinks of fear."

"O emto, ensi fy." {Fear for me, not you}.

"Unfortunately, I don't hear hearts. I only understand the language when you speak it. A message now to you, not your heart... hold me tightly. Daylight will be here soon."

Leontine leans forward, wrapping her arms around the folf's neck. There will be no better folf-belt than that.

The folf bends its knees and leaps straight thru the Water Steps. They are quickly threatened by an approaching wave. The folf instinctively swerves out of the way and almost flies into another rising wave.

"Ah ah?" Leontine wonders as she looks sceptically at the wave. They seem to be rising against them on purpose, nothing else can explain why there's one gaining waters right behind them, trying to sweep the folf off the air.

The waves come in different shapes and sizes but the folf is not bothered.

"Twesi twés siaweien e ketwél fyes?" {Is it trying to kill us?}

"Welcoming you, that's all," the folf reveals.

"Huh?"

"Speak to it."

"*Sifo twesi*?" {To it?} Leontine asks before she's suddenly bathed by a small portion of water.

The water is freezing cold and Leontine shivers instantly. On comes another and Leontine gives up on doubting the folf.

"*Eśipi*!" she yells, pointing her right palm at the water. {Stop!}

The water reluctantly calms down.

Leontine is as much surprised as she is happy. "*Twesi cien htowár emto*?" {It can hear me?}

"Of course. An ocean that flows the way it does... you should know it has a mind of its own."

"*Bisi twém sevsi hwasi sevtwéspiewer, ensi emtwéndi.*" {But I'm with a heart whisperer, not a mind whisperer}.

"Oh humans... you set up many compartments of yourselves. Your ghost, soul, body, mind, heart and head... and they all think independently and speak for you."

"Haha!" Leontine giggles. "*Htodi sevsi bifodiei,*" {The head is with the body}

Leontine spreads her arms as the folf flies further up towards the sky. In a very short while, she's completely amazed. The folf seems to be floating still as she's lost in awe of the stars and Oh's moons; she has never seen them this close before. She stretches out her hand towards a star, quite a laughable situation.

"What are you doing?" the folf asks. "That thing is still many miles away."

"*Estóemes twesies cielfoesto.*" {It seems close}.

The folf wobbles its back and Leontine almost falls off.

"*Diensi*!" screams the terrified Leontine as she grips the folf's wool tightly. {DON'T!}

"Scared? You will only fall back into Youlv..."

"Enfo, diensi siarfo emto." {NO, DON'T THROW ME}.

The folf ignores her and shakes its body some more.

"Difo en espisi! Fy sevtwél ketwél emto?" {Just stop! Do you wish to kill me?}

"I don't want to kill you... I would even die for you. Okay dump that last part... I'm not sure I can die for you. Can I be killed?"

"Diensi jéśi diarpi emto." {Just don't drop me}.

"You'll fall back into Youlv!" the folf tries to convince Leontine.

"Twe diensi ciwárto!" {I don't care!}

"You'll meet the lilies..."

"Disies wa eltweto. Sihtoei diensi efelei bio diwaei." {That's a lie. They don't come out before daylight}.

"It's not a lie. Some stay in Youlv over the night... especially the golden ones and the pink ones. They mate in Youlv or they are simply overfed to go home."

"Hmm..." Leontine finds that hard to believe.

"See for yourself." The folf throws Leontine off its back.

Leontine is far beyond shock or surprise, yes, petrified already, speechless and surely heartbroken. Her eyes are fixed on the folf, her lips unwilling to close, wondering. Her right arm is still outstretched towards the folf, hoping 'hers truly' will grab her as she falls from the night sky. The beautiful stars and Oh's moons become smaller as she descends, towards the Youlv hopefully, as the folf had claimed.

Straight into the ocean, the waters do not splash or ripple as it receives Leontine peacefully. The heartbroken Leontine is still descending, sinking thru the entire depth of the ocean with her eyes still fixed on the blurry night sky. Her head soon rests upon the soft petals of one of the sleeping golden lilies. The entire floor of the Youlv is beaming with the beauty of the lilies; quite strangely as the folf's heart had said, only the golden and pink lilies are resting underneath the ocean. The lilies pop their eyes open at once, wondering who just dropped in. Their bodies remain calm as their tiny eyeballs run from left to right.

By the side of the waters, on dry ground, Dame Nissi, Lord Omicron and Lexis come racing towards the point perpendicular to where Leontine had sunk. The three of them, suited up in their PES, are halted by Archprofessor Elise's voice.

"Yes, just there!" Archprofessor Elise screams as she tries her best to meet up with the PES propelled Rhos. She's of course accompanied by the exhausted Sextine. "That is where it fell," Archprofessor Elise adds.

"It?" Dame Nissi wonders. "Wasn't it Leontine you saw?"

"I'll assume it is," Archprofessor Elise replies.

"Well, go and check," Dame Nissi tells Lord Omicron.

"No," Lord Omicron refuses, "no one has ever swam the Youlv let alone doing it on assumption... and in darkness."

"You will not be assuming you are swimming, my daughter is in there."

"And that's an assumption."

"But the folf went up with her!"

"Yes Nissi," agrees Lord Omicron, "anything can fall fwom the sky. Let's not get distwacted fwom our objective."

"Damn it Omicwon, that objective is underwater. I'm going in," Dame Nissi declares and stumps towards the water.

"Wait..." Lord Omicron holds her back and speaks as fast as he can. "I'll go. But Lexis, we need to stop Sir Nnia..."

"...I've dweamt of today," Dame Nissi interrupts Lord Omicron.

"Déjà vu," Lord Omicron responds to her quickly and turns back to Lexis. "He may still be at the palace... not sure. But you get to Fahwenheit HQ, undo whatever it is he did there..."

"I'll do my best," Lexis responds.

"No, not your best... just get it done. You are a smart kid, undo that Gadhuvi, even if it means switching off evewybody's BEM, do it. And act normal if he sees you... just obey him until we come. Go..."

Lexis nods in affirmative. He zooms off and swiftly takes to the sky.

Lord Omicron looks at Dame Nissi and she bends her head quickly towards the water, quietly urging him to look for Leontine. We suddenly can see thru her eyes that she can see something wonderful thru Lord Omicron's eyes. Yes, a mild fear is building; Dame Nissi isn't sure of what is making Lord Omicron's eyes pop as he looks at the waters.

Dame Nissi turns to see for herself, and we too see for ourselves – Lilies rising, as spectacular as ever. The darkness of the time cannot hide their glowing wings. Dame Nissi is quite optimistic now, she may have just dreamt of this before, if she ever had any pretty dream – Leontine rising from the waters, carried by the lilies.

And so it is, Leontine's body is completely covered by the lilies as they lift her slowly out of the ocean.

"Is that my sister?" Sextine asks Archprofessor Elise.

"Aideekay," Archprofessor Elise responds as she feasts her eyes on the beautiful display of the lilies.

Leontine opens up her eyes and quickly takes control of the flight course. She goes from ascending vertically to gliding over the water, flapping her hands occasionally, admiring her reflection on the water.

"A emfoarto efeltwegiht elfyvies," Leontine says to the lilies, *"diwaei eltwesito esfóen."* {One more flight my loves, it will soon be morning}.

Leontine and the lilies soon fly out of her family's sight.

Leontine sees the folf approaching. A friendly anger stems from within her and she almost loses her flight balance before choosing to ignore the folf for now.

"Focus," the folf says to her, gliding past her and almost immediately ushering daylight into the sky.

The growing light is bright enough to cast the folf's shadow on the ground when it flies over Archprofessor Elise and the Rhos. Sextine and Archprofessor Elise quickly run to a tree and stand almost glued to it. A shadow that huge means one thing only – run first, if a tree or a house is nearby, then think later. Unless you are heavily girded with a PES like Lord Omicron and his wife, you can stand to weigh the danger first and eventually running to that tree later.

Dame Nissi keeps looking out for Leontine while Lord Omicron keeps an eye on the folf, hoping it sticks to the sky-business. There's a feeling the folf is getting closer to the ground, there's also this belief it wouldn't hunt stagnant creatures. If Leontine had spoken to the folf as Lexis and Archprofessor Elise claim, then Dame Nissi would rather wait a minute longer for her daughter to reappear.

"We need to take cover slowly," Lord Omicron suggests.

"Leave me alone," Dame Nissi grumbles, "and kill that thing."

"Sugar, I'm not a folf poacher, we need to take cover."

"Leave me alone!" Dame Nissi insists before she quickly puts on her PES mask and lights up the PES fire.

Lord Omicron unexpectedly burst into laughter; he finds Dame Nissi's decision quite amusing. We find his reaction more amusing. Dame Nissi tries to ignore him; she snaps at him twice with the tail of her eyes.

"Hmm..." Dame Nissi would rather not join him in laughing.

"Won't you guys leave that place?" Archprofessor Elise yells. "Be tempting that thing!"

"Inferno-PES?" spoofs Lord Omicron.

"Yes... *hapum! Laissez moi.*" {Leave me alone}.

"That can't stop the folf. It will soak you in the water and eat you. We need to leave the open space..."

"Leontine won't let him touch me," Dame Nissi responds stubbornly. "Look!" she points to the sky.

Lord Omicron looks up and sees Leontine flying towards them, still carried by the lilies of course; that sort of open witchcraft indeed never survived the lost earth.

Leontine lands in front of her parents and so too does the folf, landing, almost immediately, some distance away from the inflamed Dame Nissi.

Dame Nissi puts off the fire, anticipating a hug from Leontine. Leontine ignores her parents and runs towards the false prophet. Well, that is allowed. Everyone seems to accept the folf as Leontine's priority, but no, not for this – Leontine is taking out her anger and frustration on the long legs of the folf, bashing and slapping them furiously.

"Is she allowed to do that?" Archprofessor Elise whimpers as she points at Leontine.

21 MEANWHILE, at the King's palace, Sir Nnia and his coveted cohorts are in a car parked right outside the palace, waiting patiently, and the right time to strike is indeed now – 6:15 a.m. Just after the night guards hand duty over to the morning guards, there's a bit of a drag around the palace. The guards secretly sneak in and out

of the kitchen for quick breakfasts; this also gives room for the cleaners to clean every spot around the palace without having a guard standing over a dusty floor. Dusty guard shoe marks on the clean floor is quite an easy way to get a cleaner sacked around here.

Apart from the handover from a seemingly stronger nights' watch to the weaker day keepers, the King's hologram doubles are turned off, leaving only one possible king in the palace – the real king. It wouldn't have been fun chasing down the king only for him to turn out to be a hologram. With Princess Lotem-Zeta on Sir Nnia's side, there are no palace secrets anymore.

To attack the weak security inside, however, one needs to go thru the tight and unbeatable security outside. Sir Nnia wouldn't want that, especially when he already has a hologram portal implanted in the palace. Jax Lilyscent had kept one there about six days ago if we can recall.

In the car with Sir Nnia are still Princess Lotem-Zeta, Sir Luminescence, and Archprofessor Lux Eden. They all have the Holo-X^3 displaying on their sapiens, seemingly ready to deploy them into the palace.

"Don't forget," Sir Nnia gives his final instructions, "you don't go barging into walls or letting anyone punch you easily, this is the Holo-X-cube... if you hit a wall or walk into a fist, you'll waste valuable time. I don't need anyone hanging. Pwincess, you will go in first, walk stwaight to the kitchen, don't wait for us. Bwing the knives as planned, we'll be waiting for you where Jax kept the holo portal."

Princess Lotem-Zeta's hologram walks out from underneath the table in her private living room. She walks quickly out of the room and thru the corridors. Ignoring the guards – those greeting and those sneaking and hiding meals, she walks into the kitchen and straight to the cutlery shelves. She takes a tray and fills it with about twelve knives. The two cooks on duty can only question their own eyes and what they think they are seeing, certainly not the mean princess.

At the Fahrenheit Headquarters, Lexis feels uneasy with the open doors and empty halls. Though this makes his job easy but it makes him nervy and paranoid. 'What if they are watching me?' he thinks to himself as he marshals out the boldest steps his gait has to offer. He enters the office area – a huge spherical hallway housing a lot of monitors and desks, also paving way to various personal offices. This hallway isn't empty; he finds his friend, Jax Lilyscent, standing in the middle of the sphere.

"Jax..." Lexis greets him normally with a smile.

"Lexis. Back fwom the lost earth?" Jax asks him enthusiastically.

"Yes, we are. The king asked me to join you here."

"The king? Sir Nnia? Has he been named king?"

"No, but soon. They at the palace now."

"That's good! What of your popmy? It is a known fact he uses Vexim."

"Yeah... we disposed of him immediately we landed."

Jax nods in pity.

"You here all alone?" Lexis asks as he walks closer to Jax.

"Yeah, looking after Sir Nnia's gadgets until the employees come to work for today. He asked me to send evewyone home for last night."

"Quite loose... What if twouble comes?"

"Nobody knows what is happening yet. Perhaps I'll see it coming on the scween," Jax points at a screen showing live images of the building and its surroundings. "I'll shut the door," he adds, "quite impenetwable.... saw you coming so I opened the door. Sir Nnia told me it's just your popmy, Archpwofessor Elise and Leontine that use Vexim."

Lexis patiently listens to Jax blab away. He moves gradually around a single seat, caressing it gently. When his hands lock in tightly, it is a sure way to get rid of Jax Lilyscent.

BAM! Lexis smashes the seat on Jax's back and he falls lifeless to ground even before the sound of impact is done reverberating around the hall. Lexis dives quickly to the ground and pulls off Jax's BEM from his head. Jax remains motionless.

Lexis moves hurriedly towards the personal offices, scanning thru the tags on the door. From CEO to BEM Relations to BEM Behaviour to BEM Security to BEM Tech to BEM This and BEM That, literally, we are wondering if Lexis is indeed looking for an office tagged 'The King of Oh'.

"Where was the sequence initiated?" Lexis says to himself as he walks over to the office door tagged 'BEM Security'. He pulls a screen from his sapien and hacks into the computerized door.

He opens the door and beholds an empty room. The previous occupant may have just been sacked or fired or suspended or any other conjugable derivative. There is a good lead, however. We recognise the tablet lying on the table – the same one Sir Nnia had returned with from Epsilon's first trip to the lost earth ten years ago. Lexis doesn't know what it is but he looks at it all the same.

The tablet is on standby and Lexis keeps pressing the body until he feels the sole button at the bottom of the gadget. He taps it and the screen display comes on, showing a familiar message – GADHUVI-FAHRENHEIT SYNC 100%. PRESS OK TO SAVE EFFECT PERMANENTLY.

"Who becomes a king this carelessly?" Lexis wonders. He proceeds to tap 'CANCEL' on the dialogue box and the tablet pops up a relieving message – INITIATING GADHUVI DEACTIVATION SEQUENCE. This will take a long while.

Back at the palace, however, Sir Nnia is still reaping the benefits of the effects of the Gadhuvi. They all stand behind Princess Lotem-Zeta who leads a knife onslaught against unsuspecting guards as they march towards King Sigma's room.

The killer squad conceal their weapons and Princess Lotem-Zeta knocks on the door and calls on her father.

"Go and get her kids," Sir Nnia tells Archprofessor Lux Eden and Sir Luminescence.

The two men move out quickly. They sense it's safe to walk around now. The few guards inside the palace are dead.

"Popmy," the princess calls out again as she knocks calmly on the king's door.

"Give me a moment," the king's voice heralds from the room.

Sir Nnia nods at the princess. No need to make him suspect any danger now.

King Sigma opens the door, dressed in red pyjamas; his towering figure can actually be overemphasized, but not the excitement on his face.

"Lotem! You are back?" he asks before seeing Sir Nnia behind her. "Sir Nnia?" he guesses the name correctly.

Sir Nnia nods.

"Welcome back. What's up?" the king asks.

"We need to talk," Princess Lotem-Zeta says.

"Here, now? We can go to the..."

"Yes, here now," the princess insists. "It's about the lost earth, it is important."

"Fine," agrees King Sigma.

He turns back into the room and Sir Nnia swiftly attacks him from behind, sticking the kitchen knife into his back.

King Sigma staggers and groans. He throws a weak punch towards Sir Nnia but he swerves out of the way. The king tries reaching for the knife in his back, that doesn't work either.

"You stabbed me fwom behind," the king laments, "I can't even reach the sword."

"It's a kitchen knife actually," Sir Nnia informs the king.

"How low..."

"Not as low as what you did to my family."

"Your family? I have not even done anything against anyone..."

"Lol, this man," Sir Nnia laughs. "Being king cannot please evewyone... you should know that by now. Your family kicked us out! I am Nnia-Den Lilyscent... no, I'm sure you didn't expect any of us to come this far in life."

"Your family deserved what they got. I have gone thwu the details many times. And you," King Sigma turns to the princess, "you let him do this? What do you stand to gain?"

"No, don't bother about your daughter," Sir Nnia says, "she is just one of millions of people who obey my commands... and when I'm king, others who I cannot put under contwol like her will simply have to obey me for being king."

"You wish to king?"

"I am king."

They could hear Kamsi-Elle's voice coming closer, almost singing as a song, "where is the boss."

"Will you shut up?" Princess Mary-Zeta tells her at some point.

Archprotessor Lux Eden comes into the room with the struggling Princess Zeta while Sir Luminescence walks side by side with the calm Kamsi-Elle, her BEM is obviously compromised. Princess Zeta stays calm when she sees her mother and Sir Nnia standing before the king.

"Good morning boss," Kamsi-Elle greets Sir Nnia.

Princess Zeta looks at her sternly and splutters, "Seemesh."

"What do you intend to do with them?" King Sigma groans.

"You don't need to know," Sir Nnia responds as he quickly thrusts another knife into the king's stomach.

"NO!" Princess Zeta screams as the king falls dead to the ground. "What did you do that for?"

"Long live the king!" Kamsi-Elle declares.

"Ah, this little one," Sir Nnia smiles at the little princess, "evewyone should have your DNA. Your loyalty is superb."

"What is wong with all of you?" Princess Zeta asks.

"You are not using Fahwenheit. I see you choose your boyfwend's advice over your momxy's..."

"Guess it's working so far. Is that how you hypnotized them all? With the BEM? I still saw guards outside... you'll never get away with this."

"Who said I need to get away? This is my palace now."

"My momxy is heir, after her, I am. You have no claim to be king."

"We'll see about that. Oh, sowie, you may not live to see about that. I won't be needing more opposition... your argument is giving me a headache alweady." "Kill her," he orders Archprofessor Lux Eden.

Archprofessor Lux Eden pulls out a knife and Princess Lotem-Zeta helps in holding down Princess Zeta.

"Wait..." Sir Nnia stops the Archprofessor. "Let Lotem-Zeta do it herself."

Archprofessor Lux Eden holds down Princess Zeta and hands the knife over to the crown princess which she doesn't accept convincingly. She looks at her daughter for a while and then turns to Sir Nnia.

"But sir," she says to Sir Nnia, "this is my daughter."

"Yes, I know that. She needs to be dead if I must legally call myself king, and I now want you to do us the honour of killing her yourself."

"I know what you are asking me to do sir... what I'm saying is, this lady here is my daughter. I am sowie you'll have to kill her yourself," Princess Lotem-Zeta offers Sir Nnia the knife.

Archprofessor Lux Eden and Sir Luminescence are seemingly outraged and they are about to pounce on the crown princess.

"No, that's okay," Sir Nnia calms everyone down with his voice fading to himself. "That's okay. We'll go take care of a few things... we'll come back for this. The Gadhuvi has a few lapses... we'll go and fix it up."

"OKAY!" Sir Nnia's voice peaks again. "We will head to Fahwenheit HQ now, all of us here. When I adjust the pwogwam I'll love to test its potency immediately. Now listen to me little pwincess, your momxy is in a conveyor with us... all these here are just holo-x-cubes. If you as much as wink at any guard outside, I will kill your momxy before anyone gets to us. Do you understand?" Sir Nnia asks Princess Zeta.

She nods "yes".

"Lead the two kids out," Sir Nnia tells Princess Lotem-Zeta, "we'll be waiting in the car."

"Yes sir," affirms Princess Lotem-Zeta.

Sir Nnia is well aware it shouldn't take more than a minute for Princess Lotem-Zeta to march her daughters thru the palace yard and to the car parked outside the compound. He knows exactly how long to wait before carrying out his threat.

Lexis, however, is almost halfway thru undoing the entire Fahrenheit takeover. He decides to go thru Sir Nnia's tablet, not suspecting anything really but just to pass the time. He sees a folder named 'CLEONTINE'. The 'C' still doesn't make it sound any less than his sister's name, Leontine. For Lexis, it makes it look even more intriguing.

Lexis clicks on the folder after giving it a quick second thought. The folder is taking too long to open. The impatient Lexis pulls on the sides of the tablet, trying to understand its technology. The screen and flexible body elongates itself in response to the pull.

"Sapien," Lexis calls on his wrist gadget.

"Yes boss."

"Digitizer for file twansfer," Lexis requests.

The sapien responds quickly, popping up a digitizer icon.

Lexis taps on the digitizer and carries it to the tablet screen. He places the digitizer over the folder and the tablet opens up a dialogue box attempting to 'Identify recipient'.

'DESTINATION UNKNOWN. SEND ANYWAY?' is the next message on the tablet screen.

Lexis taps on 'YES' and the folder is copied to the digitizer within a second. Lexis places the digitizer back on his sapien and it announces that a document has been received, but of course with a 'Gadhuvi virus alert' message. Lexis ignores the virus warning and opens up the Cleontine folder.

His questions are not easily answered. There's an insanely long article typed in small fonts. This is unreadable, certainly no time to find out what it says. The curious Lexis swipes over to the next page and the picture of things get clearer. There's a picture of Leontine tagged 'Cleontine IV: The fourth clone'.

"Why would Sir Nnia clone Leontine?" Lexis wonders aloud.

The next three pages contain Cleo III, Cleo II, and Cleo I, and then another clue surfaces. 'Heart Whisperer Integration' is the article on the next page. Sir Nnia must have been secretly working on Lord Omicron's project. Cloning Leontine will at least ensure he makes equal or even faster progress, logically can't be slower if all factors are similar.

Pictures they say speak a thousand words. Without reading all the details, Lexis can make intelligent guesses on what Sir Nnia has been up to. The next page is even more intriguing. Lexis is however, distracted by a thud right outside the office door. He looks quickly at the tablet screen before hiding it behind his back, pondering what Sir Nnia must have meant by '*Whisperer Folfenheit*'.

The office door open slowly and in comes a slightly dazed Jax Lilyscent.

"You knocked me out?" Jax manages to put those words together.

"I had to..." Lexis explains, "Needed to pull off your BEM. Sir Nnia is manipulating evewyone thwu it."

Jax looks at the desk and pretends not to be looking for the tablet. Lexis maintains eye contact.

"Hmm," Jax can't really keep up with the pretence for long, "and where is Sir Nnia's tablet? I want to have it back."

"Oh, it that what it is... no wait... you still support him?"

"Seemesh," Jax shakes his head. "What gave you the impwession that I'm being manipulated? Where is the tablet Lexis? Sir Nnia is almost here... don't start what you can't finish."

"As far as I know, Sir Nnia has started something he can't finish... not me."

"Hmm," Jax sighs with a smile on his face and begins to crack his bones.

"You know, maybe you do need a little BEM manipulation," Lexis tells Jax, "otherwise you shouldn't be thinking of attacking someone dressed in a PES."

"Oh yeah?" Jax smiles wryly as seven others of himself walk into the room, holding steel batons, with one of them holding two batons on one hand. "Ever heard of the Holo-Q-eight?"

Lexis is rather quiet, getting ready mentally to handle what is before him. He watches one of the Jax-holograms lock the door and a baton is handed over to the first Jax.

"No?" Jax guesses an answer. "I thought you will be ahead of these things..."

"At least I know it is illegal," Lexis says calmly.

"Since Sir Nnia is king, all his works are legal, don't you think so? Now hand me the tablet."

"What I think is that this PES can kick yo'arses..."

The eight Jax-holograms burst into a synchronised laughter.

"Don't get it twisted Lexis... kick us hard or not, you are flesh and blood, we are simply technology. You will die here, but the worst for me is that I'll get disconnected, so don't bother twying to kill any of us... I am still lying down where you kept me. Once again Lexis, the tablet..."

"Please be quick," Lexis challenges them.

The eight Jax-holograms charge aggressively towards Lexis, swinging their batons towards his head. Lexis swerves out of the way and hangs on the ceiling to ease off the sudden pressure. One of the Jax-holograms jumps to no avail, trying to reach Lexis.

"You'll stay there all day? Come down!" a Jax-hologram says to him.

"You said I shouldn't bother twying to kill any of you... so, I'm not bothered again."

Lexis looks at the tablet quickly; he surely doesn't need both hands to keep hanging from the ceiling. He opens up the Gadhuvi deactivation sequence and he's slightly disappointed – it's only about 80% done. He opens up his PES and keeps the tablet against his chest and seals up the suit. He puts on his PES mask and turns his attention back to the Jax-holograms. He's caught unawares by one of them floating up to him in the air.

With his arms spread and cheeky smile, the hologram says, "Welcome to the future, Lexis. Evewything is possible." He smashes his baton on Lexis' head and it sends tiny sparks of light thru the PES.

Lexis falls to ground and recovers quickly by spinning out kicks to the approaching Jax-holograms.

The PES will indeed be a handful. Lexis draws a sword from his weapons cache and everything in the room is back on their feet now, gearing up for another go. It is faster this time, and we don't exactly follow each kick and punch anymore but we do see that the good old PES is gaining a slight advantage over the untested Holo-Q8s.

22 JUST outside the Fahrenheit HQ walls, the Rhos and Archprofessor Elise are racing towards the building before they are halted by Sir Nnia's thundering voice.

"LORD OMICWON WOE!" Sir Nnia calls out to his friendly foe, bringing him and his family gang to an instant stop.

Lord Omicron turns slowly. Sir Nnia has just stepped out of his car and he's quickly joined on the ground by Princess Lotem-Zeta, Kamsi-Elle, Archprofessor Lux Eden, and Sir Luminescence who is holding on tightly to the struggling

Princess Zeta. Sir Luminescence shakes the princess' hand aggressively and she stays calm.

"I see you bwought me the password," Sir Nnia says of Dame Nissi. "Unfortunately you are going into the wong building."

"Sir Nnia..."

"Eh eh Omicwon, men don't speak to machines at ease," Sir Nnia says as he draws the submissive Kamsi-Elle to himself, pulling a knife against her neck. "Kindly take off those suits, after which you can now beg for your lives."

Lord Omicron and Dame Nissi oblige immediately.

Leontine keeps looking hopefully at her father as he pulls the PES off. She realises a weaponized digitizer is concealed in his left hand. There are no encouraging words coming from anyone's heart at the moment. Her parents only wish she and Sextine are safe at home, Princess Zeta is hoping they all run away, Sir Nnia desires to slit her own throat himself, and his hypnotized soldiers are emotionally blank while Archprofessor Elise's heart is really not audible enough to be comprehended.

With the PES out of the game, Sir Nnia instructs Archprofessor Lux Eden to bring Sextine and Leontine over to him.

"Don't be scared little ones," Sir Nnia reassures them mischievously, "it's not time to kill anyone yet."

Lord Omicron urges them not to run but of course, Leontine can't hear him. She hides quickly behind Dame Nissi and Archprofessor Lux Eden still knows better than insisting on grabbing her near the mother. He withdraws quickly with Sextine and Sir Nnia stumps angrily towards the Rhos to grab Leontine himself.

Leontine has heard Sir Nnia's heart; she knows he wants to kill her. She moves swiftly to the unsuspecting

Lord Omicron and squeezes out the weaponized digitizer from his left hand.

"What's that?" Sir Nnia asks immediately before he begins to jog curiously towards the Rhos.

Leontine too begins to run courageously towards Sir Nnia. They are poised to meet halfway between the two parties. Leontine is anxious – her own heart is far from supportive. "Sevto ditweto! Sevto diei sevtoél!" it chants. {We die, we die well}. She'll give up anything to make it believe she can do this – to place the weaponized digitizer on Sir Nnia's neck. She has to stretch it; she has to swipe it over her weapons grade sapien; she has to leap to reach Sir Nnia's neck, and yet she has to do it before he knows it.

Sir Nnia is not a fool. He's already throwing intelligent guesses on why Leontine is coming confidently. 'A hug,' 'a kiss,' 'a punch,' 'a push,' 'a head butt,' 'we don't love you too...' well, that's how dangerous Leontine should be. No one will envision 'a kill!'

Leontine takes her eyes off the ground to pull up the right screen on her sapien. Just as the sapien pops up the 'swipe the weaponized digitizer' dialogue box, Leontine loses her footing and falls to the ground.

The digitizer falls out of her hand and Sir Nnia's eyes pop wide open; it just has to be. In a split second he imagined how the little girl was going to tag a weaponized digitizer on him.

Leontine scrambles quickly towards the small red weaponized digitizer on the floor and Sir Nnia dives to it immediately. Both get there at the same time and both have their thumb and first finger gripping a portion of the digitizer's circumference.

Leontine's homework seems to be solving itself. With the anger and desire in Sir Nnia's eyes, it is certain they both now want the same thing; then comes the stretching of the digitizer. It reaches its limit and cuts into two and the momentum throws Leontine and Sir Nnia backwards. They both swipe their own half of the weaponized digitizer across their sapien screen and roll back quickly towards each other. The aggression lands both of them a hot slap on the neck from each other; that is the kiss of death, but not quite yet.

Lord Omicron holds Dame Nissi back from reacting. He points at Sextine with his head and Dame Nissi understands what is at stake.

"The digitizer won't work," Lord Omicron assures Dame Nissi as they watch Leontine dash away from Sir Nnia who is desperately trying to understand what his own sapien is saying.

"Password boss," the sapien reiterates before putting it in writing on the screen.

Leontine stops disappointedly and turns quickly to her father and signs, "Password."

Sir Nnia begins to laugh. The weaponized digitizer on Leontine's neck shocks her when she places her hand on it seemingly hoping to pull it off.

"Don't touch it!" Lord Omicron signs to Leontine.

"Is that the password?" Sir Nnia jokes. "Go on, sign it to her and you know I'll key it in before she does, and I will bweak her neck off her body."

"I can't sign it," Lord Omicron signs to Leontine. "He'll type it in before you, I know him well."

"He doesn't understand sign language," Leontine signs.

"Says who?" Sir Nnia signs at Leontine.

Leontine cringes in disappointment. She begins to hear the heart whisperer again. "The heart whisperer!" she signs enthusiastically.

"The what? Does it work now?" Sir Nnia asks Lord Omicron immediately. "You know the consequences of killing me, don't you? Fahwenheit will make all men avenge me until there is no one left on Oh."

"Don't kill him!" Lord Omicron signs to Leontine.

Leontine raises her eyes.

"Don't listen to my heart, don't kill him," Lord Omicron signs again.

"Your heart doesn't even know the password," Leontine signs. "It is just speaking in riddles."

"LOL!" Sir Nnia laughs wickedly. "Too bad the heart doesn't key in passwords." "Come on now," he signs, "come and take this thing off my neck."

Leontine shakes her head "no". She has no intentions of letting Sir Nnia off the hook yet. If there's anything she learnt from one of her brother's numerous quess teachings down the years, it is 'never release an enemy from captivity, no matter how fragile your jail is'.

Leontine now concentrates more on listening to Lord Omicron's noisy heart and the message about the password seems to get clearer by the second – "Cancel out your names and you will have it."

Leontine pulls up a memo screen quickly on her sapien and Sir Nnia becomes more impatient. Leontine begins to type in the words Lord Omicron's heart spoke while Sir Nnia yells aggressively at Lord Omicron.

"Omicwon, you better tell her to come take this digitizer off me or I'll hack thwu this damn thing and kill her before she solves that puzzle..."

Sir Nnia's voice is quite intimidating now, it's enough to get his enemies tensed and confused. Leontine isn't moved by that. For all she knows, Sir Nnia is simply yawning harmlessly.

Kamsi-Elle jogs to Sir Nnia's side and joins him in threatening Lord Omicron. "Tell her to come now or somebody's going to die."

"This man can do it," Lord Omicron signs a warning to Leontine. "Just take it off. You'll be safer that way!"

"I rather be free than safe," Leontine signs.

"Just do as I said!" Lord Omicron signs.

Leontine ignores him as she takes a deeper look at what she had typed on the memo screen. She keeps withdrawing gently to the sides, keeping an eye on all her potential foes, including her father who may just want to keep her safe.

'Cancel out your names and you will have it' – Leontine runs her finger thru the message and takes another look at Sir Nnia who has pulled up his own screen codes attempting to hack thru the password.

Leontine cleans off 'your names and you will have it', guessing the riddle might just be a literal instruction. She switches to the password box and keys in *'cancelout'*. The sapien rejects the password with a beep.

Sir Nnia looks anxiously at her. "Lord Omicwon, you will tell me the password now!"

"She will hear it too," Lord Omicron claims.

"Your daughter can hear nothing!"

"She will form the words when my lips move."

"Hey hey!" Sir Nnia hushes him up. "I know better than asking someone to kill his own daughter. That's why we are here in the first place. I'll let you watch me do it... watch me succeed. That's why I still kept you alive."

"Let me stop her," Lord Omicron offers as he takes a step forward.

Leontine shifts further away.

"No!" Sir Nnia halts him. "You stand where you are..."

"You know I won't do anything stupid. I'll get her to you and she'll take off the digitizer."

"Shut up man!" Sir Nnia tries to concentrate on his hacking mission.

Lord Omicron is facing a dilemma. He wouldn't aid anyone in killing Sir Nnia, not until the Fahrenheit issue has been resolved. But there's more agony in watching Sir Nnia punching his screens in an attempt to kill Leontine. He looks towards the Fahrenheit HQ building, desperately hoping for a sign from Lexis.

Lexis, PES and all, is getting exhausted gradually. And with the day getting brighter, the energy of the Jax-holograms can only get better. Lexis has a sapien screen floating ahead of him. He punches in new commands to it on every slight opportunity he gets while fighting off the persistent grabber holograms. On the sapien screen floating in the air before him, we understand he's attempting to launch his Holo-X^3 hologram. The intense fighting makes the destination selection quite hard. He wishes to bring it to Unmi and, of course, to the Fahrenheit HQ. His sapien announces there's an open hologram portal within the building and Lexis keys in some special commands to force an uninvited entry thru the hologram portal. Quite rightly, it must be the same portal Jax is using to keep his eight ninjas alive in the building.

The real Jax is lying behind one of the desks outside the office. He is desperately trying to prevent the hologram portal from bringing in Lexis' hologram. With multiple clicks on the button, he finally gives up by wishfully covering the portal with his hands.

Lexis' Holo-X^3 can't be stopped. The hologram pops out forcefully, pushing Jax's hands out of the way before landing a heavy blow under his jaw. Jax falls helplessly to the ground. Lexis picks up the hologram portal and turns it off before Jax could make it back to him. Lexis' hologram and the eight fighting him in the office switch off and vanish immediately. Jax catches the falling hologram portal and begins to power it on quickly in bid to restore his apparent body guards. There's no doubt Lexis will soon come flying out of the office.

Lexis pulls out the tablet from his PES. The message on display reads 'DEACTIVATION COMPLETED. SAVE AND APPLY CHANGES'.

"Of course, you archaic thing! Lexis taps on the 'Yes' button and a 'Saving Sequence' is initiated. "Wonder who saved the changes you made initially."

Not long now, we are expecting the Fahrenheit prisoners to think free. Leontine and Sir Nnia are still trying to use the weapon they've locked on each other.

Leontine has on her memo screen, her name and that of her siblings, Lexis and Sextine. She begins quickly to cancel out corresponding alphabets from the names.

First goes the 'TINE' in Sextine and Leontine; then follows the 'SEX' left in Sextine and similar letter in Lexis, and finally the 'L' in Leon and Li cancels out each other. Leontine is left with four letters E O N I. She quickly rearranges the letters to EOIN. Sextine does have a friend called Eoin, and for no other reason, that's the only word that could be formed. She types it in quickly as the weaponized digitizer password and the sapien accepts it vocally, displaying an image of Sir Nnia and a time of ten seconds waiting to be launched.

There is absolute silence. All eyes are on Leontine, waiting to see what she intends to do with the weapon. Sir Nnia gives up on hacking thru the password. He looks sternly at Leontine his hand now placed on Kamsi-Elle's shoulders.

"You use that thing and there will be an annihilation of all Vexim users. Your family will die too, and I don't care if you are deaf. You should be well aware there's just one thing I'm saying to you... come and take this shit off my neck or I will make your popmy's fwends do it for me. You know they'll die while twying to, don't you?"

"She can't hear you!" Dame Nissi cries.

"Oh shut up woman! Then sign to her, I don't care... I don't bloody care!" Sir Nnia pulls out his kitchen knife again in anger.

We are spared the stress of wondering what next the confused Sir Nnia is about to do when Jax Lilyscent suddenly races out of the building. The sound of him panicking catches the attention of everyone and they look behind him to see Lexis chasing after him.

Sir Nnia grabs Kamsi-Elle tightly and places the knife near her throat.

"Hey hey hey!" Sir Nnia attempts to make Lexis call off the chase as Jax runs towards him and Kamsi-Elle.

Lexis is quick to understand the situation and he stops running immediately.

"Take off that suit!" Sir Nnia addresses his primary concern to Lexis.

"He's with the tablet!" Jax breathlessly informs Sir Nnia.

"What? Go get it back!" Sir Nnia roars as he pushes Jax away towards Lexis.

Jax staggers as he turns around, and just as he recollects himself, the folf comes down swiftly and plucks him out of the ground. They all look in awe as the folf leaves with the wailing Jax. The folf was already flying very low before they saw it.

"Shit!" Sir Nnia grumbles aggressively.

"That was nobody's fault," Lord Omicron explains immediately.

"Shut up! Shut up! Give me that tablet!"

"I don't have it!" Lexis attempts to buy some time.

"Go and kill his popmy," Sir Nnia orders.

Archprofessor Lux Eden, Sir Luminescence and Princess Lotem-Zeta march quickly towards Lord Omicron.

Lord Omicron gently pushes Archprofessor Elise and Dame Nissi away from himself.

"Come on guys..." Archprofessor Elise tries to reason with the advancing foes. "Sir Nnia, don't make them do this..."

"*Fydi ditweto aeśi*!" Leontine shouts from her almost-ignored position. {You will die first}.

"What did she say?" Sir Nnia asks no one in particular.

"If you don't make them stop, I will activate this thing and kill you," Leontine signs to Sir Nnia.

"And when I'm dead? Who will make them stop?" Sir Nnia asks. "Make sure you sign that into her head," he adds to Lord Omicron.

"Wait!" Lexis speaks up as he stands in the way of Sir Nnia's mercenaries. "Can you kill him?" he signs to Leontine.

"Oh kill them both!" Sir Nnia shouts and his loyalists attack Lexis immediately.

"Kill him!" Lexis signs to Leontine.

"NO!" Lord Omicron objects. "Is it done?"

"It will be done... let her kill him."

"Give me back my tablet now or Kamsi-Elle here will get my knife!" Sir Nnia threatens.

"Kill him!" Lexis yells again as he tries to prevent Sir Nnia's puppets from getting to Lord Omicron.

"I will squeeze life out of this fellow!" Sir Nnia boasts as he covers the loyal Kamsi-Elle's mouth.

Leontine is confused. Her father's heart is yet to approve of Lexis' commands and she isn't exactly ready to take someone's life.

"Do it!" Lexis signs at her again as he keeps pushing away Archprofessor Lux Eden, Sir Luminescence and the crown princess.

Archprofessor Elise stands with her hands on her head, there's no saying how confused she is.

Sir Nnia tightens his grip on Kamsi-Elle's face and she begins to struggle for air gradually. He sees Dame Nissi looking desperately to the sky.

"Don't look to the sky," Sir Nnia mocks her. "Tell your kid to give it up. The folf never hunts twice in one location."

Princess Zeta suddenly switches on. She has faith more in Lexis and she decides to help the terrified Leontine kill off Sir Nnia. She runs quickly towards Leontine. From the back of Sir Nnia and to his side, Sir Nnia throws a knife at Princess Zeta once she runs into his sights. Almost half of the blade goes into her arm and the force of impact throws her to the ground.

"Zeta!" Lexis shouts. He becomes more offensive in his fight.

Leontine's anxiety shoots up the more. She puts her finger immediately on the image of Sir Nnia's neck on her sapien and the ten seconds countdown is initiated.

Sir Nnia can feel her finger, he knows the ten seconds countdown has been initiated and he sorts quickly to do some mental battle. He lets go of Kamsi-Elle immediately.

"You can't do it," he signs to Leontine before pulling out another knife.

Leontine breaths faster as she panics the more.

"Five seconds?" Sir Nnia signs and charges towards Leontine.

Lord Omicron and Dame Nissi instantly run after Sir Nnia.

"Just do it!" Princess Zeta cries from the floor with blood still gushing from her arm.

Leontine looks at the countdown – three seconds left and she must utilize the weaponized digitizer now or at least in the next second.

The great shadow of the false prophet graces over them once again.

Impossible – a couple of seconds seem to have just skipped out of history. The fear within them causes an instant stop-and-think moment. The folf is usually more interested in the fastest creature around.

Dame Nissi is unarguably the fastest; no one is as eager as she is to get to Leontine first. She's the last to get distracted by the folf but her reaction is priceless. With everybody's heads rising to the sky to behold the creature casting the familiar shadow, Dame Nissi's eyes are almost falling off by just gazing at the shadow itself. This is surely beyond fixing one and two together to defend herself; it is a matter of acknowledging that death is hovering above her. Dame Nissi loses her footing and falls face down to the ground.

"Emexei!" Leontine shouts and everyone suddenly gets back their adrenaline.

Lexis abandons his fight and aims to help his mother up from the ground.

The countdown on the sapien is obviously up and Leontine is not sure what to do about Sir Nnia who is just a coin toss away from her. Well, there's something about this folf, and Leontine can still hear its heart.

"Enjoy yourself!" the folf's heart says to Leontine before it sweeps Sir Nnia off the ground and flies away with him.

"Jeke bisi biawengi bike hem!" Leontine shouts at the folf. {I don't mean it, but bring him back}.

Archprofessor Lux Eden and Sir Luminescence throw their knives hopefully at the folf. The folf is long gone.

Lexis continues swiftly to Princess Zeta. He bends over to her to see the extent of the wound. The tablet beeps once from his chest and he opens up the PES and brings it out.

'DEACTIVATION SAVED' is the message.

"Momxy!" Kamsi-Elle is the first to realise something has just changed about her. She runs quickly into her mother's arms. "Where is Zeta?"

"Over there..."

Archprofessor Lux Eden and Sir Luminescence look at each other, rather feeling disgusted about themselves. Sextine jogs over to Princess Zeta to help stop the bleeding.

"I will pull the knife out," Sextine tells Princess Zeta.

The princess nods courageously as her mother and sister come to her with a smile of relief.

"I don't think the folf will kill Sir Nnia," says Archprofessor Elise.

"Haha!" Archprofessor Lux Eden exclaims. "He's dead meat. He must have died when it picked him up."

"Unless he's hypertensive..."

"What are you saying, Elise?" Lord Omicron asks.

"If the folf had taken Leontine, will you still not feel safe as you are feeling now? Will you think the folf was going to kill Leontine?"

"You guys said Leontine was talking with it," Lord Omicron says. "Yes, I don't think it will kill Leontine."

"And it attacked a spot twice, and what folf speaks to people?" Archprofessor Elise asks again.

"What are you saying?" Dame Nissi asks Archprofessor Elise.

"I'm saying the nature of that folf must have been compwomised. It ignored me and Lexis under the Water Steps. We need to find Sir Nnia and end this pwoperly."

"The folf will kill him!" Sir Luminescence remains adamant. "It took the other Lilyscent too... that's obvious it's fighting for Leontine."

"Why didn't it take you?" Archprofessor Elise asks Sir Luminescence. "Or Lux Eden, or her highness... You were not fighting for Leontine."

"Excuse me, I am not on Sir Nnia's side," Princess Lotem-Zeta chips in.

"The folf must be quite intelligent and knowledgeable to know that."

"You are getting me scared, Elise," says Dame Nissi. "You suggesting the folf took Sir Nnia to a safe place? Who tames a folf to intervene on their behalf?"

"That is my point exactly! Why are we feeling he intervened on our own behalf? Did we tame it?"

"It depends on what it discussed with Leontine..."

"What did you discuss with the folf?" Lord Omicron signs to Leontine.

"Now?" Leontine signs.

"All thru the time you spoke to it," Lord Omicron signs.

"Nothing really... mine truly... he called me food. He did say he has eaten me before..." Leontine begins to suspect all sorts of things. "He said he has never spoken to any human before, but he did say we normally assume we have a spirit, soul, body, heart, head and stuff. It must have learnt that from someone else no doubt."

"I knew there's something domestic about that folf. It looked tamed to me."

"Shh... wait," Lord Omicron tries to understand these theories. "Let me get why we are suspecting this now. The folf said it has never spoken to any human before, it doesn't mean it has never heard any human before. Maybe that's how it learnt the things it said... he's been here for ages, no doubt."

"The folf may be wight when it said it has eaten Leontine before," Lexis suggests.

"How?"

"I saw a document... Cleontine... Sir Nnia made four clones of Leontine and he tested the heart whispewer on them. There are indications he did put them with the folf to see if they can discuss with it... the folf may be putting on a special BEM too... Folfenheit or something..."

Lord Omicron and Dame Nissi can't bottle up their surprise anymore.

'What?" they ask.

"...are you saying?" Dame Nissi continues. "I can't deal."

"He cloned her?" Lord Omicron asks.

"Yes, according to these documents..." Lexis pulls up the folder on his sapien.

Princess Lotem-Zeta takes the screen and moves towards Lord Omicron and Dame Nissi. Archprofessor Lux Eden, Sir Luminescence and Archprofessor Elise join them to see for themselves.

"Adonbelivit," Lord Omicron mutters as he opens the first Cleontine pictures.

"What is that?" Leontine signs at Lexis.

"Sir Nnia cloned you. He was making a heart whisperer too, and testing it on the folf," Lexis signs back.

"Where are the clones?" Leontine signs.

"The folf must have eaten them."

"That's why he said he has eaten me before."

Lexis nods.

"And that I came back deaf this time..."

"It said that?" Lexis speaks as he signs.

"Said what?" Lord Omicron asks.

"That she came back deaf this time. Maybe other clones were not deaf. The heart whispewer will be hard to work on people who can hear effectively."

"So it indeed may not have spoken to anyone before," Lord Omicron tries to establish that the folf will kill Sir Nnia.

"Yes," Archprofessor Elise says, "what if someone has spoken to it before Leontine did? It mustn't be a discussion."

"This document does support Archpwofessor Elise's fears," says Lexis.

"Shit!" Lord Omicron punches the air in frustration. "Does he know you know about this?" he asks Lexis.

"Of course. I got it fwom this tablet and it's still with me."

"No, Lord Omicwon... I get where you are going," says Princess Lotem-Zeta. "We will not sweep this matter under, no. We will not hunt for him secwetly or sneak up on him, no. A man who has murdered the king must be exposed and his potentials let known to the whole Oh. He must be found and he will be dealt with by the laws of our people. He wishes to play dead by the folf so he can plot again? He won't get that chance..."

"I understand you, your highness. I didn't know he killed the king..."

"He did," Princess Lotem-Zeta tries not to sob as she turns to Lexis. "For your intelligence in undoing the evil Sir Nnia cast upon Fahwenheit and its users, you will be awarded a knighthood, and here in the pwesence of these people as witnesses, you have been named Sir Lexis Woe, a knight of Sexat and all nations in the western wórld."

Lexis bows slightly in acceptance. The gloom on the princess' face wouldn't let anyone smile over that; it is an infectious sadness.

"And for you all," Princess Lotem-Zeta continues, "to evewyone of you who are part of the team that found the lost earth, and those who took part in this fight to keep us sane, I give an elevation of your individual titles. To any who isn't a knight, and who wishes to be, I make a Sir and Lady. Let knights be archknights and Lords and Dames be Archlords and Archdames. I think that's all we have among us here..."

"What about the pwincess?" Princess Zeta asks lightly of her own title.

"You are the cwown pwincess now." Princess Lotem-Zeta says coldly. A reminder to them all that King Sigma was lost in the process.

There isn't enough time to hug and kiss everyone goodbye; they surely will still speak to each other before the day runs out, and Princess Zeta of course needs to be taken to a hospital for proper treatment.

23

THE Rhos are home in no time. There is nothing better than being within those walls and the five of them know this. Lord Omicron and Dame Nissi drop their PES on the floor in the living room and their arms feel relieved.

"Where is my BEM?" Sextine asks immediately. "I think way awkward... I can put it on now, eh?"

"You talk awkwardly too," Dame Nissi tells Sextine. "I'm not sure that thing is safe for you."

"It is safe," Lexis assures them.

"You can use yours too," Lord Omicron says to Dame Nissi.

"No no, best Sextine tests hers first. It should be on the floor where you dwopped it."

"You dwopped it, not me..." Sextine responds as she walks in to get the BEM.

Leontine skips in too with a sense of urgency.

"Is she going somewhere?" Lord Omicron asks of Leontine.

"Ask her when she's about to leave," Dame Nissi responds.

"I saw Leontine walk on water," Lexis reveals.

"Lol... yeah?"

"Yeah popmy... the Water Steps... she went up the whole stairs."

"I need my BEM to understand this one," Dame Nissi says as she shuns Lexis' mini-testimony.

Sextine re-enters the living room and stands still, looking meanly at Dame Nissi with her hands at her back. Lexis senses mischief could be on the cards. Lord Omicron predicts a very bad joke. Dame Nissi doesn't want to bear the weight of that gaze alone.

"Did you find it?" Dame Nissi asks Sextine, gradually moving close to Lexis and Lord Omicron.

Sextine nods "yes".

"Is it working?"

"Yes..."

"Normally?"

"Perfectly," says Sextine as she reveals the knife she had earlier today. "It wouldn't have been easy to win this war, don't you think?"

"Can you put that thing away?" Dame Nissi suggests, still pretending to be calm. She is almost grabbing the suited Lexis by the arm.

"You are the one who needs to be put away!" Sextine stumps towards Dame Nissi.

"No, Sextine!" Dame Nissi panics. "Take the BEM off!"

Dame Nissi turns to hide behind Lexis and she doesn't see Sextine wink at Lexis and Lord Omicron. The men relax.

"Take her BEM off Lexis! Do something!" Dame Nissi yells.

Sextine pretends she's being restricted by Lexis as she tries to reach Dame Nissi with the knife. There is nothing yet suggesting to Dame Nissi that this is only a joke so she screams the more. But right beside her is Lord Omicron; she has lived long enough with this man to know when he finds something amusing no matter how much he's trying to pretend.

"OMICWON!" Dame Nissi thunders his name. "Do something!"

Lord Omicron is about to laugh but this prank is soon going wrong.

Like a bolt of lightning, a PES-kitted Leontine swiftly pounces on Sextine from behind. The weight of her hand pressing against Sextine's shoulders forces the knife to fall off Sextine's hand.

Sextine is screaming way louder, shorter, and faster than Dame Nissi. How does she tell Leontine that she was only joking?

Leontine throws in three quick blows towards the back of Sextine's head but Lexis blocks them.

"Leontine, stop!" Lexis shouts.

Leontine isn't looking at Lexis; there's no hope she could have heard or understood him. Sextine lifts her hands to her head and screams the more. Leontine is way too determined. She tries again to hit Sextine but Lexis is still up to the task as he blocks the quick blows perfectly.

The speed of the PES allows Lexis and Leontine to do a lot of hit and blocks before Lord Omicron could take three steps to reach them. His arm is outstretched towards them; we too wonder who he intends to grab. Leontine isn't even looking at Lord Omicron but her right hand lands a stinging knock on the back of his approaching hand. Lord Omicron spins away in pain and quickly picks up his PES to get dressed.

"Dock Sextine!" Lexis advices Sextine as he's gradually becoming unable to cope with Leontine's aggression.

Sextine squats on the floor immediately and Leontine lands a blow on Lexis' chest. Leontine raises her leg to stamp on Sextine but Lexis recovers and blocks with his own foot.

"Move out!" Lexis instructs Sextine.

Sextine crawls quickly towards Lexis' back and this gets Dame Nissi moving too.

Dame Nissi jitters off from Lexis' back as Sextine crawls towards her. The noise in the room isn't short of a panic-scream duet by Sextine the surprise lead-screamer with Dame Nissi as backup.

"Omicwon, do something!" Dame Nissi yells as she scrambles out of Sextine's way.

"Sugar, I'm getting dwessed," Lord Omicron responds.

"You don't need that PES to take Sextine's BEM off..."

"Leontine hasn't succeeded with hers!"

"My BEM?" Sextine finds her talking voice at once. "Momxy, I'm perfectly fine!"

"Heh?" Dame Nissi doesn't believe her. "*Voir cette fille.*" {See this girl}.

"What are you saying?" Sextine asks. "I've not even put the BEM on, see?" Sextine pulls out the BEM from her cloth and shows it to Dame Nissi. "I was only joking! Tell Leontine to stop..."

"How do I tell her that now?" Dame Nissi points at the aggressive Leontine who is still trying to get round the defensive Lexis.

Leontine and Lexis get into a tangle and Leontine gives him a big hug. Lexis is set to push her off but he feels her chest against his stomach moving rhythmically in a quiet laughter.

"Wait... you know she was joking?" Lexis asks before breaking the hug with the giggling Leontine.

Lord Omicron stops putting on his PES as he looks on to see if everyone is calm now.

"You knew she was joking, right?" Lexis signs to Leontine.

"Yes" Leontine nods, and she still can't contain her laughter.

"SHE KNEW?" Sextine flares up.

"Look who is surpwised... but you attacked me first," says Dame Nissi.

"I didn't bwing a PES to the joke!" Sextine argues.

"You had a knife... it's the same evil."

"You knew," Sextine ignores Dame Nissi and signs to Leontine, "and you wore that thing in here. You scared the shit out of me."

"Leave me baby alone," Dame Nissi tells Sextine.

"You should have heard your hearts," Leontine signs.

"It is not funny... that PES changed the entire scene."

"I didn't wear this for you. I'm going out," Leontine reveals.

"Where to?" her parents sign.

"To see a friend..."

"You have a friend?" Dame Nissi signs.

Leontine nods "yes" and walks towards the front door.

"Is she..." Dame Nissi mentally asks Lord Omicron to stop Leontine.

"Wait..." Lord Omicron pulls Leontine back. "Sir Nnia is still alive..."

"Maybe," Leontine signs.

"Yes," Lord Omicron signs. "Going out alone now could make him get to you."

"I am not going far... and I'm suited up too."

"Yes, the authorities could detain you for disturbing the public peace."

"Then they'll find Sir Nnia too. I am close by. Got to go..."

Leontine hurries out of the house and shuts the door.

Dame Nissi gives Lord Omicron a disapproving look.

"What... my hand still hurts," Lord Omicron complains about the knock he received on his hand.

"Hmm," Dame Nissi shakes her head, "so much for an Archlord."

"Lol," *'Archlord Omicron'* laughs. "The little miss is a lady knight now... she can do what she wants."

"Seemesh."

Leontine suddenly comes back in and gives Sextine a sapien screen containing a typed message.

"You can send that to all your friends you never have time to see or talk to," Leontine signs.

Sextine collects the screen and Leontine runs out again.

"Hmm... your daughter wishes to be a poet... hope she has let you know..."

"Yes, Sextine," Dame Nissi says proudly.

"Oh," Sextine is surprised at the reaction. "Well, this says, 'To an "old" fwend... lol...

You know I speak to you evewy day, but that's just in my head.

I call you, just in my head.

I text you, just in my head.

You do speak back, call back and text back, just in my head.

I tell you my plans, and you do the same, just in my head.

You need to hear those heart lifting conversations that take place, just in my head.

There's no other weason why I can stay for days, weeks and months without saying a word... I always forget the last time we spoke, we only spoke in my head.

You be an old fwend of mine.

Good times, bad times, whatever times, a fwend mustn't keep in touch to be tweated as a fwend.

No matter how much time flies by, if you do need a fwend's help, you can count on me, and hopefully, that won't be just in my head.

P/S: I'm not good with poems... so, you get the idea... okay, maybe just in my head.'

Okay, that's it. Well... I wouldn't call this a poem now, would I?" Sextine asks.

"Keep quiet," Dame Nissi shoves her out the way as she walks happily out of the living room.

Leontine indeed has gone to see a friend, a new friend, an unusual one – the violent waters of Youlv. Standing on the calm side of the Water Steps, Leontine takes a deep breath while admiring the stairs one more time. The voice in her head keeps rising with the same message, *"Efoélfosev!"*

Leontine smiles affectionately at her reflection on the water and sets off quickly towards the Water Steps. The PES adds to her speed as she whisks thru the water and to the top of the Water Steps. She concentrates more this time; she wouldn't want to sink again.

Beautiful as the sight may be, the waters on the other side of the stairs flow with unrelenting aggression. The waves keep rising the more as Leontine spreads out her arms, smiling and laughing increasingly. She suddenly jumps off the Water Steps and head down towards the turbulent Youlv.

A small horizontal pillar of water rises towards the incoming Leontine with other violent waves trying to distract her from enjoying her flight. Leontine embraces the pillar of water, her arms and body neither going thru nor sinking into it. She spins around with it before diving into the turbulent water. The water flows easy, not with a slower speed, but with a clearer purpose as it sails Leontine thru its surface.

We are here with Leontine but hereafter in this dream, I will be alone – unseen, unheard, unspoken, untouched, a phantom, a phoenix, whatever; and I will dream sleepily ever after.

The End.